For the Love
of Robert E. Lee

For the Love
of Robert E. Lee

A NOVEL BY

M. A. Harper

Copyright © 1992 by Meredith Annette Harper
All rights reserved.

Published by
Soho Press Inc.
853 Broadway
New York, NY 10003

Library of Congress Cataloging-in-Publication Data

Harper, M. A., 1949–
For the love of Robert E. Lee : a novel / by M. A. Harper.
p.   cm.
ISBN 0-939149-63-X : $20.00
I. Title.
PS3558.A6247937F6 1992
813'.54—dc20   92-11419
CIP

Manufactured in the United States of America
10 9 8 7 6 5 4 3 2 1

Book design and composition by
The Sarabande Press

To my sister
Donna

For the Love
of Robert E. Lee

One

Contrary to popular belief, I did grow up. Found some men, got a perm, lived in New York until it was giving me a lobotomy. Wore red lipstick and met Mick Jagger at a party once. But when I was thirteen, my motto had been "Get out." Older people never liked to hear that, especially not from a girl. They took it personally.

I took up bumming cigarettes in the girls' restroom at school. Maybe I could "get out" by degrees. Suicide by cancer. I was in the eighth grade, hormonal but happy, and enduring the Civil War Centennial at the hands of Southern history teachers. My leg had begun its slow defection by this time, but I could deny it because no one was saying anything about it: not Mama or Daddy or anybody, as if our silence would make the development reverse itself, make the muscle change its mind and come back around like somebody with the sulks who gets ignored.

So there I was, skirted and bouffanted, having to make these school-bused forays into nearby Columbia to see where Sherman's cannonballs had knocked chunks out of the state capitol building. I listened indifferently to how the Yankees had burnt half of South Carolina down, while I passed love notes to David Dale Baker. The women had worn long gorgeous skirts during the Civil War that hid their legs. That was the only thing that stuck in my mind.

And then somebody shot my President, down in Dallas.

God, he was a beautiful man and I loved him. It had seemed while I was little that I would grow old and die before Dwight Eisenhower trudged out of office. And then here came this young, smart man, with his glamorous wife and his touch football and his rocking chair and his radiant crinkle-eyed confidence. I remember sitting in front of the television set and hanging upon every crisp Massachusetts syllable that came out from between those perfect teeth. He sounded intelligent. He didn't sound like the mush-mouthed old farts we always elected to the Senate from South Carolina. He was going to make us new, this man. I was young and he was young and there seemed to me to be a rightness about his presidency.

And then somebody had to go shoot him.

Riding home on the school bus that same afternoon, my sister Beth Ann and I sat quiet and stupefied, while kids all around us wondered out loud if Johnson'd been sworn in yet and what would happen if the Russians attacked us between presidents.

The bus comes to a stop and ten-year-old Beth Ann and I go babbling about murder to Mama, scared and unbelieving and thrilled to be the first to hit her with the bad news. We three pile into the car and go bumping along in that old dirty Chevrolet to the big field where Daddy is harvesting soybeans, him looking like just a small speck riding on the distant combine that spews dust all over the gold stubble stretching away into the blue trees.

Mama looks at me in the rearview mirror. I'm biting my nails. My sweater is knotted over my skinny shoulders by its sleeves. "Don't take it so hard, Garnet. It'll be all right."

Maybe so, I think. But if something like this isn't worth

taking hard, then what is? History is being made, I'm a witness. I don't want to be a witness. I don't want things to change.

She stomps on the brakes, sticks her head out of the window, and shouts "*Rich-a-a-a-ard!*" at the combine. Daddy can't hear her. Beth Ann and I wrestle the door open and run hopping over the shorn rows in our good school penny loafers, with the combine noise roaring in front of us and Mama leaning on the automobile horn in back.

Mama lets up on the horn. Daddy sees us coming and stops the combine. All the sounds in the world stop when the roaring stops. He climbs down and is waiting on the ground when I stumble toward him out of breath, my weird leg carrying me over the rows as well as my normal one.

He waits.

"Somebody's shot the President, Daddy."

I see him slowly wipe his nose, tilt back his cap. Beth Ann creeps up next to me and stands, panting.

"Is he dead?"

"Yessir."

We all look to where the car horn is blowing again like a banshee and then it stops. Mama, straightening up her bony self, is waiting for us. I take hold of one of Daddy's big dirty hands and Beth Ann takes the other, and we walk across the field to the car in a silence that isn't even broken by birds, while Jackie stands in a bloody skirt on board Air Force One and Lyndon Johnson takes the oath of office at her side.

The Chevrolet carries us on down the rough farm road, leaving the combine sitting in the darkening field, huge and dead like a dinosaur carcass. We drive maybe another half mile through the trees and then I can hear the rumble of a second combine. Our car bounces out into the open again and stops. Daddy uncoils his long legs out the driver's side and I sit in the back seat, watching him run over the wide cut ground to tell his friend Gifford Moak the news.

I sit there, twitching my fingers in my windblown bouffant,

and I see mind pictures of Abraham Lincoln. I feel guilty. I don't know why. I feel like we weren't watchful enough. Maybe we haven't been protective enough, and somebody could've seen this thing coming. Kept Jack in Washington. I feel responsible.

I watch Daddy and Mr. Moak ambling back towards us, kicking up dust clouds with their laced-up boots, and I think about it all being a part of history. About how it will all be written down in history books someday and what a horrible shame it is that those books aren't printed yet so that someone might have read them and kept Jack home. The images of everything are freezing onto my memory: Daddy and Mr. Moak walking, and the way the twilight plays thick and purple over the distant trees, the way the combine dust hangs in the cool persimmon-smelling air and coats everything with a fog.

I will remember this exact second as long as I live, I say to myself, then realizing that the idea isn't unique and that other people between this East Coast and the West, where the sun is still high, will be saying this very thing to themselves this evening. Some people will be hearing the news at nightfall. Others will hear it early in the daylight. In a big country with more than one time zone, John Kennedy has died at different times for different people. Maybe there's someplace in the world where he isn't dead yet.

Mama, in the front seat, plays with her fingernails where the polish flakes near the cuticles. Gifford Moak leans into the window, sweaty face covered with fuzzy dust, his hair sticking straight up in back where he has yanked off his dirty cap.

"Evenin', Azalee," he says to Mama.

"Evenin'."

"So that nigger lover finally got what was comin' to him," he observes pleasantly.

The bottom of my stomach falls out.

Daddy just looks at the ground, hands in pockets. He doesn't know what to say. "Well." He scratches his head. "We just thought you'd wanna know, Gifford."

Mr. Moak grins, his rural face flat, an eyetooth gone. "I ain't gon lose any sleep over it. But I thank y'all for tellin' me."

"Got to be goin'." Daddy gets into the car and switches on the ignition. "Azalee's mother is stayin' with us this week. Probably got supper waitin'."

"Yeah," says Moak.

"Y'all come to see us," Mama says, tired. Then she glances over her shoulder at Beth Ann and me, prompting. I don't want to be nice to this man. I have known him all my life but I don't want to tell him anything now except, Go to Hell.

"Y'all come to see us, Mr. Moak," we chorus obediently.

When we get home, Grandmama Moser is waiting for us in front of our small brick house, arms folded serenely against the night chill. Her proud old face toys with a heavy-lidded smile as I follow my family into the yellow light.

"Well." I hear her stalking after us to the table where chicken and rice steam. She passes me and pauses to flick imaginary lint off of a chromed kitchen chair with the end of her dishrag. "Well. Live by the sword, and die by the sword."

"I thought he got shot," Beth Ann mutters, so low that nobody can hear her but me.

I watch Grandmama handle her stainless steel fork like solid gold all through the meal, her old lady's face wearing its satisfaction. I see Mama glance up at the same thing from time to time.

"What're you lookin' at, Azalee?" Grandmama's voice is soft, measured—countrified diction rendered in the cultured tones of her long dead well-born mother. "I made that chicken 'specially for you, sugar. Eat up. You and Richard grievin' for that papist antichrist?"

Mama takes a hesitant mouthful of food. "You wouldn't talk so mean about a dead man if Pop was still alive."

Grandmama's face flickers. She fingers her wedding ring. "Your daddy was a good man. A soft touch. Not like me. I'm a hater."

I put down my fork, remembering my grandfather, soft

7

white hair and deep voice, remembering his gentle way with hurt birds and how he always made me and Beth Ann turn loose any wild creatures that Daddy brought home from the fields. Granddaddy would heal any animal wounds with his spotted preacher's hands and then he would make a ceremony of blessing the creature and letting it loose. I can still feel the joy of the free flight away or the four strong legs running into the brush, the serene old man standing with us as we all wave goodbye.

"We would've been married fifty-four years this June," Grandmama continues, the gold ring twisting on her bony finger. "Sometimes I don't think I can stand it. Sometimes I don't think there's a God at all, Azalee."

"You girls help Mama with the dishes," my mother mutters, getting to her feet. She wanders into the livingroom to click on the television. I can hear the hushed grave voice of a newscaster from where I sit.

"Serves the papist right." Grandmama hands a dripping dish to Beth Ann, who has accompanied her to the sink. Beth Ann wipes at it halfheartedly with a dry towel. Grandmama's patrician hawk face turns its profile to the television sounds. "Nigger-lover was ruinin' the country."

Daddy dabbles in his coffee, stirring the liquid to bubbles. He doesn't say a word. The old woman gives him an arch look and then marches off into the livingroom to needle Mama.

Where is the beauty in a person like that? I ask myself. Dutifully standing, I take her place at the sink. I stick my hands into the slimy water and a phrase comes to me. From a dream, maybe, or from one of those clumsy poems I compose from time to time whenever the world gets ugly. I will probably write a Kennedy poem, I know. It will begin like this:

"Let there be a seed." I speak the words out loud.

"Daddy?" Beth Ann steps over to the table, eyes frowny under the blonde bangs, voice low. "Is everybody glad that President Kennedy got killed?"

"*I'm* not, baby." His spoon goes clink-clink-clink.

"But some folks are."

He nods. "Guess a lot of folks around here."

"Why?"

He shrugs. Beth Ann is only ten and so he shrugs.

I put down my dishrag and think about how I live in a place that isn't really fully the United States of America where Americans actually mourn the young Irishman. I live in a place where people are some other nationality. I am born of them. I am one of them. What does that make me?

Grandmama flounces back in. "I don't wanna talk about him anymore," she announces. "I'm gon be sick to death of all this by the time they throw some dirt over him."

Amen.

"Uh huh," says Daddy.

I wash a dish.

Grandmama puts the mayonnaise away in the refrigerator. "I ran into Miz Spence in town this mornin'," she speaks to Daddy over her shoulder in a subject-changing voice. "Her and Doctor Spence were just wonderin' when you and Azalee are gonna let him look at the child's leg."

"What child?"

She looks right at me. Her eyes are like hard blue beads. "Garnet here," she says to Daddy, then to me, "There's somethin' the matter with your leg."

I feel sudden perspiration on my upper lip. "Nothin's the matter with me, Grandmama."

"Richard?" The old lady points to a suddenly vulnerable spot above my left shoe. "Look how that muscle looks wasted. See it? Doctor Spence has been noticin' it at church lately and thinks y'all ought to bring her in. There's somethin' the matter with the child's leg."

I see my father's eyes follow the finger; see him start to see what he doesn't want to see, until we maybe have enough money in the bank to deal with it. I see him start to open his mouth: "Awww—"

9

It's true. There's something wrong.

Her hard, lined face keeps watching me and watching me, and I feel my suddenly inadequate leg go hide behind the strong right one. I keep my gaze on the dishwater.

Freak! My mind taunts me for the very first time. Ugly!

Grandmama goes on, standing over Daddy like a harpy: "I mean, it's just a little thing and not very noticeable yet, but you and Azalee had better see to it before it gets any worse. Remember Winona Simms y'all went to high school with? She was so bow-legged she looked like she was rollin' a hoop! Oh, and I saw Clyde Blakeney in town too, and he wants to know, can he borry your boat Saturday to take the preacher fishin'?"

I keep my eyes on the dishwater while I carefully dry my hands on the towel and rub some hand cream into them to keep them soft. *Let there be a seed/Let there be a seed.* My mind is composing its Kennedy poem while the newscast wafts from the livingroom. I imagine Winona Simms and her comical legs. That's when I finally cry.

I slip past Daddy and his outstretched arms, I evade Grand-mama's startled "Honey!" and race for the bathroom, where I slam the door and slide home the bolt and lock myself inside. Out of the corner of my eye I see my face in the mirror—contorted, ugly—while the murmur of the television set comes to me through the walls.

That can't be my face in the mirror. I am pretty, I was Valentine Queen for six straight years in grammar school. That can't be my leg. I have pretty legs. I can rollerskate and jump like a gazelle, and boys look at me on the beach even though I'm just thirteen.

That can't be President Kennedy with his head blown to pieces and everybody laughing. People loved President Kennedy.

I cry and turn on the bathtub faucets as high as they go so that the others will think I'm okay and only want to take a bath. I turn on the faucets as high as they will go so that I won't have to listen to the television set anymore.

Two

Mama was in the kitchen. Beth Ann was hogging the telephone. But that was all right. I wasn't expecting any calls.

Daddy was reading the sports page during the commercial before the television weather report and I sat across from him with my homework in my lap, chewing a pencil. I was wishing I had a cigarette.

My mind was on Kennedy. Three years later and my mind was frequently on Kennedy. Things kept dredging him up. This time it was a homework assignment. I wished at sixteen that I could let him lie, but I felt guilty when I did, like I'd lost a relative or something and then gone off dancing the night of the funeral.

"What in the world are you readin' now?" Daddy asked.

"History. Civil War. Lincoln and stuff. I gotta give a report in class for that new teacher."

"What new teacher?"

"You know. The one that came in to replace Mrs. Pitts when she left to have her baby in February. The one that the kids call a communist because he had us readin' Marx once. The one from New York—Mr. Damadian."

"Oh yeah."

I smiled. "I like him."

I had my head down but I could feel my father's glance, feel him regarding my heavy eye makeup and the black leotard tights Mama hated, the long ironed hair that Grandmama, in her few lucid moments nowadays, said made me look like a flower child.

"You would," I heard Daddy say after a moment, amused.

I grinned back. He knew where my head was at. He knew that I was a poet with hypothetical suicide on the brain. I had tried to discuss it with him once but he had hooted and laughed at me. So I didn't discuss suicide with him anymore. But I had told him all about my politics.

I leafed idly through my heavy American history textbook. "You goin' with us up to Rock Hill after church on Sunday, Daddy?"

"Wish I could. But the weatherman says that the rains are over and, if it's dry enough to plant, I'm goin' to have to be in the field."

He had religious objections to working on Sundays, but I knew he figured if God saw fit finally to give him a sunny day, then it was God's will for him to use it. I looked at him while he wasn't watching me, at his tanned sensible face and bushy black hair. He was no fool. I didn't think it was foolish to believe in God. I just couldn't anymore. It was like falling out of love.

The phone rang. Beth Ann answered. I didn't even give my blood pressure a chance to rise because I knew it wasn't for me. There was one person I wished would call me, even for just a homework assignment or something. But he never would, I knew. Oh Daddy, what would you say if I told you about Bubba Hargett? Would you squirm and get all nervous if I told you that I like to look at his crotch? Yes you would. Definitely.

Bubba Hargett. Bubba—what a stupid nickname. Beatnik poetesses did not normally go apeshit over a person named Bubba.

Supple, easy, laughing Bubba, the new kid at school. The Mississippi army brat who had lived in a million places and had lately come to light like an eagle in the midst of my humdrum classmates. Ol' Bubba, whom I sometimes imagined was watching me at peculiar moments, who would flash a predatory grin and then bend his blond Beatle haircut back over his studies to leave me abashed.

Artists should be above this kind of drooling, I realized. But I wished he would call me. Yes I did.

Who do I have to discuss such things with? I'm almost seventeen and I'm normal, even if I try to look like Judy Collins and read Nietzsche.

Oh God, I fantasize, I fantasize. During long, dry church sermons I fantasize about boys, older men, the whole species. I fantasize until a guilty warmth starts coming up from my body and I get scared that it might show on my face. At the most inopportune time: Holy holy holy.

I studied my oblivious father and craved a cigarette in the worst way. Didn't you and Mama ever feel this way, Daddy? Why can't I talk to Mama about sex without feeling that I'm standing her in front of a firing squad?

My body was something that I was coming both to treasure and hate. I had waited for breasts at thirteen and had been delighted and ashamed of the secret round soft sinful whiteness when they arrived.

My face was bony and full-lipped and I had decided that my best feature was probably my passable olive eyes. I painted them up with Cleopatra lines, then and now. The makeup hardened my expression somewhat, even in my teens—but my name is Garnet and a garnet is hard and dark red, like the color I gave my soul at age sixteen. My face suited me. I liked my face. Bubba would have liked my breasts. And face.

But, okay. There was the leg.

The calf muscle had just stopped growing. I hardly had any curve there. From knee to shoe it looked like a salami. Doctor

Spence couldn't do anything. He didn't even sympathize much. "Just be glad you can walk," he said. "Maybe you had an undiagnosed case of polio when you were little and the damage didn't show up until the puberty growth spurt. Or maybe the sciatic nerve was damaged in some way. The muscle is underdeveloped, but it's functional. You can do anything any other girl of your age can do."

Except look terrific in a pair of high heels.

"We'll keep our eye on it, Garnet. It might need bracing eventually. No big deal."

Great. What if I want to be Miss America? No big deal.

Daddy was looking at me. I didn't want him to see me patting my leg so I pretended to be searching the floor for a dropped pencil or something. Daddy didn't understand. None of them did. They wondered why I let it bother me so much. They couldn't understand that I read novels about comely bodies and drew pictures of perfect things and wrote poetry. I had an artistic intolerance of imperfection. So if Beauty was my god, then my left leg was somebody committing an indecent act on the altar with a donkey.

"It's hardly noticeable, honey," Mama told me. They meant well. I might have tried to talk more about it to them, but I didn't want my folks to start feeling guilty about putting off the original visit to that quack Dr. Spence. Earlier treatment wouldn't have done any good. What kind of treatment? My folks were not to blame. It was my cross to bear, whatever had caused it. I may have had a lot of shortcomings, but making my folks feel lousy was not one of them.

Oh God. My leg was noticeable to me. And I was the only viewer who mattered, really. "This is the only flaw," I used to tell myself in the mirror when I was locked up nights alone in the bathroom with it. I would look at it from all angles after my bath. If I really couldn't walk, or if I was really disabled, then at least I'd have the consolation of some sympathy. Or if I had been injured in some dramatic accident maybe, then at least I could look upon it with a little romance. Like an old war wound, a souvenir of Bull Run. But it came from nowhere and I'm afflicted for no reason. And if anyone ever asks me what the matter with it is, I won't be able to tell them.

Daddy was lighting a cigarette. I could've killed a baby seal for one. But I wouldn't smoke in front of him. I didn't want them worrying about my lungs as well.

I could tear up a poem when it came out wrong. I tore up my pencil sketches when I made somebody's nose too long or a mouth too wide. My left leg stood forever unfinished. Imperfect.

Daddy dragged on his cigarette. Looked at me. I had been too quiet for too long.

"What's your school report gonna be on?"

Oh, would *he* love this. He'd really get a kick out of this.

"Robert E. Lee," I said.

He saw I was serious. Then he grinned like a possum. He knew enough about the way my mind worked to see the irony in the assignment. Might as well have had Grandmama doing the life of Martin Luther King, Jr.

Lee.

That half-remembered something that lurked in Grandmama's failing mind. A name still living on the tongues of adults when Grandmama had been my age. The statue at local courthouses. The gray Christ that carried my people's burden of treason and race-guilt, who almost redeemed us in his legendary perfection. Lee was kind of like God where I grew up, even looked something like God. I couldn't recall the first time I had heard the word God and I couldn't remember hearing the name Robert E. Lee for the first time either.

I sat with Daddy and watched the rest of the newscast, hearing with a jaded ear that the Klan had bombed another black church somewhere in Alabama.

Lee.

I glanced at Daddy, chin in my hands. "I'm movin' to New York City when I graduate and I'm never comin' back. Folks down here seem hell-bent on showing everybody that we're even more bigoted, benighted, and just plain brain-damaged than they think we are."

Daddy sat there, clipping his toenails, dirty socks wadded up and stuffed into the high-top farm boots on the floor. "I'm sendin' you and Beth Ann to school with colored kids. Don't nobody put a pistol to my head to make me."

"If they did, you'd prob'ly secede." I stood and yawned.

"No," he said stubbornly. "I'd conform to the law."

"Well." I kissed him on the forehead. "You're an unusual person, Richard Laney."

He said nothing, just patted my hand in an inattentive way and watched fire roiling up from the televised church. His blue eyes were solemn. The nail clipper went snap-snap.

I let myself out the back door and stepped into the springtime grass, deep dewy, black and spongy in the dark. I wandered across the back yard far enough away from the house so that its lights wouldn't interfere with the stars. The night was warm and the big pinpricks of light up there in the coalyard sky were like stationary fireflies.

I felt small and lonely, I expected to feel small and lonely. That's why people look at the stars. They remind people, who are melancholy, that there are good reasons to feel melancholy.

Bubba Hargett might have made a night like this pass faster with laughter. But then it would have been lost, going by unnoticed. It would pass while Bubba and I stayed inside, playing my new Ravi Shankar album on the stereo. And it would never come again. Not this night. Time was like that. That's how time went.

I was seeing the light of dead stars just now reaching earth eons after the stars themselves had fizzled out. And there was no way ever to tell which ones up there were still living and which ones were actually gone.

The stars were perfect. John Keats was right. Beauty was truth, and that's all I needed to know.

You're a self-dramatizing flake, I told myself. Cut the metaphysics.

But I could feel ugliness evaporating from my mind and I spread open my arms to the sky. I even did a little dance there in its light to bug-mating music, me and my leg hidden from anybody's eyes. There in the dark I felt beautiful because for once it didn't occur to me to find myself otherwise. The female moths and I were beautiful.

Mama noticed I was carrying more books than usual when I got off the school bus the next afternoon. I saw her watching me as I clomped into the house, saw the frown between her sparse blonde brows.

"Maybe you'd better not carry 'em that way, honey. Carry 'em on your right side."

I dutifully shifted the weight, then lumped the volumes down into the middle of the livingroom floor, wishing that something as simple as carrying books on my right side would help my situation.

She dried her hands on her apron. Nubby dishwater hands. Once they had been soft and tapered and she had done some modeling for a local department store before I was born. Yet these hands were her badge of honor; she had no regrets. I loved them. She loved me. She was looking at my books.

"You got to read all of those?"

"Yes'm." I fished around in my shoulder bag for a ballpoint pen.

"Your light was on until two last night, honey."

"This is homework, Mama. Got to finish that ol' report."

"Beth Ann says she couldn't get to sleep with the light on."

I sighed. "I'll work in the bathroom tonight, then."

Pattering down the hall to the room I shared with my younger sister, I took off my short skirt, tossed it at a chair, and changed rapidly into the concealing wheat-colored jeans that unfortunately nobody but me considered proper school attire. I was happier when I came back into the livingroom, leg thoroughly hidden.

Mama peered around the doorjamb but she said nothing. I waited until I could hear a clatter of pots in the kitchen before I took up a book.

She no doubt thinks I read too much, I told myself. It's Friday night and here I am, nearly seventeen years old, with no date but a pile of mangy old books.

I didn't want to start feeling sorry for myself. Sometimes that was fun but it could get to be a drag after a while. Nevertheless I thought of my friend Anita Small who would be at a drive-in movie somewhere tonight, fogging up car windows with some heavy-breathing boy.

David Dale Baker had been on my tail for a year now but I blew smoke in his face and politely put him off. He and Doug Mitchell, and the other guys who liked me, were sparrows. I wanted an eagle. Who do you think you are? I asked myself and opened a book.

Instantly my mouth turned its white-lipsticked corners down as the name emblazoned on the title page bopped me right between the eyes: Robert E. Lee.

Oh God.

I had already rejected one book as being completely unendurable, an old sentimental thing with a maudlin title like *Lee, The Savior of The South,* taking it back unperused to the school library to exchange it for one written much later with more objectivity. Now I had to read this one. My assignment wouldn't go away unless I drove a stake through its heart.

So I opened it at random, just sticking my thumb in and letting the pages spread. It seemed as good a way as any of starting my research.

And the very first words that caught my eye were Lee's opinion of novels: "They paint beauty more charming than nature," he wrote someone in a letter, "and describe happiness that never exists."

Odd. Why's he getting all het up on fiction? I asked myself. Where's the "Let's go kill them Yankees, Cunnel!" I expected to read?

Didn't sound as if he dug real life too much. Bully for him, I thought. Real life sucks.

Hell. I shut the book again and fingered for the gray-edged photograph section that ran down the middle of the book's length. The pages fell open.

Wow. There it was. The Civil War. Wasn't it strange that there should be photographs? Made the whole thing more modern. Less remote. I saw things I recognized in these photos: Railroads and trains; rifles; utility poles; gutterspouts on the houses. Some things had not changed as much as you'd expect them to in a hundred years. Why not? Why weren't we waging war now with ray guns? After all, I told myself, we're The Future. But trains were still plain ol' trains and utility poles still looked like utility poles. Houses were still houses. Lee himself could've walked into my mother's living room and felt perfectly at home. Chairs still looked like chairs. Mama's piano was still a piano.

Of course, I would have had to explain certain things to him in detail if a jet plane, roaring over the house, interrupted our little interview.

Whoops, there he was: the old bastard. I had found a picture of him.

Maybe I had seen photos of him before. I know I had seen awful paintings of him that were idealized and cloying, done in that limp-wristed manner the way they do pictures of Jesus—lots of ethereal blue, with Lee wearing the expression of a camel whose legs are being sawed off by Saracens.

But here in this book was a Mathew Brady photograph of a virile living man. A real person. I'll be durned, I thought. I knew exactly what white hair like that felt like: soft and fluffy as cotton batting. I remembered Granddaddy Moser's fine white head bent close to my face, the scent of his toilet water. But Granddaddy had been very old. This man didn't look so old upon closer inspection.

19

He looked more like a middle-aged individual who'd had a very hard life. Funny. I had always thought Lee had been ancient. He wasn't young, no. But he was obviously not yet sixty, not if you darkened the hair in your mind.

He glared at the camera as if he wanted to punch Mathew Brady out. The caption said the picture was taken only days after Appomattox. Brady sure had a nerve, I thought, cornering this old wounded lion. Just like a modern reporter. It was like sticking a mike into Jackie's face the day Kennedy died and asking her if she'd like to comment.

But I saw what Brady must have sensed; there was more than rage in the eyes. There was a sort of disoriented and crippling pain there, the kind of pain I had seen at hospital emergency rooms and at gravesides. Somebody in this condition wasn't going to deck a photographer.

This was not the photograph of a monument. And this individual in this marvelously sharp old photograph had none of that fruity air of old-fashionedness: comical hairdo, pompous face, outrageous whiskers. Lee was peculiarly modern looking, much more so than even Lincoln or most of the other people posed in that same era by Brady. Was it because he was still in shock after the surrender and didn't have enough wits left to pose formally, to stuff one hand into his gray coat and stare off into space as stiff as a zombie?

Here I am, said the tired eyes in the photo, puffy-lidded. Your camera is the eye of the world, Mr. Brady, and I feel it heavy and hostile upon me. You have me trapped, sir. So take me as I am. But don't expect me to smile for you. I daresay I shall never smile again for anyone.

Huh. The name Robert E. Lee reminded me of bigots and murder and shame. This face reflected none of that.

Had anyone ever succeeded in easing his misery after the photo was taken? Friends or family? I didn't even know if he had a family.

Calm lined face, clipped white beard and short moustache.

Thinning white hair framing a high forehead. Large hands and tiny aristocratic feet in polished leather. Brass glitter on the useless uniform. Somebody needs to come out on that porch and put their arms around you, General.

I thumbed hastily backwards through the pages until I found a reproduction of a painting. A young man looked out from the picture in the high-collared, epauletted uniform of a U.S. Army officer, his wavy black hair in long sideburns down the lean cheeks, his face clean shaven. I read the small print under the image: Lieutenant R. E. Lee at age thirty-one.

Again strangely modern in his frank and unsilly appearance. Bubba would maybe like to see this. He's an army brat. Hmmm. I never would have thought it: high cheekbones, brown eyes, nice nose and wide mouth with a thin carefully-drawn upper lip and a full lower one. Who thinks of Lee as young? Square chin with a slight cleft in it that will eventually be hidden by that famous beard. He looks ready to trade a bit of witty repartee with the artist. Happy and open, no defenses at all. Ignorant of what is to come, and aren't we all?

"So that's what you looked like before they crowned you the Savior of The South," I told him out loud. "Bet you couldn't beat the women off with a stick."

I could hear Mama in the kitchen, the ramshackle rattle of old pots in the greasy smelling air. The phone rang. It wasn't for me.

I shifted my weight and rubbed the calf of my left leg. I wasn't prepared for a young Lee at all. That white beard had always seemed like something he was born with. Here he was, young. With a movie star chin, of all damn things.

I had been avoiding a certain word, unwilling to give him any credit at all, but I was forced to think it to myself now because there was no adequate synonym: *gorgeous*. Nobody had told me that Lee had been gorgeous. No doubt about it, the man was a storybook prince.

Poor boy, I thought. Poor poor boy. Life is gonna carve you up and have you for dinner, honey.

Three

Grandmama Moser was sitting in the dark when we paid her a visit in Rock Hill that Sunday, Beth Ann and Mama and me. Her rocking chair creaked on the polished wood floor, curtains drawn stubbornly against the spring sunlight.

"I swanny, Mama." My mother put down the foil-covered platter of fried chicken that we had brought for Sunday dinner. The sideboard was dusty. "It's like a coal mine in here."

"Who cares?" Grandmama rubbed at her face.

"Miz Spence asked about you at church today."

"No love lost between me and Eula Spence. Her daughter still courtin' that ol' widower from Gastonia who thinks he can guess folks' ages from their phone book listin's?"

Beth Ann and I exchanged resigned looks. Grandmama had gone downhill pretty fast in the last few years. Her chair squeaked rhythmically as we settled ourselves onto a faded velvet sofa.

"You ought to put your chair back on the carpet," my mother went on. I could see her peering closely at the weed-choked garden outside the window as she pulled back the funereal drapery to let the light in. Springtime used to find Grandmama outside with the azaleas and roses and camellias. This spring the garden was a neglected tangle.

"Put the chair back on the carpet now, Mama. You're ruinin' the polish on the floors, rockin' on them like that."

"Chair crawls on the carpet."

Frustrated, Mama wheeled on me and Beth Ann. "Y'all hungry?"

"No ma'am," said my sister.

"Y'all keep Grandmama company while I go fix us some dinner." Mama walked briskly off to the kitchen, high heels tapping on the floors like the clock-ticks from the mantelpiece.

"You hungry, Grandmama?" I asked.

She rocked furiously, blue-veined hands like claws gripping the arms of the chair as if she were afraid it would throw her.

Beth Ann leaned over to me to whisper, lips right beside my heavy brass earring. I could smell the childish, sweaty scent of her hair. "This isn't goin' too well, is it?"

I nudged her.

"You're lookin' poorly, Garnet," Grandmama said suddenly.

"Ma'am?" Oh great. Was there something the matter with my other leg now?

"You look right poorly, honey. Azalee feedin' you enough?"

Terrific. "Yes'm."

"She eats like a sow," affirmed Beth Ann.

My mother was calling from the kitchen: "Mama, where's the can opener?"

"Nigger maid probably stole it," Grandmama answered. "It's probably in a Jew pawn shop right now."

Beth Ann sighed. "Here we go again."

Mama was making an incredible racket, opening and shutting drawers. Beth Ann jumped up opportunistically, ignoring my restraining pull on her shirttail. "S'cuse me, y'all. I better go help Mama in the kitchen."

"There's a bowie knife under the sink," Grandmama offered.

I was trapped by courtesy, alone with my grandmother, wanting to join the others in the kitchen where it was bright and warm, where I wouldn't have to make crazy small talk.

She was looking at me, intent blue eyes on my knee.

I said, "Been rainin' up here much lately?" and pulled down my miniskirt hem as far as it would go.

She shook her head. "What's Doctor Spence say?"

"About my . . . ?"

A bony finger pointed. I fidgeted.

"I'm not goin' to him anymore. He doesn't do anything but bellow, 'How we doin', Little Lady?' and then sends us a bill that could choke a whale."

She nodded. "Doctors kept tellin' your poor granddaddy that he had gas until he dropped dead with heart failure."

"Yes'm."

"Wisht my mother had been around to take a look at him. She could draw poison from bee stings. Cain't no doctor do that. She could suck out pain from an earache. Cain't nobody do that nowadays."

"No ma'am."

"The old folks knew about stuff like that. My grandmaw, now, she was a wonder. The only one home when Charleston burnt. It caught the baby's dress on fire. Grandmaw just rubbed somethin' into the burns. They had took off towards the Mills House—only thing left standin' for miles. Used a salve made up by their old nigger woman. Don't know what it was. Fixed the child right up. General Lee himself held the baby while Grandmaw rubbed its little backside. Niggers aren't worth a durn nowadays. Only know how to cause trouble."

"The general held the baby?" I said. "Was the baby your mother, my own great-grandmother? Where was this, Grandmama?"

"Mills House. First year of the war." The old woman resumed rocking, carpet slippers making a dry scuffling noise on the floor, like rats or roaches. "He'd been sent to Charleston to see to the fortifications. Whole town caught afire, don't know how. The Mills House was a hotel. Grandmaw was runnin' down the block with the screamin' baby, dodgin' the old horse-drawn fire engines, and bumps into a heap of folks evacuatin' the hotel. Lee was handlin' that. Didn't nobody pay attention to who he was then, just another officer with no field command yet. He saw Grandmaw and took her arm and pulled her amongst his charges. Tall good-lookin' gentleman, wasn't white-headed yet. She had the baby in one arm and the pickle jar full of ointment in the other and was tryin' to get the lid open, cryin' up a storm. 'Allow me, Madam,' says he, and takes the baby, while Grandmaw gets out a glob of salve and smears it all over my mother's nekkid little fanny. 'I got a heap of children of my own,' says he, dandlin' the baby and it screamin' bloody murder. 'I wouldn't worry too much if I were you,' he tells Grandmaw. 'The burns aren't near as bad as they look.' But he found her a good doctor in all the confusion and got her a place to spend the night. She never forgot it."

"I should think not," I said, inhaling every word. I knew so little about family history. I had never wanted to give my great-aunts or uncles the chance to rant about the good old days and tell me how degenerate young people were now and how the NASA space shots were screwing up the weather. "Did any of our menfolks serve under him?"

The wrinkled mouth made a snorting noise. "Only way to beat the Confederate draft was in a hearse. Your great-great-grandpaw was an infantry captain. Captain Amos Bates Cooke. Helped organize his own outfit fresh out of the Citadel. Died at Gaines' Mill. Got the whole top of his head shot clean off. My grandpaw. The burned baby's daddy. Left his family a Bible and a picture. Picture's supposed to be around here someplace, used to be in the bottom drawer of my dresser. Nigger maid probably stole that too."

I didn't express my doubts about a black woman willingly possessing the image of my Rebel forebear. I was busy picturing the strong helpless hands in the Brady photograph holding my injured great-grandmother.

I said, "Were there any more of our kin that knew Lee?"

"T'weren't anybody that *knew* Lee, honey. Old folks used to say he was a hard man to get to know. Pleasant and friendly, but aloof. However, I imagine that you have veterans on your daddy's side too, if that's what you mean. I never knew a Laney who could keep out of a good fight." She fussed with her blouse. "My mama was friends with Mildred when she grew up."

"Mildred who?"

"Mildred Childe Lee. The general's youngest daughter. That's who I was named after."

Why didn't I just come up here and interview this hateful old dingbat instead of bothering with books? I asked myself. "Well, I knew your name was Milly—"

"I'm Mildred Lee Caskie Moser." The proud old face turned its hooded eyes on me. "That's who I am."

"Garnet?" It was a call from Mama in the kitchen.

"Just a minute!" I shouted back.

But her footsteps could be heard tapping across wood floors. I sat back in the sofa and looked up as she came in.

"Don't tire her out, honey," Mama said. "She might not feel like doin' so much talkin'. She's not used to you—"

"The child asked a question, Azalee." The creaky voice was patient but firm. "She's never asked me stuff before. Nobody asks me stuff. Get on back in the kitchen like a good girl and let me tell this child what she wants to know."

Mama gave me a shrug but her worried eyes were saying, If you get her all wound up about communists and colored people . . .

"Let us alone and fix us some breakfast, Azalee. I'll let Garnet know when I'm tired. I'll just lay down on the floor." Grandmama gave a scratchy laugh.

Mama gave us a resigned look and marched back to the kitchen. I leaned in closer. "You were saying, Grandmama?"

"Did she find the can opener?"

"Grandmama." I got up and stopped the rocking chair, one hand clamped onto its back. "Tell me about Mildred."

"Mildred Lee? Oh, she's dead. Died in 1905. Mama and she had written each other when they were young. Mildred always got a kick out of her daddy seein' Mama's bare bottom that time in Charleston. 'Course, Mama was a baby then and so it doesn't count. Mildred had a lot of friends. She played the piano. She wasn't pretty and she never married. Well, come to think of it, none of 'em ever married. Not even the pretty one."

"None of who?" Girls who couldn't get a proposal were a preoccupation of mine.

"The Lee girls. All four of 'em died on the vine. Mildred once told Mama that no fella they met could compare with their daddy. He doted on 'em. Doted on all his children. One of those girls died during the war. Cain't recollect that one's name; she was already a grown woman. Now ol' Mildred wasn't pretty; not ugly, just plain. Had her daddy's big features crammed onto her mother's little plain face. Mama had a picture of her."

Don't say it, Grandmama: Nigger maid probably stole that, too. "Did you ever meet her?" I asked.

"Law, no. Mama and she didn't see one another after Mama married and left Virginia, where her folks had sent her to school. Mama was younger than Mildred, anyway. But they wrote some. Mildred kept house for her batchelor brother until he retired. She sent my mother a sweet little baby dress when I was born in 1889. Made it herself. Folks made things in those days. Nobody had much money after the war."

"I thought Lee was some kind of aristocrat."

"Blue blood don't pay the mortgage."

"But his son didn't marry either?" What had been the matter with these people?

"Two of the boys married. The eldest never did, some ol' gal had jilted him during the war. There were a pile of those children. They were a peculiar family. They say that the oldest boy died a drunk."

"How were they peculiar?"

She shrugged. "Cain't put it into words. But the war made 'em real clannish. They stuck together and didn't seem to want anybody else gettin' too close. The mother was crippled and they all took care of her, mostly."

Oh shit.

"People took care of the old folks in those days. No one has time for old people now."

Her face had changed; I could see that the conversation had taken a bad turn while I was dwelling on crippled female types.

"Oh, Grandmama."

"Well, who needs me?" Her voice wasn't pleasant. "I buried four babies before Azalee was born. All my friends are dead. Azalee and Richard don't need me for a blame thing. Your grand-daddy has laid himself down and, God willin', I'll follow him over Jordan as soon as my ol' ticker convinces itself that there's no use goin' on with anything."

I didn't want to hear this, I wanted to shut her up. I felt guilty.

I bent hastily over the ladder back of the chair, putting my hands on the bony shoulders. "I love you, Grandmama," I lied. "I need you."

"No you don't." She slipped out from under my braceleted arms. "You don't even know me, child."

I looked down at the top of the bent white head where the parted hair was thin and tangled like the roses struggling in the garden outside. There was nothing I could say.

"Run off to New York and forget about us," Grandmama was muttering. "We've done the best we could. I know you don't approve of me and the way I think. But I was born before there were any auto-mobiles or aeroplanes or civil rights legislation or durnfool communists, and my day has passed me by."

"You've done well," I said, my gift of gab failing me for once. I knew how false I sounded.

I felt like a jerk. There was a long pause.

"You see, Garnet," she began finally, as the sounds of Mama

and Beth Ann bickering in the kitchen wafted out to us, "that's one thing that Jesus didn't preach on. He didn't understand it."

"Understand what?"

"What it's like to get old."

I wandered back over to the doorway mute, thinking about prematurely whitened hair. I stood upon Grandmama's shadow and it moved under my feet: the shadow of Mildred Lee Caskie Moser rocking, a curious dreamlike darkness, a moving stain on the polished wood floor.

Four

The winter of 1861. December.

A hundred years before my time. One-hundred-and-five years before I will stand in my grandmother's house.

I am the daughter of Azalee Moser. Azalee Moser is the daughter of Mildred Caskie, who is the daughter of Liza Cooke, who is the daughter of Elizabeth Ann Middleton. And that autumn night in 1861, Elizabeth Ann Middleton Cooke runs crazy down the Charleston sidewalks with six-month-old Liza in her arms, stumbling at gaps in the brick pavement where oak tree roots push upwards. Her mouth is open, a mewing sound comes out.

The fire is upon them. Blackened, ragged edges of the baby's white dress curl back to show blistered welts running up the child's legs. Its screams are drowned out in the clatter of horseshoes on the paving stones as company after company of firemen rush past, riding down anything in their way that doesn't heed the clangor of their alarm bells. Few men are among the shoving figures that crowd the sidewalks. Fort Sumter out in the harbor has been fired upon some time ago and there is a full-scale war on further north. Many soldiers are manning the coastal defenses and Carolina companies have marched to Richmond, Elizabeth Ann's husband among them.

Death by smoke inhalation had been her proper fate by all rights, for she had been asleep in the big bed when Providence waked her. The townhouse was empty, the servants off for the day, up the country with her mother. Needles of flame had crept unheeded up the curtains in the smoky dark. Wrapping a chemise around her mouth and nose, she had lurched across the room to the cradle. The canopy was already afire.

Unconscious, the baby lay amid smouldering fabric. Elizabeth Ann flung off the old chemise and beat out the cradle flames with her mothering hands, hating them, slapping at them, then taking up her child to flee. Detached, her mind thought of a thousand things at once: the jar of Lucy's skin balm somewhere among the shaving brushes on Amos's washstand, the whereabouts of her silk wrapper so that she needn't flee into the streets indecently clad, the look on Amos's face if he had gotten a letter two weeks from now, telling him that his child was dead.

But the child is alive, its first conscious breath a scream. Elizabeth Ann rushes out of the house in her thin flannel nightgown, the jar of skin balm in hand, her wrapper forgotten in her haste. The baby screams. The child is alive but hurt. Elizabeth Ann has already gone through the curious numbness of contemplating its death. Now it is alive—hurting. Somehow she can bear that less. If Liza dies now, it will be like losing her a second time. Elizabeth Ann doesn't think that she can bear this again.

"Amos! Amos!" she calls out futilely to her distant husband as she staggers down the hysterical street in her house slippers.

Two women—one black, one white—shove past her with a rolled-up Persian carpet on their shoulders. The sky behind her is lit bright, like Tuesday in Hades, the shadows waving all over the mob in the streets. Some people are running back towards the fire, looters or owners of threatened possessions, snaggletoothed dirty layabouts and old men with their watch chains a-jingle. Trapped horses shriek in the flames blocks away. The baby in her arms screams and fights for breath so that it can scream again.

A fleeing dog runs under her feet and she stumbles, losing a slipper. She stoops, groping for her slipper. Trampling feet, elbows, hips bash at her head and at the baby and she gives it up, losing her bearings when she straightens with a ringing in her ears. Her foot is bleeding.

Something has her by the arm. Fingers. She wrenches, snarling and terrified, but the fingers tighten to the point of pain and are attached to an arm that apparently belongs to a half-seen bearded face materializing behind panicked bodies. The arm encircles her waist and lifts her bodily off her feet. She is spun about like a rag doll, jostling against her kidnapper's hip as he fights his way through. A solid wall looms ahead of her and a knot of people stand pressed to it, out of the path of the lunatic crowd pushing past. There are women and soldiers taking refuge against the building. Children, too. She has an impression of scuffed boots and gray knees as she is deposited upon her feet among the watchers.

"Stand over here, Madam," comes a deep pleasant voice at her ear, and the arm relinquishes her gently.

She looks up at the profiled bearded face and broad-brimmed military hat. Calm eyes watch another fire company up the street come charging through the throng. "They are driving up on the sidewalks," he says, and shrugs out of his uniform coat to drape it over her shoulders.

The wind is cold here. She clutches the screaming Liza to her breast, huddling her under the soft wool. The wind whips at her loose hair. The fire company gallops past. Someone is crying. Someone is saying, "Amos, Amos."

The gray wool parts. Light falls upon Liza, cuddled there under her tent. Elizabeth Ann stares up into the officer's face and his dark brown, enormous eyes with firelight in them. They crinkle sympathetically at the corners. His hand goes gently under the coat to pull back the burned fabric of the baby's dress. "Let's have a look, Madam."

Amos. Amos. She's burned, Amos. I couldn't help it, I swear.

"General?" A young soldier stares over the officer's shoulder. "I believe that's it, sir."

Black eyes wheel around. "Yes?"

"I think we've evacuated the hotel, sir."

The officer nods. "Keep them together. We might have to move on, if the building looks like it's going to go up."

The aide turns. Elizabeth Ann's rescuer calls him back: "Cap'n Taylor!"

"Yessir?"

"See if any of these ladies have something in their belongings for burns. We have a little casualty here."

Amos's wash stand! Lucy's jar upon Amos's wash stand. Elizabeth Ann still clutches it. She sneaks it out from under her gray mantle now, amazed that it hasn't been dropped in the street.

The officer reaches for the jar, takes her by the arm and steers her over into the firelight. Sits her down on the doorway steps and then takes a place beside her. He undoes the lid without a word. It smells like hog lard.

"Wait!" she says. Elizabeth Ann doesn't want him to have to put his fingers into the stuff. She takes the jar and the lid from him, Liza in her lap. Holds the jar and lid, hands shaking, then loses track of what she is about. She needs a third hand. Her vision blurs.

"Shall I take the baby?" he prompts, not waiting for her acquiescence but taking up the child in big, careful hands and cuddling her against his waistcoat. Liza sobs. "Can you see well enough here, Madam?"

She nods, weeping, lifting the charred dress and smearing balm into the red blisters, tender fingers barely touching the skin. The infant bellows. The officer pats the baby's back, watching.

He tilts back the brim of his hat when she is done and looks down, moving her hand away from the wounds for a moment.

The gas light over the doorway is out but the flameglow is bright enough. He studies the burns.

Elizabeth Ann studies his face. The brows go up after a long moment and the corners of his mouth begin to turn upwards. He meets her eyes, smiling, something suddenly playful in his expression. "Ah! little Madam, you *have* been living right!"

"She's—?"

"She'll be fine. Dancing a jig in a week." He sticks two fingers into the pocket of his waistcoat and pulls out a handkerchief. "We need a bandage or something here. Got to keep the area protected."

Elizabeth Ann watches him tie two corners of the white cotton around Liza's little leg and then knot the other two around her other leg.

"There we are. A rather thin and baggy diaper," he mutters. "My wife would never approve, and it certainly will not do the job that diapers must do, but . . ."

His tenderness is unnerving. Elizabeth Ann breaks down totally and starts to squall louder than the baby.

He puts a warm arm around her shoulders and pulls her close. "Don't cry on me now, Madam! I'm plumb out of handkerchiefs!"

Her watery eyes peer over her forearm and she wipes her cheeks on the sleeve of her nightgown. The crow's feet at his eyes are a merry radiance. "My dear sir," she finally begins, not knowing at all what to say to this phenomenon. "My dear sir . . . My very very dear sir."

He laughs—beautiful teeth, beautiful laughter—snuggling little Liza close, her tiny fists rummaging among the dark gray curls above his ears.

"Oh, I've got children myself. Nearly grown. Too big entirely to cuddle like this, you know. Out of diapers for a very long time." He glances at her. "Do you have a place to stay, Mrs. . . . ?"

"Cooke," she supplies the surname and shakes her head.

"Well, Mrs. Cooke, if this hotel stays intact, I believe we might work out some arrangement. Mrs. Long, yonder there, has a great big room, and I think I'll have no trouble keeping Colonel Long occupied for the rest of the evening."

She nods, unable to speak.

He raises an eyebrow. "Don't cry, now."

A giddy silly smile comes to her face. She wants to kiss his hand, his feet.

He pats the child's back. "Well, Miss Baby—"

"She's named Elizabeth but we call her Liza. Amos and I."

"Well, Miss Baby Liza. How're we doing?" He holds the baby out from him a little way. She stares round-eyed. Kicks her legs. That hurts her and she starts to cry again, but not nearly as heartrendingly as before. The officer laughs and holds her close again and begins to sing softly into her tiny ear, the old minstrel tune "Little Liza Jane," rendered in a nearly inaudible but passable baritone. His eyes, however, watch the situation over the baby's shoulder and miss nothing.

Elizabeth Ann sits and shivers in the cold wind with no idea that she will be called upon a few years hence to recount every detail of this meeting for an audience of family and friends and even a reporter from the *Mercury*. She will tell them that she has never seen such eyes, that only saints or angels could watch the world with that much kindness and power. But that really isn't what she is thinking. What she has really noticed is what a fine-looking man he is for his obvious age. He is quite as old as Papa but he is the handsomest man I have ever seen.

Captain Taylor's head appears over the barricade of women again. "General Lee?"

The singing stops.

"Looks like they're standin' off the fire for the moment, sir. Guess it's safe to let the ladies go back inside for a while."

The general hands Liza back to her mother and stands, turns and tips his hat to her, then motions to the woman introduced as Mrs. Long, who takes her place beside Elizabeth Ann with a kind smile.

"Mrs. Long will see you upstairs, Mrs. Cooke," the general

35

tells her. "But be ready to evacuate at a moment's notice. This strong wind bodes no good, I'm afraid." He is watching developments up the street where a scuffle seems to be underway. He glances back down. "It appears that we military folk might have a little unofficial work before we join you."

His eyes meet those of his aides for only an instant but Elizabeth Ann notices how the younger men quickly react.

She watches the tall figure stalk up the street towards the riot in his waistcoat and shirtsleeves, broad shouldered and narrow hipped, competent. He wears no weapons and she can see that he will need none.

A hundred feet away, he turns and raises his hat. Dark gray hair blows in the night winds. "I'll find you a doctor!" he calls.

She knows that she will never forget him.

Five

Is there such a thing as genetic memory? I wondered.

I couldn't stop thinking about what Grandmama had told me. I reconstructed the Charleston fire over and over in my mind.

I couldn't have said just what there was about the story that resonated in me. But it seemed miraculous now that I existed at all. If Amos had decided to wait until after the war to marry Elizabeth Ann Middleton, there would have been no me. If little Liza's burns had become infected or if she and her mother had caught pneumonia that windy night, I would never have been born.

But a soldier had performed one insignificant act of kindness, before events swept him off to crises of his own, and I was alive. Maybe because of that one small act. Was this why I was living? Was I glad?

"His name was Robert Edward Lee and he was the ranking Confederate general by the end of the American Civil War," I read out loud from my report. Rain pattered against the classroom windows. A fly lit upon my handwriting and I brushed it away. "He invented the railroad gun and trench warfare on the modern

scale. He inflicted more casualties upon Grant's huge army in the
Wilderness campaign than there were able-bodied men in his
own. His strategy was studied by the Allies in World War One and
the British claim several Allied victories were rooted in this inspiration. MacArthur studied his campaigns. At the time of the
Allied landing on the Normandy beaches in World War Two,
General Omar Bradley psyched himself up for D-Day by reading
a book called *Lee's Lieutenants.*

"Be that as it may." I raised my left eyebrow, a maneuver
practiced incessantly in front of the bathroom mirror. "I'm not a
military student. All I know is the won/lost record. People have
their own opinions about Lee's military ability, anyway, so I'm not
going to deal with that. What I'm dealing with here is what most
people have forgotten: that as a paroled prisoner of war, this
paragon found himself taking a job as president of a bankrupt
country college at a salary of $1500 a year in an era when your
average railroad presidents made $10,000 per. And he died with-
out pardon, essentially stripped of his American citizenship. A
non-person . . . That's about it. Why was I assigned a non-person,
Mr. Damadian?"

I caught my teacher's eye with its befuddled look.

Nobody else seemed to be listening. My friend Anita was
filing her nails and Bubba Hargett was watching the rain fall. Talk
about non-persons! I thought at him. Garnet, the Non-person.
You've never even told me hello, Mr. Bubba.

"There are two kinds of people," I read on. "The carnal, who
are content with being people. And then there's the other kind,
people who try to turn themselves into walking brains because
they are scared of their bodies and what their bodies make them
feel."

That's me, I realized.

"Showing emotion, for someone like this, is to go naked."

There! Ha ha. I could sense ears pricking up all around at that.
Jackasses.

"There's nothing wrong with being naked," I ad libbed. "You just gotta be careful who you get naked with."

"Wahoo!" somebody in back cheered. Everybody laughed.

"My gosh," I grinned, "there's people awake in here after all." I ruffled through my papers but saw out of the corner of my eye that Bubba's mouth was twitching. He was listening. Now I got nervous.

"Well." I resumed my formal tone, an over-enunciated delivery with lots of final consonants that I affected whenever I became self-conscious. I loathed it. I couldn't help it. I turned into Bette Davis under scrutiny. "Lee was actually very emotional on the inside. Had a hot temper. Cried easily, something that men in his day were almost as persnickety about hiding as we are. He was a sucker for pretty women. He took an occasional drink, contrary to popular belief. And he must have lived in terror of his occasional urges to run off the rails: to slug a subordinate in the mouth, console himself with an adoring belle, or just to get stinking drunk after Gettysburg and forget the whole durn thing."

Whoops, I had almost said "damn." I wondered what Damadian would do if I cussed in his class. He was looking down at his roll book at all the names. Trying to place me, maybe.

I'm Garnet Laney, Mr. Damadian. I'm the chick who wants to get cancer. I go on:

"Lee's outer shell built up from within. It wasn't evident in his boyhood. But by the time he had finished West Point, he was already in the habit of confiding his stronger feelings to nobody."

He should have taken up smoking, I said to myself.

Bubba was watching me. I had the sudden urge to scratch my nose.

"He would have been happier if he had let some of this out. His wife spent years of their early married life away from him, spoiled rotten in childhood in the luxury of her parents' plantation, unwilling to share army life with her young husband for long. He should have been outraged. But he wrote her long plaintive letters and physically ached for her at the lonely military outposts. And he could have been firmer with his junior officers during the Civil War: Longstreet and Stuart lollygagging at Gettysburg, for instance. He should've put his foot down to everybody from time to time. Hauled some rear ends into courts martial. Taken a mistress."

Damadian was staring at me. Maybe I've gone too far. But I could hear Bubba's delighted snort from where I stood. Now my frigging nose itched like it was going to fall off.

"Yet Robert was Lighthorse Harry Lee's son," I went on, "and hence he would always have to be beyond disgrace. Lighthorse Harry, cavalry hero of the Revolution, was George Washington's protégé—ol' George had been in love once with Harry's beautiful mother. Harry was an irresponsible rake who used up the family's whole share of human failings. Harry chased women. Was a compulsive gambler who lost all of the family property to stupid financial speculation. He had been Governor of Virginia once, but he was thrown into debtors' prison right after Robert was born. Ultimately he abandoned his wife and five children and ran off to Barbados. He never came back.

"So there would be no human failings allowed Harry's youngest boy, just six years old when his father abandoned him. None would be allowed and he would ask for none. His personality must gleam like the flashing yellow glitter of his epaulets. He would polish his soul as relentlessly as he polished his brass . . ." Careful, careful, too much rhetoric, I reminded myself. You've been reading too many Victorians lately. "For it would take more than conventional behavior to redeem the unsavory memory of Lighthorse Harry. Harry would have been enough for any family, but there was also Robert's elder half-brother Henry, whose very nickname became a dirty joke in the South: 'Black Horse Harry' Lee, another thoroughgoing deadbeat, who became famous when he was hauled into court on a paternity rap. He had fathered a child by his underaged ward after—you guessed it—squandering her entire inheritance! His wife was a dope addict, she didn't take much note.

40

"Sex and money! Money and sex! These were carnal people, chillun. They dragged their shame out into the light and held it up for everybody to see, while the youngest boy tried to turn himself into solid marble."

Kids could do a lot of things in self-defense. Kids could get all weird if they felt like outcasts.

"Is it any *wonder*—" I let my voice rise for a big finish. "—that this repressed child became one of the most sheerly aggressive commanders in military history? What enormous reserves of hostility he must have had to draw upon! God help the Union generals who had to face Robert E. Lee on a battlefield. They didn't know what they were up against."

The classroom was utterly quiet. I collected my papers and indulged my masochism by glancing at Bubba Hargett. He wasn't looking at me anymore, he was watching the rain.

I thought, I've just tried to tell you something, Bubba Hargett. I've just tried to tell you something important about myself and I don't even know what it is.

My fingers rustled my notebook pages, failing to locate my pencil and my belongings on the slick wood surface of the podium.

I slunk back to my desk, weak-kneed, feeling (I swear to God) like I wasn't wearing any clothes. Naked. My face got hot.

It wasn't until I took my seat and put away my notes, that I raised my head, feigning composure, to discover Bubba's pale eyes locked on me.

Six

🌿

Elizabeth Ann Middleton Cooke isn't born yet. But her mother is a little girl running about the gardens of a South Carolina lowlands plantation house. The air of 1823 is in her lungs. The lace edges of her snowy bonnet flutter at her cheeks.

Miles to the north lies Alexandria, Virginian village on the Potomac. And inside a modest townhouse, in the quiet of a darkened hallway, a small ill woman sits by a coat rack, waiting.

Ann Carter Lee. Always waiting for something, in her patient Scots way. She sits in the dim light until her youngest son comes bounding down the staircase.

"Ready?"

Ann nods. He lifts her in his arms, her small booted feet dangling, and carries her to the door.

"You done forgot your muff, Miss Ann!" the maid, Nancy, calls after them. "You better bundle up, it's still right chilly outside."

The tall boy turns at the threshold so the maid can slip the warm fur over Ann's weak gloved fists. "Don't you be keepin' her out too long now, Mr. Robert," Nancy mutters, fluffing the cloak collar tighter around Ann's throat. "You heard what the doctor says."

"I shan't." Impatiently, he shifts from one foot to the other.

"Goodness sakes, boy, stand still!" Nancy's fingers are trying to tie bonnet strings under Ann's chin.

Robert waits, eyeing the hall clock. His eldest full-brother Carter is The Brilliant One; Smith, The Handsome One. And Robert? Robert is the sort of child, Ann thinks, who will bring you a bouquet of nasturtiums and unwittingly trample all over your garden. And you'd better not mention the trampling, or he'll be out there with spade and watering can in the middle of the night trying to rectify the damage.

Old Nat has the rickety carriage waiting for them at the curb. Robert deposits her onto the worn leather seat and stuffs her skirts inside before he hurries around and into the street to climb in beside her, whistling. The carriage surges away.

How old is Robert, sixteen? He is quite tall for sixteen. Ann is disturbed by his adolescence. He is high-spirited, sometimes a mite rowdy. He needs a father's firm hand. Well, no help for that. His grown-up half-brother Henry Lee has already given him The Talk, in two words only: "Do *not*." It is left up to Robert to apply that short sermon to whatever his imagination suggests.

Ann hands him her muff and, by the time they reach the river, she is trailing one gloved hand in the early spring wind. The sun shines under her bonnet, a pleasing blindness. When she can again see, she sees that the boy has become a hussar with the muff stuffed down over his wavy hair like a Cossack's hat. "Don't do that! You'll stretch it all out of shape! Give it here."

"Versatile garment," he remarks. Holds it out to her. "Looks like dog fur."

"It's bearskin. Cost me a great deal."

"Not as much as it cost the bear." He sighs through his teeth. Pulls some of the hair out of the muff. "Lookathere. He had leprosy."

"It's old. I purchased that thing before you were born."

Schoolboys loaf by in their hobnailed shoes, metal scraping the bricks of the sidewalks, fishing poles over their shoulders as they amble to the river. Robert watches. Makes himself stop watching. Plays with his thumbs.

Ann looks at her lap. "I'm sorry," she mutters, understanding.

He doesn't answer.

She was able to get around quite well when Carter and Smith were growing up. Carter and Smith got to fish and shoot quail and swim in the river whenever they pleased. But now she lies abed in the afternoons and watches Robert from her window as he makes his after-school trips to market for her and the girls, shopping basket on his arm, keys to the storeroom jangling in his pocket as he sprints up the sidewalk. On his way to mingle with housekeepers and elderly black cooks at the stalls where he will count his change and search for bargains in wilted vegetables and day-old eggs. Ann will hear his heels smacking the brick pavement upon his return, keys turning in the storeroom lock, and he will closet himself afterward for a while with the books to record the day's expenditures, juggling the bills that are overdue. Finally Ann will hear him bounding up the stairs to poke his head in her door and give her a solemn wink. It's always dark of an evening when his work is done, the old horse looked after, his pet rabbits fed, a broken shutter or a loose handrail repaired, and Ann's medicines mixed with his large bony hands. He has even taught himself to sew and mends most of his own clothing. Once in a while he will pick nasturtiums.

She clears her throat, upset. "I am not very scintillating company, I'm afraid. Perhaps we should return."

He makes a rather crude but sincere sound of denial. She doesn't have it in her to reprimand him.

Hawks are wheeling over the woods across the river. He gazes to the southeast. She wonders how much he thinks about Stratford. She gave birth to him there in the chill of winter, ill with pneumonia, weeping and not wanting another baby, *any* baby, certainly not another troublesome boy. Suckled him despondently in the sole heated room, where most of the furniture was gone and weak flames flickered in the grate. The old lands and big house are lost to them now. Robert hasn't lived there since he was three. But he told Ann once in a black mood that everybody has to have a real home somewhere, and she suspects that Stratford is the place he clings to in his mind. It doesn't seem possible that he can recall it in such detail, but he remembers the cherubs over the nursery fireplace and the horse chestnut tree Ann planted on the lawn herself when he was still in dresses.

The carriage wheels spin past the yards and walled gardens. She feels him staring at her. She looks up into his round eyes and sees herself mirrored there in twin pools of shiny blackness, Ann sitting abandoned on the creaky springs like a china doll, its face white and unsmiling.

Robert takes her hand. "I hope Papa's in hell."

All the joy goes out of the day. "Don't say such things."

"I hope," he amends, "that Papa did not gain admission to heaven."

What am I going to do about you? she thinks. My sassy little benefactor, my goodhearted friend? Look at how fast you are growing up. There's nothing left for you, child. Carter has squandered it all. He scrapes by at the Law, now, pursuing young ladies. Smith has gone to sea. Annie and Milly have pedigrees and can always attract rich husbands who fancy impoverished gentility and want to trade their fortunes for our ancestors. But what's to become of you? You are content with so little, your rabbits and your dog and your hand-me-down clothes . . .

"Look at that ol' mule yonder, Mama," he interrupts her worries. "He fairly is the spitting image of Mr. Leary, the school-master, don't you agree? Especially the learned expression: the compleat Irish scholar in a reverie of Plato!"

How to get him educated? I can get him married off with no trouble, I think. Wash and Mary Custis have a daughter he rather likes, and she stands to inherit a good bit. A religious and high-minded girl, who will know how to curb these sassy tendencies and settle him down. But college? What is he without college? A planter's son needn't attend college but he is no planter's son and we have nothing to plant, except a city lot full of nasturtiums and snowball bushes. Even that much is not *ours;* we live in a borrowed house rent-free upon the charity of my cousin who is too kind-hearted to turn poor relations out into the street. Dear God, I own *nothing!* Except Nancy and Nat. I can't afford to feed Nancy and Nat, but she pleads, "Don't sell us Miss Ann, please. For the love of God, they beats house niggers in the Mississip!" Nancy cries until I am about to lose my mind. The proceeds from their sale would be gone for debts in a fortnight, anyway. How much do we owe? To whom? Only Robert knows, I guess.

Robert is still raving on about the schoolmaster mule: "A pair of spectacles would properly—"

"How are your marks?" she interrupts.

He blinks. Shrugs with his brows. "Excellent."

She nods. Puts on her stern face. It is the expression she uses in consultation with Henry Lee, Robert's half-brother and legal guardian. "I think he wants to be a doctor," Henry has confided to her, "but that is of course out of the question. He might try for a West Point appointment, Ann, you know. I pledge to do all in my power to contact the necessary officials in that eventuality. He could leave the Army after serving his required time. Go into civil engineering. Engineering would be the branch of service he should push for. Robbie wouldn't find any lucrative civilian future in artillery, for instance."

"But is he intelligent enough?"

Henry pauses at the question, astonished. "Oh yes, dear Ann. Our Robbie has quite a head on his shoulders. Haven't you noticed?"

No. Not at all. Ann hasn't noticed. She hopes, yes, but it is heart that she sees. Every family has a child who makes valentines for Mama. In this family, that child is Robert.

"It will not be easy, Madam," says Mr. Leary the schoolmaster. "I do my best, but I am not the equal of specialists in places like New York City or Baltimore. Still, I believe that Robert is intelligent enough, even with my poor tutelage, to pass the entrance exams if he studies very hard in preparation. And perhaps the military service of his father might still mean something to some politician. The government will pay for his education if he passes, Madam, you understand. And I believe he can pass. He draws conic sections for me like Michelangelo."

Ann studies Robert now. Michelangelo conic sections do not seem possible. This is a plodding child. A dutiful child. A boy who foxhunts with well-to-do relatives but on *foot,* for God's sake, since he cannot afford a horse, running two miles without stopping, with no sense of humiliation, no loss of dignity, ending up with the hounds at the kill before the riders arrive, dogs slobbering all over him.

God forgive us, she thinks. Harry and me. Harry for being Harry and me for loving him. We have collapsed around this child's ears like a burning building.

Robert tilts his face up to the sun in a squint. Ann sees Harry there, the stubborn posture, the fine long-nosed profile. She thinks about the locket that George Washington, Harry's late commander, gave her on her wedding day.

I did not want Robert when he was born. I did not even have a name for him. I had to name him Robert Edward, after my two brothers, when I could not think of anything else. I had pneumonia, God forgive me. I was wishing I were dead. Harry was wherever Harry went in those days, sleeping with whomever Harry slept with. Scheming with our livelihood, gambling for a fortune, hah! And if I had him here with me right now, alive, I would kiss the dust from his boots. I would lick his boots clean like a dog.

Hold your head up, Robert! she would insist when he was a small boy just beginning to be aware of the gossip. Hold your head up and be proud of the great deeds your papa did! Don't speak of his weaknesses. And don't feel obliged to hit Cousin Edmund in the mouth every time he alludes to them. Don't let Edmund see how much he disturbs you. We'll get by.

So she clothed him in the short pants outgrown by Carter and Smith, taught him his catechism and prayers, helped him with his lessons, and held her own head high. Made Robert understand that he must care for his sisters when she was gone, and sent him off for his early tutoring to her sister-in-law Elizabeth, with the injunction to "whip and pray." She attempted to make Carter feel intolerably guilty for wasting so much money at Harvard (Harry's choice, although Harry had been a Princeton man himself), saw poor Smith off to sea, taught Annie and Milly French and piano, and let Robert run the household. Ann, raised genteelly upon a Virginia plantation, kept her misery a secret in the middle of the bleak nights, lying forevermore solitary in Harry's big feather bed. One kept up appearances, at all costs.

She was pulling it off, she thought, learning to deaden her expectations and carry through on pride alone, when Robert had asked her, "Will you leave me too, Mama?"

She had put down her darning, appalled. The dark little boy had stood solemn in the doorway, absurd in his adult stance, his shabby clothes. "For if you will," he had continued in a middle-aged manner, "perhaps you might warn me first. I must find Annie and Milly and me another place to live, you know. It might take a little time."

Not yet nine years old, and he might've been Ann's grandfather.

"Never!" she had promised when she could find words. "I'll never leave you, Robert! I love you!"

A lie, she thinks now, sitting in a dilapidated carriage. A lie. I am leaving you a little more every day, dear child. I think I am dying. Dear God, don't let me until I can find a place for my poor son.

Robert doesn't notice her closed, pained eyes. He is thinking about West Point. About his father the famous soldier. About fine gold-laced uniforms and blooded horses.

About tearing downhill with straining horseflesh under him, sparks flying from hooves as he bends over the animal neck, long fingers against the sleek sides, with the reins held loose. Wind whipping his hair and his splendid uniform, mouth open in a shout of wild free joy that blows behind him in echoes to the Tidewater.

Seven

Perhaps Mr. Leary was a better schoolmaster than he thought himself to be. Or perhaps Henry Lee's confidence in his little half-brother's intelligence had not been misplaced. At any rate, the United States Military Academy was prepared for intelligent cadets but not for perfect cadets. For twenty-three years it had awarded demerits for the normal inattention of the young—irregular margins on academic papers, sloppy salutes, tardiness, badly cleaned muskets—as well as for more serious infractions like drunkenness or insubordination. The idea was for an ambitious plebe to accumulate enough merit points to outweigh the demerits on his record. That was the idea. What to think about a nineteen-year-old boy who finished his first year with no demerits at all?

Was it a fluke? He had the Academy's full attention now, was scrutinized at drill and in the classroom and at the mess hall. And with only a Southern small-town education, he was academically an astonishing Number Two in his class, edging upon the Number One set by a fellow from New York nearly three years his senior. Well, however it was done, it is done: Cadet First Captain

Robert Edward Lee graduates as Adjutant of the Corps, second in the class of 1829, without having received a single demerit in all four years of his Academy career.

But there are no Lees on the Plain among the parents and friends to see him take his diploma. Widow Lee's youngest son accepts the document with gloved hand and makes his way alone to his quarters where his few belongings are already packed. He is oblivious to the hoopla. Guts churning: bad news from home.

A new second lieutenant in the Army Corps of Engineers, he bids goodbye to comrades in a low hurried drawl and gathers up everything he owns at blinding speed, building a small fort of luggage at the threshold.

"The Marble Model seems uncharacteristically distracted," observes an idly interested underclassman lounging against a barracks wall with chums.

"Wondering, no doubt, how to manage the baggage while he walks home on the water down the Hudson," remarks another. Several of the boys snigger.

The first cadet raises a brow. "A thoroughly good chap, actually, our Model. Explained Euclid to me last term in a way that Old Tedium never could. If I were ever tempted to turn queer, that's the man I would turn queer for, I vow."

His classmates had dubbed him The Marble Model because someone there once likened him to Michelangelo's *David;* his polite aloofness has something of marble in it, besides. A certain cool purity, an unchanging calm. It causes no one to hate him, but very few get to know him well. He has shared none of the nightly bull sessions, for he is always in bed at lights-out with his lights dutifully out. He never parties at Benny Havens', because Benny's is off-limits. It occurs to none of the boys that what they take for rectitude is actually abject terror; very few of them attend the Academy with so few alternatives.

An irrepressible young Georgian named Jack Mackay has not been deterred by the stony surface, however, and has come to call him "Bob". Jack is also a widow's son, a middle male child in a house full of sisters, and the two have become close. Joe Johnston and Hugh Mercer, Southerners all, round out the small circle. But it was Jack to whom Robert had mentioned Molly Custis one evening, leaning back in his seat and doodling hexagrams upon a copy book.

"But do you love her?" Jack got right to the point.

Robert shrugged. Doodled. "I've known her since we were children. My mother admires her very much. She's very bright. Digested Spinoza without a belch."

"Good God, man, it isn't your mother's choice to make! Do *you* love her?"

"I expect so. I've never been in love, really. Haven't had time for it."

The hesitancy in the low voice confirmed Jack's longtime suspicion: Robert Lee was still a virgin. And not too happy about it. The silence between the two lengthened as Jack puffed out his cheeks and blew and blew and Robert's pen scratched.

"If you were in love, Bob, you would know it, old man."

Robert didn't look up. "Who else would have me?" A quick laugh, like a bark.

Jack, flabbergasted, could only slap his knees for a moment. "What the *devil* are you talking about?"

The pen went round and round in a spiral. Robert laughed again, humorlessly. "My father, I suppose." And Jack Mackay knew then that they aren't speaking of poverty here, although that is certainly a legitimate consideration; they are dancing carefully around the disgrace of a sad bad old man who has been dead for years and years . . . whom Bob will not discuss. Oh, he'll tell you if you insist about the sword George Washington gave old Harry and how tall old Harry was, et cetera. And then—*wham!*—The subject slams shut and suddenly you'll find yourself examining the merits of international trade or the Dulcinea theme in Cervantes, or some such damn thing.

But *damn* this warped logic, when Bob hasn't a penny to his name and is only twenty-one and already deathly afraid of Marrying Beneath Himself!

What's the infernal hurry?

"You need some fun," Jack observed now, out loud.

"Yes," Robert agreed. "Desperately."

"Well? How about it? I know a couple of jolly barmaids here."

A shrug. "One does a disservice to one's children if one behaves badly."

"One needn't write out a full confession for one's children. Need one?"

Robert's lips twitched, corners upward. "Jack, I don't want my children to have to slink around some day, avoiding questions about one parent. *Either* parent." He slapped the copy book shut. "What was that you said earlier about Napoleon at Marengo?"

And the subject is closed again. Jack says to himself, Good Lord, Bob, how many times have we hurt you with our innocent questions about a Revolutionary War hero, made *you* "slink around" with our thickheaded curiosity, made you wish — ? Jesus! I'm sorry to my soul, old man. I can't even tell you I'm sorry. That good-humored reserve of yours does not permit an acknowledgement of your own hurts, does it? It would hurt you to hear my apology.

Much has been expected here of General Lighthorse Harry Lee's son and he has delivered much, and the cadets, who suppose that such a paternity has made the West Point experience easier for this boy, are unaware of the terrific hazing he was put through his plebe year by upperclassmen who wanted a shot at a bona fide hero's whelp.

The gray group outside the barracks on graduation day sees no hurt in The Marble Model — only haste. Bad news from home.

A steamer and a stagecoach and a long solitary ride, and Robert is soon standing by a bedside at Ravensworth in Virginia where Ann has come to die under the roof of kinfolks. She lies under the coverlet like a fallen branch, emaciated, depleted, cold even in the summer heat. Trembling, Robert dismisses the servants and rolls up his sleeves to mix her medicines again. She watches him push back the dark blue wool above sinewy forearms laced with black hair. He is in uniform, for her, and she burns with a fierce pride. She has waited long for this day, hung onto life with her fingernails until he could come home and tell her, "Mama, I've finished."

She can sleep. It's done. But he anchors her longer, willpower keeping her alive by its resolution. He won't let her nod, he keeps relating one anecdote after another to make her smile. Reads out loud to her. Tells her of his hopes. Teases her about the supposed admiration of some old widower who lives down the road. "Ann Carter," he wags a finger in her face, "your flaming escapades are the talk of two counties."

Day after weary day her dark shrouded eyes follow him around the room as he putters and laughs and trembles. He straightens the coverlet and smooths Ann's wilted hair under the lace cap.

"Robert," she manages the name. "I did not want you when you were born. Did you know that?"

"No," he says. "Shhh. Rest." But her confession injures him.

And the day soon comes when he is there with her and she stops breathing. There is no drama, nothing transcendental. The next breath is simply not drawn, as if Ann in her stupor has made a decision not to draw it.

He has been trembling for days and now the tremor works its way through him as he waits for her to breathe again. His teeth chatter audibly and he clamps his jaws shut to listen for the next hiss of inhalation through the peeling lips, knowing that it will not come, insisting to God that it *must* come. Surely it will.

He believes he is praying but what he is thinking is, Dear God I hate You I hate You. Oh Mama. Oh please Mama.

But now he is the only person in the room. The thing on the bed isn't Ann.

Function, he orders himself. *Function!*

But nothing will except his eyes.

Eight

Nat, the family coachman and man-of-all-work, has had worsening bouts of consumption all winter. When Carter Lee discovers that Robert has been posted to Cockspur Island near Savannah upon his first engineering assignment, he suggests that Robert take Nat to that gentler climate. The family is breaking up, young Milly going to Baltimore to stay with married Annie, Robert leaving. The few dresses and tablecloths Ann has willed them are parceled out. This is the end of anything like home for these people. Robert and Nat push off south, the old man coughing all the way.

"*Eat,* Nat," Robert insists, dishing up the stew he has prepared for the two of them, fumbling with the medicine bottles the apothecary has sold him.

"Don't worry none about me, young Marse." The old man turns over in bed, waving Robert away with a pale-palmed hand. "I just be down in my back a little."

"Nat," says Robert, "I can't lose you."

Skinny old black arms rise from the sheets. "Come here, son."

Robert bends into the embrace. The sick old man pats his back, reassuring. "Just got a little croup, son. I be fine in a day or two."

But no. Nat is laid in the alien Georgia soil, far from home.

Robert sketches turtles in his off-duty moments, hard-shelled creatures who carry their homes with them. He has looked many a turtle in the eye.

One early holiday lures him back to the Old Dominion upon business with his brother Carter and he moseys over to Arlington again to plague the Custises. An old militia major, "Wash" Custis is never very glad to see him, but his wife and daughter break out in unaccustomed finery for dinner and sit up late with Robert afterwards while he reads out loud to them from some cockeyed British author that Mrs. Custis fancies. Major Custis has har-rumphed off to bed, but lamps are still lit in the parlor and drawing room. It is a sad, odd night on the whole; nobody mentions the scandal Henry Lee has lately been embroiled in, nor Robert's profession, nor how he is billeted. Another sordid Lee scandal; another impecunious Lee in the parlor—what else is new? But the ladies are attentive, and they have not thrown him out.

"Robert must be tired, dear," Mrs. Custis speaks up when he gets to the end of an interminable chapter. "Why don't you see if he will take some of that fruitcake, on the sideboard, in yonder?"

Molly gets to her feet. Robert stands. "Allow me," he says.

"You may help," she says over her shoulder, her pretty dress of some sateen stuff rustling in the semi-dark hallway like soft leaves. She is tall for a girl, and usually cares nothing for clothes or the latest Paris hairdos, but tonight she is dressed to the nines. He follows, admiring her shoulderblades and narrow corseted waist. She turns and flushes, plain face all coy and discomfited.

They face each other by the sideboard. "Will you marry me?" he says.

"Mercy!" she exclaims. "This isn't how it's done."

"Shall I kneel?" He is serious. He has no idea how this is done.

"Fetch me that knife over there, please."

He does so. She whacks at the cake like a woodsman.

"I'm not making a jest here, Molly. Will you marry me?"

"Of course." She hands him a slice. Bugger the cake. Her skin is creamy in the soft light. Their hands touch. He tries to kiss her.

"*Not,*" she admonishes, cool and warm, "not until we are properly betrothed."

"And when shall that be?"

"And perhaps not even then. Proprieties must be observed, Robert. Papa is going to be difficult about this." But the triumphant way she takes his hand, and pulls him back into the parlor to mama, makes him start thinking shameful thoughts.

"I *love* him!" He overhears her arguing with her father some time later, knowing that old Sam Houston has also been courting her, wondering if Sam Houston loves her and wondering if *he* loves her. "Papa, I've loved him for years! I've got him where I want him now, Papa, and you shan't make me back down on this!"

Good Lord, Robert thinks. What have I gotten myself into?

He returns to dismal Cockspur Island and the mud of that damned fort, feeling like a man who has just stepped upon a bull alligator. Perhaps it will all blow over. He sketches alligators. Molly writes him glowing letters, assuring him that she will live entirely upon his army pay, and he looks around himself at his squalid little quarters in the swamp and the mud and wonders if the girl has perhaps stepped on an alligator herself and just doesn't know it yet.

This is the frame of mind he is in when Jack Mackay returns home to nearby Savannah, looks him up, and hauls him off one day to meet his family in town.

Mercy, what a family! A flock of the prettiest girls Robert has ever seen, and a jolly mother who loads down Robert's plate with her homemade pie and laughs about how "Jack always used to fetch home stray puppies, and we loved and kept every one of them!"

Jack himself is full of the devil and able to laugh more than any human being has a right to. What a glorious uproarious house it is—the girls at the piano, Mrs. Mackay bawling a lusty opera, the windows rattling and Jack languishing by the fire.

And Eliza. Small, dark Eliza. A rosy beauty and a joyous gamine. Jack's sister has tiny white hands and a talent for artwork and the sweetest voice and shapeliest form ever to sashay down the pike. Maybe Jack knows what is happening as he sits and smokes, watching, for he seems amused and slightly concerned. Robert's infatuation is in his eyes all the time.

Nights are hell. Robert finds himself having embarrassing dreams about her. He wonders if this is a sin, but he has no means of controlling his sleep. There are wet places upon his sheets. Life is marvelous.

Jack warns the girl he's engaged when she pins Robert's mangled little bouquets of violets on her dress, and again after he spies the pair of them out back in the garden, hands entwined, and when the two of them begin to exchange letters and sketches across the miles that separate Cockspur from Savannah. "Go easy on him, Eliza. Beware."

"Bobbert," says Jack one weekend during a respite from the happy Mackay uproar, "I've got to talk to you, old man."

So it all boils down to Molly Custis, Martha Washington's great-granddaughter, "A brilliant choice," in the words of Carter Lee. Haven't I got this all backwards? wonders Robert. What in the world am I doing? I am fouling everything up again.

A memory moves behind his eyes as he does another sketch for Miss Eliza: "*You*, sir!" shouts his beleaguered father at him from the Stratford steps of his past. "Did you strike your sister?"

"Yes, papa?" answers the child from the lawn.

"I say, did you strike Ann Kinloch? She is wailing in the hallway like one murdered, and I won't have it! Do you hear me, sir?" The old man's face is red as the very devil's. His malacca stick taps the steps in a rage.

The small boy searches his mind. There are blackberries in his palm and the juice dribbles out from his clutch onto his stockings. No, he hasn't hit anybody today. He hasn't even seen Annie since breakfast.

"Did you, Smith?" bellows the old man. There is a suspicion

of whiskey on the breeze. "I've a lot on my mind, and I won't stand for any uproar! *Did* you?"

The purple juice runs into the child's shoes. "No, Papa."

The old soldier flails about with his stick. If he decides to make the effort of descending all these stone steps, he might hit the child with it. He has done so before. There are heavy chains hanging from the doors behind him, employed at need to keep the sheriff and irate creditors out, to buy old Harry a little more time. All the cows have been sold, most of the furniture. Eviction will soon follow. His bulky body, in its outdated knee-britches, makes the chains clank a bit with all the stomping and stamping, but the pale blue eyes look far away and befuddled—hurt. "I won't have you lie to me, Smith. Damn you, sir!"

The child has squeezed the blackberries into mush. He whispers. "I'm not Smith, Papa."

"Speak up!"

"I'm not Smith," his voice quavers. "I'm Robert, sir."

"I meant 'Robert', I meant 'Robert.' Don't sass me, damn you! And keep your hands to yourself, whoever you are! I need peace and quiet!" The stick points at the child like a musket. "Do you understand me?"

Small lips shape, Yes sir. No sound comes out.

The memory goes. Robert studies the finished drawing. It, at least, has turned out rather well. Robert has promised Jack Mackay to forego violets and stick to artwork. He examines the piece critically and tries to imagine what it would look like if it were engraved upon a page in some book. People live happily ever after in books. Perhaps it would be nice to live in a book.

He leaves the sketch in his quarters when he goes back on duty later. It is a drawing of Napoleon's death mask, imagined by Robert in sadness and finality, with features that resemble his own.

An odd subject to depict for Eliza, perhaps. But she will keep it for the rest of her life. It will someday find its way onto a printed page in a book, and Garnet Laney will see it there in 1966.

Nine

I sat scrawling a poem in the margins of a book the next Monday afternoon, one of those lousy baleful adolescent poems, all about death and the absurdity of life. I knew it was rotten. I was rubbing an eraser across it when a shadow fell over the page. Shading my eyes with a ring-encrusted hand, I looked up into the sunlight of the schoolyard.

Mr. Damadian stood there. "I've been meaning to speak to you about something, Garnet."

The lunchtime crowd swirled around the nearby Coke machines. I could hardly hear his voice above the raucous laughter. He stepped closer to my bench.

"I want to ask you something," he said.

I moved over and he sat down beside me, looked off across the schoolyard and played with a button on his jacket while I wondered, Am I in any trouble?

"Shoot," I told him.

He grinned. "Does that mean like 'Oh, heck,' the way I hear you guys use it as a mild expletive? Or was that a 'shoot' like—?"

"Fire away. Shoot."

"Oh." His broad cherub face creased pleasantly. He looked a lot younger up close, couldn't be much more than twenty-four. "Well, you know that Mrs. Pitts coached what passed for a debate club here before I came in to replace her. Now they want me to do it—coach the debate club. Well. You can't make bricks without straw."

"Nossir." Hmmm. He wanted me to run my mouth for him.

"Well, we can't do much this year. No experience. Mrs. Pitts knew even less about debating than I do. We'll just knock about on the edges of state competition and lose a lot of matches."

"Yessir." Forget it, Damadian, I thought. I'm too busy being melancholy and interesting to take up debating. Debate is for nerds.

"But I'm trying to recruit some new blood. That new kid from Mississippi—the Hargett kid—he's done some debating and seems receptive."

Now I was all ears.

"We'll do some practice matches. With schools like Dreher High—they were State Class AAA Champs last year, I understand. We'll get our noses bloodied, but the experience will be valuable."

"Yessir." Yes yes yes. I'd debate the devil for Bubba Hargett. I closed my book and buried it in a stack of its companions on the paint-flaked wood beside me. Damadian didn't see I was already hooked. He was winding up himself for a hard sell.

"Garnet, I've got to go to Washington, D.C., sometime this summer to hit the Library of Congress for my Master's thesis. There's going to be a National Debate Workshop held at American University there in August. So I thought . . . Have you ever been to D.C.?"

"Nossir."

Heck, I was thinking, Washington Schmashington; I'd go to Leningrad for Bubba Hargett. C'mon, Damadian. Get to the point. No need to be coy.

"Well. I need you, Miss Laney. If I could pair you with Hargett, I'd—"

Oh jubilation! Oh, too good to be true! I didn't *believe* what I was hearing: they'd just handed the keys to the candy store to the local diabetic. Close your mouth, I reminded myself. Don't let him see that your blood has turned to jello. "I don't know nuthin' 'bout no debatin', Mr. Damadian."

He laughed. "Doesn't matter. Your current phraseology may not indicate it, but I have recently been privileged to hear you speak quite eloquently—"

Thank you thank you, Robert E. Lee.

"—and I think that you have an adequate mouth."

I giggled. Couldn't stop it. The delight poured from me in asinine gurgles, like I was a cheerleader reading *Winnie-The-Pooh*. "Thank you, Mr. Damadian."

He rubbed his blunt nose. His dark Beatle bangs blew over his brow. Cupid was a short Armenian history teacher and he was sitting right here beside me.

"That speech you gave on Lee, or whatever it was, it wasn't what you'd normally expect from an eleventh-grader. It was very . . ."

"Outrageous. I'm sorry."

"It was cheeky, it was cheeky. I gave you an A-plus. I've studied history for years and never heard anyone approach Lee in such a vivid manner. You guys say 'cheeky' down here?"

Vivid. Vivid. "Nossir."

"Well, I don't think we said it in Flushing, either."

"I thought I heard that you were from New York," I said.

"Flushing's New York. Flushing, Queens."

Sounded glamorous. Flushing—Queens—New York. I wondered if he had ever been to the coffeehouses in Greenwich Village where poets and artists sat up until three o'clock in the morning and talked about Life and Art and Love and Death. I couldn't believe this was happening to me. Ten minutes ago I was nobody. Now I was *vivid*.

"How'd you end up in this backwater of civilization?" I asked.

"Well . . . Got out of the Peace Corps and just came on down. My wife was a campaign organizer for Lyndon Johnson here."

"From one banana republic to another, huh?"

"That's about the size of it."

Uh oh. Suddenly I was on the defensive. "Bringing enlightenment to another set of natives, huh?" Tell me *no,* Damadian, I thought. Tell me I'm not a native. Tell me how enlightened I am. Vivid.

Oh shit, I could see it in his eyes: I had thought maybe he was down here because he liked the climate or something, but he had come to save us. There were little smiley lines around his mouth where the razor had missed a few beard bristles.

"I really like you people, Garnet."

I fiddled with my pencil, wondering how long he would tolerate Grandmama and Gifford Moak. "You didn't think you would before you got here, in other words."

"No. Frankly I expected *Tobacco Road.* Weekly lynchings. I don't know. But you guys aren't as vicious as you're cracked up to be."

I couldn't look at him, I felt my cheeks hot, thinking: I hate this place but it's my home. It's for *me* to criticize. Don't discuss it in front of me like this with no idea that I might want to contradict you. I won't contradict you, but I am embarrassed by your assumption, Mr. Damadian.

"Robert E. Lee," he mused, oblivious, thumbs drumming out a solo on the wooden seat. He laughed—a sudden squawk. "I thought I'd get the usual Lost Cause crap from you . . . something reverent and irrelevant about the old buzzard."

Now don't jump on Lee, I thought. Don't make me mad.

"You haven't seen any of us in action yet," I interrupted, tying a little knot in the ends of my hair and then untying it. "I hope you never have to see any of us be mean. 'Cause we can be meaner and eviller than anything this side of the Hot Place."

He looked at me intently. "Why do you do that?"

"Do what?"

"Lapse into dialect when I make a point. You keep doing it. You can speak perfectly well when you want to."

I rubbed my cheeks. Yankees were born psychoanalysts. They also possessed no manners.

"You people," he continued, "are going through a social upheaval right now with the civil rights thing."

I sighed deeply, disgusted with both him and myself for bringing up the whole regional subject in the first place.

"Now, I don't condone what I've heard about. What I see on television. But it seems to me that this particular community has so far handled itself with—"

"I'm not talking about just that. I'm talking about the kids here who call you a communist."

I had wanted to jolt him. But he was amused. "I'm a carpet-bagger, huh?"

Why couldn't I cut my losses and just shut up? I wished that he would take himself away from my bench before I really made a donkey of myself. Surely I was not that fascinating.

"Thanks for the oblique warning, Garnet. I still think you people are charming."

"God help you," I muttered.

"Well." He stood. Put his hands in his pockets. I looked up at him, eyes squinting in the sun under my Cleopatra painted lids.

"Well. Are you with me, Miss Laney?"

You bet your carpetbag. "Yessir."

I watched him out of sight, and that was that. Kept watching. Couldn't see him anymore. Smug ol' Cupid was eclipsed in the crowd.

I opened the Lee biography again. I looked for a chapter on love.

Ten

He sits in the June sun at Fortress Monroe in 1832 and squints against the light reflected from paper. The letter flutters and he presses it down against the notebook on his uniformed knees while he waves his pen in the air, trying to find proper words. Someone walks by and a shadow falls across the letter. He pulls his boots in further out of the walkway so that no one will fall over him.

The pen point flicks into the ink bottle and then decisively touches the paper: *Molly, we have been writing mighty short letters to each other lately,* he scribbles his fine slant. *I think your last was even worse than mine . . .*

Someone is standing over him. He shades his eyes with the letter and looks up.

"Bob. You coming with us tonight?"

"Perhaps."

"They're roasting a pig, I hear. Harriet says I mustn't even bother to show my face at home unless I talk you into accompanying us."

The speaker leans in his stance a little so that he can nosily scan the words of the letter that shields his friend's face. Automatically, Robert brings the paper down to protect its contents even as his dark eyes blink, all innocent.

"Your Mrs. Talcott is a difficult lady to refuse, Cap'n." He puts down his pen and his lips part in a smile. The tips of his teeth gleam.

"Oh, she is that, Lieutenant." The captain hitches up the knees of his summer trousers and crouches so that his voice can fall. "And the scintillating Miss Sally will be there."

"Indeed?"

"Ready to verily entertain your every whim, Bob my boy. Ready, no doubt, to repeat a certain questionable invitation concerning a bedchamber."

Robert smiles. "You have a most long and indelicate memory, Cap'n Talcott. Sir."

Talcott grins like a fox, long sharp good-humored face and hooded eyes. "Got to keep one step ahead of you wretches, let you know who's in command here."

His subordinate laughs.

"The party promises to be quite a show, Bob. You recall a cadet named Farrell in your class at the Point? Big ugly fellow?"

"From Rhode Island. Brains of a mantis."

"The very man. He's here from the War Department. Quite a lady's man, supposedly, though God knows what the dear creatures see in him."

"His father possesses two shipping fortunes and several senators, I believe," mutters Robert. "Perhaps therein lies a certain appeal."

"Well, we're to be blessed with his presence at our provincial little soirée tonight and he positively lusts after my Harriet. Met her yesterday, purportedly fresh from a duel over a brigadier's wife at Fort Hamilton. Slobbered all over her hand like a Frenchman."

"Choose swords, Cap'n. He's the only man of my acquaintance to ever successfully touché himself." Robert pauses to dot an

66

I in his letter. "And faithful Lieutenant Lee, ever courageous, shall be your second. Provided you leave me your house in your will."

Talcott laughingly puts the toe of his boot against his lieutenant's shoulder and feigns a push. "That ready to get me out of the way, eh, Iago? I've given Harriet the very devil over Farrell and she ups and assures me that she'll never cuckold me with anyone but you! What say you to that?"

Graceful hands fly at the boot and grip it. "I'm going to wrassle your foot right off, Cap'n." He twists. "For impugning the honor of The Beautiful Talcott."

The young Connecticut captain is laughing and dancing up and down on his one free leg and if Farrell from the War Department could witness the scene, he would have serious questions about discipline among the Fort Monroe engineers. Muffled guffawing echoes over the compound until Robert turns his superior loose to save his wrinkling letter.

"So you shall accompany us, Lieutenant, and stave off a duel?" Talcott pants. "In which I might possibly get my posterior shot off?"

They break into laughter again like schoolboys. Talcott rubs his nose and tilts his cap to a more dignified angle. He lets his laughter fade and glances at the letter.

"So when is she coming back, Bob?"

There is an awkward pause. "She doesn't say, Cap'n."

"Perhaps I could find you two larger quarters. I know she found the accommodations here appalling."

Robert shrugs. "She says she just wants to stay a while longer with her parents. I feel like a tyrant, insisting that she rot here in poverty. She wants to bring her servants. Few of the wives here have servants. Where in God's name will we find room to house a servant? But I'll leave her the apartment and camp out on the parapet, if it will make her happy."

Talcott crouches again. "Women don't take to army life. Not at first. But she'll come around. You'll see."

Robert studies the instep of his boot. "Your Harriet just dove on in. Molly and I have been living apart for six months now, sir. Is this 'separation'?"

"Look. Come along with us tonight. You could use an outing. And the ladies will wilt and pine into their wine if their Virginia gallant locks himself away in his quarters with letters and blueprints and books. You flummox me, dear boy! They chase you like a pack of wolves, despite your damnably little feet! Surely ladies must know what is said of men with little feet."

"Perhaps they'd rather recall what is said of men with enormous noses."

"Hah! Well, come with us then and titillate them with your nose!"

"Very well." Robert slams the letter shut inside the notebook. "Done. I guess I mustn't allow the ubiquitous Farrell to steal a march on me."

"The ugly Farrell."

"The ugly ubiquitous Farrell."

Talcott waves and saunters off and Robert sits motionless for a moment, watching his friend, biting his lip. Then he positions his notebook on his knees and takes up where he left off. He sits bareheaded, looking at the letter closely, black hair blowing a little over the white skin at his forehead where a visor has divided paleness from ruddy sun tan.

He is twenty-five years old and has been married exactly one year to a stranger. The Molly Custis he knew as a child is gone and the Mary he married is someone who took along her mother on their wedding trip. He doesn't know too much about women, but he never supposed that one would be so delicately cold whenever her husband said, "Take down your hair, Moll," and locked himself up with her in the bedroom. Molly is dutiful but unenthusiastic. Maybe virtuous women are made this way, teasing and flirtatious, but too refined to respond to the rough realities of marriage. He can accept that. Perhaps he has not been enough of a gentleman. Perhaps he was too carried away initially after the wedding. Approached her too often. But he can't help thinking sometimes that maybe Eliza Mackay or Harriet Talcott would have laughed with him in the dark and helped him take off his nightshirt.

Now Molly is pregnant, in her sixth month. She doesn't seem to like being pregnant, either. Her letters are fretful and pettish and she complains of her health. And it is a sure thing that she will be wife to him in name only until after the child is born, even if she does decide to favor him with a visit.

Let me tell you Mrs. Lee, he writes her, *no later than today did I escort Miss G. to see Miss Slate! Think of that Mrs. Lee! And hasten down, if you do not want to see me turned out a beau again.*

She is a peculiar girl, but she is steady and wellbred and pious. She will be the perfect mother for the little son he expects. He plans his boy's education and has already purchased a few toys, things that will suit even if the boy turns out to be a girl. No matter. Whatever it is, he will hug it and love it and will never have the heart to spank it, and he or she will certainly have the best of everything with Custis money and Custis prestige.

He finds himself speaking to his unborn child sometimes as he supervises some of the construction on the fort or takes his solitary meals. He wants to leave something fine behind him so that the child can say, "My papa designed this . . . My papa built that."

There is no name for the feeling he wakes up with in the middle of the nights here, but it is like smothering.

At the party, Misses Sally and Rachel predictably flirt, and he flirts right back. He even becomes slightly inebriated with the wine punch, but alcohol has never agreed with him. It makes him stupid.

He gives up and leaves early, escorting a lady back to her quarters, the wife of an absent officer. She has befriended both him and Mary many a time. So it is with pleasure that he later answers his own door to find her on the porch. She has discovered that her Yorkshire terrier has somehow escaped in her absence and she is dreadfully distraught.

Robert offers to help her search for the dog and is pulling his tunic back on over his shirt when she pushes past him into the apartment and takes a flask of brandy out of her handbag.

"My word!" she says and sits on the edge of his mattress. "What a miserable, ascetic, disgustingly neat little room!" She laughs. "Looks like your sweet little wife could render it more homey. If she ever sees fit to return."

Robert isn't thinking clearly. The wine has him muddled. "Uh . . . We can alert Cap'n Talcott, Madam. Perhaps he and the others at the party will organize a search."

"No hurry." She smiles brilliantly. Pats the place beside her. "Come sit with me. I am quite upset. Come tell me what you hear from little Mrs. Lee. When is her confinement to be accomplished?"

"Uh." He thinks. "September."

"I hope the baby will have the good fortune to look like you. Has anyone ever told you, Bobby, that you're a very pretty little boy?"

"Not since I was six. If we hurry, Madam —"

"Oh, *do* sit down! Partying makes me very weary. I always find it such a bore. Jojo cannot get very far, his little legs are so short. I . . . can he get out of the fortress?"

"Probably." Robert is suddenly wary. Her distress, so heart-wringing five minutes ago, has alarmingly lessened. "He can fall into the water and drown."

But she takes a pull at the flask and looks around herself. Studies the volumes racked neatly on a nearby shelf. "*Marcus Aurelius.*" She points. "What's that?"

"Stoic philosophy." He sits politely beside her.

"How dull. Have you read *Fanny Hill?*"

Oh Lord, he thinks. "No, Madam."

"You really must. There is a strapping country lad in one passage who reminds me of you."

"Well, actually I grew up in a small town." He draws away as she moves in closer, noticing too late that he has made the mistake of sitting near *Marcus Aurelius* against the wall. Soon there will be no more room for discreet retreat.

"Are you frightened of me, Bobby? Are you frightened of your old Auntie?"

"—but actually I WAS born in the country, actually—"

Old Auntie can't be much above thirty-five and she is a really fine looking woman and getting better looking by the minute.

Loud fiddle music wafts in from the nearby frolic. And salacious laughter from far off, uproarious and hooting.

Her hand is cool as its palm caresses his cheek. "Don't be uneasy. I promised little Mary—you call her 'Molly', I forget—I promised I'd take good care of you. And here you are, always working so intently. Have some brandy. It's superb for the digestion, really."

"Dogs can fall into quicklime. Dogs can fall into mortar. I knew someone whose dog—"

Her hand is undoing his collar band. He can barely breathe. Starts to stand, and then realizes that he is in an embarrassing condition.

"It's really quite late, Madam," he stammers, "And I'm sort of married, and your poor dog is drowning."

"Dogs can swim, love! For hours and hours. And hours."

He wishes that he could think of something Man-of-the-World to say, but he feels provincial and downright maidenly. He can't decently stand up, not in front of her, until this condition passes. And it doesn't look as if it will anytime soon. She is opening his shirt placket.

Her fingers rove over his pectorals. "You're so *strong*, Bobby! What did they feed you on in your itty bitty town?"

"Cornbread. Chicken backs." Her breath is hot on his neck. Hell hath no fury— She can start shrieking rape, he realizes. I'm dead.

She titters, charmingly. "Chicken *backs?*"

"There were a lot of us. Not enough meaty pieces to go around— Really, Madam, I'm unaccustomed to this sort of thing and perhaps it would be wiser if I saw you home."

"'Meaty pieces.'" She bends, pulls his foot sideways into her lap, and wrestles with his boot. "Such a provocative term! What's the matter, dear? Don't you find me just a tiny bit appealing?" The boot strikes the floor.

"Yes, Madam. A large bit. Appealing. Very. I'm not much of a Romeo."

She laughs. Her cool touch tickles the sole of his bared foot. "Please don't be a prig, darling. We're both lonely. And this is such a little sin, really." She reaches for his other leg, pulling it over the first and nearly flipping him onto his stomach.

He feels like an idiot. Need seduction be so inelegant? His socks aren't perhaps as clean as they could be. "You've tied me in a knot here," he observes to the lady while she tugs the other boot free.

Papa would not have said that to her, he rebukes himself. Papa would say something suave. Delicate but risqué. And take the initiative.

The lady has begun to perspire. Robert studies her dé-colletage as she pitches the second boot across the room. There is really quite a lot of Old Auntie stuffed into that bodice. The initiative and Auntie there for the taking.

Ann Carter Lee has not raised her boys to be rakes, but neither are they yet Victorian. An army installation is a place of incessant card parties and amourous intrigues. Bible-spouting Molly is horrified by both, but Robert likes to observe and some-times participate, exploring his own self-imposed limits in the fields of horse-racing and wine. He uses a "damn" occasionally, but only in male company. He has lost some money on the horses. He does not visit fancy women, but tonight he can find no limits and thinks that maybe he might have to rethink that position if Moll can't be persuaded to return, because it isn't humanly possi-ble to keep ignoring these bold nymphs who dog his step and

parade themselves shamelessly in his dreams. Sometimes he wonders if perhaps he is abnormal in his susceptibility to feminine
charms, but his natural reticence keeps him from comparing
notes with Jack Mackay or Andrew Talcott; and it doesn't yet
occur to him that his startling good looks provoke behavior in
women that neither Jack nor Andrew elicit.

At least Old Auntie is no innocent whom he can lead astray.
Half-brother Henry, his onetime legal guardian after Lighthorse
Harry's decampment, was not so fussy; the underage mistress
with whom he tampered is irreversibly ruined at age sixteen and
has shaved her head! Moral watchdogs have hounded Henry out of
Andrew Jackson's administration for disgracing a pathetic ward,
an innocent child. Robert doesn't know what to make of Henry.
The whole business, the terrible questions from new acquaintances that begin, "Are you related to—?" have tormented him for
years like a half-pleasurable itch that can't be scratched.

Robert had adored Henry, his kindness to Robert's mother
and her young brood, his willingness to send them an occasional
cheque when it had been no responsibility of his to keep them fed
or housed. Robert remembers the feel of Henry's large kind hands
lifting his own seven-year-old self into the saddle, the blond
handsome man tolerating "Little Robbie's" prattlings and dark
presence with unfailing good humor. Now all of those good days
are long gone. How was it that generous Henry failed to keep his
pants buttoned? Can it be that sometimes it is simply impossible
to keep one's pants buttoned?

It seems so. Auntie has sprouted about twenty frenzied
fingers and breaks a nail having a go at his military button
holes. Robert is happy to finish the task for her. Ravenous,
in fact, fumbling with each small maddening disc, panicked
that he may explode before he can get the damned things
undone. His brain has shut entirely, just struck its tents and snuck
off with all thoughts of Molly and Old Auntie's absent husband (a cruel martinet rumored to beat the woman when he is not
occupied with his "laundresses," the sort of man who will cer-

tainly murder Little Robbie if he ever finds out about this interview).

The two wear so many clothes that they are both on hair triggers by the time that they can get at each other. In an era when a man can see a good deal of a woman's bosom but her legs not at all, and propriety hides his throat and even his forearms from feminine view, arousal is no great effort. Ladies frequently swoon. Sensitive German poets glimpse female ankles and go mad.

It's like the Fourth of July, all fireworks and gunpowder and joyful noises, and the deed is done on the Fortress Monroe mattress with a great crackling of its humble cornshuck innards. Old Auntie laughs and cries, mashing Robert's face into her breasts and crooning, "Such a sweet boy you are!" while he tries to breathe. His brain is still on leave.

When they recover themselves, the lady departs in newfound flusterment and the two of them are too killingly embarrassed to do more than mumble apologies and assure one another that nothing of the sort will ever happen again, all the while avoiding each other's eyes and chalking up the whole experience to the evils of alcohol.

"Your honor, madam," Robert hears himself muttering inanely, "is safe with me."

When his wits return, the very first thing they afflict him with is a terribly clear picture of his mother's face.

And the nausea hits him like lightning. All the roast pork he has eaten, the cake and wine punch come out of him in a gush, leaving him with a frightful mess to wipe up from the bare wood floor. He is glad for once that he has never been able to afford the carpet Molly wants.

But he wonders what Miss Sally will be like behind locked doors.

Eleven

"Lookahere," Grandmama said, as Mama and Daddy and Beth Ann drove away, headed in the Chevrolet to the hamburger place to get us all some lunch. "I've got some things to show you."

She had been having a lucid day so far, had not said "nigger" once. When I turned, she had a paper sack in her hand, its corners so worn and fuzzy that the white tissue inside stuck out all over.

"What is it?" I asked her.

"Not out here." She moved the sack out of my reach. "We might lose some of it out here. Let's go inside."

She had my curiosity all stirred up. I hadn't wanted to be here: my first debate club meeting, a picnic, was scheduled for the legal holiday tomorrow afternoon and I preferred to be home, deciding what to wear. But Grandmama had me all curious now; something in the sack was clanking.

"Hurry!" she told me as I took her skinny old arm and helped her back up the steps. "I don't want Azalee to come back and catch me goin' through this stuff."

"Why not?" I opened the door for her and we moved into the

75

living-room. She made her way very slowly to the velvet sofa and I followed.

"Cause old folks who do this are usually about to die." Her small eyes were on my face as I sat down beside her. "It'll upset her. I wouldn't upset Azalee for the world."

"Are you about to die?"

"I don't know." Her claw hands curled around her secret in the sack. "Maybe. I was born in 1889 and just plain ol' common sense tells me time is about to run out. Nobody needs me now. I'm ready."

I didn't know how to react to her. She was very matter-of-fact as she up-ended the sack into her lap and let the wadded contents spill out into the lap of her seersucker dress.

"I went a-lookin' for this after ya'll left last week." Her fingers slowly unwrapped a small rectangular object. "I found it in the pie safe. Found a lot of stuff. Look here."

Her palsied hand held up a murky picture.

"It's what they call a tintype, I believe," she said, as I gingerly took it from her. "That's my grandpaw. Captain Amos Bates Cooke. The burned baby's daddy."

Once the back of it had been covered in velvet but time and moths had eaten it to stubble. The gilding had worn off the frame but still gleamed in a few crevices of the ornate scrollwork. Her hand shook as she relinquished it to me.

"He was just a *kid!*" she said as I studied the thin buoyant face, the small goatee, the boyish heavy-lidded eyes. I could see some of my own features in his face: the sleepy lids, the lower lip. It was eerie. "My mother never knew him," Grandmama was saying. "He was killed at Gaines' Mill after only gettin' to see her once on a furlough. She was fourteen months old. Grandmaw took the train up to Richmond. Look at him, Garnet. How he holds that sword. Look at how bright his buttons are. Look at how bad he wanted to join the fight. The young fool."

There was something wrong with her voice. I looked up to

76

see moisture oozing from the crinkled eyes like blood from a wound.

I didn't know what to do.

"When I was young," she went on in a stronger, more determined tone, wiping at her face unashamedly, "the older people were still grievin' about that war. There were so many old maids, so many widows who never remarried. We lost a whole generation of boys."

I returned the picture to her, my fingers careful not to leave prints over the image.

The clock ticked in the hallway.

"So many wars," she said. "They're crankin' up one now over yonder in Indochina or somewhere. So many durn fools always wantin' to crank one up. The ones who start 'em don't never have to fight 'em. They stay home in their easy chairs and talk all fine about patriotism and I-don't-know-what-all while somebody else gets up on the firing line."

I never knew what to say to Grandmama. She was like a creature from another planet sometimes.

While I was trying to think of something witty, she wrapped Amos back up and started to undo another little bundle. "My own uncle went to Cuba to fight the Spaniards," she was saying while old hands fumbled with aged cellophane tape. "He couldn't wait to git on that boat, to show everybody in Washington that a Carolina soldier could be loyal to the Stars and Stripes once again. He showed 'em, all right. Got decorated twice and lived with one arm gone 'til the end of his days . . . Here."

Now she handed me a silvery thing. Sharpness somewhere pricked my fingertip and I saw that the object was a kind of brooch, all tarnished. It was shaped like a heart, like half of a large locket. There were letters engraved all over it, some singly and some in pairs. I held it up so that the feeble light from the dirty windowpane could shine upon it.

"That belonged to my grandmaw, Elizabeth Ann," she said

as I examined it. "I think that there were two pieces once, but no one in my day knew what had happened to the other half. Somebody made a pin out of it. See those large initials? Those are Grandmaw's. She gave this thing to my mama when she was on her deathbed. Mama had her own initials cut into it then: E.C.C. for Elizabeth Cooke Caskie—Liza wasn't her proper name—and she put her husband's right beside them. When each kid was born, their initials were engraved onto it, too. Here are mine right here: M.L.C. I always meant to have Samuel's—your granddaddy's—put on there next to mine. But time gits away so fast and he's gone now . . ."

The things seemed to throb in my palm like a real heart. I was silent.

"I never gave it to Azalee. She was always so hard on me about things like this. Said I live in the past too much. Well, I do. All old folks live in the past, Garnet. When you haven't got a future, what else do you have? Where else can you live?"

I looked at her face over the pin and wondered if she had been pretty when she was young. It occurred to me suddenly that there was a young Milly Moser inside of her, a young woman like me trapped in that failing body and confused mind. And the things that she was telling me, things that had happened so unimaginably long ago, had happened for her only yesterday.

"Take it." She closed my fingers around the pin. "Take it and have your initials put on it. Put your husband's on it, too. And then, when each little baby's born, stick 'em on there. You are my oldest grandchild. I want you to have it."

I didn't know what to say. I suddenly envisioned that unbroken chain, that great dance of life engraved on the heart, with people finding partners and having children, and then those children finding partners and having yet more children. Mildred Moser was passing the dance on to me, expecting me to find a partner of my own and join in. To find my place in the unimaginably long procession of family, people living and dying and carrying on through their posterity.

Would I ever join in, though? Would I ever fit myself into the great struggle? Who would I pass this brooch on to when I died?

My scalp chilled where little shivers touched it as I imagined all the living that went into making this body that I inhabit. All the effort that would come to nothing if I died dead-ended, died like a barren branch. I wanted a cigarette real bad.

"Life is so short, you see," Grandmama was saying now. "You won't realize that until it's too durn late to do anything about it. But I saw Elizabeth Ann Middleton in her coffin. They held me up to it—I was too little to look over the edge by myself—and they said, 'Here is Grandmaw. Say goodbye to Grandmaw, Milly.' I saw her, Garnet. She was born in 1840. And I knew her."

I don't know what kind of reaction she was trying to elicit. But I envisioned her now as a little girl looking on the dead face of my great-great-grandmother, and I saw beauty there in that long unbroken chain from Elizabeth Ann to me. I was wounded somewhere. Wounded by the stately beauty of it all.

Mildred Lee Moser, lifted up to say goodbye to a grandmother born in 1840. Only yesterday.

Life was short. And so far, mine had meant absolutely nothing.

Give this pin to Beth Ann, Grandmama, I thought. She will not be wounded. She won't reflect upon any of this the way I do. She'll get married right out of high school and have lots of kids and won't spend all her time trying to find meaning and beauty in everything, the way I do. She won't ever have initials engraved on this thing; she'll always be too busy for that, washing out diapers and watching television and happily aging. She won't be a dead end. I have closed my future off to myself. I don't know why.

I foresee all the wars and births and deaths and effort to come. I'm not up to it. Each initial on this pin represents unbelievable struggle to me. Give this to someone who doesn't see the struggle, Grandmama. Give this thing to someone who won't be touched.

But while I sat brooding she was unwrapping yet another

antediluvian treasure, happily undoing the tape, glad to be in the presence of someone who could feel the worth of these things.

I wanted to turn on the radio or something. I needed to light up a Camel, hear some rock and roll.

"Now this," she was saying, "this is another thing that I want you to have. It should go to you because I think you'll appreciate it."

She held it up; I was bewildered. It looked like a large spider, spiky pieces sticking out in all directions from a central point, brown and shiny like the carapace of a bug.

She saw my puzzlement and laughed. Then gathered up all the long spiky points, flattened the object against her knees, and finally spread the spikes out in a semi-circle. The thing had become a fan.

"This here could go in a museum," she mused, rubbing the tortoise-shell surface made by the overlapping veins. "It used to have a ribbon through it to hold it together, but I guess it rotted away a long time ago. Here's the original tassel, though. Used to be black. It's kind of a dark red color now . . . Faded."

Garnet, I thought, touching it. The color is garnet.

Except for the missing ribbon, the fan was entirely intact. Someone had taken good care of this object. People had lovingly watched out for it through all the years, keeping it from the bumps and gouges that they could not keep from themselves. The people had died but the fan was intact.

"This came to me from my mother, Liza," Grandmama said with pride, "and I want you to have it. I want you to re-string it. Sometime. Put a narrow black silk ribbon back on it. That's what was there originally."

I took it up. The veins fluttered. Grandmama was breathing noisily beside me.

"Mildred Lee gave that to Mama when they were friends. That thing has seen many a year come and go. It's special, Garnet. It's a mourning fan. All black and tortoiseshell. Folks used to believe in going into mourning. You didn't want to carry no fan with feathers and frills, you understand."

"No ma'am."

I could almost sense what was to come. I could feel the pattern in things now.

"Mildred Lee had no children. She gave away a lot of stuff to the U.D.C. and museums in New Orleans and Richmond and God knows where. But she gave this to Mama. Thought Mama would want it. Mama put it way back in the back of her dresser drawer and didn't let none of us kids touch it. Mildred carried it to her daddy's funeral in 1870."

The tortoiseshell shone on my knees.

"She used it that one last time, and never used it again."

All the tears shed on that fan. No wonder the ribbon had rotted. "Well, it should be in a museum," I muttered, afraid to touch it now, afraid of it.

"Hogwash," Grandmama snorted finally. "If Mildred had wanted it in a blame museum, she woulda given it to a blame museum. This here meant something to her personal. Museums are full of statues. Stuff like that. Old dead history like the kind of junk you read in books. Stuff that never happened. This here fan belonged to a person. It was used at a very private time. It involved people. Just plain ol' people. That's all there is to everything: just plain ol' people. My mother had lost a two-year-old to the typhoid, and here comes this package from Lexington, Virginia — 'You'll need a fan, Lize,' Mildred wrote, 'and some gloves.' Mama and Daddy were bad off, him farmin' that burnt-out land. Mama wore the gloves every time she went to church. Never used the fan. It wasn't meant for a museum. It was just meant for funerals."

Lee's funeral. I could hardly believe what I was holding. It was like a piece of the True Cross, like one of those relics that you know can't really be what people say it is.

I was very afraid of it. It was mine now and I was afraid to touch it.

"Garnet," Grandmama's voice sounded very odd. I wouldn't look at her. "I come from another time. Another country, almost. You'll never understand what somethin' like that fan there meant to the old folks when I was young. People loved that man. People used to talk about sneakin' up behind him at church in Richmond or somewhere, just to touch the hem of his coat so they could tell us children that they had touched him. Mothers brought their babies to him to be blessed. He never understood it, Mildred never understood it. He was just her daddy and she loved him. But he meant somethin' deep to your forebears, meant somethin' fine. And when he died, the dream died. And folks were just poor again, ragged, just plumb beat all to hell. I'm one of the last. One of the very few left alive who can look at this thing and cry over it. So take it and try not to think about how foolish I sound now. Old folks like me git all worked up sometimes over nothin'. Just take it and keep it, and maybe take it with you to my funeral when I die."

So there had been John Kennedys in her day after all. Another kind of John Kennedy had walked the earth once.

Dreams died, and you went on living. People shouldn't put their dreams into the hands of another human being who can die at any moment and take them with him. But they do. I had. I thought of Jack in Dallas.

"He was just a man," Grandmama repeated, sniffling. "Just people. Just Mildred's daddy."

We heard the car rolling into the driveway. Beth Ann's loud chatter came to us through the closed window. Grandmama and I started talking about the weather.

Twelve

The sun reflected gold on the waters of Lake Murray. The silver heart-shaped pin shone at my collarbone.

I was the only girl who had come in jeans. All the rest were decked out in pastel Bermuda shorts, tanned bare legs exposed to the low spring sun. I wouldn't have been caught at a dog fight in Bermuda shorts, not even if I had had pretty legs. No, I was an intellectual—in full Bohemian uniform this evening, long Isadora Duncan scarf around my neck, heavy earrings clanking at my cheeks. Unbound ironed hair getting into my hotdog.

"You glad you're with us?" Mr. Damadian asked.

I nodded. He had paid for this debate club kickoff out of his own pocket and the fare wasn't fancy. But there were plenty of hotdogs and Cokes to go around. The guys who had brought dates were down at the dock, threatening to throw the girls in. Bubba wasn't one of them. He had not brought a date. Good God, I thought suddenly. Maybe he's gay.

I looked down the slope to the edge of the water, where Damadian's wife Betty was throwing sticks into the lake for their

Irish setter, Banshee, to fetch. Bubba had the Damadians' three-year-old son on his shoulders and was running up and down the shore making *vroom-vroom* noises, his light hair glistening like wheatstalks while the kid on his back shrieked and laughed.

I was an uneasy stew this holiday Monday evening, too mixed up to even finish a Coca-Cola. I kept opening fresh bottles and then forgetting where I had put them, leaving them to the sweat bees and the flies.

Did Damadian call these things "sweat bees" where he came from? Did they even have them in New York?

Uh oh. Bubba was wandering up the slope with David Dale Baker, beautiful muscular arms dangling at his sides. I made myself stare back up the hill as they approached.

"Hey, Garnet Laney," Bubba Hargett spoke his first-ever words to me as he casually sat on the grass by my side. "I hear you and me are gonna be the next South Carolina debate champs."

"Izzat so?" I flashed him what I hoped was a blasé, sexy smile. My upper lip got stuck on my teeth.

David Dale sat at my other flank. He thought I was Elizabeth Taylor. Good. I needed David Dale Baker for moral support right now.

Oh Jeez. Bubba leaned over to finger my pin. I'd never been so close to him before.

"What's that?" His hand was six inches above my left nipple.

"Somethin' my grandmother gave me."

He moved his hand away. "Looks real old."

"It is. Been in my family for years."

There. Was that so hard? I asked myself. No. Well then, find your latest Coca-Cola and take a nonchalant pull. Be cool.

I kept my gaze straight ahead on the lake. The kids at school believed that two aspirin and a Coke would make you slightly high. I had taken six aspirin so far this evening.

A canoe paddled by strangers floundered awkwardly across

my line of sight: a boy my age and an older woman. They were doing as wretchedly at canoe-paddling as I seemed to be doing at brilliant repartee.

"You like old things, huh?" Bubba was saying mercilessly. "So do I."

Hell's Bells. Gay boys owned half the antique shops in Columbia.

"You a Civil War buff?" he asked.

"No," I said. "Yes!"

He opened a Coke. "So's my dad."

"Yeah?"

"He's writin' a book on Joshua Chamberlain. He's been peckin' away on an old Olivetti for as long as I can remember."

Okay. I was supposed to be a Civil War buff. I got the picture. I remembered Bubba's face during my Lee report. I took another cool slug of my drink. "Chamberlain . . . Chamberlain . . . Whose command?"

"Grant's. Meade's at Gettysburg. Then Grant's."

"What's a Mississippian doin' writin' about Grant?"

Bubba smiled a smile that could melt wax. "I'm the only Mississippian in the family. Dad's from Maine."

"Ohhhh."

"Mom's from Tennessee. And my kid brother's a Texan. The army sees to it that you move around a lot."

I felt suddenly provincial. "Jeez. You must've lived a lot of places."

"Uh huh. I'm always the new kid at school."

"Mr. Damadian says you've debated before. Where'd you debate?"

"San Antonio. My old high school. Took up debate during our last tour of duty there when I couldn't play football anymore. Hurt my blame knee." He unceremoniously rolled up the leg of his Madras plaid pants and showed me and David Dale several crisscrossed red stitch scars. "Had surgery. Middle linebacker mopped up the thirty yard line with me."

I grinned. It was his left leg. Life was full of coincidences. And most gay boys never got wrecked by linebackers.

I did feel a trifle high. Maybe the kids were right about aspirin.

"You wanna dance?" He pointed back up the hill to where several couples were doing the Dirty Dog to a record of "Mr. Tambourine Man".

"Sure." I scrambled to my feet. Shoot, I could dance. Especially with my leg covered so nobody had to puke at the sight. I bade David Dale a giddy goodbye and accompanied Bubba to the cement dance floor.

"They say this song's about takin' drugs," said Bubba as he got into a pretty good white-boy groove. "Would you ever take drugs?"

"Know anybody who's got any?"

He laughed. Loudly.

I was Queen of The World. This is too easy, I thought as I shook my skinny hips. I'm being set up for something.

"What's your mom think about South Carolina?" I asked my new debate partner between record selections, brushing the hair euphoriously out of my eyes.

He put another quarter into the juke box. "Don't know. I don't think she's ever been here. She's in Tennessee and I don't get to see her much."

Something flickered in my memory. A dream, maybe. I had not slept too well the night before. I had kept dreaming about my stupid fan and Grandmama and lots of weird stuff.

"My folks are divorced," Bubba went on, leading me out again onto the dance floor as the juke box whirred. "My kid brother lives with Mom."

I mumbled something about being sorry and we started to dance again when the music got going, but all at once there came a shout from downhill. I turned around.

David Dale had popped to his feet like a giant Slinky and was shouting something incoherent, hands waving out towards the water.

"Ants," said Bubba, hand on my elbow. "Ants in his underwear."

"Somebody's overturned out there, I said!" David Dale shouted back at us and then to Damadian who was downhill, frozen over his charcoal fire.

I ran down the slope, Bubba right behind me. I followed David Dale's pointing finger and could make out a stirring black smudge way off in the brilliant ripples.

Damadian was already sprinting down to the water's edge where the adjacent Baptist summer camp had beached its canoes after a weekend outing. I felt wind whipping by my legs and Bubba was overtaking him with a cheetah lope, bad knee and all. The two dragged a canoe to the shallows and clambered in and pushed off from the bank like pulling guards.

I was thrilled. I had wanted an eagle.

"What is—?" Betty Damadian shaded her paling face.

I turned. "It's a kid and a lady that I saw earlier, I think. They paddled past here a little while ago like a couple of spastics."

We dashed down to the shore, me feeling guilty for that remark (What if the poor things actually were spastic?). The rest of the debaters were on hand now, David Dale hoisting little Tommy onto his shoulders where he could watch his daddy be a hero. Bubba and Damadian strained at their paddles, way out there.

Then came a lot of flailing around in the low blinding sunlight. The lady was wearing a life jacket but seemed already to be in shock. The boy, not jacketed, clung to the side of his capsized canoe. I shaded my eyes and bit all of my white pearl lipstick off. Neither Bubba nor Damadian seemed able to heft that rigid woman into their craft. Her heavy legs thrashed and she floated crazily in the cold sunset water, one leg kicking up now and the falling sun flashing off the metal brace around the calf . . .

"Godawmighty," whistled David Dale, "she's crippled."

"Hurry up Bill dammit!" Betty was shouting. Leaned over to me, lips at my cheek: "That cold water could give the old babe a heart attack."

A metal brace. I felt totally unreal.

Bubba was futilely pushing and pulling out there and I was in the water with my sandals off before I knew what I was doing. There was a slack inner tube around the gatepost at the Baptist camp dock, still partially inflated after some child had ringtossed it there one day the previous summer. I found it somehow in my arms and then I threw it onto the surface of the water.

"Garnet!" I heard David Dale behind me. *"Hey!"*

But I bellyflopped easily into the rubber ring and the cold evening water washed over me in a splash. Kicking out with both of my legs, I pulled myself through the water in a determined breast stroke, the goose pimples rising all over me as the awful cold bit into my skin.

"BILLLLLLL!" Betty's shriek flew over my head.

But I was too far out into the lake to be stopped. I was getting farther out, farther into it, all the time. And I was strangely excited, the star of my own movie.

Damadian and Bubba were wasting time. They were doing it wrong and all four of them were soon going to be in the drink, I told myself as I blew air and droplets of Lake Murray out of my mouth and nose. That damn Yankee didn't know nothin' about nothin'.

Bubba saw me as I grabbed hold of the side of Damadian's canoe and tried to slip the inner tube out from under myself and underneath the dazed woman. The lady had hold of Damadian's hands in a death grip and was about to pull the little ignoramus over the side with her, while Bubba was leaning back in the vessel in the other direction trying to counterbalance it, but the canoe was rocking and wallowing about to beat the band and there went the fool inner tube squirting up and out from under my control.

I couldn't hold onto both it and the bobbing canoe too; this was like wrassling two wet seals. Damn. I sank straight down and then came up again like a cork, blowing.

"Durn it, Bubba!" I hollered. "Hold this thing steady!"

He nodded. I sucked more air. Reached up over the gunwale and slapped Damadian on the leg. "One more time!"

He looked down. I patted the slack inner tube. "Pick her up one more time, I said!"

Bubba leaned back for balance and Damadian's puny biceps flexed. The heavy woman came up out of the water just far enough for me to stuff the rubber circle under her body. She fell back into it as if it had been an armchair and sat there in the cold water, senseless and catatonic, while I tied my long Isadora scarf onto the tube behind her.

"Here, Bubba." I handed him the end of the scarf.

Damadian started to paddle, towing the victim to shore. That lady could have been me in forty more years or so, brace around the leg and all. This was oddly like saving myself.

Well, we weren't done yet. I swam to the capsized canoe where the boy still clung and shivered. "Help me right it," I told him.

He answered back in a foreign language that sounded like German. He doesn't speak English, I mused, dog-paddling now for dear life. That's real cute, God.

I rocked the canoe angrily up and down and nearly threw him off of it and finally he understood what I wanted to do and helped. The canoe was full of water when we got it righted, but there were flotation pockets in the aluminum sides. It would stay up. So I gripped one side of it and the kid gripped the other and we swam it to shore.

I tried to apologize to the kid for swearing at him: it wasn't his fault that he spoke no English. I was patting him on the back and he was grinning like a German shepherd, when the debaters pulled us from the shallows.

★   ★   ★

The Damadians made a big fuss and plied me with coffee. I got to sit in the front seat of Bill Damadian's car as they sped home with me, my bare feet and wet jeans thrust under the blower of the heater. Up ahead, the flashing lights of the ambulance, carrying the woman and her son, lost themselves in the evening glitter of the modest Columbia city skyline.

"You okay, lady?" Damadian lit a cigarette.

"Yeah. Yessir. May I have a little drag on that?"

He smiled, gave me the cigarette, and lit another for himself. "A strange thing," he said. "They were German or Dutch or something."

"Probably exchange visitors from the Baptist bible camp," Bubba remarked from the back seat.

"Well, they didn't look Southern Baptist to me. Hey Garnet, you cold?"

"Nossir," said I, freezing. My long heavy hair was like an ice pack. "Thanks for the cigarette, Mr. Damadian."

"'Bill'," he corrected me expansively. "When you save somebody's life with someone else, you call him Bill."

"I'm all right. Bill."

"But not in class." He smirked into the rearview mirror at Bubba, crammed in the back seat with little Tommy and the Irish setter. "You guys don't call me Bill in class. Too progressive. Smacks of communism."

I heard Bubba chortle and then he was digging his foot up between the seat cushions from the back. I could feel the pressure on my rear end and wondered if it was deliberate or if his feet were just cold like mine were.

An anticipatory warmth nevertheless started someplace near my stomach and began a disgraceful crawl downwards.

Calm down Garnet you twit, I told myself. Look at you. You look like a drowned refugee. Bubba can't possibly want to get into your waterlogged britches.

"Where exactly do you live, lady?" Damadian punched my

arm lightly. "I've got to make some directional decisions here soon."

I stubbed out my smoke. "Go on out Bluff Road and I'll tell you when to turn."

"You're a farmer's daughter!" crowed Bubba when we pulled into the scenic Laney driveway and came face-to-face with a John Deere tractor parked out under the shed.

"Yeah." I scrambled out of the car. "And I've heard all the jokes."

I thanked Bill and Betty for an unusual evening and Bubba walked me to the door. I did not ask him to. But I noticed that he kept to the shade and finally steered me carefully behind the shrubs at the porch, out of the glare of Damadian's headlights.

"You sure are somethin'," he said, hands in pockets. "For a little bitty ol' girl, you sure can swim."

"Used to swim a lot. When I was little."

"Before you got hurt?"

My throat went dry and no words would come out immediately. I wet my lips, the only dry spot on my whole durn body. "I never got hurt. I didn't go out for football."

"Oh."

"Nuts." I touched an earlobe with a nervous finger. "I've lost an earring."

"Can I see?"

I looked up at him in the dim light and he was embarrassed about the leg business. Maybe more than I was. I didn't move and his tentative fingers twitched back my damp stringy strands of hair.

"Yep. It's gone. You still got your heart pin, though."

"Yeah." I touched it.

"Well," he said, "that kid and the ol' lady'll never forget this evening. Nor their angel with an inner tube. It was worth an earring."

I tried to feel something about saving a life, if that's what we had done. I wondered what that boy's kids would turn out like. Wondered if they'd be glad to be alive when he'd tell them someday about the American girl with the long scarf who'd yelled at him like a screech owl.

The air was cool and scented with early spring flowers.

"You are a very lovely girl, Garnet. You know that?"

I looked up. Bubba's head loomed over me.

"Not pretty. 'Pretty' is too common a word, Garnet. You're like an old picture with that pin on your blouse. You know?"

"Stuff it, Hargett."

He laughed. "That tough-cookie stuff don't fool me. I've been watchin' you for weeks, girl. You're bout as tough as a month-old puppy. Cuter, too."

I punched him sappily on the arm. Giddy.

"Ow! Damadian's waitin'. Can I maybe kiss you goodnight?"

I didn't say yes but I didn't move. I couldn't believe that he really wanted to do it. But his arms did go around me as Damadian's horn started to honk. My cold mouth pressed to his warm one. I was nervous, pure as the proverbial driven snow, except for a few past games of handsy-feelsy with David Dale Baker and Doug Mitchell. I felt out of my depth. But my mouth knew what to do, and it astonished me by opening to his caressing tongue.

He does want me, I realized. But if I am good enough for him, then is he good enough for me?

My unconscious wanted to speak his babyish name, to put a label upon what I was feeling as his hands snuck over my wet soggy self in the dark. Bubba Bubba, I tried to think. But it came out Bobby Bobby.

He walked stiff and frustrated and happy back to Damadian's car to yell long loud goodnights into the air at me. I stood in the shadow of the bushes by the back door and fingered my initialled pin.

A rush of déja-vu wallowed over me in such a sudden insistent wallop that I felt my knees give out and I squatted there in the yard while the tail lights turned to red pinpricks. The pin was cold in my fingers.

A dark memory stood with me in the night, a ghost who had been living somewhere just out of my reach for weeks and who had now come forward on this nutty Monday to claim me.

Good God, I laughed, crouched there in the dewy grass with my hair dripping. I didn't feel at all like laughing but I laughed anyway. There was no correct response to the knowledge that I had somehow fallen in love with Robert E. Lee.

Thirteen

Robert is thirty-one years of age.

He has been sitting for a portrait all day. The session has been tedious, but he is waylaid on his way upstairs to change clothes by his little boy, Custis. An impromptu game results in Robert's crawling all over the floor in his dress uniform.

Finally he climbs the stairs, two at a time, and marches down the hall of his sister's Baltimore house to the room he is sharing with Mary, all the while undoing the high stiff collar that digs into his jaw whenever he looks down. He passes a dim hallway mirror and salutes himself as he strides by, pleased with the portrait and the entire world. He is taking his growing family with him to his post in St. Louis and he is jubilant.

"I'm going," are Mary's first words to him when he pops into the room, whistling.

He hasn't known she'd be there waiting for him. He turns to stare at the young woman sitting round-shouldered in the windowseat.

"Not *going*," she amends then, hugging herself and looking

out over the garden. "Not back to Arlington. I meant I've decided to go with you—to St. Louis."

"Oh." He resumes fooling with the collar. "I wasn't aware that there was ever any doubt."

She doesn't answer.

His tunic unbuttoned, he begins to undo the black stock around his throat. "You don't want to go. Is that what you're saying?"

"St. Louis is too far removed from my parents. That's all I said at breakfast." She plucks at her full challis sleeves. Brown corkscrew curls bob at her pale cheeks. "My aged parents. Who won't live forever."

"Molly—"

"They love you like a son and never fail to give you the benefit of every doubt. They know you must have some good reason for insisting that their grandchildren grow up amongst savages."

He jerks at the black silk. "Then go back to Virginia."

"Wanderers upon the face of the earth. That's us. It's all very well for you. And it might be acceptable for me. I'm not strong, but I can endure."

"Then go home." He rips at the cloth and flings it off onto the top of the dresser. "I certainly don't expect you to bear my cross."

"I can *endure*," she raises her soft slow voice, "a certain lack of security. But the children. . . ."

"You knew I had no money when you married me."

"Let's not commence that argument again. We don't lack for a thing, we have a perfectly good home. Mama and Papa love you like their own son. Perhaps you don't chose to accept—"

"Arlington belongs to your pa. It isn't *mine*."

Mary looks at him leaning over the dresser with his back to her. There is a chicken feather stuck incongruously into the black curling ends of his hair, a remnant of the pretend-Indian game played with Custis. He sees his reflection in the mirror now, sees the feather, too, and plucks it. Mary notices a vein starting to throb at his temple, the backs of his ears becoming red.

"Your father warned you not to marry me," he says in a conversational tone. The anger is gone from his voice but Mary knows where to look for it and she finds it in the set of his shoulders. "We all know very well that 'soldier' is just another word for 'gypsy'."

"Robert, for goodness—"

"What kind of a man would I be if I shirked my duty and went off to live upon your father's bounty? Isn't there an unpleasant name for fellows like that?"

She puts a hand to her forehead where a headache is coming.

"Is it so unthinkable," he goes on lightly, rummaging in the top drawer, "for a poor soldier to live with his wife? Or has that practice perhaps fallen out of fashion? Forgive me, but I am hopelessly behind in current social trends."

The razor edged sarcasm makes her whimper a little, knowing the way he can cut her to bloody ribbons. "I—"

"Cohabitation is out of vogue—" He smacks the stopper back into the cologne bottle Mary has left open. "—and no one told me."

She takes a breath. "I told you that I would go with you this time. So stop your theatrics."

"But I wish you to *want* to come with me. How dreadfully old-fashioned."

She watches him for a moment as he neatens up her scattered belongings, idly arranging her brushes and bottles into precise military rows.

"Stop it," she says.

He glances up, deceptively mild. She looks away and stares out of the window, her sharp plain face trying for control.

Finally she can ask "Why in the world did we get married? What ever could've been in your mind?"

"You're my family." His voice is low. Hesitant.

"Perhaps that is not enough . . . for me."

"I needed you, Molly."

"And you still need me."

"Yes."

" 'Need.' An entirely different thing from 'want', Robert. I know you. You don't want *me*. I *hate* those inane parties *you* adore. I'm no good at the giggles and the winking. I'm not sociable. I find most people connected with the service to be unbearably stupid. I know you feel compelled to make excuses for me to your *stupid* friends. I've proven to be a very poor heroine for whatever little drama you are staging."

"You're my wife. I love you. That's God's own truth, Molly. What in the devil do you want me to do?"

She sits there with her chin propped on one hand, thinking about the cadet who used to come riding to her Arlington door. Not the only suitor she had by any means, and certainly not the most suitable suitor. But she thought, even then, that she would defy father and mother, and heaven and earth, to run away with her soldier. Cherishing him, cherishing something clean and poetic and strong about him. Longing for the day she could escape with him to some Walter Scott bower of roses and hear the lovely words of pledge and endearment pouring from his clean lips. But he utters no poesy, and the bower consists of a dingy bedroom in a crowded army fortress. He just needs her and uses her, coming home silent and mudcovered after a day devoted to steam piledrivers and construction, and it's not enough. There is no romance in need.

It's my fault, she thinks now. He wanted family. What did I want? A fantasy? I don't know anymore.

"You won't *try!*" he snaps. It is blurted out, almost of its own accord. "You won't even *try!* How the devil can there be any warmth betwixt a man in the middle of the continent and a woman way back in Virginia? How am I to conceive a consuming desire for your company if I'm unable even to remember what you look like?"

"Well, if you love me as you claim, I don't see how you can keep uprooting me so coldbloodedly and denying me a home! Children need security."

97

"I needed none."

"If your marriage vows mean anything at all to you, which I have good reason to doubt, then you can learn to sleep alone in St. Louis and rejoice that your family is secure and happy at home in Virginia! Any other arrangement is pure selfishness, Robert."

"Oh my *God*."

"If you don't care to leave the army and accept our home as your own, then that's your business."

"Anywhere, any blessed place a man has his family with him, is *home*. My God." He tosses his head. He splats an open palm down onto the dresser top. Bottles overturn.

"Don't you try to make me feel bad, Robert Lee!" She loads some heavy ammunition into her anger. "I'm not the villain in this piece! I seem to recall a time when you didn't miss me so much, unless those abundant rumors were further off the mark than rumors ever are. Me, huge with your child and sick as a dog, sweltering at Arlington, while you—Dear God, my breeding won't permit me to speak the words! How could you? *How could you?*"

He sighs. Rubs his face and looks at the moulding around the ceiling for a moment. "There is no excuse for what I did. I sinned. There is no excuse for sin. I've hated myself for a long time, Moll. But that was six years ago."

"Has it ever occurred to you that I would have been well within my rights to take the children and leave you altogether? *Has that ever occurred to you, Mr. Lee?*" she shouts.

A child's sudden wail sounds down the hallway on the other side of the closed door.

Robert appears panicky, his eyes accuse her. "You've disturbed Rooney."

"Well, let him bawl! Kitty will care for him. I have no one to care for me."

"That's very unfair."

"No, it was *you* who made me ill—giving birth to Mary so soon after Custis, not an ounce of consideration for anything save your own bestial pleasure. I'm still not well. You and Custis drive me insane in the afternoons with the whooping and the noise, as I lie here and try to find some relief. And now here's *Rooney,* another screaming brat. No doubt I am fated to give birth to yet another, somewhere among strangers and hussies and ruffians, on some godforsaken army post! Who knows if I shall survive it? Has that ever occurred to you?" She waits, furious. "*Look* at me when I'm talking to you!"

He rubs his face again. "Ahhh, Molly . . . Molly. I'm just lonely. Not depraved. I grow lonelier every day. I lie awake sometimes at night in St. Louis and become afraid that if I close my eyes I might die in my sleep alone. Isn't that ridiculous? Die absolutely alone."

"Don't cry 'orphan' to me. I am sick of it."

He looks startled. Stabbed.

She realizes the cruelty of her remark but she isn't sorry. She lifts a hand to her cheek where the skin under the eye has become wet and glistening.

Robert puts out both hands and leans against the mantelpiece, head bowed. "I've never wanted to hurt you, Moll. For God's sake, don't goad me into it."

"Stop taking the Lord's name in vain and listen. I said I was going with you. And I've gotten as far as Baltimore, haven't I? But you can't force me to want to do it, Robert. I *don't* want to. If you would stay at home like other husbands, things might be otherwise. But you won't. So there it is."

He reaches for the doorknob. She speaks again.

"I am not cut from the same bolt of cloth as that Harriet Talcott and all of those silly, frivolous army wives." Her voice cracks. "I am only Mary Custis. Plain and unalterable."

He glances back over his epaulet and sees her sitting there small and hard in billowing challis. And suddenly he wants to throw her onto the high canopied bed and rip into her crinolines and take her murderously like a small white fort.

Her hands cross defiantly, over the cameo on her breast, and hug her thin shoulders.

She quietly weeps. He turns from her and lets himself out into the hall.

But what she cannot see, once he has closed the door behind himself, is Robert suddenly bending over there in the empty hallway, doubling up as if he were in pain, mashing the palms of his hands against his face to hold back the roiling inside.

The heels of his hands leave red marks on his cheeks when he straightens, after a long moment, and steps to the dim hall mirror, sniffling, sprucing up his tieless uniform. *I did not want you when you were born.* His mother's deathbed confession comes clawing.

Who is to want me, then? he thinks at his own woebegone reflection. Who is ever to want me?

He paces slowly down the hall until he can breathe without catches, and is satisfied at last to pass the mirror one more time and find no expression at all in his own eyes. He nods at himself and goes calmly back downstairs to hug Custis over and over until the little boy laughs.

Fourteen

Robert and she dance. Markie Williams doesn't bubble or giggle or squirm the way young ladies her age often do. She has never been one for silliness. Robert doesn't mind silliness, but he has watched this cousin of Molly's growing up for five years now and he admires her dry wit and her self-possession— something that he hopes will rub off onto his own little girls. The eldest is just ten and none show signs yet of developing anything like female accomplishment. Cousin Markie, with her good taste and deportment, might teach them something inadvertently.

"Isn't this delightful, Cousin Robert?" Her face is just a foot from his own. She is becoming quite tall. She dances well and shows evidence of potential bellehood, but her reluctance to cut herself loose from the family and make acquaintances among these New York fashionables tonight is counterproductive. She would rather be housed up here with the Lees as planned, but the situation is tense in that household and Markie has become a house guest of the soirée's hostess.

"Thank goodness you came," she tells Robert. "I couldn't bear to sit out a single waltz."

He had taught her to waltz himself, back in the Arlington parlor, upon her earlier visits there. She had been a gawk at fifteen. Well, perhaps not a gawk. Markie was never gawky. Perhaps a tad stiff. A tad nervous. He smiles to himself now, remembering. "It's puppylove," Molly had whispered to him once, amused. "The poor child is quite taken with you."

That had been news to Robert. "Never! I frighten her!"

"Oh, no. Her mother says—"

Her mother. A neurasthenic Custis relation who has all of the joylessness of these spoiled people. No wonder the little girl is a bundle of nerves. She needed fresh air, Robert decided. The opportunity to be herself.

Most young ladies do not waltz—a newish touching dance where the partners embrace—with any but family members, and so the floor is not as crowded as it has been for the reels. Young fellows duck out the back for a cigar and a brandy, leaving the girls to *yoo hoo* up and down the sidelines and compare their dance cards. The matrons sit fanning themselves. Robert thinks for a moment and then steers Markie out into the middle of the floor where people can see her, a graceful maneuver that swirls her ruffles up against his uniformed knees. His mind goes back to Fort Hamilton, out there in New York Harbor. He is sure that his architectural renderings are affecting his eyesight, and that the miasma on the waters will probably give him malaria. Molly hates the place. Having left several of the children down home with her parents, she will probably shove off south herself any day now. Her displeasure is breathable.

Robert and Markie waltz. Onlookers pause in their conversations to regard the couple: rosy beautiful girl moving like a pastel moth, supple faultless officer in dark blue and glittering brass.

"F. F. V.'s," mutters a lady to her neighbor, forever enamored of First Families, "and did you see his *wife*? Poor dowdy thing in a frock two seasons out of fashion."

"He married her for her money," is the rejoinder. "Lees always marry money."

The ladies watch suspiciously as Markie tilts her head back and wispy little tendrils of hair float around her face. Her laughter wafts through the room like scent.

"I hear he's got a brother in the Navy who's even better-looking than he is." The voice is whispery behind the fan. "But I don't see how that's possible."

"You know," mutters the first lady confidentially, watching the radiant pair, "if I were Mary Lee, I'd get myself back in here *right now*. And I'd purchase myself some prettier dresses."

The piano and the fiddle are relentless. Robert says, "You really must let an old man sit out a few and find yourself a younger beau."

But Markie is bored by all of the inane talk she gets tonight from men her own age who run on about cotillions and British Royalty and the likelihood of a war with Mexico. Her father is a soldier. Cousin Robert is a soldier. She doesn't want to hear of wars. Men get shot in wars.

"Don't abandon me, Cousin," she pleads, fan dangling at her wrist where it swings into his elbow with a steady thwock-thwock. "Don't throw me to the wolves. Buck up!"

There are awkward boys around the punch bowl, pimply, fuzzed with sparse shadows trying to be moustaches. They don't look like wolves to Robert. Spaniels, maybe.

Robert says, "This is the fourth blessed waltz in a row, Miss M.! You're going to bust a stay!"

"Cousin Robert!" she hisses with mock disapproval. "I am scandalized."

She laughs, but he is sorry now that he made the jest. It seems improper suddenly to consider Markie in her corset. Mercy. She's like a daughter.

"Actually," she confides over the music, leaning in so that her nose is at his collarbone, "I've been trying to shock you for years."

He grins, helpless. "Well, you mustn't give up."

She looks over his epaulet at the old biddies against the walls, reveling in this public attention from the officer called The Handsomest Man In The Army. She can recall hiking up her skirts in her hoyden days and running breakneck down Arlington Hill, out in the fresh air, while old Great-aunt Mary, Cousin Molly's mama, stood up there on the portico like an old biddy with that old-biddy look on her face. Markie wouldn't be surprised if Cousin Molly turned out to be an old biddy herself, with her prim blue stockings and mangy calico. Too bad, too, because Markie adores her sharp wicked tongue, her good sense, her talent at watercolors. Her taste in husbands—

She had been scared of him at first, scared of his intense eyes and his silence, and of the remote way he would move around the periphery of the family upon his rare visits home. A body might visit Arlington as much as a dozen times a year and never catch him there. It was his portrait on the wall that Markie had fallen in love with at adolescence; the actual man was dark and morose, something out of Lord Byron. With as much personality, apparently, as a stone. Yet . . .

Major Custis would putter around the garden and paint his dreadful pictures of George Washington and invite perfect strangers to the house at all hours to see his Washington memorabilia. Mary would keep to her room or throw herself into her roses and needlework, always fussing about some ache or pain or other, while the little Lees ran wild with the black children, and had their dogs and cats and horses and games. The servants gossiped on the stairs in the endless lazy afternoons and the gardeners chattered outside. And nobody at all ever paid much attention to a quiet soldier stepping around the edges, unless it might have been Markie's father, sitting with the man over a chess game and a glass of wine in the plantation office. The ringing laughter astonished Markie and her brothers, who would creep up close outside the windows to hear army reminiscences and spicy stories they could never quite understand. They would peer in through the glass at their merry papa and Cousin Mary's husband, sitting at his ease with his chair tilted back, cheeks pink with glee, anecdotes pouring out, and his marvelous boyish laughter making his face look the way it *should,* like a prince's.

She was sitting in the grass in front of the house one day when she was fifteen, pencil and paper on her knee, trying to draw the façade of Arlington for her little brother Orton. She couldn't get the columns right. They looked like watermelons. She erased and erased and was about to discard the whole thing when Cousin Robert materialized over her, bareheaded, in his rumpled linen riding clothes smelling of horses and fresh sweet hay. He had crouched. "May I show you something?" He was pointing at her sketchbook.

She handed it to him without a word, embarrassed, and watched him flip to a fresh page, where he began to render the Arlington columns faster than lightning, and perfect: round and straight and shaded, so real that you could touch them. All the while explaining about how light falls upon one side of an object, and about the Greek visual concept of *entasis* — not treating her like a child, either — his quiet low voice hypnotic as he drew in the house around the columns and finished up with a *unicorn* on the porch! And that marvelous laugh . . . the sun in his face, and his hair blowing into his crinkly eyes.

She feels someone else's eyes on her and turns in her dancing.

"Cousin Mary has come back inside," she says. All the life has left her voice. "She's over there, watching us. I think she must be ready to leave."

"Oh me."

Robert spots Mary then, huddled at the edge of the dance floor, her face sharp and tired. Her eyes are waiting for his and they lock onto him like a trap the instant he looks. She snaps open her fan and looks pointedly away.

Robert sighs and regards his partner. Their waltz winds down like a watch spring. Markie grips his gloved hand. Her eyes are sad. Woman eyes, gray-green. Her delicate pointed chin looks fragile and white as an eggshell. The lights of the chandelier throw red hellfire sparks all over her thick brown hair. How old is Markie now? he thinks. Twenty? Good God. He remembers Eliza Mackay at age twenty. Mary Custis at twenty.

He clears his throat, disturbed. "Perhaps I should—"

"Well." She stands still. The room is full of Yankee strangers.

"Whom shall I leave you with, then?" he smiles tightly, creases in either cheek bracketing his newly-grown black moustache. "Would Mr. Van Altt amuse you sufficiently?"

"Mr. Van Altt is an ass."

"Now now. You mustn't hold his species against him." He leads her by the hand to a knot of people where he inserts her into a conversation against her will. He bows his way out of the conviviality and is turning to go when Markie takes him by the arm and lowers her voice. "Cousin Robert?"

But her face goes all confused when he glances back. She looks down at her gloved thumbs. Smiles lamely. "Forget it, forget it. I'm sorry. Go on." Her eyes flick in Mary's direction. "Good Lord, I'm never going to get married."

He laughs. "Some young Romeo will snap you up into matrimony within a year. Like a trout on a cricket. Goodnight now, Sweet—"

"I don't think so," she mutters at her feet. Shrugs, bare shoulders moving like ripples on milk. "Not if I'm waiting . . . for someone special, Robert. Go on home. I had a nice time."

She has left off "Cousin". His unadorned name hangs between them like a light. There is a dangerous warmth in her face.

The ballroom is hot. Suffocating. He feels jaded and a little crazy, raw and full of the devil. No no no, he insists to his devil. This is *Markie,* you idiot! Little Markie. Not some teasing soubrette.

Go home. Fetch your wife and go home.

But she raises her eyes just then. Her face is very pale above the lilac ruffles over her breast, sweet and lonely. He resolutely bows with just his chin and makes himself walk away. He affects nonchalance when he offers his arm to an unsmiling Mary and makes for their hostess and then the open door.

Lord, he *loves* Mary. She is a fine, spirited woman, easy (too easy) on the children, tough in the face of her worsening arthritis. But why does she rag him so? Not easy at all with *him,* ever. Nothing he does pleases. He has been completely faithful to her since those indiscreet evenings at Fortress Monroe. Utterly faithful. His thrifty tightfisted way with a dollar has kept her in dowdy calico and kept Arlington House in one piece when Major Custis lacks cash. What is the problem, then?

She doesn't love him back. He can't blame her.

Some fault in me, some taint, he thinks now. I know it's there. She knows it's there. I don't know what it is, is all. I wish she would be specific and perhaps I could correct it.

"I've never met such stupid, boring people in my life," Mary mutters during their silent carriage ride back to their rented house. Robert affects indifference. But it isn't indifference he feels. Dear God, it is hot sweet honey and loneliness inside him. And he knows that he will never get to sleep unless Mary admits him charitably to her bed.

Fifteen

I stood at Bill Damadian's desk and shifted from one foot to the other. Lack of sleep had made me spacy. I was only a little uncomfortable with the discovery that I had fallen in love with a dead historical figure. It seemed that every infatuation brought with it its own justification. My friend Anita would no sooner flip for a guy than she was rationalizing, saying, "Garnet, I love him because he's Italian." Or, "He's gonna major in business administration like me." Or, "Garnet, I love him because he's not a virgin and he'll know what to do on our wedding night."

The emotion always came first, but it came equipped with a raison d'etre. And I was following that pattern this morning as I stood in front of Damadian's desk. I had already started to rationalize. Giddy, smiling that dopey sick-cow smile that I had so lately been smiling for Bubba Hargett, I was ill and metaphysical.

Only the faintest part of me was protesting the ludicrousness of my situation. Love had an enormous survival instinct.

I felt good. Yes, I was in love with a dead historical figure— my God!—but that was no sillier than having a crush on Ringo

Starr or Paul Newman, was it? No girl I knew, who had gone apeshit over Paul Newman, would ever get to meet him. So what was wrong with the way I felt?

I was apeshit over someone special. And I felt good about it. Felt good about loving him, because he wanted to be loved. It would tickle him to death to know that a girl in the future succumbed like so many before. What a boost that would give his ego. He always impressed girls, even when he was old and had lost his looks. But *I* was special. I lived in the future. I had succumbed at incredibly long range.

Garnet, said my rational part, you are completely nuts. You ain't got all your oars in the water.

The final bell had rung and the classroom had emptied out fast. Bill Damadian was collecting his things for lunch.

I stepped forward. "Bill."

"Well, Esther Williams! How's it going? You going to make it to the meeting to elect our officers on Wednesday night next week?"

"Does a bear shit in the woods?"

He laughed. "Why do you always think you have to come on so strong?"

"Hey now. Stop analyzing me and listen. I need your academic expertise. I gotta ask you a question."

"Hokay."

I moved closer to his desk. "What can I read that'll tell me something about time?"

He rolled his tongue blankly around in his mouth. "Time zones, you mean? Date lines?"

No. I shook my head. Earrings tinkled. "Time. What it is, exactly. The nature of time itself."

"Time theory?" He blinked. Tapped a pencil against the palm of his hand. "How the ancients told time, or what?"

"Well . . . If that's all there is."

"You could read some physics. You know. Einstein. You familiar with the Relativity Theory?"

"I know about it. We've never studied it. There aren't any of Einstein's books in the school library."

He snorted. "Any resemblance between this institution and a school is purely coincidental. Go to the University of South Carolina Library. They won't let you check anything out, but you can sit and read to your little heart's content. Could you study Einstein, though, Garnet? Understand it, I mean?"

I frowned. "Not everybody at this institution is a moron."

We walked to the door. He turned out the overhead lights. "What in the world are you investigating, lady? Is this independent research or what?"

"Well, hey Bill," came a voice from down the hall.

We looked around. Bubba stood there, looking real good, and I felt only a faint little twinge. Oho. I was free. Hello, Babycakes, I thought. Look how I look you in the eye. See how I'm not turning into jello anymore.

Bill glanced at him. Paused. "Yeah?"

"Just wanted to say hey."

"Well, hey Bubba."

Bubba took tentative hold of my elbow and propelled me down the hall while I could hear Bill's shoes squeak behind us. He stopped to talk to the algebra teacher and we two ambled on down the emptying corridor for a while, side by side, my bracelets clanking against my books.

"I like your hair that way," Bubba said.

I put a hand to my head where the hair was rolled back, away from my face and pinned up in a plump knot at the rear of my skull.

"Real pretty," he said. "Old fashioned like. Suits you."

"Thanks."

He put a hand on my arm. His heavily veined wrist was appealing and frightening in its obvious maleness. "You doin' anything after the debate meeting on Wednesday?"

"Goin' home."

"Wanna go get a hamburger with me or something afterwards? If we're gonna be a team, we gotta get down to brass tacks. I can take you home later."

What an ego boost to be able to say Yes without going all to giggly pieces. I nodded, my nonchalance genuine.

"I can ride you home today too, if you want," he went on. "I've got my car outside."

I was tempted. I wanted to be seen driving away with Bubba Hargett. "Better not," I said. "If I don't turn up on the school bus after Beth Ann gets off, Mama's liable to call the highway patrol."

"Yeah. Well. Okay." He pushed the hall door open for me and we stepped out into the sinful spring sun. "But be sure and put Wednesday night on your calendar."

I looked at my watch. I was already late for chemistry class. "Hey." I held his arm as he turned to go. "Somethin' I've always wanted to ask you: What is your right name?"

"My given name?" His blond hair fell over his temples as he stood closer to me than one person usually stands to another. I stood my ground. We were nose-to-collarbone. "It's Charles. Charles Hegler Hargett."

"Oh. I had a hunch it might be . . . oh hell, forget it. Lots of Heglers up around Rock Hill and Lancaster. My folks are from up around there. Any of your kin from up there?"

"Dunno. Mom has cousins all over Tennessee."

"Nice name. I like it."

He waved and sauntered away. Looked back once. Waved again. And disappeared behind the crepe myrtle bushes at the corner of the school building.

But no. He wasn't Robert. Out of sight, out of mind.

A person in love becomes more attractive or something, I realized. Bubba had never really even looked at me until I gave my Lee report in class. I must have already been a little infatuated that day. That's what Bubba had come on to. People are weird, I thought now. They don't want something until someone else wants it. Or until it's gone.

Thank you, Robert. For the first time in my life I know that

I'm pretty. Leg and all. You loved something essential in women and that essence is mine because it's my birthright and I'm claiming it.

I felt so good and so drugged that I decided to skip my chemistry class altogether. I decided to sit outside under the shade of the pecan trees and fan myself languidly with my re-strung fan. It and I had a new lease upon this bowl of cherries.

And by the time I consulted Einstein, I knew that I would have an air tight rationalization of why it was okay to feel the way I felt. I wasn't an intellectual for nothing.

Sixteen

The American army's march from Veracruz towards Mexico City has been murder, under a blistering sun that kills six men in a single regiment in one day. The mules give out. General Scott never thought it possible to sweat so much, to be plagued with such fleas, to be so constantly thirsty.

Santa Anna's artillery checked their progress at Cerro Gordo until Captain Lee hatched a plan to get in their rear and presented it to General Scott. Skeptical but desperate, Scott then saw this lone engineer take charge of a unit and advance heavy artillery up the side of a mountain with pulleys and ropes and their own straining backs, for God's sake. "Like Bonaparte crossing the Alps," observes Quartermaster Ulysses S. Grant. That dirt-covered engineer with the Virginia drawl will bear some watching. Scott has found a new weapon.

All of the other engineers under Lee's command are ill. Several have had to be invalided back to Veracruz. Scott wonders what has kept this one on his feet.

When Santa Anna backs himself into a heavily-defended

Mexico City, it is Lee that Scott calls for. Lee's reconnaissance has uncovered a mule track through a lava bed that will place American forces in the Mexican rear. Would General Scott like to hear more? General Scott would. Does General Scott believe that a sizeable force can be hauled over the boulders into Santa Anna's rear? Not really. But Lee has Generals Cadwalader and Shields and Persifor Smith in place by nightfall, their batteries in position. Rain has started falling, a tropical August thunderstorm.

"Come dawn," observes General Cadwalader, "we're going to find ourselves trapped in here if we lose the initiative. Santa Anna will bomb hell out of us from Rancho Padierna."

General Scott is to make a feint on the front, while the main attack will be delivered from the rear—this lava bed. What time shall Scott make his diversionary move? No such attack can be coordinated without communication from Scott's headquarters. Smith and Cadwalader and Shields hole up in a church. Rain pounds. They expect a staff officer will arrive from Scott any second. None does.

Someone spits tobacco juice in a brown arc that puddles on the floor. Cadwalader taps a pencil against a rough map.

"Scott's maybe three miles away," mutters Smith. "His staff can't find us in the dark, perhaps."

Captain Lee hauls out his gold watch by its chain.

Smith eyes him. "What do we do now, Captain?"

They don't say it, but the thought is clear: You got us in here in the first place, Captain Lee. You're going to get us drubbed if Scott doesn't open up before the Mexicans discover us.

"Damn," says General Cadwalader.

Lee stands. "I'll go. Sirs."

Maybe that's what they've been waiting to hear, yet it doesn't seem like such a good idea once he has said it. Crossing the lava field in the daylight has been a brutal exercise, even for mounted men who could see where they were going. For a man on foot, in the dark and in the rain . . .

Shields rubs his face. "Ol' Fuss-and-Feathers'll have our

scalps if his pet engineer here falls into a ravine and breaks his damned neck."

"I know where the ravines are, sir." Lee puts his watch away. "In theory."

"You ever been possum huntin', sir? I've been all over Virginia in the dark."

"Virginia." General Shields grins.

Cadwalader cleans out his ear with his pencil point. "Scott's got to move by daylight, gentlemen. Time is running out. Use this man. That's what Uncle Sam pays him for."

Smith stretches. "Uncle Sam pays him to tell me where the hell I am. I don't know where the hell I am or where the hell Scott is." Smith laughs, punch-drunk, exhausted. Dirty and apprehensive. "What would you need, Lee?"

But that captain is already on his feet, looking around the adobe walls at the gear piled on the floor. He finds his visored cap and gun belt. "Oh . . . two or three men, sir. Whomever will volunteer. I'll take care of it."

"Equipment?"

"Light as possible, sir. Can't get mounts through there now. We'll have to feel our way."

The firm way he dons his dusty cap betrays no apprehension. Smith's aide sprints off to recruit volunteers among the sappers and redlegs. Lee salutes the war council from the carved wooden doorway. "Have the men stand to their guns at four A.M., sirs. I'll be back as soon as I can."

"Don't you use a pine-knot torch when you hunt opossum?" Smith calls after him. He looks at his companions.

"Are you a betting man?" Cadwalader says as the door closes behind the engineer.

"I am, sir. But I won't give you odds. Enemy recon is all over the place tonight. And the pedregal—that lava field—well, it might as well be the surface of the moon."

"Sir, one hundred dollars says he pulls it off," says Cadwalader.

"Done, sir." Smith sighs. "Let's give it another four hours. And then prepare to defend this miserable ground as best we can until we can figure out a way to effect a retreat."

There are no stars and no moon as Lee's little party sets out. No light at all except for sudden stabs of lightning that illuminate a nightmare landscape of jagged boulders. A compass can only be glimpsed for a second at a time and then the rain water, pounding upon its crystal, distorts the needle into a shivering black dot.

"Godawmighty," mutters an engineer lieutenant, water pouring down the back of his neck like his native Niagara Falls. His boot soles slip and slide over unseen, knife-edged rocks.

There is no way to keep to the mule track. Captain Lee is taking a short cut, anyway. In truth, there is no way to find the goddam mule track, and its twists and turns eat up precious time. Robert tries to picture the land in his mind, the way it looked in the daytime. When the sky flares, sometimes he finds himself at the edge of a black gully and he raises a hand so that the others will come no nearer until he has decided to climb down it or jump over it or back up and seek another way.

Actually, he is in his element. He has never known before what his proper element might be, but this brutal martial life seems to be it. He trusts his own stamina, arms and legs strengthened at construction and piledriving, and he trusts the map in his brain. Nobody can hear him over the torrent, but he is singing.

He has spent the last several years bored, supervising the building of one fort after another, expecting to rot at his drawing table eventually. Until suddenly the United States picks a fight with Mexico. Captain Lee suspects that the war is not moral but political. Politicians, however, never ask soldiers their opinions of foreign policy. And Lee can't deny that a part of him welcomes this dubious crusade.

The Mexican girls are sun-warmed and wear no stockings. He enjoys looking at them, and he contemplates touching them.

He is teaching himself Spanish to facilitate his party-going in this easy exotic locale where the residents welcome gringo gentlemen, enemies or not.

And what a marvelous respite war itself is, from the temptations of bare brown legs! For the first time, he is under fire. He has built military roads and established artillery batteries in a storm of lead. It scares him some, yes, but the fear clears his mind wonderfully. He has no time now to mull over Mary's chronic illnesses or wonder how best to keep the children, seven of them so far, out of trouble. He has made out his will, bidden them all goodbye, and has trooped off into a peculiar new world that consists only of the present. Far away from Mary and her discontent. Far from his father-in-law who never tires of telling him how to conduct his life. *"Fare thee well, for I must leave thee./ Do not let the parting grieve thee . . ."* He recalls the old song words with relish as he stumbles over the rough terrain.

Mary had said an uncharacteristically heartfelt goodbye to him with the newborn baby Mildred in her arms. There had been fear in her. Yet he has waited a long time for this war. On the day of his departure, him crying poormouth to his brother Carter and still unwilling to live off Custis money, he had resolved to make his mark. Forty years old, it's now or never.

It won't come again; get on with it, man.

His brother Smith is here with the Navy, was ashore at Veracruz with the marines behind the cannon, and the two had shared something savage in the bombardment, faces blackened with powder smoke and white teeth stark as they shouted to one another, "Hey, get down, ol' man! They've got our range!"

"Fare thee well, for I must leave thee./ Do not let—"

Pain. A sharp edge gashes through his glove and into his palm. My first wound, he thinks, feeling for another handhold. Give that man a promotion.

Lightning strikes nearby with an apocalyptic crash and the soldiers see him in the pink glare for a second, poised hands-on-hips, staring off into the storm towards Scott's Zacatepec camp, rain pouring off the sides of his cap visor, hair plastered against his neck and cheeks.

"Hope to God the Cap'n knows where in hell he is," shudders a man in an India-rubber poncho, watching the engineer for any sign of indecision. There is none. At least none that he shows them.

But the blob of Robert's compass occasionally indicates one direction while his gut screams for another. Sometimes the compass wins, sometimes it's his gut.

Captain Lee feels his foot sliding down a steep slope in the blackness. A sixty-degree angle, his instinct tells him irrelevantly. *Fare thee well, for I must leave* —

A loud shout sounds behind him. He gropes back to help the fallen. Damn, tilted jagged rocks everywhere, and he can't see a one of them. Seventy-four degrees *exactly* his detached mind computes, when a sudden incline throws him onto his knees.

"You're bleeding on me, Captain!" hollers the downed man beneath him. Lee fastens his hands around the lieutenant's wrists.

Yes. Black blood—from his hands? His knee? "You all right, Lieutenant?"

"Beg pardon, sir?" he yells.

"You hurt?"

"I'm tolerable, sir!"

Lee hauls the man up, panting, and faces him towards Scott's camp again. The soldiers, appalled, stumble after him, waiting for each new lightning bolt to show them how to get to where he got to in the dark.

The mission is a failure. A flat, all-for-nothing failure.

Smith's information is old. Scott is no longer at the Zacatepec headquarters. He has returned to his old camp at San Augustin before this nightfall, three more miles away.

Three miles further, across the black pedregal? Sweet Jesus.

The volunteers' faces grow pale when they hear the news. They collapse under a crude shelter in the middle of the night, seeking coffee, gulping dry air, muscles twitching with exhaustion.

Lee paces the floor, dazed, slapping his cheeks with both bloody hands to wake himself up. He places his dripping cap onto his wet head and steps unsteadily back out into the rain, aiming himself at three more miles of lava. He doesn't turn around to see if any of the volunteers are with him.

Duty has been satisfied; no one will ever point any accusing fingers at him if he goes back inside to share the coffee. But he sets out again, too punchy to wonder about his motives. No other course of action occurs to him, except the wish that he could grow wings and fly.

This time he is alone. His men sleep in puddles on the floor of their shelter. This time he knows that he could die out there.

Promotion is slow in the peacetime army and he has never developed the knack for the politicking and the ass-kissing that it sometimes takes to boost oneself up the brass ladder. He has preferred to believe promotion is made upon merit. Mary tells him that he is a fool and he knows that she is right. "Papa knows many many important people, Robert," she reminds him pointedly.

Well, damn Papa. If it takes a special dispensation from politicians to make him a major, he'd rather remain a captain. And he has.

He has lain awake nights, thinking about Lighthorse Harry's stay in debtor's prison and his dalliances and the whole sordid mess, his abandoned mother left with too many children and calling herself a widow before Harry actually died and worrying herself sick that her boys might turn out like their spendthrift gambling womanizing utterly charming father.

I am mightily like you, he says to old Harry as he stumbles through the rain. I want to be calm and pure and pious like your idolized George Washington. But I'm mighty like you instead, Papa.

Many things flit across his fatigued mind, Mary among them, Mary and his growing sense of déja vu among the medicines and linens of her sickroom. She is beginning to smell like his mother: camphor, lavender, herbal teas with lemon.

I am at last beginning to understand you, Papa, he thinks. And it makes my soul tremble.

Hands slashed, knees cracked open on the rocks so many times that they threaten to no longer hold him up, he crawls blind across the lava. The wind batters when he struggles to stand. He does not know whether his eyes are open or shut. All is black. The lightning has stopped. The rain pours into his nostrils and gasping mouth and he senses that a man can actually drown like this. He can vanish, and nobody will know how he met his end or where. It's like a fistfight with the very earth, an unseen opponent, and his back tells him if he stumbles one more time that he'll break in two.

There is no one to witness his indecision; he staggers in a circle when he loses the way, spinning unsteady as a drunkard, fingers outstretched and twitching.

His head is down so that he can breathe. His eyes are shut because they are useless.

Help me, Dear God, he prays. Please help me, God.

Help me, Papa, you bastard.

An aide conducts an apparition into General Scott's headquarters nearabout midnight, a semiconscious Shakespearian ghost, water pouring off it in rivers. It flings bloody droplets all over Scott's bedding when it attempts a snap to attention.

"Great God Almighty!" Scott gapes in the candlelight. Takes hold of the sodden shoulders with his gigantic hands and steers the messenger into a camp chair, summoning astonished officers with a bellow.

Scott has sent out no less than seven staff officers since sundown this beastly night to make contact with Generals Smith and Shields. They all had given it up after a few hundred yards. The night and the ground and the darkness has beaten them all. All but this pet engineer with his sudden, white countryboy grin under the black moustache.

"Great God!" Old Scott laces black coffee with a hefty dollop of brandy and kneels himself to pour it into the man, watching the throat constrict, studying the droopy eyelids with his own probing gaze. "Where are they, Bob? Have you artillery in place?"

"Yessir. Yessir."

"Can you—?" He studies the battered knees, face all concern. "How am I to get my orders back to them?"

"I'll take them, sir. They are expecting me." The coffee-and-brandy is doing its work. Lee roughs out a map on Scott's camp table and begins explaining the plan, gathering his strength to make the crossing one more time. Scott does a dance of delight in his robe.

The successful assault is made at daylight. And the push for Mexico City goes on for days, with Captain Lee bringing up the guns and directing troop movements, disregarding the spray of musket balls that edge in ever closer, until a spent one finally glances off his jaw, just at his left ear, and smacks into his collarbone as he stoops to find the range for a battery. Never stopping to have the wound dressed, manic after forty-eight hours without sleep or food, he can't sustain the blood loss. He is in the middle of a shouted sentence when his eyes suddenly roll back into his head and he pitches headlong from his horse like a sack of potatoes. Under General Scott's very eye.

He is a brevet full colonel before he hits the ground.

"I think a little lead, properly taken, is good for a man!" Colonel Lee will later exult that evening, arms spread wide in bed, feet up, the creases in his cheeks deep happy notches that wrinkle the bandage. He'll be in the saddle again the next day, in full dress uniform for the ride into the city, the blue bruised collarbone bothering him not at all.

Winfield Scott is to become a tiresome bore upon the subject of this engineer in the years to come, "the very best soldier in Christendom," is the way he characterizes the man. "The U.S. government should insure Bob Lee's life for five million dollars a year."

Someday he'll even tell Abraham Lincoln: "God Almighty had to spit on His hands to make Bob Lee." Not a man in the army, in fact, will forget the name or the reputation. Not George McClellan. Nor George Meade. Nor Quartermaster U.S. Grant.

Seventeen

Bubba and I were sitting rather chummily on a bench in the schoolyard, near the Coke machines, while he tried to read me a quote from Wernher Von Braun on nuclear delivery systems. We were supposed to be working on our debate presentation during our one mutually free period of the day. Bubba might have been at work on a debate; I was helplessly writing a poem in my head.

I had been up all night with my head in the timelessness of Relativity. I hoped that Bubba wasn't noticing how catatonic I was. I wanted him to go and I wanted him to stay and I wanted to tell him the magical thing that was happening to me. But that would be a mistake. No matter what I would ultimately think about my state of mind, I knew that I mustn't ever tell anyone. No one would even understand.

He scribbled the Von Braun quote out onto an index card while I slapped the wooden seat gently in rhythm to the verse uncoiling in my mind.

"Hey, Bill!" I heard him call, and he nearly knocked me off

my side of the bench as he hastily moved papers and notebooks to make room for the Ubiquitous Damadian.

Let there be a seed, chanted my poet brain.

"So, Scarlet Laney, how did you find Einstein?" Damadian leaned across Bubba to address me.

"Looked in the card catalog."

He laughed. Offered me some of his grape soda. I shook my head. Bubba took the bottle from him and helped himself to a loud slurp. He handed the drink back to Damadian slowly and looked at me, bangs in his eyes.

"You're readin' Einstein?" Bubba said.

"For debate." It sounded reasonable.

Damadian frowned slightly. "You don't need to bust your brain with Einstein, lady. All I want is a good, well-crafted, affirmative speech on nuclear disarmament. Don't get it so complicated that the judges can't follow."

"I didn't find out anything I can use," I said, doodling on the back of Bubba's note card, sketching a perfect little turtle. "I just ended up readin' about his thought experiments. You know."

"Bubba, does this little broad ever make you feel stupid?"

Bubba grinned. "Heck no, Coach. I ain't ever stupid." He sidled an arm over the bench, back behind my head. His face radiated a kind of hesitant pride as he pushed at my shoulder. "Thought what? Thought experiments?"

Don't beam up at Bill as if you own me, Bubba Hargett. As if I were a smart dog who has just done a trick and made its master look cool. You aren't my master.

"Einstein did certain experiments in his head," I began, trying to keep the annoyance out of my tone. "He called them—"

"*Thought experiments!*" crowed Damadian.

"Aw, that was easy," Bubba chided. "Wait 'til we git to the hard part."

They giggled. I hated to hear men giggle. It sounded so ineffectual.

"Go on, Garn," Bubba nudged me, sensing my displeasure. "Go on. I'm sorry. I'm interested. We'll be good."

"Well . . ."

Okay. I would tell them what I knew. Just to show Bill Damadian that I could read and comprehend physics, if nothing else. I hated that carpetbagger look of condescension that crept into his round little face sometimes.

"Well," I began again, "one of these thought experiments dealt with an imaginary railroad track. A man stands off to the side of this railroad track, see, and he witnesses lightning striking the track at two different points. But simultaneously."

Bubba rubbed his jaw where the warm day was glazing it with a moist sheen. "And?"

"So there's another man riding in a train on the track itself. And he, too, sees the two bolts of lightning. But he doesn't see them simultaneously, he sees them in sequence." I warmed up. The idea was turning me on. "You see, since he's moving away from the lightning behind him, moving in the train very fast towards the bolt in front, it takes longer for the light from the one in back to reach him. So he thinks that the bolts have occurred at two different times. Not all at once, like the man off to the side thinks."

Bill was amused. "What does this have to do with nuclear disarmament?"

"It has nothing to do with nuclear disarmament. I told you that."

"Just a long shot," he said, knowingly.

Long shot, my ass, I thought, and wondered if Albert Einstein was ever in love with a dead person.

"But both men are right, then?" Bubba said. "Is that the point?"

"Exactly."

"So time is all relative, huh?"

"That's why they call this stuff Relativity."

Bubba laughed but Bill picked at a cuticle. "What does this mean to you, lady?" he muttered.

I could have told him that it meant that I was less and less in love with a dead man. And more and more in love with just a man. Period. An extraordinary man who had charmed my great-great-grandmother and who only happened not to live in 1966. He could be any age for me that I wanted him to be. I could be any age for him.

I looked at my lap. "It's just an interesting idea," I said. "An interesting idea that can't be proved."

"Has poetic possibilities," Bubba remarked.

"Yep."

Bubba nodded. "Could explain ghosts. Or multiple dimensions. I've read a lot of science fiction. Hey, can I read some of your poetry sometime?"

"Sure." But not the poem I was writing now. It wasn't for living eyes. I was writing a letter to the past.

"Well." Damadian glanced at his watch. "Free period is over for me. Got to get back to my next class of cretins."

Bubba got reluctantly to his feet. "You gonna sit out here all day, Garnet?"

"My lunch starts now. I'll see you in geometry."

"Don't forget about our date on Wednesday night, hear?"

"I won't, I won't. Go! Go! You'll be late." I gave his hand a dutiful squeeze as the bell rang and broke the bird-twittering silence to pieces.

I sat on my bench, grateful to be alone, finding it increasingly hard to be alone and more necessary now than I had ever thought it would be. I needed time to myself, I needed places where there was no Damadian or Bubba or Beth Ann asking me things or routing me out of the bathroom at home—my solitary refuge.

It took a lot of aloneness to think things through, to versify and dream and nurture the outrageous thoughts I was compelled now to entertain. But I was happy, I was self-contained, I carried around the comfort of my ludicrous secret obsession like a turtle did its shell. I could crawl into this love at any time of the day, I could give myself the names of women long dead and instantly feel the excitement Robert must have felt whenever those names were uttered within his hearing. I felt connected. I felt needed. And I felt perfectly sane.

I would write down my poem tonight as I sat in the bathroom, after everyone had gone to bed.

These were the most private thoughts I would ever have. I could discuss religion or politics with anybody. Someday I would be intimate with a lover or husband and tell him about how my leg used to hurt me and other middling little secrets like that. But I would never confess what I was feeling now, I knew. It wasn't just that people would misunderstand and find it ridiculous, it was also that I had found a new core to my being and it didn't belong to anybody but me. I was living within the circle of a magical attachment, and it touched everything around me with beauty and poignance.

I opened one of my books to a photographed portrait and sat looking intently at my soldier, at the implied great human dance of continuity of which he and I were a part. I touched my heart-shaped pin.

Yes, I did feel a little uncomfortable and guilty thinking what I was now thinking, knowing that it was incongruous and absurd to be thinking such a thing about an historical figure and the Christ of my people. But I couldn't stop thinking it and I didn't want to. It was a normal thought for a young woman.

I was wondering what Robert Lee looked like with his clothes off.

A train whistle sounded in the deep woods behind the schoolhouse, beckoning and reasonable and untellingly lonely. And I stood off to the side of Einstein's railroad track, letting two histories merge into the present.

Eighteen

Maybe this is the ideal way to love someone, I told myself on Sunday afternoon as I sat in the back seat of the Chevrolet headed for Rock Hill and my grandmother's house. My father and mother were idly arguing about something up front and Beth Ann was dozing on the seat beside me, mouth open and eyelids twitching as she watched something in a dream. Our small tape recorder, full of Sunday hymns and sermonizing for Grandmama, lay on the cushion beside her thigh.

The ideal way to love, I repeated to myself silently. No surprises. You know the person's whole life from beginning to end. Know how they'll look when they get old. Know how they turned out. What they were worth. No disillusionment.

I shifted position, tucked my left leg under me, pleased and yet saddened by my rhetorical assessment.

But of course there is one small insurmountable difficulty, I realized again: Such affairs are unavoidably Platonic.

Oh Law, I am nearly seventeen. What is it in me that turns its back on a perfectly good Bubba Hargett and wants something it can never have? What is it in me that wants to kiss a dead face—No no, *not* a dead face, not a moldy rotten corpse. A live needy body with a living face.

I've become a necrophiliac, nearly. Terrific.

Would ol' superior Bill Damadian think Robert Lee was a hick if he came into our classroom tomorrow? How would Robert talk? Would he talk like me, or would he talk like Damadian? Would he say "hoose" for "house" and "oot" for "out" like Uncle Walter from Richmond? He was educated and was stationed in places like New York and St. Louis. How much of their accents would he pick up? But maybe accents were even broader in the nineteenth century, without radio and television to homogenize everybody. He probably sounded like the biggest hick who ever lived. Damadian would have a fit.

I had gotten hold of the tape recorder the previous evening, one of those little reel-to-reel jobs that the church occasionally donated to shut-ins like Grandmama. I had listened to my own voice for the first time in my life and heard it the way everybody else heard it. An appalling experience. It was the voice of somebody on "The Beverly Hillbillies", the voice of a girl from somewhere so far back in the Southern woods that she could have never seen the sun for all the pine trees in her way.

" 'To be, or not to be,' " I intoned into the machine in an effort to at least sound English if I could not achieve Midwestern, secretly trying to find a voice there in the bathroom after my parents' light was out.

"Phony talk!" Beth Ann had suddenly hissed through the locked door. "Go back to Liverpool!"

"This is the question: whether or not to open the door and smash your little sister in the chops."

"The rain in Spain falls mainly in Lake Champlain!" Beth Ann cackled. "Hurry up and come outta there. I'm 'bout to wet my britches."

"Be patient!" I answered, with the microphone still on, and then replayed the two words after hearing Beth Ann's sullen footsteps go back up the hall. The phrase, so sharp-sounding on my lips, twanged and drowsed out of the tape recorder like somebody's bad performance in a Tennessee Williams play.

Well, hick or not, I mused now: When Robert E. Lee said something, people jumped.

My mother broke into my backseat reverie: "Y'all comb your hair. Beth Ann's looks like a rat's nest. We're almost there."

I pulled out a compact and dabbed more eyeshadow over my lids. Beth Ann stirred and fluffed out her blonde bouffant. I put away my cosmetics and turned my attention out of the car window onto the hill country where spring lay heavy. Each tree seemed about to break under the weight of green and the clouds draped over everything like a wedding veil.

Dixieland, I thought with a hatred and yet a hot love that oppressed me. Lush home of prayer and murder. Once its own country for four brief years, until people who were always truly right about everything, like Damadian, ended the delusion. And quashed my wrongheaded soldier.

I hated spring. It always made me maudlin.

The Chevrolet rolled into the wooded Moser driveway and I got out with my family, laden with the tape recorder and foil-shrouded platters of fried chicken and potato salad.

I felt my father's eyes once and he smiled.

Nancy, the maid, had dressed Grandmama Moser in a frilly blue negligee and had braided her white hair into fresh coils. The wrinkled woman looked wax-like and dead for a shocking moment when we walked into the bedroom. She was propped up and still against white pillows in a darkened void. Her veined hands rested on the counterpane.

"Hey, Mama." My mother bent to kiss the sunken cheek where a dot of rouge testified to either Nancy's efforts or Grandmama's improbable vanity.

The blue eyes swiveled then in their deep sockets. One of the hands reached out to me with a tremor.

"Hey, Grandmama. I'm wearing my pin. See it?"

"Garnet?" came the voice in a half-question.

"Yes'm."

"There's somethin' the matter with your leg, honey."

My father's big palm caught the reaching claw and nestled it, imprisoned. "How you feelin' today, Miz Moser? You look might pretty."

"Garnet." The cracked voice was pitiless. Her eyes were on me no longer, they ranged around the darkened room.

My mother's sudden muffled sob broke the stillness and her high-heeled footsteps sounded like rifle shots as she fled down the hall. Daddy dropped the wrinkled hand and hurried after her, his murmurings flying back to us in a deep incoherent echo.

I watched Grandmama watching me. I tried to feel something.

It's inevitable, I told myself. She's going. Maybe we should just let her go.

"Lookahere, Grandmama." Beth Ann plopped the tape recorder onto the counterpane in her practical way. I both admired and resented her determined insensitivity as she pushed the ON button. "We got Preacher Watts' sermon here for ya. It's a doozy. On covetousness and wantin' things we're not supposed to get. Just like Granddaddy used to preach."

Oh Mary Custis Lee, I thought, you didn't know what you wanted. You had the best of us. The most perfect one of us. The only one of us fit to be called Great. And you treated him like an old tennis shoe.

I could hear my mother crying now somewhere down the hall as the sermon unwound. I left the house by the back door and crept guiltily into the garden when I could stand the sound no longer. Feeling like Judas as I lay in the grass hidden by the wild weedy roses, I put Bubba Hargett on instant replay.

I thought about the upcoming Wednesday night date, wondering with a knot of anxiety in my stomach just how long it took for a man to make love to a woman. Not the "make love" of the Victorians, the brief fearful kisses and the fluttery fully-clothed words, but the mechanical, obligatory fumbling on the back seat of an automobile that a person was going to have to learn to lightheartedly master if she was going to be part of my generation. I wondered how much it would hurt the first time.

I've got to *know,* I said to Mary Lee. I've got to know something of what you had. And I knew what I might do to Charles Hegler Hargett in the freedom of 1966, how in my imagination I might make someone else out of him. For this is love, I said to myself in Grandmama's untended rose garden, fingers plucking at the petals. This is adult love with all of its implications. And it is valid. It is valid. Einstein and Bubba Hargett could give something back to me that time had taken away.

Nineteen

It is a procession up the aisle of a swaying railway carriage.

"Oh, I beg your pardon, sir!" stammers a very young girl who has just hit a dozing passenger in the leg with a crutch. She turns. "Pa?"

Colonel Lee is trying to keep his balance upon the lurching floor, another girl in his arms. It is the family's annual trek from Virginia to West Point. Brevet Colonel Robert Edward Lee, Mexican War hero, is currently Superintendent of the United States Military Academy. The army doesn't know what else to do with him. The girl with the crutch is fanning the cinders from her face.

At the front of the car a huge young man is juggling hand baggage and trying to spy out seats for his followers: seventeen-year-old Rooney Lee, dying to be a dragoon but settling for his second term at Harvard College instead when his grades fail to win him a West Point appointment. He has found one seat near the middle of the car and has plumped a bag into it. Now he beckons from his advanced position and cups his hands to shout discreetly at the man whom he tops by several inches. "Hey, Paw!"

Robert Lee is trapped in the middle of the aisle, hemmed in by children. He is carrying his nineteen-year-old daughter Mary who has injured her foot. The color is high in her cheeks: she knows that she is being stared at.

Her father risks lifting a foot to push at the rear end of the small boy who blocks the aisle in front, a friendly blond-haired little boy who has struck up a conversation with the curious people seated on the aisle. A raffish-looking small mutt dog is clutched in his arms, hind legs dangling down.

"Robbbbbb!" hisses injured Mary at the curly blond head below.

Rob throws the dog over his shoulder, where it grins sloppily, and he starts up the aisle towards his big brother.

His father follows in his wake, trying not to bang Mary's bandaged foot against the plumed bonnets of the seated ladies. He is in civilian dress, black-suited, his high collar rising to his jaws from under an impeccable black silk cravat. But his ramrod posture speaks of a lifetime stood at attention. The sleeper's wife glances up at him from moment to moment in shy little takes, admiring. His black hair is flecked with silver at the part and the temples. He has a profile like on a coin. He possesses the broad shoulders, nipped waist, and short muscular legs, tapering down to tiny feet, that Victorians on both sides of the Atlantic portray in fashion illustrations as the beau ideal of manhood.

The seated female passenger is no fashion plate. She is portly and she is flustered when the man looks down suddenly at her. Though she is not a handsome woman, for a brief instant she feels like one.

"Pa!" complains the young lady in his arms.

"Easy, Roon . . . Easy . . ." the man mutters to his taller son as they maneuver injured Mary into a seat where Rob has already encamped with his dog. The dog pokes its head out of the window and flaps its pink tongue at the cinders flying in.

"We can't tote this gear any further, Pa," comes a voice from the rear aisle. Two girls stand there, the younger nearly buried under the bundle of family cloaks and greatcoats, the fifteen-year-old balancing with Mary's crutches in the crook of one arm and her father's high silk hat in the other.

He takes the clothing burden from the younger girl. "Here, Agnes."

The woman passenger smiles at her. "My goodness! You seem to be undertaking quite an expedition, dear! Where are all of you going to sit?"

Agnes shrugs. "Oh, this is *nothing*. You should have seen us when we went to Fort Hamilton! We have to go up in shifts. Mama travels with enough trunks for three stagecoaches. My eldest brother Custis was a cadet at West Point—that's where we're bound—and so he's up there already. Mama and my littlest sister Milly and Grandpa are coming up later."

"Agnes!" warns sister Mary, self-consciously.

Agnes waves goodbye and moves up the aisle.

"Wonder where they left their niggers?" The woman's husband mutters as the unruly procession makes its way further up the aisle.

His wife digs at him with her fan. "Hush! They'll overhear."

"I don't give one pinch of owl dung," he sniffs, angry. He has read an Abolitionist editorial just that morning and has crumpled the newspaper in his hands. He is outraged with some of the things that are going on in this country, this Pennsylvania merchant. Outraged with the high-and-mighty ways of slave owning gentility who buy their leisure with the sweat of black imprisoned bodies. It's not Christian. He catches the deep irritating Southern voice of the man in the aisle, apologizing to a preacher he has inadvertently elbowed in the ear.

The sleeper leans close to his wife, his finger pointed at the straight black-clothed spine in front of him. "Look at that fellow. Bet you he's never done a day's work in his life."

The woman looks. "He has beautiful manners. They have beautiful manners down there."

A smell of cold grease wafts back to them. The tall young

man has taken a leg of fried chicken from a hamper. He lounges against the forward end of the car, munching. His father joins him, having settled the girls, and their billowing skirts and the cloaks and baggage, into the available seats. It is late summer, 1854, and the train chuffs through Pennsylvania.

The large family gradually entrenches as passengers disembark at Philadelphia. Colonel Lee finds a seat next to Annie, the crutch-bearer. Rooney and the lunch basket end up by Agnes on the cushions directly behind.

Rooney leans forward. "Want some dinner, Paw?"

The Colonel shakes his head. Pats Annie on the knee with a wink: "We made it, sugar. You tired?"

She looks up and grins her shy grin, one eye scarred by a childhood accident involving a pair of scissors. She ducks her head whenever she thinks anyone is staring at her disfigured face. Gentle Annie will give out and die during the war at age 23.

Agnes sits in the seat behind. Pretty Agnes will grow up loving her wild cousin Orton Williams, Markie's brother, only to see him hanged as a spy by the Union.

Rooney, who sits gnawing at a chicken leg, is destined after all to be a cavalryman who will endure the deaths of his wife and children from his cell in a Union prison where he himself will await possible execution. His older brother Custis, just graduating from West Point at the head of his class, will also be a Confederate general. He, too, will be captured by the Federals and falsely reported dead to his father just before the surrender at Appomattox. He is doomed to alcoholism.

Little Rob fondles his dog. Rob will forego college at age eighteen to serve as a gunner private in the gray ranks, where he will fight and go barefoot just like the sons of sharecroppers. Little Mildred, Molly Lee and daughter Mary will be homeless fugitives soon, trapped in the final Richmond conflagration with the roof smoking over their heads, no home at Arlington to go back to ever again. And Colonel Lee . . .

Colonel Lee can't yet see the future.

He pats little Annie's knees and thinks about how much she looks like his mother, the original Ann, Ann who never knew her grandchildren. He leans back in the cushions on this dull day, on his way to a dull assignment, ambition stilled for a moment by the drowsy rocking of the train and the comfort of having most of his family with him.

Annie takes up his hand and strokes it in the light, lazy way he likes. His mother used to rub his arms and hands that way when he was little, just barely touching the skin, and he has calmed his own children this special way since they were babies. They unconsciously return the favor sometimes, small fingers running idly over the horseman's calluses on his palms, drawing lazy circles over the hairy knuckles.

He shifts position and a paper crackles inside his coat pocket: Markie's latest letter, picked up in Baltimore, the handwriting large and bold, the words blunt. Markie writes like a man. He can read her letters without his new reading spectacles, steel-rimmed embarrassments that stay stashed in his breast pocket unless print is absolutely too tiny to be deciphered at arm's length. His wife caught him one night recently, holding the newspaper out at his fingertips until his arms got tired and he had to give it up, settling the spectacles onto his nose until he heard her making a peculiar sound and he glanced up over the rims to find her watching him over her knitting, face crinkled in amusement. "I swan," she had chortled, "I swanny to my soul, you are so *vain!*" And he had stared at her round-eyed over the edge of the lenses like an owl, until they had laughed at each other across the room; and he rose and came over to kiss her cheek for no reason.

They are polite, even affectionate. Mary is enjoying the Superintendency at West Point far more than he is. Her down-to-earth careless dress and chatty intellectualism prove motherly and welcoming to many a young cadet far from home, and she certainly knows how to set a table, thanks to George Washington's china and the grace of her class. She discusses problem cadets with her husband in the evenings, offering suggestions for modifica-

137

tions of their behavior (mostly involving God and the Bible), and listening to his concern over young James McNeil Whistler who can draw like the devil but will probably flunk out. Perhaps it is partnership she craves from Robert. Inclusion. She most certainly does not crave more motherhood.

Oh God, the cadets, those ubiquitous and impressionable cadets observing his deportment and conduct—to say nothing of the children, their pride in him, and their illusions. The customary female servant would not elicit any note whatsoever from his fellow officers, but these young idealistic eyes everywhere are quite another matter. He doesn't like giving Mary any satisfaction in spiritual matters but he has started to pray with a vengeance nonetheless, day and night. Sometimes he feels God there in the dark, listening, and sometimes he knows he's just talking to himself about how unfair life is, how stalled his career seems to be and how, if he leaves the army, he'll only be Mr. Mary Custis, feckless planter, gentleman wastrel.

And of course he tells God all about Markie Williams, who writes him every month. About how besotted he is with her and how wrong he knows it to be. But the girl is incorrigible—her blunt letters are proper and ladylike but full of words like "my heart" and "adoration."

Her father has been killed in the Mexican War and now her mother is dead. She is rudderless. Colonel Lee knows very well what it is like. He is thankful that he can put several hundred miles between himself and Markie during this West Point tenure, but that's the only good thing he has found about the job.

Even now, he is putting about rumors that he hopes will reach the ears of Secretary of War Jefferson Davis that he would not be averse to duty on the Texas frontier. He is plotting his escape from domesticity. From Mary.

From Markie.

He might even succeed in getting himself killed, but he doesn't think so. Comanches aren't good shots. And the heat, dysentery, and deprivation are old friends. Maybe God lives in Texas.

He is still not making enough money to support his family like Custises. Arlington House had been like a battle zone upon his return from Mexico. Mary was constantly badgering him about Mexican women when all he wanted to do was put his arms around her, the older children were ill-at-ease over his graying hair and unfamiliar ways, and the smallest, Rob and Mildred, did not even know him. Major and Mrs. Custis were adamant about not relinquishing the family to his questionable supervision. Maybe they had been half-hoping that he'd be killed in Mexico. He had had all he could stand after only one week. God Almighty Himself would have to be his family at Fort Carroll in Baltimore. Worse yet, his best friend, the irrepressible Jack Mackay, was dead in Savannah of consumption, and Andrew Talcott had left the army.

The train whistle wails.

Oh Mary, Mary . . . I feel lonelier with you than I do without you, he thinks, as he leans sleepily against Annie who rubs his hands. We married too hastily, Mary. You should have had Sam Houston. And *I* should have had the time to grow up, to stop wanting the things I cannot have, to appreciate what God has given me. To learn to be what my mama wanted me to be.

Oh Heavenly Father, let me be *good*. Not covetous. Nor ambitious. Nor lustful. I am slipsliding into hell with my papa. And he'll probably just cuss me when he sees me there.

Twenty

🌿

They sit in the long grass of Arlington Hill where it overlooks the Potomac. Markie Williams is sketching again. She has much improved over the years. Her lips pucker as she erases several extraneous lines and finally she says, "There," puts down her pencil, and turns her sketchbook around to display the work to her subject.

Robert shoos away the cat he has been scratching and takes up the drawing. His face shows no expression as he studies it. The silence between them lengthens. He is due to leave in two days for Louisville, and there to take temporary command of the Second Cavalry for frontier duty down around Texas, a new line officer after a career with the Engineers. He has been agitated for a week, uncharacteristically testy.

"Perhaps I made the face too full," Markie says.

She looks back down at the portrait he holds in his hands, upside down from her point of view. The yellow cat walks across it, using it as a bridge over Robert's lap. He pushes the cat away gently, a small frown beginning between his brows.

Markie sighs. "Let me do another, Robert."

"No." He moves the sketchbook out of her reach.

"Well, what is it, then?"

He looks up. Then the black eyes go back down to meet the eyes in the portrait. He taps the face on the paper near its chin. "It looks like my father."

A shadow comes blowing at them from the other side of the river, a high cloud pushed along by a damp spring wind. Markie waits, picking up a small penknife to sharpen her pencil with no-nonsense hands—a thirtyish Markie, no longer so very young.

"This is curious," he says at last. "They always told me that I looked more like my mother. Papa was blond and blue-eyed, had rather pursed lips, much as if he were brooding all the time. Like my brother Smith. Smith has Papa's mouth."

"Well." Markie closes the penknife and tests the pencil point on a fresh page. "Sometimes a portrait will clarify small resemblances that go unnoticed to the eye. I've seen a painting of Harry Lee. I do think you look somewhat like him. Shape of the eyes, if not the color."

"He was fifty-seven when I last saw him." Robert squints against the sunlight. "I was about six. He was a very big man, I think. Or perhaps I was just very small."

Markie removes her bonnet and places it on the grass. "He stood no more than five-foot-nine, according to Cousin Mary."

"She doesn't remember him. I don't know if he ever came over here after she was born. He'd gotten into some political trouble that ended in a riot. His face was permanently scarred—he was a terrible-looking thing, I tell you—and I remember him quite well, roaring about the house in his misery, disgraced and disfigured. He didn't go out all that much after that. Finally he left us altogether. To recuperate in the Caribbean, he claimed. But he didn't come back. Can't say that I was sorry, the way he used to treat my mother."

Birds twitter in the trees.

"He wrote my brother, Carter, that he was coming back to us when he died. Carter was his favorite. He never wrote me at all," Robert mutters.

"Could you have read a letter at age six?" Markie smiles. Robert doesn't.

"I could read some at four. I was eleven before he died. He got as close as Georgia and died on the way. Why did he wait five whole years to start for home? We needed him. If he needed us, why did he wait so long?"

Markie doesn't know what to say now. She has never heard him speak plainly of his family, has never heard him talk this way before.

"I am forty-eight years old, Markie. I wonder if I, too, shall someday wander off."

But she sees the mood he is creating for himself. Lays a quick hand on his sleeve. "Don't. Don't."

"There are bloodthirsty Comanches out there in Texas," he laughs, reacting to her sudden seriousness. "I might get killed."

She smiles because he wants her to. "Possibly."

"And then what will happen to Rooney? Bless his heart, he incurs debt the way other people breathe."

"Aw, Roon's a good boy," she says.

"Mary, she'd let him get away with I-don't-know-what-all and then hire him a good lawyer. I've told him: 'One more time, boy, and I'll set you afire.' I mean it."

Markie thinks of her cousin, Mary, sitting ill and remote, day after day, in the big old house, where she passes the hours with her old father and his reminiscences of George Washington. She is unwilling to trek off to the frontier with her husband and wonders still why he won't stay home and live in one place. She is unable to play Stern Parent with her children in the absence of their idolized father and is, as always, upset by the gossip that circulates about their separation every time Robert departs for another post alone.

Markie feels a sudden quirky sympathy for her older female cousin, above and beyond the familial fondness she has always had for the woman. And yet it lurks, deep in her mind it lurks: the anticipation that Mary Lee might someday soon peacefully succumb to her illness, just never wake up. Markie goes cold with guilt and pushes the thought away.

Robert looks distracted. "My mother worked her head off to hold my family together. She tried. Some people won't try."

"You hate yourself for wanting to go to Texas?"

He plucks a blade of grass and pinches it between his teeth. "It gets harder each leavetaking. I hate to go. I *want* to go. You'd think a man would get used to this hating and wanting. But it's worse than ever this time."

"It's your duty to go. My papa was a soldier, remember. I understand things like duty."

He chews on the piece of grass. She feels his eyes.

Miss Martha Custis Williams—Markie, who has raised her younger brothers after the death of their father in Mexico. Markie, who volunteered some years ago to stay at Arlington and look out for old Major Custis while Robert dragged Mary off to West Point. She had told herself she was only trying to ease Cousin Mary's concern about her elderly, widowed father. But it had been Robert all along that she has intended to please.

He looks right into her. "You understand rather a lot, my girl. Entirely too sharp for a broken-down ol' man to keep ahead of."

"My word," she tells the purring cat, "he's fishing for compliments."

The young men have come over the years, "Marry me, marry me," on their tongues, and she has found them all somehow too short or too tall or too fat or too stupid or too lazy or too—

I am wasting my life, she thinks. I am wasting wasting wasting my life and I am a wretched wretched fool.

Robert takes the yellow cat onto his linen knees and watches the river. Markie watches him watching, and then snatches up her pencil to reflect the lines of his face on the paper. He is cool and quiet, elegant, yet there is some strange violence coiled inside him.

"You know, I was terrified when I left home as a boy to go to

143

the Point," he says, not moving, conscious that she is sketching him again. "I used to play Artillery with ol' Rose—that's what I nicknamed Smith—when we were little. And once a particularly effective *feu d'enfer* of mine blasted out his front milk teeth. I played with Papa's sword until he caught me with it and caned me. But I never really meant to be a soldier. It was terrifying, leaving home. And yet I was fascinated by the terror. Wanted to go so bad it kept me awake nights.

"My mother was sickly. Like Mary. I had always taken care of things for her—housekeeping and bookkeeping. I quite frankly couldn't see how the devil she'd get along without me. 'Oh, we'll be fine, Robert,' she said, 'I'll even find myself a companion who eats a great deal less!' Took the wind out of my sails and pushed me out into the world at the same time. Made me feel how glad she was to see me try my hand at something I might prove to be good at."

Markie recognizes a lecture. "Why are you telling me this?"

"To show you that no one is indispensable. To tell you that people who really love you want nothing more than to see you lead your own happy life."

"I have no life to lead. I'm an old maid."

He says nothing.

She goes on tonelessly: "I will stay where I am needed."

"Well, bully for you." There is an odd tone in his voice. "I'm more selfish. My mother kept the true extent of her debility to herself. So I left her."

Markie looks up, confused. "Wait. Wait. We're talking in circles."

"She died immediately after my graduation. I don't think I'll . . ."

Markie can see it coming, he has trapped her into some kind of accusation.

"I don't think I'll ever . . ."

There is a difficult moment. His expression does not change, he simply stops speaking. Markie cannot draw until he goes on. She leans over to rub the cat.

"What a strange world it is," he remarks. "Don't you find it so?"

She tries to keep her voice light. "I think some people are very strange. I think some people are very *wrong* about things. I think some people are too hard on themselves."

"Strange," he says, not listening. "I've got at least one half-brother I can never acknowledge, a brother of mine born into bondage because his mother was black. Now how can that be right and Christian, pretending not to know that my own brother can be bought and sold like a horse? I don't know who owns him now. My father sold off all our people for debts. And look at what I do for a living—what a strange profession. They got me out of my own clothes at the Point and they gave me a uniform that matched everyone else's. They fed me and educated me and browbeat me and the upper-classmen rode me into the ground until I vomited into my pillow one night."

"Oh Robert!" Markie puts a hand on his arm but he pays no attention. He is not trying to elicit sympathy; she takes her hand away.

"I submitted with a vengeance so that I could show my mother how well I was doing. Oh, I used to go home on furlough and try to tell her and my sisters about it, about how they were teaching us to die in that place. About how they hoped for another war as soon as possible so each man could move up another rank as the officer ahead of him got killed and vacated a command." He laughs softly. "But as soon as I would get home, there would be Mama, sitting by the fire and chattering with the girls, teasing me about my courtships and the length of my side-whiskers, in that happy ignorant way of gentle women, and I'd forget what I had to say."

He looks down at the cat, but Markie, sketching again, orders, "Sit still!" The air in her ears has begun to hum with pre-thunder tension.

"When my mother later died . . . well, we had no home together anymore and we had to go every-which-way. So I took instant hold of the next best thing to keep the army from swallowing me alive: unfortunate Mary Custis. We were as mismatched as two people could be and still be of the same species. She hasn't known one single happy day as my wife. And that's the certain of it."

Markie puts the pencil down carefully in the grass, the bright gingham of her dress billowing over it. She considers her words. "That's not true, Robert, and you know it."

"It's common knowledge. You're her kinswoman. Surely you've heard what's been said, I've given her nothing, I don't know how to give her anything. How she's ill, getting worse all the time. Dear Jesus, I'm killing her, Markie. And I don't even care."

Suddenly he muffles his face with his big hands and lets his shoulders bend him nearly double.

Markie is like a woman struck by lightning. She cannot think, cannot feel, she is stunned and acting on instinct when she takes strong hold of his shoulders and tries to pull him against her. His arms clutch. The buttons of his waistcoat grind into her bosom.

"*No no no!*" she shouts. "You're not killing her! She's not Army—that's all. It's no one's fault. We're Army and she's just not. It's not your fault. She loves you—!"

"I'm not worth it. Selfish *hypocrite* . . ." It is spewed out in a tortured voice not his at all.

Markie fights her own rising grief. Old Maid Markie, unmarried because she has been waiting for this embrace for fifteen years, but not wanting it—like this. Not wanting to watch him flay himself. She tastes salt in the deep creases under his strange eyes.

He moves and her lips brush his. Those sad guilty black eyes seek some sort of permission, then he kisses her squarely on the mouth. The effect is like a lit lamp thrown onto dry straw. Their arms snake around each other and they fall sideways into the deep grass, his moustache like stiff wool, hard lips forcing hers back away from her teeth, tongue filling her and pushing into her throat

146

(a detail omitted in the French novels Markie reads—shocking in its rawness and yet terribly effective). Is this seduction? she wonders, feeling no sense of sin. Only wild bliss and the urgency to get the thing over and done with so that no more years will be wasted while she withers on the vine of maidenhood.

But the fright at how easily it can actually happen! How *soon*. Tonight perhaps, when the household is sleeping. Suddenly she is not sure that she is ready or that she can bear the guilt that he has borne for decades.

Before she can decide he breaks free of her hold and straightens, with an effort, to sit upright beside her, head bowed, knees drawn up. She can sense the fright in him too, his fear of himself. He has blushed a deep pink.

"Was that hello or goodbye?" she asks softly.

"I am capable of depravity that you can only guess at," he sniffles, wiping his eyes on his sleeve like a child. "But I certainly never premeditated proving it upon demand."

"It's all right. You've been under considerable strain lately."

"It's *not* all right!" He keeps brushing at his cheeks with his fingertips. "You cannot imagine how close to ruin we are. Because of me. Texas is not far enough away. Dear God, I'm not fit to live."

She is wild with love that night, awake and waiting. He does not come to her.

Markie sees little of him the next day as he packs his gear and searches the house for his misplaced shaving brush, buys horehound candy in Washington for the younger children when he reports to his superiors there, instructs Major Custis in the mysteries of the planned central heating system he will not be here to help install, and stores personal belongings with mementos of Mexico in his trunk upstairs.

He encounters her in the second-floor hallway sometimes, stepping hurriedly around her as if she had typhoid. Finally she can stand it no longer and she grabs him roughly by the arm.

"It's not *my* fault, either."

His voice is mild and perfectly blank: "I blame you for nothing."

Oh heavens, his breached defenses are repaired, and he has retreated again into unassailable gentlemanly deportment. She could kill him.

"I could kill you."

"Come here." He pulls her inside the doorway of his bedroom and kisses her on the forehead like a brother. Agnes and the maid Kitty come chattering down the hall and pass the open door where the pair stands, his hands holding her cheeks. "Are you still my friend?" His voice is very low.

"Forever."

"Markie . . ." He isn't hiding his embarrassment. "When one part of me unravels, then all of me starts to go. I mistook your . . . solicitude . . . for something else."

"You mistook nothing. I love you, Robert."

"Markie, there's a taint in me. I ask God to save me. I don't believe He will. I am the most selfish person you will ever meet. You don't know me, Markie."

"I do know you! I love you. I love you," she pleads.

He pushes the open door of his bedroom, disturbed. It swings shut with a squeak. "Oh Markie, *please* don't—!"

"Just stop avoiding me."

"I don't want to evade you. The problem is quite of the opposite."

"Why do you hate yourself so?" She is baffled.

He turns, walks from her to his bed and begins to plunder his belongings on the spread: shirt collars, underwear, his Colt revolver. "You might take Mary to the Springs in the summer if her pains flare up. Withdraw whatever you need from my account at the bank in Alexandria. Here—" He presses his gold watch into her hand and closes her fingers about it. "This goes to Custis if I don't get back. I want him to have it."

She nods, mute. The watch ticks in her hand like a small heart.

"I can't disturb Mary with that possibility, but you and I both know—"

"Robert, I am no longer young. Look at me. I'm not a child. I know my own mind, however wrongful its inclinations might be."

"Some things must never be said, Miss M. Some inclinations must never be indulged. That doesn't mean that they are not felt." He stoops to stuff a saddle blanket into the trunk on the floor, his back to her. "Don't encourage my faults, for God's sake, if you are my friend."

"Mine need no encouragement. I'll write to you while you're in Texas. I'll write to you and pray for you every single day until one of us is dead."

She has to strain to catch his words; he kneels on the rug and rattles around in the trunk, hands doing one thing and mouth another: "You are my rose. Dearest heart. Touch a rose, and it turns brown. Dearest heart. I will not turn you brown."

Good heavens, there is no way to tell how much of this he means. He seems devoted entirely to the trunk and to the spurs and gear it contains.

"I never knew," she says, "a man so utterly delighted to exile himself."

"Leaving you does not delight me." He straightens. Puffs out both cheeks in a huge sigh.

She ties two of his socks into a knot and begins to match up the remainders while he meticulously folds his new pair of pants to preserve their knife-edged creases. "Well," she mutters, "then at least concede that you are spoiling for a fight. And since you refuse to fight with Mary or me, the wild Indians will have to do."

One of his brows goes up. "I thought you said you understood, Miss M. This is what I do for a living."

"God help the poor Indians."

"This is what I do. I'll chase perfectly innocent Indians around the wilderness to satisfy some . . . I dunno." He mates his white dress gloves palm-to-palm and slaps them down on the bedspread. "I badger my children about faults which are mine instead of theirs. I harangue Mary until she's frantic, when she has done nothing at all wrong and never shall. I *adored* the war. Mexico. I am some sort of heathen ingrate, I think."

She can see how much he anticipates getting into the field again as a cavalryman, after all the years of engineering drudgery. He will be upon grassy plains where he has never been before. He will have his narrow cot under canvas and an end to complicated folderol, like women and children and where his duty lies in this troubled house. Time falls away from his face and he looks to her suddenly boyish, sweetmouthed and childish. She looks closely; his lashes are graying.

Her vision blurs for no good reason. Tears slide hot down her cheeks.

"Oh, please don't start that up yet!" he begs, holding his revolver in one hand, a pair of drawers in the other. "There is plenty of time for everybody to blubber their heads off tomorrow morning, including me!"

"There are Comanches out there, Robert! And Mexican bandits!" She thinks of all the horrible things that could befall him. "And maybe cholera. And heat-stroke."

"And camels."

She is derailed. "What?"

"Camels." Mild mischief shows in his posture. "Jefferson Davis is bent upon experimenting with camels. For the War Department."

She stares.

"Camels," he repeats. "You know. The large desert creatures with humps."

"I could kill you. I really could."

"Well, we all have to die sometime, don't we." He squeezes the bullet mould and lays it on the bedspread. "Soldiers mustn't die in bed like old women; people will say that you did not perform your duty. Society cannot accommodate a bunch of retired killers. Let's see now, what am I forgetting?" He paces, smacking one fist into the palm of the other. "I've got the roof here fixed so that you all won't mildew . . . Perhaps Custis can get transferred to Washington City and be the man of the family for a while. He's a better farmer than I am. You might even teach him to polka; he can't dance a lick."

"Are you coming back? Are you ever coming back?"

"I'm just in the way here," he mutters. "Mary is sick of the sight of me."

"Well, I am sick of *everything*. I am sick of you crucifying yourself for your own humanity! Sick of Mary crucifying herself because she is not Great-grandma Martha Washington and you are not George. I'd like to knock both of your heads together."

"Somebody needs to do it," he agrees. Shrugs. "Too late. Too late."

"Well, you may succeed in dumping the family upon Custis's shoulders, but if you think I'm going to *rot* here—!" She puts a hand to her forehead. His defenses are impenetrable. "Maybe I shall just pawn your watch and run away to Paris. Study my art in some atelier. Find myself a continental lover to turn me brown."

"A young Frenchman should suit you nicely," he mumbles. "They have a certain charm, I'm told. All that hand-kissing. They know what to say to ladies whom they love."

"*What's the matter with you?*" she shouts suddenly, unable to keep it back any longer. She throws the balled-up socks onto the bed.

He doesn't move. Just stares stupidly at the socks, blinking.

She wrenches open the door and flees down the hallway, races down the back stairs and past a startled Mary who has been cutting flowers. Markie sweeps, panting, into the sunny garden, gathered skirts swirling petals from early roses.

His watch ticks in her damp hand, ticking away the beginning of the years to come. It will tick on until Major Custis suddenly dies and Robert is called home to settle the estate, having been named legal executor of the will and left with virtually nothing in it except the responsibility of coping with one of his pet

horrors: debt. Arlington is $10,000 in debt. But Mary will sum-
mon and he will answer, coming home unshorn and sunburned,
and silent. Seeking God in this duty. Penance.

It will take him two years of extended leave to right the mess.
He'll still be there, repairing the house and farming the unprofita-
ble lands (at his wit's end, trying to free the Arlington slaves
according to the will's terms, at the same time he needs all the
labor he can hire) when the summons appears from General
Winfield Scott's headquarters calling him back to active duty to
command a detachment of Marines at the arsenal at Harper's
Ferry, a stronghold where an Abolitionist visionary named John
Brown is mounting a slave insurrection.

Colonel Lee will take John Brown. Brown will be hanged.
John Brown's body will mold in its grave but his soul will go
marching over the land. Glory hallelujah.

Twenty-One

My hair was piled up on top of my head, the way Bubba liked it, and I had come to the debate club meeting that Wednesday afternoon in a blue granny gown that ruffled around my ankles, ready for romance, perfumed in Emeraude by Coty. I sported my heart pin. I had no idea what I was doing wrong here, but I was doing something wrong.

Bubba took the podium with his speech as second affirmative, and Damadian's stop watch clicked.

He looked great, all square-shouldered in his pale blue button-down shirt and madras tie. He sounded great. His drawl speeded up at the podium. His consonants appeared. He kept his head up and looked the judge right squarely in the eye. I wondered if he had heard the sniggering.

Bubba had ten minutes exactly to bolster the resolution in favor of nuclear disarmament that I had just presented in my own ten-minute speech. Debate was like a tag team match, sort of. You couldn't win one all by yourself. But you could lose one to the other two-man team all by yourself, sure enough. And I was positive that Bubba was losing ours for us.

The little snots from Hampton High were the best negative team in the state. The Hampton coach was reading a magazine in the back of the classroom. Bubba droned on about how Pakistan and Egypt and Israel would get the Bomb and blow us all to kingdom come unless we disarmed, and how chemical and biological weapons would be impossible to control unless the community of nations first learned to limit the proliferation of nuclear weaponry, et cetera.

I could read it in the eyes of the little snot seated at the table across the room from me. His glossy rich-kid cheeks creased with a smirk as he passed a note to his partner. Bubba was getting sidetracked.

Oh hell, it wasn't as if it were all his fault. Debate speeches are crafted in tandem. One partner takes no position that the other partner isn't privy to. Bubba had discussed chemical and biological weapons with me. It wasn't as if he had just pulled the subjects out of a hat.

Buzz buzz buzz, went the little snots. Damadian frowned and made a mark upon his note pad, deducting points for the noise. But I knew that they were ready to pounce as soon as Bubba sat. They would righteously complain, one by one, that the Richland Creek High School second affirmative had introduced elements irrelevant to the resolution being debated. They would be right, too. And there was nothing I could do.

Damadian caught my eye. It's only practice, read his brief expression.

But I didn't know whether I was feeling embarrassment for Bubba or for myself. It was as much my fault as his. Yet his lips were the ones speaking the words that would hang us.

The classroom was dotted with our own people: David Dale Baker and his lackluster second negative, Doug Mitchell, a bunch of sophomores who couldn't win roles in the drama club productions, and two freshman geeks each about three feet tall. I was the only female.

We seemed to be mostly nerds. We were not the popular nor the sought-after. Only Bubba and big ol' brainy David Dale had anything like charisma.

I met Damadian's next glance with a what-the-hell-am-I-doing-here stare. I was miffed. I wasn't ready to be disillusioned. When I closed my eyes, I felt my mascara'ed lashes interlock.

Bubba finished his speech upon the exact flip-over of the ten minute time card, and sauntered over to our shared table, while the second negative scrambled to collect his note cards and then trotted gleefully to the podium for his speech. This is when they would start laying the ground work for their rebuttals. I could smell blood in the water.

Bubba drew a little cartoon tin can in the margin of my notes and labeled it *Hampton Speech*. His shoulder scraped mine. *Finito* he wrote.

Hampton was anything but. They were setting us up, paragraph by paragraph. I moved Bubba's hand out of the way and drew a tiny noose.

Damadian shook his head at us, flipping his time card for the benefit of our opponent. He wanted us to be orderly and quiet.

Bubba noticed now that Hampton High had us. He stopped drawing cans.

Bubba said nothing to me when we learned we had lost, and were told the margin of points we had lost by. The Hampton High coach finished his magazine article and cruised out of the building with his killers. Wrong wrong wrong. Everything was all bollixed up. I sat at my desk and bit my lipstick off.

"I don't think y'all oughta mention chemical and biological weapons in the future," David Dale volunteered. "Somebody'll kill ya."

I stuffed my note cards into my index card file box and

slammed the lid upon a couple, dog-earing them forever. "No shit."

Bubba stood, trotted for the door, threw up his lunch onto his Weejun penny loafers, and then galloped down the hall for the Boys' Room. He abandoned me like a dead skunk.

I made my mind go blank, but it wouldn't blank out all the way. It indicted me, the newly-elected president of the debate club. It indicted me with a crime that I didn't understand.

"I'd better call Mama to come and get me," I said, once the last debater had filed out of the classroom.

"I'll take you home," sighed Damadian. "But I want to talk to you first."

I lifted my head, feeling my face redden and wishing I could stop it. "I don't think I wanna talk, Bill."

"Garnet. This is none of my business. But you can't play games with this guy."

I fumbled in my purse for a dime to call my mother.

"Honey, I think there's more—"

I threw my purse onto the floor. "I've made a fool out of myself again . . . God damn everybody on this whole stinking planet . . ."

He stood several paces away from my childish snit. Sniffed once or twice. Studied me. "Let's talk about debate, then."

I looked up, wary, his practicality reminding me of Beth Ann. "You must be the fastest subject-changer in the business," I said dully.

He shrugged. "You don't want to talk about Bubba. Very well. Let's discuss debate."

"I just wanna go home." I reached down for my shoulderbag and then looked back up, curious about his ironic tone. "What about debate?"

"What does 'compromit' mean?"

I shrugged.

"You used it twice tonight. I don't know what it means, either. And neither will a real judge. I don't think it's even a word."

"I don't recall—"

"And 'adjure.' 'I adjure you,' you said. And 'sanguine'—you use that one a lot. Have you been reading Webster's for fun lately or what?"

"I read too much. Everybody says so."

"Well, lady, the topic is nuclear disarmament. Space Age stuff. Let's leave the Victorianisms out of our deliveries from now on."

I thought about what I *had* been reading lately. I could quote several of Lee's letters in my mind, full of words like "compromit" and "adjure." I sighed, felt totally naked in front of this man who had witnessed my wallflowerhood tonight and who was criticizing my speech again.

I think if I had a gun I'd shoot this guy, I thought. Or shoot myself.

"Want a Coke?" Bill dragged his little ice chest out from under his desk.

"Okay." I looked in my bag for aspirin. I was his prisoner.

He knocked the caps off two bottles against the metal rim of the blackboard and handed me one. The warm May night was coming down as it neared seven o'clock but the sky was still red in the west with the lengthening of days. "We'll finish these off and then hit the road."

I was very low. We left the Coke bottles on his desk and locked up the classroom and let ourselves out of the building. He carried my large purse for me and helped me into his little Valiant. He hefted the shoulderbag onto the floor by my feet.

"Heavy," he grunted. "What's in it?"

"Oh *nooo.*" I reached inside and felt for the little tape recorder, took it out and pressed all of its buttons. It squawked. "Thank God. It still works."

"It's cute." He trotted around the front of the car and climbed into the driver's seat beside me. "What's it for? You going to blackmail somebody?"

"I'm working on my diction."

"Why?" He backed the car out of the space and steered us toward the highway.

"I wanna sound smart. I thought that me and Bubba—"

"You *are* smart."

"We sound like mush mouths."

"Leave it alone!" Red lights from a neon sign played over his face as he passed a truck stop on Garner's Ferry Road. "You're going to get too self-conscious and end up sounding affected. 'Adjure' . . . Christ."

We raced down the highway in silence. Bill took a short cut through Atlas Road and came out at the intersection with Bluff Road that had at one time been known locally as Bloody Bucket because of all the auto accidents that had occurred at that intersection.

"Better be real careful here," I muttered, looking out of the window on my side at the lights from a truck bearing down. "Don't pull out onto the highway until you can see six miles both ways. Three teenage boys came barreling down Bluff Road here when I was a little kid and wrapped themselves around one of those pine trees yonder eight feet off the ground."

"Any survivors?"

"Are you kiddin'? 'Hair, teeth, an' eyeballs all over the highway,' to quote one of Brother Dave Gardner's routines."

He eased the Valiant out and made a careful left turn. I had to smile.

"You live on this end of town long, lady?"

"All my life. Farmers don't move." I pointed back at the junction behind us. "There used to be an old wooden frame store that sat right back there. Gatherin' place for all the idle yokels in the neighborhood. One of those old general-store-type deals, with Red Man chawin' tobacco signs all over it."

He laughed.

158

"And we used to see mule wagons go up and down Bluff Road when I was little," I went on in a monotone in the deepening twilight, about mules and old drivers clopping slowly down the highway with a patter of mule shoes. "Old men . . . some black and some white, just moseying along the way they had a hundred years before Bluff Road was paved. And Atlas Road was dirt when I was little. Called Lover's Lane. You could actually hear whip-poorwills out here on moonlit nights. The cars and trucks weren't so many and didn't go so fast."

"Wow." Bill shook his head. "Did you know any moonshiners?"

"No!" I was irritated. "Don't believe everything you see in the movies." Then: "Yes, I knew of a couple or three. A still once blew up right across the road from the high school. Everybody found out about that one."

I saw him smile.

"Don't smile that way," I muttered. "Where would you be without Elvis Presley?"

I saw him chew that one over. "Don't follow you, lady."

"Elvis Presley. Pecan pie. Most of your big time race car drivers. The Charleston, the Black Bottom. Jazz. A thousand Miss Americas. Country music and the Grand Ole Opry. James F. Byrnes. Bear Bryant. Say, 'Thank you.'"

He grinned. "I could have done without the Grand Ole Opry."

"Things used to not change here so fast. Before Kennedy died, I didn't think anything could change here at all."

"I like the way you think, lady. I want to read some of your poetry sometime." He turned the car into my family's driveway, the long farm lane that ran behind the pine trees and soybean fields up a gentle slope where our house sat quiet and yellow-windowed in its greenery. He stopped the car and turned off the engine.

"I was so happy when I was little," I mused. "I read a lot and planned to be Nancy Drew—or Snow White—when I got big.

Nothing bad ever happened until Granddaddy died, and Kennedy died, and this damned ugly *leg*—"

"Garnet." He put a quick hand on my arm. "The leg has nothing to do with Bubba Hargett. I want you to know that."

"I don't want to talk about it." I struggled with the door handle.

"Bubba is a straight arrow, Miss. He wouldn't want to intrude where he isn't really wanted. And you've been giving him some mixed signals lately. I've seen it, Garnet. You act like you don't hear him."

I looked at him. "Ann Landers in drag."

"Garnet!"

I tried to get out of the car again. The door wouldn't open.

"Are you in some kind of trouble, lady?" Bill's round face was earnest.

"I'm a virgin."

"Well, *call* him. Tell him that you're sorry he's sick. If there's anything that Betty or I can do—"

"Get me out of this doggone *car!*"

"You have to mash that handle really hard. My son Tommy hit it with a tire iron."

I mashed it, really hard, and the door sprang open. I nearly fell out onto the gravel. I reached down for my shoulderbag. "Tell your pal Bubba that I don't care if he moves to the moon. He ain't the only fish in the sea."

"You have a mean mouth," he said. "Hell needn't have that fury, lady. You haven't been scorned. *Talk* to him."

I climbed out of the car and stood, looking back through the window at the small man with the Beatle haircut. "I'm doin' okay," I said. "I'm goin' steady with somebody else. That's all. A *soldier.* Tell Bubba *that.*"

"Yeah?" He leaned on the steering wheel. "Here at Fort Jackson?"

"No!" I answered, having nothing to lose, excited a little with spite.

I could put them on in the most royal way, I realized. I could put them both on with the pure truth. What the hell. I fairly danced with cleverness, utterly rancid little smartass that I had become.

"He's a lieutenant. Lieutenant Bobby Lee. At Fort Monroe. In Virginia. I don't mess around at Fort Jackson, you can catch *cooties* that way."

He was supposed to drive away now, but he didn't.

"Goodnight, Bill," I prompted, evil in my giddy omnipotence. When would I learn that I was a whole lot dumber than practically everybody else? "See ya tomorrow."

"Lady," he said, "Fort Monroe isn't used much anymore. It's a registered National Historic Landmark."

I swallowed but kept my face impassive.

"What does your soldier do, Garnet? Is he an engineer?"

"Should he be one? We need a lot of engineers to fight the Russians or what?"

"There was a famous one by that name. At Fort Monroe. Over a hundred-some-odd years ago."

I smiled weakly—who could have come up with a witticism after that?—and said to myself, What on earth made you think you could con this know-it-all historian? When will you learn to keep your big goddam mouth *shut?*

"Whose name," Bill went pitilessly on, "just happens to be plastered all over the books you've been reading lately. Oh my God, *you're serious!*"

I was so embarrassed that only my bones kept me standing upright, because my soul was down in my shoes.

My voice was a croak. "Goodnight, Bill. You're insane."

". . . and that report you gave in class. And your archaic vocabulary!" He was laughing and shaking his head, and laughing and shaking his head, and I wanted to kill myself. "*Why?*" he said, trying not to chortle.

There were many reactions he could have had, but he was only twenty-five years old. Still, laughing was the wrong thing to do. My feet found themselves and I took off for the house.

"Garnet!" I heard him shout after me. *"Lady, I didn't mean —!"*

But I scrambled into the house and pushed past my flabbergasted family and made it into the bathroom just in time to lock the door and entertain the worst case of diarrhea that it had ever been my misfortune to experience.

All of my guts were coming out.

"You got the homework assignment for Damadian's class?" Bubba's voice came weakly over the phone.

I fumbled for my notebook, nervous, glad at the genuine hoarseness in his voice but feeling my fingers vibrate nonetheless as I rooted around in my shoulderbag for my notes. "Yeah," I muttered. "Just a sec."

"How've you been?" He sounded awful. Like a toad.

"Okay." It didn't seem possible that the sound of his voice could still cause me this much anxiety. But I saw the garnet ring on my finger doing the Watusi and I thought, This is merely a physical reaction, Robert. You know how these things are. They can be mighty powerful.

"All right," I told Bubba, "Damadian wants us to finish the chapter on the Depression and then answer that bunch of stupid questions on page 410."

"'Finish the Depression,'" repeated Bubba, faraway. There was a pause. Then he said, "I've finished with my depression," and he laughed.

"Oh?" I waited. Twined the phone cord around my wrist.

"Yeah. I feel like hell. Throat all raw. But good ol' Joanne Barringer has brought me some soup. Several times. Just like Mom used to make. Full of slimy okra. Great for the throat."

Jo Barringer. Treasurer of my Sunday school class. She wore a 36-D.

You are a dog in the manger, I thought at myself as I felt my mood plummet. Your chance with him has gone forever but now you're pissed that Jo Barringer is chasing him around.

"Good," I lied.

"Yeah. Well. Sorry about last Wednesday night. But I just was too sick."

I was tempted to say something uncalled-for about being stood up but I bit my lips just in time. Let it go, I thought, trying to be gallant and mature and worldly. If Robert could let Markie go . . .

"Garnet," Bubba began after a moment, tone changing. "You're supposed to say that you miss me or somethin'. Aren't you?"

"I miss you."

"Well you don't sound like it."

What do I want? What do I want? I was thinking as I said, "We all miss you. David Dale misses you."

The voice that came from the other end was full of machismo, trying not to show any hurt: "Nice to know. Nice to know how much everybody likes me. Joanne Barringer ain't content with missin' me. Fixes me soup."

"*Stop* using that ignorant word. 'Ain't' ain't a word. You wanna win debates or be a shitkicker?" I said, hurt in turn.

"Well." He breathed noisily into the phone, didn't say anything for a long time. "Sorry to take up so much of your evening."

"'S'all right."

"Well." He just kept on breathing.

"Can I bring you anything?" It broke out of me. I couldn't help it, couldn't think straight. "Debate stuff? Anything? I've got a tape recorder here. Maybe we could listen to ourselves and see where we need to polish."

"'Debate stuff,'" he muttered in the same tone that people use when they say, "Adolf Hitler." "No. That's okay. Don't worry. I won't let you down, Garn. I'm not gonna forget how to debate."

I had taken the wrong approach, had been altogether too businesslike. I grasped at a straw, saying, "I could bring you some ice cream and we could play my new Jefferson Airplane album and maybe you'd feel—"

"Don't bother." I could barely hear him. "Joanne's stuffing me with all the fat goodies I need. I don't want to put you out."

I could see the headlines: GIRL POET SLASHES WRISTS·

Suddenly I didn't want to lose him to the telephone, didn't want him to hang up without knowing how much I had fantasized about him all these months. Mama, I thought wildly, I don't know how to play these boy-girl games.

He was saying nothing. He was giving me a chance to commit myself, to jump in and strip myself naked and give myself away. But there was this pain in my wasted calf muscle and I told myself, No no, he couldn't possibly care for you, you mean-mouthed incomplete repulsive piece of shit.

"Well . . ." he said. And I said nothing.

I let him say goodnight. I didn't let myself feel anything.

Twenty-Two

Winfield Scott, hero of two wars, onetime Presidential candidate, sits in his Washington office, General-In-Chief of the Army, seventy-five years old and hugely fat and with a crisis upon him, with gout, with years and sorrow weighing him down.

"I will repeat myself, Colonel Lee," he is rumbling, his face like a mashed-in melon, flattened pugnacious nose very red. "Lincoln is offering you command of the army that is to be brought into the field to put down this rebellion. I know this for a fact."

"With all due respect, sir." Lee still stands at attention, shocked to his marrow. Certain politicians have been feeling him out upon this issue for the last few days. But he hadn't believed it until now. "I am merely Lieutenant Colonel of a Texas regiment who—"

"At *ease,* I said. Sit down, Colonel."

Lee sits immediately on the caned seat in front of the old man.

"Now. Don't tell me that you're not up to it. Don't gainsay me, Colonel Lee. For it was my recommendation."

"With all due—"

"Humbug!" Scott rumbles and helps himself to a fistful of chocolates from a cut crystal candy dish on his desk. "You saying you *don't* know what an impression you made upon me in Mexico, Colonel?"

Lee fingers the long scar in front of his left ear. "Not really, sir."

"Modesty becomes you," The general chews, "but let me make myself clear. I won that fight because of you. I had presidential ambitions afterwards. Because of you. You are the closest thing to a one-man army I have ever seen."

"Sir."

Scott's eyes narrow, bushy beetling white brows twitching. "I still need you, Colonel. I'm too old to fight this fight that's a-coming. And it's going to be Armageddon."

Things dash around in Lee's mind. He has spent the last few months again in Texas, after John Brown's capture, cut off from newspapers and politics, glumly planning his retirement. And then come these orders from Scott to get himself back to Washington with all haste, where he has found the country just falling to pieces over the South Carolina secession. Unbelievable. Officers choosing up sides, Washington City itself an armed camp.

Command? Command of an entire army, under no one's orders save Scott's? The old man is senile, Lee reasons. I've never commanded anything larger than a *regiment,* for God's sake, and then only second-in-command. Not a brigade, not a division, let alone a corps—just a regiment of frontier cavalry. I might actually laugh if he were not he and I were not I. Dear ol' Fuss-and-Feathers. I am dearly fond of him, but he is quite mad.

"Let me tell you." Scott is leaning close over his desk, his corpulent old face grim. "I was in uniform when you were still in short pants, and I know my men. People say your daddy was a hell of a soldier. Well, you'll make your daddy look like a parson at a church picnic if somebody gives you the chance."

Lee blinks, browned features impassive under graying hair.

"I'm giving you that chance, Bob." Scott's voice is low. He

holds Lee's eyes and won't let him look away. "Don't let me down. You've got the genuine warrior's talent, Bob. You've got murder in you. Don't let me down. You've never let me down."

Mary, Mary you'll never guess. I'm a full general. General Lee, son of General Lee, if you please. What would your papa say? He never expected me to amount to anything. I'll buy you a fine townhouse in Washington City. General of the Army, can you believe it? We'll take the chicks to visit Europe once the rebellion is put down and I'll hire you an Irish maid and take you to the best doctors in London—

"I can't, sir," Lee hears himself mumbling.

"What? Speak up!"

He feels his lip quaver. Makes it stop. "I can't do this, sir."

"Can't?" The General-in-Chief is pale.

A pigeon flies past Scott's open window. Lee stares after it and speaks. "Virginia will probably secede too, General. My people are all there. My father-in-law willed properties to my sons, sir. They'd have to forfeit everything if I brought them north to side with me."

"Dammit, this is more than a question of property—!"

Oh Dear God. My life is this army. "Sir, I can't lead an invading army into Virginia. I can't fight against my own kin, sir. How can I fight my own sons?"

"I'm a Virginian too, you remember." Scott's voice goes soft. "But we swore to defend the United States when we took up this profession. A solemn oath."

"No one ever told us that the enemy would be our own people, sir."

Scott's brow was furrowed. "No."

"Begging the General's pardon, the General's family has lived in the North with him for many years. The General might not have the ties—"

"I have *ties!* I have ties." The old man leans back in his chair. It squeaks under his fat body. His face is stricken. "Great God! I never had a son, Bob. All I've ever had is this army. I used to watch you in Mexico and wish that you were my—"

167

And this old man is the closest thing to a mentor I've ever had, Lee realizes.

The general's chair squeaks. *Squeak squeak squeak.* "Great God, boy! The United States educated you!"

"I know, sir."

"Your daddy fought with George Washington to *build* this nation!"

"Yessir."

"You can't just turn your back on your country now, when she needs all the good men she can lay her hands on to stay alive!"

"I can't turn my back on my people, sir. I can't fight my children."

Scott sighs, a deep unhappy *whoosh* that sounds like a steam engine giving out. "Well. I feared this. I flat feared it. You're making the greatest mistake of your life, son, mark my words. Won't you reconsider?"

Lee shakes his head. Shrugs shoulders under the epaulets of his blue uniform.

Scott's eyes meet his. "Very well, Colonel. What do you propose to do instead?"

"Obtain leave and go home, sir. Wait it out and see what Virginia does. Perhaps she will come to her senses."

Scott shakes his massive head. His face is reddening. "Haven't you understood a goddam thing I've been saying? You can't just turn down a President and then trot off home all winsome, like Young Lochinvar, to put in a crop! Great God, Colonel, I thought you were supposed to be *smart!* You can't keep your commission and continue to draw pay if you're unwilling to perform the duties required of you!"

Silence. Everything is going right into the outhouse. Christ there it is. My whole life. Gone.

"Now can you? In all honor?" Scott stares at him, eyes red at the rims.

Lee makes his face behave, it will be too embarrassing to

both of them if he shows how stricken he is. "Nossir. Definitely not."

Guess what, Mary? I've left the army like you always wanted. No, no pension. No retirement. I've resigned. Fifty-four years old and no prospects. Don't know how to farm very well. Don't know how to do anything except one thing and now I've kissed it goodbye. How will I ever . . . ?

Mary totters up to him on her crutches when he tells her of his resignation. Her small brown eyes swarm like bees with stirred-up anger. Anger at something. But not at him.

She puts her arms around him for the first time in years and he feels a wiry strength in her arthritic shapeless body. He pats her back and feels worse for her loyalty. Worse for her strength. It would be easier somehow if she cursed him.

He is awake all night up in his room, trying to write, trying to pray, pacing the floor and trying to find the words to tell his Unionist sister, Ann, and dearest Markie that this decision has been forced upon him.

But he looks at his father's sword, hanging up there on the wall, and he knows that nothing has been forced. Not with that brave little crippled woman downstairs in the house and little Annie, with her scarred face, in the way of a Union invader gathering just across the river. Not with Custis and Rooney and young Rob in the Tidewater, all of military age and persuasion, all Southerners. Agnes and Mildred and daughter Mary here, in the way in the way . . . in the way. An army on the move is a terrible thing, no respecter of persons or property, no friend certainly of pacific Arlington that sits up here on its hill and waits for the blow to fall.

He crosses the floor to the sword and takes it down, fitting the hilt into his hand and feeling the heft of it. No forced decision, this.

The sword gleams in the lamplight.

God help anybody that threatens these people, in this house.
Anybody at all, even General Scott. I've got murder in me and I
feel it, sinful or not. Dear God, I will stand here and dispatch
whomever I have to. Let them set one foot across the river . . .

Twenty-Three

"Just forget it, Bill. I was kidding."

I was in Damadian's car again, being driven home again. Still embarrassed. Determined to brazen it out.

Bubba was still home, sick. The stuff had turned into influenza under the careful ministrations of his dad, Major Hargett, and Jo "Clara Barton" Barringer. I didn't have the guts to go see him. I had actually cranked up the pickup truck one night and had backed it out of the driveway, but then I thought about rejection and I got no further. I felt like a complete fool. And Bill Damadian wasn't helping.

He had been excruciatingly nice to me all week in class, I'll say that for him. Had kept his distance at lunchtime, leaving me to the questionable blessing of my friend Anita and her nonstop monologues about clothes and boys and the Barringer-Hargett romance. Anita was not privy to the knowledge of my aborted date; Bill had kept what he knew to himself and my attitude towards him had softened somewhat for that.

But he knew the other thing, the irrational thing, the obsession that I had been forced for the first time to view through another's eyes and see how ridiculous it was. And for that, I nearly hated him.

Isn't it funny how we always make somebody else bear the blame of our own peccadilloes? We don't hate ourselves for unacceptable behavior; we hate somebody else for finding out.

Yet, not once, before the previous Wednesday, had I thought of my love for Robert as really ludicrous. Yes, I had kept telling myself that it was. But I had never *felt* the truth of it. It was crazy — yes. Certainly neurotic. I had known that. But now it was ludicrous. The comical kind of love, like talking to Paul McCartney, that adolescents indulge in. And I was post-adolescent and I was still feeling it. It was getting stronger. The only thing I could do was to act nonchalant around Bill, go on about my business with as much dignity as I could dredge up, and deny it and deny it should he ever mention it again. I had been afraid to ride home with him tonight, afraid that he would. But to avoid him would be to admit more than I cared to admit.

So of course he mentioned it not two seconds after the Valiant made that turn onto Bluff Road at the Bloody Bucket junction. There was no jollity in his manner at all. He just said, "Tell me about Lee."

"You're a historian. You know more than I do. Just forget it, Bill," I said wearily. "I was kidding."

He lit a cigarette. "Nope. You weren't kidding. I had no idea how much you weren't kidding until you ran off to the house."

"Well, maybe I don't want to talk about it. Okay?"

He reached over to turn down the car radio and then deliberately drove on past my driveway.

"Hey!" I said. "You've passed—!"

He was shaking his head vehemently. I had never seen him do anything that could be called vehement. "We've got to talk. I hurt your feelings last week." He made a U-turn at the Orphanage Road and barreled back up the highway towards town, passing our farm again at sixty miles an hour. "You said last week that you felt you had made a fool out of yourself. Well, lady, you aren't the only one who feels like a fool."

I sat cornered on my end of the seat, sighing, wondering how I could escape his well-meant perpetual analysis and get him to take me home so that I could lock myself in the bathroom.

I said, "Playing father-confessor is not a required part of teacher-student relating. Don't make a mountain out of a molehill. I just made up a stupid story to save my face. 'Bobby' Lee, for God's sake! It was a put-on and you saw through it. Next time I'll tell a better lie."

"No. There's more to it than that. You're nervous even now. I can tell. You're not using hillbilly talk. Robert E. Lee as your secret steady date—that's just too wacky to be fiction."

"Thanks," I muttered, my arms and legs all crossed and entwined about each other. I couldn't look at him. I felt like he was probing all of my humiliating places, X-raying the fillings in my teeth, looking in my ears for dirt, sniffing at my underwear.

Why are you doing this to me? I wondered. Why do you liberal Northeastern types always insist upon honesty? Don't you know that we've built a way of life down here based upon the Graceful Lie, to keep from chafing each other raw in the heat?

"I mean," he went on, oblivious, "it's not like you had said 'Johnny' Lennon or Yelverton A. Tittle. There are no Robert E. Lee fan clubs."

"Yeah there are. And the members wear white sheets."

He gave me a look. "I upset you Wednesday night. And I'm sorry. I feel terrible. I didn't mean to hurt you."

I sighed. "God. As long as you're kidnaping me for a therapy session, could we please stop at McDonald's? I'm starving."

I was hoping that we would run into somebody we both knew at the burger joint where the highschool crowd hung out, hoping that a diversionary chat and a milkshake with cronies would get Bill off the track. I felt like he was raping me.

But there were no familiar cars there as the Valiant pulled into the parking lot and the yellow lights played over Bill's face like auroras. I felt a muscle twitch under my eye. Bill switched off the engine and threw an arm over the back seat.

"Would you laugh," he said, "if I told you that I once had a thing for Doris Day?"

"Probably. I don't believe it anyway."

"Well, I did. Still do, to a degree. Saw that thing she did with James Garner last year at least three times."

I smiled.

"You find that funny, see, Garnet. And I know that a lot of people would find it funny. So I don't tell anybody. If it was Brigitte Bardot, or maybe even Petula Clark, no one would find it funny. But it's not Brigitte Bardot. It's Doris Day. You see what I'm saying?"

"I see that you're a sucker for apple pie and freckles."

"Okay." He leaned forward, earnest. "It says a lot about me. I was just a fat little Armenian kid. My dad owned a deli. Doris Day was like those few blonde WASP goddesses that sat in my high-school class and always seemed to be out of reach. You get what I'm saying?"

"Is Betty Armenian?"

"Betty's Italian. She's no WASP goddess. You don't marry your fantasies."

I thought about Mary Custis.

"Look." Bill put his fingertips together. "I loved Betty because she lived down the block and liked pastrami. I didn't ask her to fit some inner image— Oh hell." He lit another cigarette.

"I'm not a Muboogabooga tribesman and you're not a Peace Corpsman bringing me Western enlightenment. Why do you think you always have to make everything better? Huh? You're a nice guy. We like you. You don't have—"

"Look—" He scattered ashes out into the warm noisy night.

"Are you trying to tell me that I'm working on some unconscious inner-image thing? Is that it?"

"Read Carl Jung, Garnet. Robert E. Lee is about as archetypal a figure that ever existed: the white-bearded Old Man as

Wizard, Patriarch, Merlin, Gandalf, Moses. It's Magic. Wisdom. It's tribal. Atavistic. Especially for you, with your hang-ups about the South."

"Bullshit."

"I'm telling you, lady, that Carl Jung—"

"We gonna eat or what?"

"Hey, I just thought you'd like to talk it out with somebody."

"We don't talk things out down here. We internalize. We're taught tact and manners and to let each other keep some dignity. Please take me home."

He sat there for a moment. Then he bent over so that he could pull his billfold out of the back of his gabardine slacks. "You hungry? Go get us some food."

I left him sitting moodily behind the steering wheel and came back laden with burgers and fries and shakes. He took the cardboard tray from me so that I could scramble once more into the vinyl seat beside him.

He stuck a french fry into his mouth. "You see a phone anywhere back there? I'd better call Betty and tell her not to wait dinner."

"There's one over there, but it's busted."

He looked at his watch. "Eat fast, then. It's pushing eight."

He looked so crestfallen sitting there with ketchup on his lower lip, this strange small man with the exotic name and the city voice. He was trying to take responsibility for my welfare the way he tried to do for Bubba and for all of us. But I wasn't letting him. I was flogging him with a stick. I felt bad. And maybe, just maybe, I needed . . .

I blew a long breath. "Okay. You win, Sigmund. I know it's not healthy and I'm kinda scared of it, if you wanna know the truth. It's getting out of hand."

"What's getting out of hand?" He looked up from his food.

"My obsession. My whatever. I can see myself in a few years—if something doesn't give—mooning wild-eyed around

Lee's grave in Virginia. Living on acorns. A Tennessee Williams heroine, gracefully mad."

His voice was mild. "Don't make a joke out of it. I know you don't think it's funny. I don't either."

I said nothing.

"It's hard to get yourself taken seriously by anyone when you're your age. I'm only twenty-five, Garnet. I'm still up against it."

"But you don't know what *this* is like. This isn't just a dumb crush, hon. I don't know what it is. But it isn't that. I'm not going through some kind of innocent juvenile phase."

"You, of all people I know, would not be susceptible to what is legitimately called a phase. I would bet my life on that."

"I refuse to give much credence to anything opined by a man who fantasizes about Doris Day. Want the rest of my fries?"

Bill chortled and I saw him look out of the car window at all of the kids milling around in the muggy May night, restless and erotically aware of each other in a nervous supercharged way.

He said, "Lee was an interesting character. I used to think he was a stuffed shirt, so little of anything warm and human comes down to us through the legends. The complete antithesis of Lincoln. You notice how Lincoln and Lee dominate the imagination? Grant and Jefferson Davis recede into the background, comparatively. And yet I used to wonder where Lee's strange ability came from. That audacity. What West Pointer in his right mind would have taken the risk he took at Chancellorsville?"

"But he won."

"Oh, yes lordy," he drawled.

I had to grin at his mimicked Southern accent.

Bill gulped another fry. "He seemed so calm and cold. So organized and machine-like. At least, that's the impression I got from a superficial look during my undergraduate days. And yet he could do the weirdest things on a battlefield."

"Uh huh," I agreed.

"All that effort for nothing. A man in his fifties, sleeping out in a tent in the heat or the snow for four years, with all of that incredible responsibility on him. Jesus. It would've killed me. No supplies, no rations, no matériel, an outnumbered army paid in money not worth the paper it was printed on. Against the whole northern United States, with over twice the South's population and unlimited factory resources. And he almost pulled it off. *Jesus.*"

"Surely you're not going to shed any crocodile tears for the Lost Cause."

"What did he fight for, Garnet?"

"Not slaves. He was a professional soldier. He owned no slaves, really."

Bill scratched his chin. "That's important to you, isn't it?"

"I couldn't be me and sympathize with him if he had."

"Lincoln was ready to give him field command of the U.S. Army when Lee just took off for Virginia and resigned his commission. Threw away a whole career. Why?"

I didn't really know. Yet I understood something fundamental out of my own meager experience, something that I had seen in my grandmother's face. I fingered my heart pin, remembering. "He was like everybody else. Just trying to get by. People get pushed and pulled by the things around them and don't know what they're doing. They just want to muddle through the bad times any way they can and then find a breathing space when it's all over. People just want to be happy. Most of them don't know how. They don't see where they're headed. They just want to be needed . . ."

I thought of something: "Let me tell you an anecdote." I wiped my hands on my greasy napkin. "Mrs. Chesnut, the Confederate diarist, wrote about seeing Lee for the first time in Richmond. He hadn't yet assumed command in the field, he was just Jeff Davis' military advisor. Mrs. Chesnut and a bunch of ladies were in a carriage and he rode up alongside. One of the women knew him and began to tease him about being ambitious. Everybody was super ambitious then, all fighting over position in the new Confederate hierarchy. But he laughed and told her that he didn't want anything out of it all except a little home of his *own* at the end of the war. A little farm. With home-produced eggs and cream and fried chicken. Not just one or two fried chickens, he told them. But *unlimited* fried chicken."

I let the warm night come in the windows over me but I felt cold.

"Such a mundane little dream, Bill. And I think he meant every word of it. He never had a home. That's all he fought for: home."

Bill turned to look at me.

"Grandmama tried to tell me once," I went on in a flat monotone, "that sometimes you have to get what you need in this life or it kills you. Sometimes what you want is so simple and basic that it looks like God would relent and let you have it. I guess you gotta have incentive. But if you lose out—Ahhh. If you lose out, then you're in real trouble. You end up with nothing. Maybe it's better to go through life not wanting anything, not loving, not needing anything or anybody at all."

Bill rubbed his eyes. They glittered in the carlights. "Is that what you're doing, Garnet? Learning not to need?"

"I don't know."

"Well, you're not going to get anything, riding Einstein's railroad with a dead man."

I bowed my head. "Dammit," I sputtered, "I'm crying all over my stupid hamburger."

Bill sat there for a long strained time and then one of his hands reached out and touched my shoulder.

"Don't!" I said. "Be careful! There are kids from the high school all over the place here. You wouldn't last another week at Richland Creek High School as a commie child molester."

"I'm sorry."

I cut him off with an impatient wave of my hand. "It doesn't matter. Take me home." I balled up my hamburger wrappers with a vicious crunch, stuck out a braceleted arm, and pitched them into a garbage can.

He switched on the ignition with a jerk at the key. Something stirred deep in my memory. A dream, perhaps. Strong hands touching me. I hugged myself. Lights swam by me as the Valiant fled into a stream of smooth traffic.

"I'm sorry, Bill."

We turned back onto Bluff Road and rode in silence. Am I trying to escape wanting something? I pondered as the little white car whizzed over the creek bridge at the U–Tote–'Em Truck Stop. Spanish moss hung over the turgid backwater, nameless shredded things hanging in the moonlight.

Is that what I've been doing, insulating myself from real life? Does all of this come from my fear of wanting something?

But I *do* want something, I thought now, trembling in the heat. I want something very badly.

I can't touch you, Robert. Not even through Bubba Hargett. I'll never be able to hold you and comfort you and rock you to sleep in my arms after the war, when the nightmares come. There is no way to make love to your body.

The body is gone. I'm in 1966 and I don't know how to get off Einstein's goddam train. But souls don't die. I know they don't. Einstein said matter and energy cannot be either created or destroyed. One is merely converted into the other and then back again. I feel you so close to me sometimes. A soul that carries that much is too preoccupied to die. You're in the 1800's and I'm in the 1900's and yet I feel you reaching out in all directions, just as if you were in this car with me, silent in the back seat.

Maybe when a heart really breaks, maybe little pieces of it fly off all over the place. Maybe a little piece of your heart has hit me.

I don't care what Bill thinks anymore. This isn't a matter of fantasy, it's a matter of life and death. You are alive in me now and I'll be damned if I'll let a little thing like a century kill you again.

I will burn like fire. I will burn like the sun. I will turn my energy loose and I will find you. Sleep dearest heart. I will give you a home.

Twenty-Four

He hasn't grown a beard, exactly. He has just stopped shaving. Beards are shaped with a razor and confined to one's chin. This exuberant hedge grows as far up on his cheeks as it wants to, and as far down his neck as it pleases. He takes a few moments once in a while to trim it with scissors, but has given up the idea of maintaining a natty Van Dyke during hard campaigning. There is no time. Besides, the tomfool thing is *white*.

Tonight, beard and all, he rides back to his headquarters at the Hogan house and the jubilation of the young staff officers, Long and Marshall and little Walter Taylor, who playfully calls him "The Great Tycoon" behind his back.

Meredith will be frying fatback and laying out the mess utensils. News of the Gaines' Mill victory has already been dispatched to President Davis in Richmond. McClellan's huge Federal army of 120,000 men—the largest and best-equipped army yet seen in North America—has been stopped a mere nine miles from Richmond's gates. It has taken quite some doing. Lee has begun his offensive with only a fraction over half that number, and has been assailing McClellan day after day with such vicious resolve that the Federal general is convinced the rebels must have fully 200,000 men in his front. What a laugh. Nowhere near even half that, especially not now. Lee's casualties have been horrifying. The railway station back in the city is buried in wounded. No help for it. If McClellan is not stopped here, then the war will be lost before it has hardly begun.

We've stopped him, Lee acknowledges now as he rides. Now I must eradicate him. End this deviltry before any more people bleed to death.

He has been in command less than a month.

He can hear the wounded plainly out there on the dark field, so many of them, crying and hollering as the night comes down. The sound will grow weaker throughout the night until it ceases altogether, while the stench will become so evil in tomorrow's June sun that green volunteers will faint. This sound and this smell are familiar to Lee; he has been living with both since Mexico, not knowing that he was but discovering it now to be an unexplored but definite part of him — like the soles of his bare feet.

The gray horse is reined to a standstill and Lee dismounts, removing buckskin gauntlets and tucking them under an elbow so he can rub his tired eyes. He glances up at the stars that show through the clouds and the cannon smoke still thickening the distance. Astronomy was his favorite subject in his West Point days. He hasn't thought about astronomy in years.

Lanterns flicker way off in the blackness, medical details and messmates of the missing who stumble through human debris. What do they think war *is?* he wonders, pondering the civilians who start such things. Banners? Bands? Brave patriotic verse, for God's sake? I'd like to fetch Davis back out here — yes, he and Lincoln both — and rub their noses in the blood of these dying children.

He reaches around the horse's tall neck with both arms and hugs, mashing his nose into the sleek stiff hair. "You're very fortunate to be a horse, Mr. Traveller. Oh yes. You'll never be tempted to run for Congress and turn into a pompous swine." He smiles a little. "Not," he amends, even for Traveller, "not that I actually think Mr. Davis is."

A young man somewhere far off in the hot darkness cries loudly for a drink of water. It sounds like Rob. It can't be Rob, but Lee feels his stomach lurch and he wants to ride out to the sound, canteen full, and pour blessed water into the boy, no matter if he's in a blue uniform. So many crying now. He feels empathic pain he's never felt before, almost physical in its intensity.

The lanterns of the medical details double and then triple, shimmering. He blinks. Dashes fingers at his eyes and finds them damp. Damn your soul, he berates himself. You know why they're out there. Who gave the order?

He swings back up into the saddle in the outdated dragoon mount he was taught in his cadet days, making himself calm again. The staff might come looking for him at any moment. Lord, I'm tired. When did I get this *old?*

A hale and athletic fifty-five, not an ounce of fat on him, he can still get by on four hours of sleep a night. Yes, and stay in the saddle for eighteen hours a day. And pore over his maps in the evenings and understand them better than the ground knows its own self. But this *reluctance,* now . . . No, not reluctance. He was not in the least reluctant a while ago to throw his troops like hailstones into the enemy fire. Second thoughts, perhaps? Yes. Second thoughts. There had been no second thoughts in Mexico. Only an old man has second thoughts.

Personal danger doesn't really frighten him. It speeds his blood up some, and he expects to be hit sooner or later, but it doesn't matter when his blood is up. It will come when it comes, he says to himself, always close to the front, where he can see and hear his crazed skinny troops piling into McClellan's lines like all hell breaking loose. What matters? The boys in the night matter. Mangled boys, gray and blue.

Blue. He looks at his thighs. Blue pants. Mary has stripped the U.S. Cavalry stripe from them.

And Mary. Where is Mary tonight? Under the roof of which kinfolks? Saying God-knows-what, thinking what sort of resentful thoughts while the Union buries dead soldiers in her front yard at Arlington?

If I had to do it all over again, he thinks. If I had to do it all over —

"General Lee?"

He turns. Walter Taylor is there upon a soft-snuffling horse, his dark, thin face patient and questioning. The night is very hot. Taylor's face gleams with sweat.

If I had to do it all over again, I'd make just as big a mess of everything as I did the first time . . .

Lee unslings his field glasses and fumbles for his canteen. Taylor's eyes are in shadow, the eyes of a young man not much above twenty-one years. The canteen sloshes. "Major, there is a boy somewhere out there . . ."

"There are a good many boys out there, sir. We've hit them hard, sure enough."

Lee's eyes are stern, glowering brows, rigid mouth set, and he holds Taylor's glance.

"Begging the General's pardon, sir," Taylor amends. "I did not intend to be impertinent, sir."

He hears the sigh come from the bearded lips. The face softens, becoming almost loving as the big eyes look up at the stars. "No impertinence, Major," comes the slow low voice. "Quite pertinent. Quite." A large warm hand, almost hot, squeezes Taylor's biceps for just an instant. "Go eat your supper, Major. I'll be along directly."

Taylor isn't stupid. The smart thing to do is to ride away. He flicks the reins and moves off into the dark, thinking: the devil's got hold of the Old Man again and we'd better give him a wide berth when he gets back.

What could get into a man like that? Damndest thing I ever saw or heard tell of, him whuppin' ol' McClellan every way you can think of . . . ordering General Magruder to march his troops around in a gigantic circle until the Yanks thought he was putting a godamighty *horde* into place in front of Richmond, having Stonewall pretend to threaten Washington until Honest Abe called off some of McClellan's people to its defense. And boy! Don't you imagine that made ol' McClellan eat gall? We been attacking for days, just pouring it into the Yanks like I–don't–know–what, betcha ol' Jeff Davis is down on his knees right now, thanking Almighty God for a veritable miracle. No miracle. General Lee. General Lee. Good gracious, you'd think he would whoop and laugh and throw his hat into the air, wouldn't you? What gets into a man like that?

The place on his arm where Lee held him is still warm. Taylor rubs the muscle and feels the parental heat lingering there. Smiles, finally.

Gotta make sure he gets a good night's sleep, he tells himself. He's going to be wanting to whup McClellan's ass again in the morning. Depend on it.

Twenty-Five

Bubba showed up at school the next day, not diffident or uneasy as I might have expected, but brash and thoroughly his old self. He was a little thinner from his illness, but he cornered me in the library among the classical music stereo albums and casually outlined a new angle of attack for our debate strategy. He was as unconcerned and easy as if the past weeks, since the canoe accident, had never happened.

Bill must've talked to him, I reasoned, watching Bubba go bopping down the hall to his next class. Can't think what Bill might've told him. Something on the order of, *Start all over and give her time,* maybe.

I've got a fairy godfather now. No doubt he is going to play Cupid until I am ready to shoot him. God save us all from carpetbagging Peace Corpsmen.

I might have thought that way, but I was actually becoming rather fond of him. I liked to watch his teddy bear face in class. Liked to hear the tough and tender way he lectured us.

I checked out a couple of record albums from the library and took them home, where I played them through on the small stereo in the den until I found what I was looking for.

"Whatzat junk?" Beth Ann stuck her head in the door at the fifth straight playing of one selection.

"Schubert." I leaned back in the rocking chair and put my hands behind my head, my feet up on a pile of magazines stacked on a faded footstool. "The *Marche Militaire*."

"La de dah. You gon play it till I can hum it by heart, huh?"

No, I thought, I'm going to play it until *I* can hum it by heart.

My mother came into the room with the new copy of *Life* Magazine. "This just came today. Lift your feet up."

I lifted my feet and Mama slapped the periodical down on the footstool. She straightened, hands on aproned hips. "I used to play that on the piano." She was listening, staring at the turntable where Schubert went round and round.

"Too much Culture in this room for me." Beth Ann tossed her bushy bouffant and ambled to the doorway. "Call me back when you put on the Beach Boys."

Mama looked at me. "You done your homework?"

"Yes'm."

"Supper's ready and your daddy'll be home any time now. Better get washed up."

"Yes'm."

I hummed the *Marche Militaire* while I helped Mama set the table. I whistled it later while I took my bath. Girls don't whistle, I could recall Grandmama saying, and I whistled with a vengeance until I thought my ears would split in the little wet room. I dried myself off and rubbed cream into my skin until I was greased up like a carnival pig, wondering if *Marche Militaire* had been something Mildred Lee could play on her piano. It was full of the innocent naive war glory of the 1820's, when her father had been a West Point cadet, with banners waving and flower garlands, long lines of young men, white gloves at their trouser seams. It had no Vietnam in it. No Korea, no second thoughts. No brutality or blood or broken intestines. It was a seductive anthem of the days when people had found war beautiful, a pre-war march, not something played for veterans limping home with bodies maimed and eyes glazed. People didn't usually find war attractive once one had actually gotten underway. Schubert had to have been a civilian.

I wandered humming into my parents' room in my terrycloth robe for evening devotions, my mind far away, my heart willing to go fight the Russians anytime, anywhere.

Mama already had the Bible open to the designated chapter. Her lined face was tranquil, blonde hair looped up in curlers. "Where's Beth Ann?" she asked me, sitting on her side of the bed where my father lay dozing, arms over his face against the light.

"I'm coming!" Beth Ann shouted joyously from somewhere in the hall and then bounded into the bedroom in fluffy pink mules with high heels.

"Cheez," I muttered.

"Y'all settle down." Mama looked closely at the printed Presbyterian devotion schedule. "Was today May tenth?"

"Yes'm." Beth Ann picked her toes. "Two more weeks and school is out."

"Richard, you awake?"

"Uh huh," Daddy muttered.

Mama squinted at the small print in the King James Version. "Fooey. Where're my glasses? Get my glasses from the dresser, please, Garnet."

I looked. "They ain't there, you left 'em in the livingroom. Here, Mama. I'll read it. Daddy's falling asleep."

I took the Bible from my mother and sat back down. "Where's it at?"

Mama peered again at the devotion schedule. "Psalm 144."

"That's gross," said Beth Ann.

I glanced at her, still picking her toenails, and I cleared my throat. Nightly devotions meant little to me in themselves, but I did like the sense of peace they brought me every night when the last thing we Laneys saw before going to sleep was each other.

The exhaust fan hummed from down the hall and pulled in cool damp air through the wire screens where big flying bugs plinked against the mesh at the windows.

"Beth Ann?" warned Mama.

My sister put her toes down reluctantly.

"'Blessed be the Lord my strength,'" I read out loud in my smooth debating voice, seeing the irked look come over Beth Ann's face and fighting a smile, "'which teacheth my hands to war and my fingers to fight.'"

The page blurred without warning as if someone had switched off a light. I faltered and looked up at the moths circling the overhead fixture and then back down. The print had become all murky. I blinked. Held the Bible close and then held it away until it was at arm's length.

"Honey?" Mama was staring at me.

"'Bow thy heavens, O Lord, and come down,'" I continued when I could focus. "'Touch the mountains, and they shall smoke.'" Oh God Oh God, I thought, I'm going blind at ten o'clock on May the tenth. Or this is epilepsy. "'Cast forth lightning, and scatter them: shoot out Thine arrows, and destroy.'"

I heard music and I heard a song. I heard singing.

The Bible fell from my lap in a thin-papered heap. I looked up at my mother and the déja vu was overwhelming, some part of me feeling that it had played this scene before. "I can't read any more," I said to her calmly. "I can't see the page."

They must have seen my face quite clearly. Daddy flung himself out of bed in his boxer shorts and Mama had me by the shoulders, shaking me and hugging me and Beth Ann was frozen whitefaced over her bare feet. "What do you mean, you can't see? What do you mean, you can't see?" Mama was tugging at my eyelashes.

"Didn't Granddaddy used to read that psalm?" I prattled while they turned my face up to the light, "Didn't Granddaddy used to read that psalm?"

"Does your head hurt any?" Daddy was asking.

"No," I said. I realized now that I was crying. No wonder I couldn't see.

"She fell asleep readin', she's tired out." Mama told him, pulling me up against the soft skin at her neck where her yellow hair hung in curlers. "Let's go make us some coffee, honey," she crooned. "It's all right."

I started to bawl in earnest then, it had been a long time since I had held onto my mother and smelled her perfume and shampoo. Her warmth opened floodgates. My daddy's heavy hands rested on my shoulders.

"I love you all so much," I coughed, like somebody about to embark upon some long journey. I tried to see over my shoulder where my hair was in the way. "I love you too, Beth Ann."

"She's havin' a nervous breakdown," my sister announced.

I laughed unconvincingly. But I could see her puzzlement and her terror—I could see normally now. And I did love her. It had never been important to tell her so before.

They walked me into the kitchen like an honor guard but I turned on them, weary. "Go to bed, y'all. You gotta get up real early, Daddy."

"I just wanna know what in the dadblame—?"

I smiled at him and found a little bravado that had snuck back. "I'm okay. I just fell asleep and then woke right back up and didn't know where I was. I'm getting as spaced-out as Grandmama."

"People do that in cars sometimes," Beth Ann nodded, unconvinced. "Like R.J. Crenshaw when he mowed down all those mailboxes up at the dairy."

Mama put coffee water on to boil. "Go to bed, Richard. You too, Beth Ann. I'll be along in a minute."

But Mama sat with her chin in her hands long after the other two had gone back up the hall, watching me sip at my coffee. The night pressed in against the kitchen window and I felt myself shrink back, oppressed, not having been afraid of the dark ever, not even as a baby.

My mother stirred finally, rubbing her eyes under her glasses. "Maybe it's female problems."

"Probably."

"I get right edgy myself at certain times of the month. Did something in there scare you, honey?"

"Hey." I put my cup down and took Mama's dishwater hand and patted it, speaking in my bluffest voice now. As normal and nonchalant as I could make myself. "I'm an artist, Mama. I'm sensitive and temperamental and all that bull. Now I'm gonna finish my coffee and then take my edgy self to bed. You go on."

"Well . . ."

I could see her thinking about having to cook breakfast for her farmer husband at four A.M. "Go on, Mama. Do I look like I think the boogerman is gonna get me?"

"If you're sure that you don't need to talk about anything. 'Cause, honey, I want you to know that you can always come to us and talk about anything at all."

I laughed, a No-I'm-not-pregnant laugh.

Mama smiled tiredly and padded off in her worn house slippers, and I sat at the table in the lighted kitchen.

Twenty-Six

A man can get used to almost anything.

By autumn of 1862, Lee has learned what switches to pull.

This new gray army is like a steam invention, bristling with levers and handles and gauges. It won't respond to discipline in the same way as a body of professionals. It takes subtlety to move it, inspiration to fire it. There is no master machinist to show Robert Lee how to use it, so he has tinkered and experimented and rebuilt it himself to his own instinctive specifications. No one knows its limits, how far it can be driven until it wears down. And fueling it is difficult in the extreme. But it runs and is picking up momentum, and the quiet pride that its inventor/operator takes in it continues to grow.

He is, in fact, running this army like a family. "My boys," he says to himself with amusement when they pass in review with the seats of their pants ragged. "That's all right, boys. The enemy never sees your backsides."

There they go, a full-size army of amateurs led by a handful of West Pointers, and planters like Wade Hampton who turn into able officers under fire. There they go, a horde of piratical cavalry and farmboy sharpshooters who can pick off a rabbit at a hundred yards with a shot through the eye, delivered from one of these new rifled muskets. They live on cornbread and bacon when they can get it, field peas when they cannot. They are clothed in a hodge-podge of tatters, remnants of worn gray uniforms mixed in with civilian garments. Gone are the flashy Prussian-style outfits and the absurd Turkish Zouave harem britches. ("Their ladies have clothed them for a costume party," Lee remarked, stunned by the new volunteer regiments marching into Richmond a year ago.)

Young scions have brought along their body servants. The hillbillies tote their squirrel guns. The Texans keep their Bowie knives in their belts. They are barefoot, filthy, skinny as scarecrows.

But they have been drilled to within an inch of their lives. You cannot move 50,000 men across country and get them to form battle lines under fire unless everything is choreographed be-forehand. And they have been taught to dig entrenchments, even the pretty young aristocrats who object to "Nigger work." Lee has made them drill and dig and dig and dig, until they call him the King of Spades.

There have been setbacks and false starts. The recent invasion of Maryland in search of recruits and to forage has ended in costly stalemate at Antietam Creek. But two Northern generals have wrecked their careers tangling with this army so far, and several more will be put out to pasture in the foreseeable future. Generals McClellan, Pope, Burnside, Hooker, and Meade will be among the disappointed. Lincoln changes generals after every battle. *I'm afraid that sooner or later he will come up with someone I don't understand,* Lee writes to his wife.

Yet the Confederates make do with the same old com-manders. Stonewall Jackson, that iron Calvinist who seems never to smile and never to regret, appears as another name for terror in the gleaned Northern newspapers. But the name of Jackson's com-mander is becoming synonymous with the word "Magus." The short, neat syllable "Lee" reverberates through the Union with mystery in its sound.

He has been scanning a New York newspaper this chilly autumn night, wondering why the reporters ascribe clairvoyance to him and then go on to detail all the movements of the Union Army so thoroughly that Mary herself would have no trouble following them. He is dumbfounded upon finding an engraved portrait of himself, a likeness based upon a decade-old Brady photograph, showing hair still black and chin still bare, with liberties taken around the mouth and eyes to make him look as fierce and unscrupulous as possible.

"Robert Lee as Attila The Hun," he says to himself, pitching the paper onto his cot and getting down to paperwork as the single candle in the tent gutters in a cool draft.

His hands ache. He injured them months ago at Second Manassas by tripping in raingear that didn't fit. The splints and bandages have just come off. He curses himself for the millionth time. Would Attila have tried to overtake a horse while wearing rubber overalls? Irritably he rubs the sore place where the bones were broken and settles his reading glasses onto his nose. He is a little seedy, a little rumpled, a little slouchy in his plain checked shirt and gray frock coat.

Attila The Hun as a country preacher, he smiles to himself.

A few low laughs come from outside, and what sounds like the clink of a whiskey demijohn against brass cuff buttons. And then comes Jeb Stuart's unmistakable baritone giving an instruction to somebody. The Stuart staff has evidently come to serenade the Commanding General again. Oh me. He has postponed work on his reports for too long already this evening; he flips through the papers on the rough table and wonders where Major Taylor has put a missing sheet.

But he can hear them out there, louder now, boots scraping on the rocky ground as they push into the circle of firelight. Walter Taylor is probably out there with them. Lee considers calling but stops himself. Taylor might be functioning as chief of staff but he is only a boy and Lee remembers what it is like to be a boy in the army. He thinks of Harriet Talcott with her regal little face and about officers' wives of questionable virtue. "Never had to worry about Molly that way, thank God."

He puts an aching hand to his forehead and wonders if Markie has married and if she is happy. One of her brothers has stuck by the Union and her home is in Washington City. So there have been no letters since hostilities began.

Perhaps she is my enemy. I have become such a tabloid monster. There may never be any more letters in that bold unfeminine handwriting.

His thoughts go to Eliza Mackay, his first love, his Georgia love, who kept his sketch of dead Napoleon and used to tuck little clumps of violets into the palm of his hand when nobody was looking. He can remember the feel of the flowers against his life line, tender and dewy like parts of a woman.

Aware of an unsuitable stirring at his groin, he guiltily adjusts his posture.

Shame on you, you old fool. One would think that this sort of reverie might abate as one got older, he thinks to himself. But it never does.

He tries to read a long impassioned complaint from some disaffected officer who doesn't think that Jewish soldiers should have been granted leave for Yom Kippur—*It is incumbent upon us, sir, to lead them to the Truth . . .* —and he scrawls a dressing-down in the margins of the fellow's letter, his initials large and angry.

The Truth, indeed, he thinks; and Pilate asked our Lord what is truth and He never answered a word.

There is a jarring note or two of music from outside, the twanging strings of Sweeney's banjo. A clamor of male voices in the high joshing falsetto yelps peculiar to Southerners who are bent on having a good time. The raw plucking settles into a breakdown and there is laughter, and then the banjo jangles into Stuart's theme song, "Jine The Cavalry."

Lee scratches his gray head with the stub of a pencil. Lice again?

They are all singing at different pitches. Someone has a fiddle and Perry, the black valet, is providing hambone percussion. Walter Taylor's light voice is edging into harmony with Stuart's ringing baritone on "Alabama Gals, Won't You Come Out To-night?" There is a tap-tap-tap of a rock, or something, against what sounds like a stoneware whiskey bottle.

Lee smiles, wryly, as he thinks, Those people in blue uniforms have to make do with "Hail, Columbia."

Panting and stomping—they must be dancing, some of them. That arms-close-to-the-body mountain clog step the Scotch-Irish brought with them, interpolated with African flair. Lee's own toe begins to tap the plank flooring beneath the camp stool, and it comes to him, in spite of himself, that life is exceedingly good sometimes. The weather is dry and cool, morale amazingly high. Lee knows all of the tunes that Sweeney is playing and he hums along, enjoying the sound of his own voice.

The men fall silent immediately when he flings back the tent flap to come to the firelight, spectacles removed, the flickers burnishing his sun-brown face and satisfied smile. They stand—not exactly at attention, since some of them are a little too taken with whiskey and high spirits to be rigid. And when does he ever require rigidity?

"At ease," he mutters pleasantly.

Jeb Stuart removes his plumed hat and sweeps the ground with it in a goodhumored bow: "An humble serenade, *mon général.*" His young face is hidden in its ridiculous whiskers. How in God's name does he get the ends of his moustache to curl in corkscrews that way? Lee wonders.

The whiskey sits at Sweeney's feet. Lee folds his arms, one eyebrow up.

"Well, gentlemen. Shall I thank General Stuart for the fine music tonight? Or should I maybe thank that jug?"

Stuart hoots and slaps his knee. Lee knows very well that the young man has vowed never to touch the stuff, but the fumes out here are enough to fell a mule. And *somebody* has been touching the stuff.

"Want a snort, sir?" grins a woozy Major Taylor from the dirt near the fire, lounging with his back against his saddle.

For a moment Lee looks as if he does want to join them, to sit relaxed at the fireside and tell them his anecdotes about drunken turkey shoots in Texas and the time somebody reported to Winfield Scott's Mexican headquarters in his drawers. But none of them expect him to join in. They are not Jack Mackay or Andrew Talcott or Captain W. George Williams, Markie's father. Most of them have never seen him drink anything stronger than buttermilk, except Walter Taylor and Charlie Marshall. They have witnessed the occasional glasses of wine at dinners, with no discernible effect except the general's tendency to stop war-talking with the menfolks and switch to chitchat with whomever happens to be present in skirts.

He can see that they don't expect him to join them. They have their own ideas about what is in character for him and what is not. You must not shock the young, he reminds himself. They are not adaptable.

Walter Taylor lolls at his ease, glad tonight to have his career as a banker suspended, happy with the vision in his eyes of the Old Man so near and so contented. Stuart's staff doesn't know the Old Man the way he does, doesn't know how to identify his secret moods. Someday I'll write a book, Taylor thinks now, and set everybody straight. Marse Robert isn't a plaster saint. He can get every bit as mad at me as my pa ever did. And when he's happy . . . Taylor smiles to himself and remembers last night in the general's tent—the matter of a certain hapless colonel's battle report. "Major, what does this word look like to you?" the Old Man had asked him.

Taylor studied the dreadful scrawl under the general's index finger. "Hmmm. Can't make it out, sir. The context of the sentence suggests—"

"Looks like 'pickpockets'."

Actually, it looked more like Hindu or Arabic. "Doubtless he means 'skirmishers', sir, I should think."

Lee squinted through his reading spectacles and held the foolscap paper out at arm's length. "'I had deployed my *pickpockets* across the Turner's Fork Road.'"

Taylor had felt a grin coming. Looked up and caught Marshall's eye.

"No wonder he got a good drubbing," the Old Man muttered, peering at the script.

Marshall laughed, inserting a small question mark into the text next to the mysterious word.

"Our good colonel recruited that regiment himself," said the Old Man, observing. "I mustn't argue with his assessment of their civilian occupations."

"Of course not, sir," Marshall smiled from his lap desk.

Lee had looked up at Taylor. "Major Taylor here allowed Colonel Pickpocket his-very-own-self to deliver that to me this afternoon while I was trying to give myself a haircut, you know . . ."

"Did I, sir? My apologies, sir! I had no instructions to the con—"

"I know how you operate, Major." There was devilment at the corners of the bearded mouth. "You say to yourself, 'Let's see. How am I to inconvenience the old fellow today? Perhaps he would find a visit from an incompetent blockhead exceptionally diverting.'"

"Sir, I never!" Taylor laughed. "Ah, begging the General's pardon—"

"'—especially if the old fellow is backed up to a mirror like an acrobat with his shirttail out and galluses a-hanging.'"

Marshall began to chuckle, and Taylor knew that they were all being silly, and he treasures these silly moments with the real Robert Lee, because he understands that few others ever get to share them. Fewer even suspect their existence. "You know why

Marse Robert cuts his own hair?" Colonel Long had once volunteered. "Because the Richmond barbers were *selling* it! True!"

Now Taylor sits at the fire and exults: There's no finer man than Robert Lee. No finer place to be anywhere than the Army of Northern Virginia. Hallelujah!

I wish he'd take a little spirits now and then, though. Whiskey. I worry about him sometimes. He won't let himself relax much. He never leaves camp.

Taylor watches the Old Man nod pleasantly at them and then fade back into the weatherstained tent marked "U.S.," like all of their scrounged wagons and most of their mules. After a while the serenade resumes.

Lee just can't work with the music outside. He begins a letter to Mary to tell her that he received all of those socks she sent. Little Mildred has sent some for the soldiers, too, but her knitting is odd. She doesn't reinforce the heels. He decides not to inflict her defective articles upon needy privates. He'll keep these for himself. His own have given out.

Now he trails off in mid-letter, sidetracked into thoughts of the army. The cold weather is coming and they'll be in winter quarters by the Rappahannock River soon and many of the boys won't have enough to wear. It's rumored that McClellan has been removed from command (again) by Lincoln and that General Burnside is now in charge of the blue army across the Rappahannock. Burnside will probably want to start something before long to show Washington that he is a real go-getter.

I've got to keep my mind upon what I'm supposed to be doing, Lee tells God silently. Or I won't be any good to anyone.

He opens his battered Episcopal prayerbook to the bookmark stuck perpetually into the passage that he reads almost every night. He kneels on the hard rough planking where the splinters prick through the threadbare cloth at his knees while the banjo jangles outside, asking God to get him back Up There, back to that high cold plane where he doesn't feel or remember. Back to the place where the strength flows from some mysterious reservoir in him until he can demand killing from his army and exult in it like an Old Testament prophet.

The power flows out—through Stonewall Jackson, through Pete Longstreet and Powell Hill and Jeb Stuart and Dick Ewell and Jubal Early, out through the eyes and hands of the youngest and skinniest private in the banjo-jangling army. On to the snows of Fredericksburg.

"'Blessed be the Lord my strength,'" he prays in a whisper, folded hands white-knuckled, hearing in his memory the artillery at Sharpsburg as he recites the words of Psalm 144, feeling its vehemence flood his arteries, "'which teacheth my hands to war, and my fingers to fight. . . .'"

It will be winter before he catches the strep throat that will lead to rheumatic fever. It will be early spring before he has the first heart attack.

Twenty-Seven

It didn't take a genius to see that I had a few screws loose. And they were getting looser all the time. I started to check out library books that dealt with adolescent psychology, searching for myself, but I didn't seem to be in them anywhere. I threw myself into an orgy of television-watching until my eyeballs wanted to explode, gobbling up *American Bandstand* and *The Andy Griffith Show* and *Star Trek,* as if my life depended upon it, needing to put myself in touch with my times as viscerally as I could. I took to reading comics, for God's sake, and *Mad* Magazine, and there was not enough Motown in the world for me. Re-rooting my interests in the twentieth century was conscious labor, and I hated it. But I kinda liked *Star Trek.*

I was driving myself crazy. It was an excruciatingly hot day, the kind of day that left me helplessly wondering about nineteenth-century women and how they could have possibly endured such heat in their starched and crinoline modesty, sans air conditioning or even electric fans. I was hurrying across the schoolyard to the bus after the final bell, imagining myself in a sweltering hoop skirt, with no antiperspirant either—although they did have primitive deodorants. I held my tortoiseshell fan at half-mast and I was ready to go home, when I heard Rainer Phillips' voice, low and mean, asking somebody, "Who you callin' a nigger?"

Little genetic alarm bells went off in my brain. But before I could react, Bubba Hargett came out of nowhere and took me by the arm. "Let's get outta here, Garn."

I turned. Jeff Moak was the person Rainer had addressed, I saw. He was opening his car door, lip twitching, not twenty feet away from me, where he regarded Rainer hunched up in the heat by the curbside of the parking lot. A kid behind me went into full cry: "Somebody go get a teacher! Somebody go get a teacher!"

"Garn Garn. You see what happened?" There was an agitated tug at my bare elbow. I looked over my shoulder at my friend Anita's beet-red face.

"Jeff, he was backin' his car out," Bubba pointed, sweat making snail-trails over his jawbone, "didn't look where he was going, I guess. Almost ran over Rainer Phillips. Rainer cussed him."

Kids, like sharks drawn by blood, were closing in from all sides to the edge of the parking lot by the cafeteria, where the pecan trees threw dusty shade over the birdshit-spotted gloss of the automobiles. Two black guys were standing shoulder-to-shoulder right behind Rainer, empty fingers twiddling at their sides.

"That stupid Jeff," Anita growsed at my elbow.

"Jeff's gonna get his stupid butt stomped in a minute." Bubba jingled his car keys. "And folks with sense had better git as far away as they can. C'mon. I'll take ya'll home. Don't fool with the buses."

"No!" I shaded my eyes, searching the growing clot of onlookers for a blonde bouffant. "Can't leave Beth Ann! Y'all go on!"

"*Get a teacher!*" Rainer's sister Laurine was yelling out of the window of her old Plymouth, her dark face silhouetted against the blaze of the afternoon. "Get a teacher, somebody!"

"You goin' to let me git back in my car and go home?" Jeff did a John Wayne imitation for Rainer's benefit, thumbs hooked into belt, pelvis thrust forward. "Or you goin' to do somethin' you gonna greatly regret? It don't matter to me none either way, Phillips."

"Man, you called me a nigger! I don't take that offa *nobody!*"

Yes, we did talk like that; yes, this kind of thing happened in those days. We had gotten almost as good at dodging rocks thrown at the school bus by the black kids in Arthurtown, as we had gotten at diving under our desks for a Nuclear Attack Drill. We deserved the rocks.

"Rainer?" Laurine called from her Plymouth.

"You hush up!" he yelled at his sister, not turning around. "Ain't nobody goin' to try to run me down with his automobile and then call me a damn *nigger!* Ain't nobody gon do that!"

"Well, hell—that ain't the whole story!" Jeff shouted, face reddening. "You cussed me! Called me things I wouldn't even call a blame dog!"

"Man tries to run over you—"

I stuck my fan back into my shoulderbag. It had survived Reconstruction and two world wars and I didn't want to see it get broken to bits in a pennyante race riot.

"Damn niggers all over the place! Can't back my car out without squishing one!" John Wayne was totally gone. Jeff's voice was tinged now with hysteria as he belatedly noticed Rainer's friends closing in. "Nobody ast y'all to come to this school! Who ast y'all? Nobody wants you here! And I ain't gon stand here and let no nigger cuss me like a damn dog!"

"I don't *BELIEVE* this!" Bubba was muttering in my ear.

I believed it. He had been moved around too many places by the army. He had forgotten how weird people, who have known one another all their lives, can get when they stay in one place too long. I stood on tiptoe looking for Beth Ann in the sea of faces where several white boys were pushing through the mob to stand at Jeff Moak's side.

"Can you *believe* this, Garn?"

"The fool," I said. "The goddam fool."

"Clear out! Now everybody just clear on outta here!" boomed a sudden adult voice, and Shotgun Harman, the State Championship football coach, came bulling through the students with Bill Damadian right behind him. "Move! Move!"

I saw Jeff look up at six-foot-four-inches of constituted authority bearing down on him like a wounded grizzly.

"Coach, I—!"

"Didn't you hear me say *move?*"

"Hey, Rainer?" Bill Damadian crooked a finger and pointed significantly at the car where Laurine Phillips waited a safe distance away. His voice was Peace Corps bland and matter-of-fact.

"Stay outta this, li'l White Man." Rainer stood his ground, face like an African war mask. "This ain't yo scene, man. This ain't yo scene."

Bill's face changed imperceptibly as I saw him slowly realize that he was indeed a small young white man in the middle of hostile black bystanders.

Oh nuts, I thought, feeling a sudden strong affection for the teacher. He came down here to save us. To witness our degradation. And now he can't think of anything to do.

"You gonna git us on TV, Jeff?" Coach Harman was hollering, planting his solid lineman's weight between the blacks and the whites. "You gonna git us on Walter Cronkite with the fire hoses and the U.S. Marshals? That what you plannin' on doin'?"

Somebody laughed nervously.

"*Shut up!*" Jeff wheeled on the crowd, veins standing out on his neck. "Just shut the fuck up!"

"Ahhhh Christ!" Bubba groaned.

Coach Harman reached out to grab Jeff and he made sure that he had the boy's arms pinioned, but Jeff's friends still stood free, muscles jumping in the heat. Harman nodded to a football player, who ran for the principal's office.

Rainer was sullenly edging towards his car and Laurine when one of Jeff's buddies — Stanley Dawes, large and pink and torpid — pointedly put his booted foot up on Jeff's bumper. A Rebel flag bumper sticker glowed there, red and threatening, beneath the punctuation of his leather sole — stuck there on the greasy chrome like a warning beacon.

"That's right, nigger," he said easily, fake-genial. "Run on home with yo tail between yo legs. My daddy knows where you live."

I took it all in: Stanley with his foot crowning that bumper sticker, Rainer trying to do the right thing. And a sudden rage churned in my gut. I jerked and staggered against Bubba, nearly fell, recovered, and then thrashed my way through the crowd.

"Hey Garnet!" Bubba grabbed for me and missed, fingers sliding off my slick perspiring arm.

My voice was so thick when I got close to Stanley and Jeff that I couldn't say anything. I didn't know what I wanted to say, anyway. Bill Damadian stood there watching me, face bleak, and I was humiliated that he had to be there to see this with his Northern note-taking brain, to see my peers act out all of his cherished fantasies about Southern brutality.

Shotgun Harman held Jeff by the arms but Stanley stood free with his foot on the bumper and the son of a bitch laughed in my face.

I was astonished myself when it happened: My be-ringed hand flashed downward and peeled the red bumper sticker free of the chrome. I straightened up and stood breathing hard for a moment, feeling curious eyes eating into me, and I smoothed out the plastic with its printed flag face down against my thigh. Coach Harman turned to look at me and Stanley. Stanley chewed his cud and everybody seemed a little calmer now that they had something new to stare at: the school's first Flower Child doing something characteristically weird, smoothing out that wrinkled bumper sticker. I felt the tension being drawn into me and I smiled noncommittally while I felt my blood pressure go down a little. Someone waved on the edge of my vision. It was Bill Damadian.

"You're beautiful when you're angry, Stanley," I told him.

He grinned. Somebody chortled. Stanley reached out and pinched me right on the side of my butt. "Anytime, Sweet Thang."

"You lay a hand on me again and you'll draw back a nub, Bo."

"Wooooo!" yelped somebody in the crowd. Several kids applauded.

"Garnet!" I could hear Bubba.

"Stanley," I went on, conversationally, while he chewed and smiled, his eyes at a condescending half-mast. "My great-great-granddaddy Died at Gaines' Mill for this." I turned the flag with its cross face-up and then hugged it to my chest where my fingers continued to smooth out its dog-eared corners against my heart-shaped brooch.

And Robert Lee, I appended silently, my sweet incomparable Cousin Robert wrecked his life for this rag. "And I'll be damned," I went on out loud, "if I'll see it sullied by any stupid bigot hoodlum."

"Garnet Garnet Garnet!" Bill Damadian sounded off like a siren.

"I'll be goddamned if I will," I insisted in a new mean voice, my vision clouding until all I could see was a smoky fog with two hateful eyes looking at me out of it.

"Gimme back my flag, baby—now." Jeff's voice filtered through, calm.

"You don't know what it means," I told them. "You aren't fit to show it."

What am I bothering with them for, anyway? I asked myself. Neither of them has the brains of a tapeworm; you can't reform tapeworms overnight. But I wish Bill Damadian could see that many of us—me, Bubba, Beth Ann, Anita—aren't remotely like these cave men.

205

Are we?

Are we?

What am I holding this thing for? Who am I defending it against?

"Nigger lover!" jeered Stanley.

God, they've spoiled our flag, and it's really an attractive flag. Doesn't anyone really read history? They've taken this symbol of a squelched revolution—and revolutions are as American as apple pie—and they've made it something ugly and obscene. Another swastika. The Confederacy, benighted as it was, had plans underway to free its blacks when it went out of existence. Some of them were freed. Some of them were even drilling in Richmond as Confederate soldiers. This flag was hopelessly wrongheaded, but innocent of real hatred until somebody went and splotched it all over with the blood of lynchings and smeared hate all over it like stinking shit.

Poor great-great-granddaddy. Poor Amos Bates Cooke. He died for a shit-smeared rag and I can't even be proud of him for it. I feel foul and smelly just holding this poor little Kill-John-Kennedy flag.

Yes, I'm a nigger lover. I come from a long line of nigger lovers. The niggers nursed our babies and rocked us to sleep and grew our crops with us and laid us out when we died. And made the salve with loving hands that Elizabeth Ann and Robert Lee smeared all over Liza's burns.

Christ. I'm gonna hit somebody.

"Laurine?" I called over my shoulder. Took my eyes off of Stanley. Walked calmly over to the black girl in the Plymouth, while Coach Harman must have wondered whether or not to lay hands upon a female student. I handed Laurine the flag. "Hold this a minute for me, hon."

"Lord hamercy!" Laurine's slim two-toned fingers recoiled from the piece of plastic as if it had given her an electric shock. "What I be doin' with *this* thing?"

She showed her teeth and let it fall distastefully to the ground.

Several bystanders giggled. I thought: Bad move, Garnet, that's like asking a Jew to hold Hitler's headquarters banner. Now *everybody's* mad at you. Democracy in action.

I went back to the guy with his foot on the bumper and the world went into slow motion. I could see every pore on his nose.

Calm me down, Robert Lee, I thought. You have enough self-control for both of us.

It wasn't calm I found, though, as I probed my psyche. It was anger, a sea of it, an ocean of it behind a cracking dam: anger with no target. It couldn't all be coming from me, I had not lived long enough or been wounded deeply enough to amass all this rage.

Oh boy, I thought miserably, remembering the Bible fugue. Oh boy, oh boy.

You're imaginary, Robert. If I can turn you on like this, I can turn you off. This is no place to fantasize. God knows they probably think I'm crazy as it is.

What is happening to me? Get out of my head! I put you there, you're not really there.

"No!" I shrieked, loud. I ripped my fist back and hit the face in front of me as hard as I could.

Twenty-Eight

There were cheers for me that hot afternoon as I made my way through the crowd to Bill Damadian's classroom, where he pried the flattened rings off of my swelling hand with a screwdriver. The cheers were from the kids who had found common ground in my ambiguous act, from the ones who had gotten bored and tired of waiting for Jeff and Rainer to trade punches, and from guys who warmed to Women's Wrestling. I had acknowledged the cheers with a weary wave while they tilted Stanley's head back to keep the blood off of his shirt. I later accepted my suspension with stupefaction, Bubba's startled eyes fixed on me. Stanley, Jeff, and Rainer were all suspended too.

Daddy got off the phone that night with somebody after we could hear him loud and hot over the sound of the television. "That was Ewell Dawes," he told Mama. "She broke Stanley's nose! She broke his blame nose! He wants me to pay—"

"I'll pay every cent of it," I told him. "I'll pull weeds and slop the hogs all summer, Daddy."

"You're durn right you will! You don't go around punching people in the nose, no matter what cause you think you got! What you watchin' T.V. for? You gonna have a lot of schoolwork to catch up on."

"Yessir." I wouldn't look at him.

Mama looked like she didn't know whether to laugh or to cry.

They talked far into the night behind the door of their bedroom. I couldn't sleep. I sat on the bed with my hand in a pickle jar full of ice cubes.

Beth Ann was awake. She turned on the light and sat up. "I been wishin' for years that somebody'd close ol' Stanley's big mouth for him."

"Yeah," I said. Had to laugh after a while. "Looks like I aimed a tad too high."

"That's fine. Never liked his nose either."

I wondered what I would do if my hand continued to swell and got stuck in the jar. It was my right hand, the one I applied my makeup with. Would anybody recognize me if I was forced to go back to school without my Cleopatra armor?

"Reckon Ol' Man Dawes'll burn a cross in our yard?" Beth Ann sat immobile under the lamp on the sidetable, a lamp with a frieze of Snow White and the Seven Dwarfs lollygagging around a flyspecked shade. I watched my sister carefully apply a dab of peach pearl nail polish to each of her toes, Michelangelo working at the Sistine ceiling.

"What is it with you and your feet?" I stirred the ice cubes in my jar. "You got a fetish or somethin'?"

The blonde head didn't move. "What's the matter with *you?* You been actin' like a zombie lately."

"No I haven't."

"Yes you have. Just like Grandmama."

"Grandmama's senile, Beth Ann."

"You've caused Daddy a lot of trouble. He has enough worries already."

My hand hurt. "Where's the tape recorder?"

Beth Ann looked up. Frowned.

"Look. I'm sorry. I'm sorry about everything. But I'm not goin' to get any sleep tonight. My fingers are killin' me. I wanna write a poem."

Her light eyebrows rose. I took my hand out of the jar, waved reddened fingers in the air, spilled some cold water on the rug. "I can't hold a pencil! Where's the tape recorder at?"

She pointed at the dresser with the nail polish brush. With my good hand, I took the machine out from under a black-and-gold crepe paper pompom.

"How late you gonna sit up?" Her question stopped me at the door.

"What's it matter? I'm suspended; can't go to school in the morning. You go on to sleep, kid. I'll stretch out on the living-room sofa if I feel sleepy."

"Betcha you're the only girl who ever got suspended from Richland Creek High School for *fightin'*."

I returned my sister's proud and wicked smile, and closed the door behind myself, then padded down the hall in my bare feet.

But the poetic catharsis did not come. I sat in the dark by the light of the low-tuned television set for hours, clicking the recorder off and on. The stream–of–consciousness stuff that came out was such a bunch of juvenile drivel that I popped myself woefully on the cheek with my good hand and erased the junk. My fountain of poetry seemed dried up entirely. I dozed and spoke and dozed and spoke, and finally heard:

I am a woman.
I am old with the century.
I am booking passage to the moon next week.
I was a woman.
I grew old with the century.
I married an admiral and took steamers to Europe.
I am a painter, my brush will not be stilled.

I've limned your image.

"Come soon," you told me, "Or you won't see me again."

I did not go.

I limn your image.

My tongue will not be still.

I am going to the moon with the Class of '67, geriatric in my weeds.

Let there be a seed.

It wasn't exactly a poem, and it wasn't exactly good. But it was Markie. I had been waiting for her to come out. Markie and me.

This is schizophrenia, I realized.

I clicked off the machine and sat with knees drawn up under my chin. The window fan droned in the kitchen and an electric clock whirred on the bookshelf by my ear.

Clocks don't tick any more, I observed. They whir. We're in a whole other kind of time.

It was days before they let me go back to school. I sat in Bill Damadian's class until the last debater had filed out, ignoring Bubba's parting glance and fiddling with my pencil until I could face Damadian alone.

"I think I'm going crazy," I told him without any preliminaries when he had bidden the last straggler goodnight and had come back in to flop onto his desk top.

He said nothing, just dragged his everpresent little ice chest out from under the desk and offered me a Coke. He puffed out his cheeks and lit a cigarette against all school rules.

I watched him. "Gimme one," I said.

He lit it for me. Its blue smoke uncoiled.

"What makes you think you're crazy?"

I hauled my heavy shoulderbag up onto the desk top and took out the tape recorder. Punched at a button listlessly. He listened.

"Nice," he commented when the poem had droned away. "Something of yours?"

"Sort of. I collaborate with a dead lady."

He smiled.

"I collaborate a lot with dead people lately."

"That doesn't make you crazy, lady."

I told him about the Bible incident. About the odd uncurling idea that had gone through my mind before I had decked Stanley Dawes. I looked up into his face from under the painstakingly-drawn eyeliner I had had to execute with my left hand that morning.

"Garnet Garnet." He smiled faintly. "Teenage crushes do not a crazy person make."

My voice was high and tight: "Can you honestly tell me that this is a teenage crush? If you can, I want to hear it. There's nothing that I would like to hear more at this point."

"Look—"

"My sister has a crush on Ringo Starr. She doesn't go around punching bigots and freaking out over Bible verses . . . And thinking she's some . . . some deceased old maid!"

He stared up at a flickering fluorescent light that was about to go out. The smoke from our cigarettes brushed it like a pale silk scarf.

"This is all I can think about, Bill." I looked at the swollen knuckles of my right hand. "Everything I do now is tied to it. I wear my hair up because that's the way women wore their hair in *his* day. I debate with *his* vocabulary. God help me, I even sit here and treasure the ache in my stupid hand because *he* once broke both of his. Even such an idiotic little coincidental tie as that seems precious to me."

"There's nothing crazy about imagination, Garnet Laney. You're an artist."

"So was *she*—Markie. So was Eliza Mackay, so was Mary— she did watercolors and wrote verse. So was *he,* when you come right down to it!"

"Yeah, but you have a streak of self-dramatization in—"

"There's *insanity* in my family, Bill! My grandmother—!"

"Your grandmother is *senile*, Garnet! Christ! Do you *want* to be crazy or what? You act disappointed when I try to tell you how normal I find you!" He held my eyes and wouldn't let them go. "Jesus. Lady, you have such an improbable personality, I can't tell you. You don't need to go around here all dressed up like a beatnik and acting like Blanche Dubois to get attention. Try to relax for a little bit. Give yourself a chance."

There was nothing I could say. I looked at the ceiling for help.

He stuffed some exam papers into his briefcase. I got to my feet and dragged myself to the door.

He looked up. "You got a ride, lady? I can give you a lift."

I could feel it coming. Stopped it in my throat. Then let it out on impulse and heard it rattle the windows: *"Goddammit Bill, don't you see what I'm saying? Haven't you been listening?"*

He sat small on his desk, leaning as if he had been blown back a little by the blast.

"Why does everybody always urge people to *talk* to them," I went on, voice stifled, "and then act like they don't hear what is being said?"

"Look. Sit down."

"You're the only one I can talk to about this," I muttered as I walked back to my seat with numb feet. "The only one, Bill. Don't turn me away, 'cause I'm not talking to anyone else."

He lit another cigarette and gave me one before I could ask.

"Garnet." He blew out thoughtful blue smoke after we had sat a long time in silence, getting lung cancer. "It's just possible that you might be a medium."

"A medium what?"

"A *medium*."

I sat there and thought about little old ladies with Ouija boards. Laughed finally at the ludicrousness of it and rubbed my tired face. "Is there such a thing?"

"I honestly don't know."

213

We sat there looking at one another. Things froze for me. The shared look could have lasted an hour. I didn't know.

"Well," I said finally as the implications sank in. "That beats being crazy all to hell."

"I think you could use some help here though, lady . . ."

My eyes narrowed. "A shrink?"

"Help I am not qualified to give you. Counseling."

I shook my head, vehement. "Out of the question. I'm not goin' to go to any shrink and worry my folks into an early grave. They've already got enough concerns. Totally out of the question."

He stood up abruptly and paced the room, spewing smoke like a wornout Buick, hands jingling agitatedly among the keys and coins in his pockets. He stopped at the open window and wheeled. "Jesus! You tell me you're crazy! What do you want me to do, Garnet? What do you want me to fucking *DO?*"

I didn't know exactly. "Just listen," I mumbled. "Just listen to me sometimes. I don't know."

He stood there at the window looking out at the night and I suddenly had a premonition of him dialing a phone number, tonight or tomorrow, asking my mother and father to come to his classroom some evening for a conference: Now about your daughter, I could hear him saying while Daddy's hand tightened on Mama's cold one. About your daughter. I think she's going through some kind of little problem.

Maybe I was more clairvoyant than I knew.

"No," I said to Damadian's back, to his hunched shoulders under the white dress shirt. A dark patch of perspiration on his back looked like the continent of South America. "You got to keep all I tell you confidential, Bill. I don't care how much you think I need help. You got to keep all this to yourself."

The irritated way he looked at me over his shoulder said plainly that he didn't "got to" do anything at the request of a minor. Not when his judgement dictated otherwise.

"You don't understand, Bill." I felt the odd strength rising. "You *have to.*"

I saw him react to my tone. My voice stayed low and cool, the idea flowing out now fully-formed and unshakable: "You have to," I repeated, not liking what I was about to do but doing it anyway because I had no choice, "because if you say anything at all about this to anybody, Bill—ANYBODY—I'll tell people that you tried to touch me—"

His head visibly jerked.

"—that you tried to take advantage . . ."

He fell back against the windowsill. Whispered to the overhead lights: "Oh *shit!*"

I felt a void. An ache. Thought of him small and well-meaning. Bill Damadian. Always well-meaning. I wanted to touch him. "I know you're trying to help me, Bill. But I can't let you help. Not in the way you plan."

He pulled his watchband out and let it snap back against his wrist. "You're a little bitch. You know that? A rotten little bitch."

"Funny." I stood up, weak. Squared my shoulders. "I would have used a stronger word."

"Get your things. I'll take you home."

I made myself not cry. It was the hardest thing I had ever done up until now.

We went out into the hot night and I wished that I could find a big bathroom somewhere, big enough so that I could crawl into it and hide in it until I was ready to come out. Or stay there with my books and my leg for the rest of my life, writing the same poems over and over.

Twenty-Nine

The Battle of Chancellorsville will be Lee's masterpiece, but it will be won at great cost.

General "Fighting Joe" Hooker has been assuring Lincoln all week that an enormous Federal victory is in his grasp. It certainly seems so. The formidable Union army is on the move across the Virginia countryside when Hooker makes his error, tangling up his troops in the miles of jungly woods known locally as the Wilderness. There is no talk of masterpieces when that piece of intelligence is reported to Lee's headquarters. Not when Goliath stumbles for a moment and David has only a heartbeat in which to sling his small stone.

General T.J. "Stonewall" Jackson bends over the map, hands on knees. Bright hard blue Scots-Irish eyes watch Lee's finger trace the unthinkable improvisation.

It occurs to Lee now that perhaps the man is trying to find the proper words to make the expected deferential objection. Jackson is a bona fide hero, a veteran's veteran, with the fierceness of a pit bull dog and the best military mind Lee has ever seen or heard tell of. Surely Jackson knows that only a lunatic would send off half his outnumbered army on such a route when facing a force the size of Hooker's.

Well then I'm crazy, Papa, Lee tells Lighthorse Harry in his mind. But I don't know what else to do. Did you know what this is like?

He waits for Jackson to look up, for the blue gaze to come out from under the dusty cap visor.

If Jackson has a better idea, Papa, I'm going to listen. If any barefooted private out there has a better idea, I will listen. What I am proposing sounds insane indeed, even to me. If *you* can hear me, don't listen.

But when Jackson finally raises his head, his crooked teeth are gleaming in a humorless smile. He touches the visor of his cap slowly, voice soft and utterly pleased. "My troops will move at four A.M., sir."

This man is as unbalanced as I am, Lee thinks. Looks up into Jackson's not-unhandsome hatchet face, the jutting brows and sharp nose and high cheekbones planed cleanly. Some people in this army do think Jackson mad, with his hypochondria and his religiosity and his inability to forgive. General "Pete" Longstreet thinks both of them are crazy, in fact, both Lee and Jackson; and he fears the way they bring out the madness in each other. Long-street would be reaching for a shot of whiskey right now if he could see the look that the two share.

Lee loves Jackson, simple as that. He is not old enough to be Jackson's father, but he worries about him the same way he worries about Custis and Rooney and Rob. Jackson is a perpetual misfit, an eccentric who has the knack of rubbing everybody the wrong way, and he doesn't seem to care whether he has any friends or not. An orphaned hillbilly from the mountains, he has raised himself to respectability by the force of his own implacable will and has made so many enemies doing it that Lee wonders how Jackson will manage in eventual civilian life. There is something in the man that reminds Lee of his own father—maybe a harshness, a gambler's willingness to lay everything on the line. Although Jackson seems to have little of the charm that Harry was noted for, his tender behavior around his little wife Anna and his infant daughter makes Lee wistful in an unnameable way.

They bed down near each other tonight and rise again before dawn, sipping coffee in the early May chill, pulling up empty wooden cracker crates to the fire and sitting close together to talk while the staff officers and a mapmaker whisper in the blackness. Jackson, enamored of the map, unfolds it and traces the chancy route again and again.

"This is the one thing, Ginral, that they'll never expect us to do." His bony finger finds Hooker's right flank and lands upon it with a stab. He laughs softly, his face like a sabre.

Lee holds up Jackson's finger in mid-march. "You know what I want done. And it's got to be done immediately. If you can pass your infantry from my right to Hooker's right—"

"We'll move at daylight. Wagons and all."

"You'll be seen. No help for it."

Jackson glances up. "What would you think if you were Hooker and your scouts saw us moving like that, Ginral? What would you think I was doin'?"

Lee grins. "Retreating."

The grin is contagious. Jackson's cheeks crease. The firelight on his bearded face is red and dangerous. "What force are you goin' to give me, sir?"

"You're the one who has to carry this out, General. What would you propose to make the movement with?"

"With my whole corps, sir." The answer is quiet and ferocious. "Let's make 'em really squeal while we're at it."

This thing is reckless enough to begin with, thinks Lee, tilting back his hat brim and rubbing his forehead. And now he wants to execute it with two-thirds of my entire army. "What would you leave me, then?"

"Anderson and McLaws."

Hooker will murder me where I sit once he breaks out of the

woods, Lee reasons, trying to rub life back into his tired eyes. If I'm going to strike him at all now, I have to give Jackson enough force to make it count.

He removes his hat and flops it onto a knee, running fingers through his gray hair. He can hear Jackson breathing.

"Well," he sighs finally, resolving to take the two incomplete divisions himself and hold off the entire Union Army while Jackson disappears into the woods with the rest. "Go on."

Jackson issues immediate orders through his staff and gets his raggedy troops started down the road to Catherine Furnace, thinking constantly of the Warrior God who toppled Jericho. Praying for his men and praying especially for that quiet grayheaded soldier back there in the clearing who is going to hold his position in the face of 138,000 men with only 14,000 Rebels. Jackson estimates that his march might take eight hours or so, eight hours during which Hooker will have the opportunity to eradicate the 14,000 so completely that it will be as if they had never existed.

He rides his scraggly sorrel by the columns. "Close up, men. Close it up."

Hooker is either overconfident or outgeneraled. The troops that make up his right flank are cooking supper that evening when rabbits and deer start to pour out of the woods, overrunning the campfires; and the Union boys are laughing and chasing down unexpected game, when hairraising shrieks sound from the trees and armed two-legged animals break upon them.

Bacon is trampled; stacked arms are inaccessible; lines of defense are impossible to form. Officers scream orders but there is nothing to do but to run for it, and the rebs are squatting, reloading, tearing cartridges open with their teeth and firing into the mob that gives mile after mile of ground.

Lee has heard the steady gunfire. He has been listening for it all day, praying for it, Anderson and McLaws bedeviling him with nervous couriers and the sun moving across the sky and going down while he sits like bait in his own trap. One determined push from Hooker will break the lines wide open.

Horses snort ominous warnings in the flower-smelling air. Agitated pickets potshot. It is near dark when the distant woods open up—Stonewall—and Lee leans, head down, against a scrubby oak, blood pressure going back down. He orders his puny divisions to attack Hooker's front.

"Ol' Stonewall's curled up their flank like a cheap rug, sir," Captain Wilbourn gives Lee his report in the early dark of that next morning, crouching by his commander's side in the weeds. "Hooker's whole right is plumb gone."

Lee sees something else in the man's dirty face. "What is it, Cap'n?"

"Stonewall's been wounded, sir. Shot in the arm, I hear. Don't know how."

Wilbourn sees emotion cross Lee's grave features, and then it's gone. Lee looks at Wilbourn's lathered horse, the white sweat on the dusty flanks. "See to your horse, Cap'n." He takes two biscuits from his saddlebags and hands them to the officer. "For you. Breakfast."

Wilbourn starts to gratefully protest but Lee is fetching him coffee like an orderly. There is no time for Lee to brood about Stonewall's injury because the implacable tomfool sun is going to be up soon and the two wings of the army are separated by two miles. I'm in a ticklish position, Robert Lee thinks as he puts the coffeepot back to the fire, the roasted corn "coffee" bubbling again. Does Hooker know it yet?

I know what I would do if I were Hooker. I'd re-form my right with all possible speed and then squash each part of Confederates before we can reunite. Jackson's corps has lost the initiative.

Jackson. Thomas Jackson. Dear God, it should have been me.

Listen to me for a moment, Dear God, and hear me out while I get these orders ready for a courier. No time to kneel properly, begging Your forgiveness, we'll just have to make do as we are . . . Tom Jackson has never done You any harm that I know of, and I've done You a great deal. A minnie ball in the arm is a painful business and Tom Jackson doesn't deserve it. We cannot spare him, Dear God, not even for a week.

He unhorses Jeb Stuart of the cavalry and places him in command of Jackson's corps, sitting stranded on Hooker's smashed flank in the woods. Stuart has orders to push eastward. No time now for the banjo: he sings, "Old Joe Hooker, won't you come out and fight?" a capella in his ringing baritone as he throws the last of the reserves into the push.

"Ginral Lee knows what to do," the troops keep telling each other as they trot into the undergrowth at the double-quick with their shiny Enfields capped and ready. "Marse Robert knows what to do."

Lee moves Anderson west to meet them, trying to close the two ends of this iron ring with his bare hands.

Lee of the legends: Fifty-six years old, just a fraction under six feet tall in his size 4 1/2 C cavalry boots, one hundred and seventy pounds when he has enough to eat. He has weathered the recent heart attack very well, the medical officer unable to diagnose the trouble for what it really is. *The doctors have been tapping me all over like an old steam boiler before condemning it,* he writes to Mary. *But they pronounce me tolerable sound. . . .*

Actually, he is nowhere near sound. The occasional twinges in his chest make him doubt himself sometimes, and the doctors warn him against stress. What a laugh. He decides he has rheumatism, because dwelling upon any other explanation of the pains in his arms and back is pointless. What does it matter, anyway? He has never expected to survive this war. What the hell.

The heart trouble manifests itself in one unforgettable aspect: the rather sudden blossoming of his iron gray hair into snowy white. Without his hat he is recognizable at great distances, and the troops scramble to get a good look at him whenever he rides by. They speculate upon the holiness of his face and trade stories in camp about how he sends all of the food and supplies, given him by admirers, to hospitals for the wounded. Some of them tell of receiving socks knitted by the mysterious Mrs. Lee and many of them have felt a warm hand on their shoulders before battle, turning flabbergasted to see their commander standing next to them without fanfare, sharing the hailstorm of artillery or bad weather. He doesn't smile much and he doesn't talk much, they notice. And when he does speak, his voice is very slow. But he sure to God *thinks* a hundred times faster than he can speak. And he looks a lot younger up close.

They know he's been sick. He sure as hell doesn't *look* sick. Few photographs really capture his likeness. They record a rather average-looking individual, most of them; what the soldiers write about and remember all their lives is a white-haired vision. They revel in the beauty they see in him.

Sometimes he will rein up and take off his hat to the gawking boys, and they accept that salute from him with yells that leave them spent and hoarse.

He is dimly aware of the effect he has upon his men but doesn't understand it. Generals come and go, after all. I would not be in command of this army now, he thinks, had Joe Johnston not been wounded. And when I am hit, they will fight as well for the next man as they have for me. That next man should definitely be Jackson. I'll have to put a bug in the President's ear the next time I'm in Richmond. Please, not that blockhead Braxton Bragg. I shall make it a point to come back and haunt him if he puts someone like Bragg in charge of my boys here. I shall clank and stomp and wail for all I'm worth.

Death frightens him, yes, but not nearly as much as bungling this war. Whenever his courage gets a little thin, whenever artillery shells have exploded too close, he jots down little memoranda to himself at odd hours, private musings and Stoic quotations from *Marcus Aurelius,* and Bible passages—all about the rightness of a soldier's death. Tucked into his saddlebags, his will sons find the papers there and decipher the elegant scrawl. They will speak of him with pride and will lead visitors to the grave, where he will lie forever in the free soil of Virginia, in the Confederate States of America, in the nation of his children.

Just take me before I foul up, he reminds God, strengthened and serene. You know best. Whenever You see that fatal error coming, say to Yourself 'Robert Lee is putting his foot in it and it is well nigh time he covers himself with glory,' and send me a quick piece of metal. Better yet, send two. I am difficult to deactivate.

But now at this moment he is very much activated, galloping breakneck into the Chancellorsville clearing, Traveller carrying him with surefooted speed to join Jeb Stuart in the treeless space where the Chancellor house burns like hellfire. Musketry has set the Wilderness aflame. Tree sap crackles overhead like lightning. Stuart waves his plumed hat, howling victory, white teeth gleaming in his reddish beard like a wolf's fangs.

The smoke-blackened soldiers see Lee materialize against the ferocious inferno engulfing the house and the woods. The graceful hand lifts the wide-brimmed hat from the white hair, the hard thighs grip the rearing silver gelding. The graverobber scream of their war yell carries insanity to the sky with the smoke. They whoop, thousands of them.

He cannot think of Thomas Jackson now, who, unknown to him, is dying of his wounds and pneumonia. This godawful noise, this crazy pandemonium, does not permit thought. This is the highest, most perfect celebration of The Present outside of a bedroom, and it is better than laudanum or wine or sex and nobody who has sat out a war will ever understand how crystalline a moment can be.

He can hear his boys, the wounded ones lying in the leaves and the able ones who come running up to Traveller's flank to hug his knees and thighs. He hears with dizzy awe the earsplitting love from them all. He waves his hat in tribute to them, young men in their floppy rags, toothbrushes in their lapel buttonholes, dirty hair sticking out every-which-way from the holes in their hats, until they get hold of his hands to shake and kiss, leaving their saliva and blood on him.

He has yearned for a home all his life and has found it among these thousands of sons.

I will not fail these men, he vows as his vision blurs red, Traveller spinning him in the hysteria while hands grab at him and clutch. Dear God, I swear it: I will not fail these men.

Thirty

The school term ended and we all went home. And Grandmama Moser decided one day that week to throw her food at the wall. On my seventeenth birthday, Mama and Daddy drove up to Rock Hill to fetch her. By nightfall she had been admitted to the Columbia Hospital.

Beth Ann and I sat outside on the hospital steps in the viscous muggy dark, waiting. Inside the fan-cooled lobby we could hear the squeak-squeak of nurses' shoes on the tiled floor and the public address system whining out the names of unknown doctors. Outside, the fireflies flickered among the banana trees and the traffic swished by in a hazy superheated swoon.

My sister and I had not exchanged a word since our parents had disappeared inside with Grandmama's maid, Nancy. I could hear Beth Ann sighing. I fanned myself with my tortoiseshell fan and read my book by streetlight, troubled, brushing away small moths that lit upon the page. Beth Ann stood up finally to run after fireflies in her bare feet.

"You gon step on a piece of glass," I called after her.

She glanced back once over her shoulder. Then she ran down the sidewalk and out over the dewy grass without a word.

I thought, None of this is my fault, is it? I wish it were. It'd make more sense somehow. I never wanted to cause any worry for Mama and Daddy, but they're worried anyway.

I looked at the book in my lap while gospel music from a car radio tamped down the dull noises from inside the building. A sudden hot wind, moist like steam, blew the pages open to a new chapter and the lines from a letter written long before even Grandmama Moser had been born: *Oh, Markie, Markie, when will you ripen?*

"I'm seventeen," I muttered out loud to the letter. "Pretty durn ripe."

Oh, Markie, Markie—

I rubbed my dripping temples. "Bill can't be right. Part of me can't be her. Part of me can't be you or anybody. Can't be. Can it?"

Can it? Oh Lord, I don't know. I haven't any answers. I can't even ask the questions.

What in God's name can be taking them so *long* in there?

A shadow fell over the page and I looked up. My father stood on the top step, hands in pockets, perspiring and uncomfortable in his city clothes. He pulled at the knees of his trousers and sat down on the step beside me. "Hey," he said. "You hungry?"

"Is Grandmama goin' to die, Daddy?"

Beth Ann had come softly out of the dark on bare feet and stood now in the shadows at the bottom of the steps, rubbing one bare sole against her other ankle.

Daddy looked at her. "If she does, it's because she wants to. Doctor says there ain't a thing wrong with her, clinically."

Beth Ann chewed her lip. "C'mere, Daddy," she said finally. "I think I've found a glow worm in the grass. What does a glow worm look like?"

But he was looking at me, lighting a cigarette, stuffing the matches back into his shirt pocket. "Azalee's not taking this too well, y'all . . . I expect a lot out of you girls the next few days . . ."

"C'mere, Daddy," Beth Ann kept insisting. "I think I found a glow worm over yonder."

He got heavily to his feet and took her by the hand. I watched them move silently off in the dark over the sparkling grass, Daddy's lanky farmer's gait contrasting with the coltish long-legged steps of my blonde sprite of a sister. They disappeared under the black dark of the banana trees.

I sat there with my book, unable to follow. I felt like a passerby at the scene of an auto accident who wants to help but is mortally scared of all the blood.

Grandmama's voice came out of my memory: Nobody needs me, and that's the God's own truth!

She's right, I thought, hot breezes loosening my pinned-up hair. I don't need her. I took her mementos but I don't need her for a thing. I'm a selfish bitch. I don't like myself anymore.

Who am I?

The book upon my knees fell open again. Pages fluttered. I read:

You have not written to me for nearly four months and I believe it is equally long since I have written to you. On paper, Markie, I mean, on paper. But oh, what lengthy epistles have I indited to you in my mind! Had I any means to send them you would see how constantly I think of you. I have followed you in your pleasures and your duties, in the house and in the streets, and accompanied you in your walks to Arlington, and in your search after flowers. Did you not feel your cheeks pale when I was so near you?

"I am not pale and I'm nobody that you know, Robert." I spoke to the wind, thinking nonetheless of Bill Damadian for some reason, some fleeting related memory that I could not quite put my finger on.

I heard Beth Ann's chatter coming from a little distance away and I snapped the book shut. She and my silent father trudged towards me, hand in hand. The tired sag of Daddy's shoulders cut me like a blade. Beth Ann twittered beside him, cool and buoyant because she could not be otherwise. My sister was not constituted for darkness.

I am not at all like them, I remarked silently to the God I didn't believe in. What else did You do to me when You gave me this funny leg?

I made my voice light as they neared: "Did ya'll find the glow worm?"

"Naaaah." Beth Ann plopped down on the bottom step. "It was near the sidewalk down there at the corner, but it's gone now. Musta been a cigarette butt."

Daddy's hooded eyes swiveled around to meet mine. I gnawed at my cuticle until it tore into living flesh.

"I want you to behave yourself, Garnet," he said. "You got any problems, you come to me. Give your mama a rest, now. You hear me?"

"Yessir."

He patted my hand. "You got to punch out any more big-mouths, you come tell me and let *me* punch 'em out. All right?"

I laughed because he wanted me to. I thought: He won't say anything from here on. He'll keep his worries to himself. Mama must be feeling pretty bad.

But I have the power of words, me the big poet. The debater. There are things I could say right now about Grandmama that could destroy everybody's composure, even Beth Ann's. I could talk about loneliness, and what it must be like to grow old, and how wounding a death is for the survivors. Especially a nebulous death-in-life like this one.

My my my. I feel my own cold, bitchy eyes at the point of misting up. I do have the power to wound. I could say: I don't care.

I suddenly visualized Lee young, as in the painting: Lieutenant Lee, with his naive eyes that had read happy novels and thought they knew how the world worked.

Oh me, we have this much in common, you and I. We do all

the wrong things for the right reasons. You have the power to unwittingly wreak havoc on a colossal scale, I on a somewhat more mundane level.

I went into the hospital corridor to the phone booth on Grandmama's floor. I had remembered the thing about Bill Damadian, the formless memory that had struck me earlier. I was about to put a dime into the pay phone when I saw Daddy coming.

"Happy birthday, Garn," he said, recalling what day it was.

I looked up into the rough tanned face and found irony. I smiled. I bent down to hide the dime in my Mary Quant shoe.

"I'm going to take us all out to supper tonight for your birthday, if we ever get out of here." We walked slowly back to the door of my grandmother's room. "Call ol' Bubba and ask him along, if you want."

"I think Bubba's dating Jo Barringer now, Daddy. And we can't go nowhere, Beth Ann didn't bring her shoes."

He leaned against the wall while I thought about Bill Damadian, remembering the something he had mentioned a long time ago. Nancy the maid came around the corner from the nurses' station, black face grim, jaw set. I wondered if some white women had maybe been giving her trouble about using the ladies' room. She wasn't happy, that much was clear. Daddy opened the door to Grandmama's room for her. She passed in with muted thanks and did not look up.

Daddy stirred. "I guess I better go back in. See if I can't get Azalee out."

"Beth Ann in there?"

"Don't know. They wouldn't give her a visitor's card. Said too many of us were up here already. I think she might be in the lounge with a Co'-Cola . . ."

A howl sounded from inside the room. I could hear no words in the sound but I sensed them: No one needs me anymore. Why am I alive?

Guilty sweat sprang out of my pores and ran down my nose. I wiped my face on my bare arm. A clatter of glass came from the room and Nancy pushed her way out, clapping her net-and-flowers Sunday hat back onto her head where it had been knocked askew. She fumbled indignantly in her purse for bus fare.

"Dirty nigger!" screamed Grandmama unseen in her thin voice. The door swung shut behind the maid but still I could hear it: "Dirty nigger!"

Nancy shot Daddy a quick look. "I'm about two seconds from *quittin'* this job, Mr. Laney."

"Wouldn't blame you. Need a ride anywhere?"

She shook her head. "I got a brother lives over near the Benedict campus. I be stayin' with him, close by. Doctor say Miz Moser be here for a long time."

Beth Ann came pattering up eating a candy bar as Nancy strode off down the hall. Another muffled outburst came from within the hospital room.

"I'll see y'all in a little bit," said Daddy with his hand on the door handle. "Lemme go check on your mama."

I saw Beth Ann's brows lift. She made slurping noises as she licked at the chocolate melting in her hot fingers. "You better break out the strait-jackets."

Daddy grinned. "Sounds more like I'll need a whip and a chair."

He disappeared into the sinister room and we stood there together in silence. Beth Ann slurped at her candy. The slurps got louder. I looked at her eyes. The kid was doing it on purpose.

"Ain't you gonna tell me to stop?" she muttered after a while.

I sighed.

Slurp slurp.

"Whaddaya want me to say, Beth Ann? That this is all my fault? Okay. It's all my fault. I did this deliberately. I made Grandmama flip out. Through voodoo. With poison pen letters. Whatever you like."

She stopped making the noises but her maddening blonde brows went up again. I fastened onto her eyes—level, serious. "What do you want me to *do*, Beth Ann?"

She shrugged. "What does it matter? You don't care about any of this, anyway."

"Don't care about any of *what?*"

The sticky childish fingers took in the whole hospital with a gesture. "This. Grandmama. Mama and Daddy."

I pushed back my hair. Angry. "The devil you say."

"You're a million miles away. You sit with us and eat with us and you just go through the motions. You don't give a durn. You just wanna go to New York and let the rest of us rot here and you couldn't care less."

The small portion of truth in that assessment hurt me. "But I *do* care, Beth Ann." I heard pleading in my own voice. I hated to plead in front of her, I hated to look weak when I should be wanting to slap the silly smile right off the kid's face. "I do care about all of you. Why do families *do* this to each other?"

Beth Ann balled up her candy wrapper. Sweat dripped down the channel of my spine under my cotton blouse and rolled past my bra hooks.

I touched her with a quick hand, needing to touch something real and breathing, afraid of a rebuff. She pulled away from my reaching. And then Grandmama's grief came howling at us down the hot airless hallway along with the muted radio gospel music and the soft black laughter of the orderlies. We clutched each other. Beth Ann's small hands dug into my forearms.

"I'm scared, I'm scared," she muttered, rigid in my arms now. I could feel her shoulderblades like little wooden staves, unbending but fragile. "I'm scared Garn and you're not helping."

I shivered. "I'm scared too."

"I don't wanna see Mama go through this, Garn. I don't wanna see her and Daddy ever get old and unhappy like Grandmama. Ever. Ever."

"You see?" My teeth chattered. "You see? There's such a thing as caring too much. It makes cowards wanna run away. Cowards like me."

"Well I don't wanna see you go off anywhere where I can't

follow. You always used to run off and leave me when I was real little. And I'd cry because I couldn't keep up."

I hugged her tighter.

"You get further and further away every day. Don't go off where I can't follow, Garn."

"I'll try not to. I'm trying not to," I lied.

She stepped back away from me, regaining her old bravado. "This is gonna be a long summer. I wish I was old enough to drink."

"Go in there!" I pushed her to the sickroom door. "Git Mama and Daddy outta there and let's go hit Burger King."

She saluted grimly and let herself through the door. I waited until she was inside and then I ran flying down the hall to the phone booth. Fumbled in my shoe for the dime.

Bill Damadian had mentioned something to me on the day he had asked me to join the debate club. I had been so moony-eyed over Bubba that I had let it go in one ear and out the other. But a piece of it must have lodged in my brain nonetheless, because something in the Markie letter had begun to dredge it up. Hadn't Bill mentioned something on that spring day many weeks ago about a debate trip after school was out? Some kind of debate shindig that he wanted to take his club members to. In August. In Washington, D.C.

I dropped the dime into the slot with steady fingers. Bill had probably forgotten, it had probably been just a recruiting ploy. All notions of debate stuff had probably passed right out of his head as soon as he had locked up his classroom for the summer to go home to Italian Betty.

He said he had to go to the Library of Congress to work on his graduate degree or something, I remembered. He's got to go up there anyway, then, doesn't he?

I knew that I could no longer let my obsession drag on inconclusively. I would have to confront it. I walled myself inside the glass phone booth and dialed.

Bill would probably be playing on the floor with little

Tommy and the dog when the phone rang. But with my new and disturbing ascendency over him, I knew that I would make him remember his Washington notions.

And I would hold him to them.

Washington, D.C., was right across the river from Arlington.

Hold on, Robert, I thought as I could hear the Damadian phone ringing. I'm on my way. I'm not going to let you down this time. This life.

Show me what to do when I get there.

Thirty-One

Everybody will later blame everybody else for what has gone wrong at the Bloody Angle. Ewell will blame Armistead Long for moving the guns back from the toe of the salient, and Allegheny Johnson will blame Dick Ewell for not reacting to his reports of heavy Union troop movements in the dark woods in his front.

Hindsight notwithstanding, the Confederate lines are broken in the dead of night on May 11, 1864, near Spotsylvania, where Lighthorse Harry Lee was once jailed. And all the Yankees on the planet are breaking through now. Nearly two thousand exhausted Rebels are killed or taken prisoner as they wake from their muddy sleep in the fog.

General John B. Gordon will live to write about it, Gordon the thirty-two-year-old Georgia ex-miner with a clear eye and a way with words. He advances a single brigade from his division to check the enemy pouring through the gap. Gordon screams at his staff, over the sheet-lightning of musketry, to bring up the last two brigades and form a breakline. Gordon's division constitutes General Lee's only reserves. Lee's orders are calm: Throw them in.

Outnumbered by Grant by more than three to one this spring, Lee has built the most extensive system of field fortifications ever seen in warfare to nullify Grant's numerical advantage. But digging in like this in front of Richmond means an end to maneuvering, and sometimes young General Gordon buries his irreplaceable dead and wonders what tomorrow will bring.

We have only a sword, he thinks. And we are being bludgeoned with a sledgehammer.

Tonight he wrestles his pitiful reserves into position, the wet fog streaming down the back of his neck as the sky grows lighter. The unseen Union artillery lobs shells into his ranks and his horse steps over a fresh corpse with white rafter ribs. Gordon can see the glistening viscera inside like chicken parts.

The Union gunners are finding their targets, and pieces of people, metal, and belt buckles, and soft sticky red meat, are beginning to fly through the wet air. The men are veterans; their heads don't flinch, but their eyes do. A boy who can't be much over fifteen regards the empty space in front of him with the stolid expression of an animal.

You can tell our dead from their dead a mile off, thinks Gordon. Their dead are always naked because we loot the bodies for pants and shoes after the shooting stops. Their dead turn black in the sun and putrify fast—ours just dry up, so dessicated are they by their scant diet. The Fed and the Cornfed. Our poor scarecrows are mummified before they die.

"When you go in, aim low. Fire at their knees!" Gordon can't hear his own voice; he knows he is shouting by the pressure at his neck. A teenage corporal throws a homemade deck of cards into the weeds, unwilling for Mama to find this sinful kit among his personal effects. Somebody laughs.

Gordon pats his own pockets, wanting to die with the daguerreotype of his Georgia lady. They pick off the officers first, he knows.

A shell explodes overhead. Too high.

"You c'n do bettern'n that, Yank!" guffaws a dirty Carolinian.

The boy with the animal eyes looks up. Then turns eyes-right, with a glimmer of something across his face in the fog. It makes Gordon wheel. And then jerk at the reins of his mount.

A horseman rides out of the dark mist, a silver man on a silver horse. Chills go down the back of Gordon's wet neck.

And the men start to make a sound like the sea.

The hoofbeats of the gray gelding are drowned out in the gunfire. The hooves pound soundlessly over the swirl of mist, and Gordon feels the blood drain from his face. He has looked into the cold black eyes as the rider passes and has seen nothing in them, no sign of recognition.

"GENERAL LEE?" he shouts. Gives his mount the spur.

Lee has ridden to the center of the battle line, reining Traveller up with his face towards the enemy. The proud profile etches itself against the growing light, static like a statue. Gordon sees the gauntleted right hand come up and take the gray hat by the crown, lifting it off, and the blowing white hair blazes in the morning. The troops roar.

A lathered horse splashes at Gordon's right, there is shouting — Young Colonel Walter Taylor, knees covered with mud, dark face red and panicked: *"God's sake, help me Ginral Gordon, I can't do nothin' with him. Marse Robert's gonna lead your charge!"*

Mounted officer, thinks Gordon, a mounted officer like *that* one ain't got a chance. That horse and that whiteheaded man are about the most conspicuous target God ever made.

Taylor's mouth is at Gordon's ear until his curvetting horse pulls him away. *"Don't put your hands on him, he's strong as a damn ox and he'll fight you."*

God in heaven, thinks Gordon.

"— second time he's done this. He tried to take Gregg's Texans in last week."

Taylor fights his horse, shells plow up the ground all around and the animal's eyes roll.

Gordon does not wait for Taylor. He bangs his heels into the side of his mount and makes for Traveller at a gallop, before Lee's golden spurs can connect. Time seems to stop. Gordon's eyes rivet upon the small booted feet in the stirrups where the silver sides of the horse breathe in and out.

Faces blur white as he flies past the troops and rides across Traveller's front, hand grabbing for the right cheek of the bit. The gray horse tosses his head and pulls Gordon half out of the saddle but he hangs on, eyes lifting to face the chiseled rider.

You can't fight the whole goddam Yankee army by yourself, old man! he thinks in a panic. Tell us what to do and let us do the fighting. We'll come to a full stop if you get yourself killed.

"I ain't gon let you lead my men, sir. Now that's my job!" He screams to the expressionless black eyes. *"These men here are Georgians, Virginians, Carolinians. They've never failed you on any field, sir. Now you know that! They ain't gon fail you now!"*

The shells are coming in and finding their targets. Gordon hears shrieks and the *clump* of bone smashing. Lee's mouth moves. Gordon can make out no words. The face is too serene, deep crow's feet at the eyes unstressed. Gordon wonders: Has he lost his mind? Doesn't he know he won't get two hundred yards before they cut him down with a million minnie balls?

Gordon can hear him now: "Get out of my way, General, or I'll set you afire!" It isn't a loud shout but it carries. The black eyes flicker something deliberate and fatal.

Great God, thinks Gordon. He knows.

He's doing what he thinks he's got to, devil take the consequences.

Lee reaches for the restraining hand but can't make the distance and Gordon sees his jaws tighten. He thumps Traveller in the sides with his spurs and the horse tries to rear, throwing foaming saliva all over Gordon's straining arm and shoulder.

Taylor comes pounding up, hands groping for whatever he can grab.

"We ain't gonna fail you, sir!" Gordon shouts again, head turn-

ing in desperation to the troops behind him, trying to make eye contact with as many thunderstruck soldiers as he can. *"Will we, boys?"*

"Hell, no!" yells an old sergeant.

"General Lee to the rear, Sergeant," Gordon orders.

"General Lee to the rear, sir!" the noncom salutes in affirmation, and breaks ranks to grab Traveller's bridle.

The boys behind take up the cry and become a mob, surging like a wave of reaching hands and openmouthed faces, as they press in on all sides and turn the prancing gray horse around by the force of their arms and backs. Pushing and pulling. Some of them clinging to the reins or to the legs in the stirrups, opening a passage to the rear and passing the horse from hand to hand. Gordon watches the white head recede into the distance, sees it turning always over its shoulders to face the enemy, arms pinioned by tattered muddy boys with terror in their faces.

They'll stop the Feds, Gordon realizes. We'll stop 'em right here. We'll stop 'em for Him.

He puts a hand to his face. He is weeping.

Thirty-Two

I watched the Virginia countryside flash past the open car window as if it were doing the rolling and the Valiant was standing still. Bill had the radio on; the Lovin' Spoonful was singing about summer in a city.

Bubba Hargett and David Dale Baker traded jokes in the back seat. Bawdy jokes. I didn't listen.

"See if the tarp's coming loose!" Bill was shouting at me over the wind and the radio.

I stuck my hand up out of the window and felt for the flapping edge of the canvas that covered our luggage on the auto top. The August sun on the chrome stripping burned my forearm. Even the seventy-mile-an-hour wind couldn't blow the heat away.

"S'okay," I mumbled, drawing my hand back inside.

"What?"

"S'okay!"

Bill glanced over at me with a peculiar look. I caught it out of the corner of my eye. I knew that there were things he wanted to say to me. But he wouldn't say them in front of the others.

I had told him the same lies that I had told my parents: that debating might someday prove a good way to get a college scholarship, should I prove good enough at it; that I and Bubba and David Dale owed it to ourselves to attend this workshop with the cream of highschool competitors from all over the country; that the trip itself, to the nation's capital city, would be educational. But I knew that Damadian wouldn't take long to figure out a more fundamental motive.

"I feel right bad, leaving ya'll like this," I had told my father truthfully the night before my departure, throwing my long granny gown into the little suitcase on the bed. "Hope Grandmama'll be okay. I'll call you while we're on the road, let ya'll know where we are so that you can reach us if anything . . ."

He pulled the door closed behind him, shutting out the sound of the television that came from the livingroom, now converted into a sickroom for Grandmama Moser where the old woman sat and stared at Merv Griffin, unseeing. "We'll be okay," he said. "Azalee's a little tired. But . . ."

I waited.

He lowered his voice. "But I'm glad you got a hobby that takes you out of the house, Garnet. If ol' Miz Moser at least had a *hobby* . . . She don't even knit, she just sits there and stares at the walls."

I went to him then and had hugged him.

"Just come back safe," he smiled, patting my scrawny back. "We'll be okay. Just have yourself some fun and come back safe."

I don't know, I don't know, I told myself as I rode in the overheated car and Virginia rolled by me. I don't know if I'll come back safe or not.

"You guys ready to stop yet?" Damadian was yelling to the back seat.

"Just find us a motel with a swimmin' pool," said David Dale.

"You tired, Bubba?"

"I can take over drivin' again for ya, Coach, if that's what you mean."

I leaned towards Damadian. "How far away are we?"

"Sign back there on the Interstate said about sixty miles. We could stop any time now. Hit D.C. in the morning when we're fresh."

"Let's go on into town!" David Dale leaned over the seat back, his large face at my ear. "Sample the big city night life. What's the drinking age in Washington?"

Damadian grinned into the rearview mirror. "Your parents'd have my ass. You stay out of bars, sonny."

Bubba leaned out of the window, the wind combing his shiny hair. "Motel rates might be cheaper out here in the boonies."

The sun was getting low and it glared into my eyes. Virginia was making me nervous. We were rolling through the battlefields now, rolling over a sign-crowded highway where artillery horses had once dragged limbered twelve-pounders. I could almost see them out there in the dusty heat among the mirage shimmers.

These haunted old fields, I thought, growing cold. I reached over and turned up the car radio.

"Registration for the workshop doesn't start until tomorrow," Bill shouted back at Bubba over the music. "Opening dealies are tomorrow night. We'll get there in plenty of time if we stay in one of these—"

"Oh for God's sake!" I broke in, exasperated, nervous. "Then stop! Does *everything* have to be a debate around here?"

Bill became quiet. The quiet lasted well after I was settled into a Holiday Inn single next to the big room Bill was sharing with the boys. I was nervous still, glum and chilly in the air conditioning, taking my toothbrush out of my little overnight kit when the knock came at my door.

I opened it and Bill shuffled through. I had known it would be Bill.

"Want to go grab a bite in the coffee shop?" He stood uneasily on my carpet with his hands in his pockets.

I put down my toothbrush. "Where are the guys?"

"Doing bellyflops in the pool."

"Wait a minute," I muttered. "Let me brush my hair."

He sat on the bed. I had hoped that he would wait in his own room, but he flicked on the color television set. "Wow," he called. "They've got color sets here. This place is costing us a fortune."

My electric hair crackled around my scalp as I pulled the brush through it. "You shouldn't let David Dale pick the motels. He has expensive tastes."

Bill lit a cigarette. Eyed me as I moved from the dresser. "You have a good summer?" he asked finally.

"Tolerable."

"Sorry about your grandmother's illness. When you called that night in June—"

"I just wanted to hear you say that this trip was still on. I needed something to look forward to."

I put my hairbrush down. He kept sitting there, crunching the mattress on the very edge of the immaculate bed.

"Ready, Bill?"

"I've been doing some reading over the summer." He fumbled at his pockets for a light. Another cigarette glowed orange at its tip. "Jung and so on."

"Jung At Heart, huh?"

"Puns do not become you, lady."

I took three bangle bracelets out of my luggage and slipped them over a ringed hand. "I would kill *babies* right now for a cup of coffee."

He laughed and accompanied me to the coffee shop. No more was said about Carl Jung.

But I sat up late that night in my room, busy with a poem, coffee and adrenaline making sleep impossible. I didn't want to risk sleep, anyway. I was afraid that I would have strange dreams out here in these haunted places.

I still did not know when I would make my move, how I would manage to give Bill the slip so that I could go to Arlington alone. But I knew that a way would be found. And I realized that I was frightened, a little.

Time is made of heartbeats, that's all it is.
And if it's not that, then it is Nothing at all.
Where will I go when my heartbeats stop?
When time isn't?
The ground won't hold me, I know that.
I am electric, I belong to the skies.

I scrawled the words hurriedly, trying not to think about tomorrow, knowing that my poem was awkward and puerile but rushing into it for solace. And then the lines segued.

Footsteps quick on the floor by your room.
The house is empty.
You are somewhere down the hill
Across the river, in wool and brass
And your distance.
I pause at your door and go in to sit
In the clock-ticking stillness,
To be alone with your absence.

The Markie poem again. The Arlington poem. I stopped and read, internalizing the images of the empty hallway and the deserted stillness.

This is where I will be tomorrow, I thought. Alone in a hallway outside a room that has been empty for a hundred years.

My hands fumbled at my shoulder bag and extracted a photographic reproduction torn from a book, the edge of the page raw and ragged. My eyes slowly fell. Sleepy. I turned the photo over and over in my hands.

Maybe I am only a neurotic kid with a Jungian crush who is going through an identity crisis. But, hello . . . I know you. And I do love you so much, I said to the image in the gray tunic with the field gear slung across his body, face calm, one gloved hand on the hilt of his sword. Slim and straight and elegant, hair and beard gray but face still young — General Robert E. Lee, larger than life,

243

photographed early in 1863 before the first heart attack—winning. He is humiliating every army that Lincoln sends against him.

I felt empty and foolish and was glad that there was no one around to see the look on my face.

If only I could touch you. If only I could help you in some small way. I think I would gladly trade my life for that.

I turned the photograph over again and started to slip it back into my bag. There was a pencil mark on the back. Just an accidental line that cut across the print. I looked at the line closely because it went through the word "infinite". An inadvertent underlining. I put the photo away.

I sat on the bed for a long time remembering Einstein. I took out a pencil, looked at the room. All of the doors and windows were closed, the air conditioning hissing through some unseen vent that I could ignore. The room was the inside of a cube.

My eyes followed the wall surface to the ceiling. Down the opposite wall. Across the floor: The inside of a cube. I was inside a folded surface with no beginning and no end.

I was thinking like an engineer.

Suddenly I stood up and went to the closed white door of the bathroom and drew a thin horizontal line on the paint. I stepped back, taking several deep steadying breaths, and then addressed the line again. I made it longer until it stretched some four inches. I could hear myself breathe, a harsh rushing in the silence.

Impulsively, I drew a small crossmark on the line, about an inch from one end, and labeled it with the initials R.E.L. Then I matched it with a similar mark an inch from the other end. My hand shook a little as I wrote G.M.L. by the little cross. As an afterthought, I put arrowheads on both ends of the line, so that now it became something that pointed in two different directions.

And then I stepped back and dropped the pencil into my purse, thinking.

"This is probably how Nietzsche went nuts," I said when I understood what I had done.

There it was upon my infinite wall, a penciled timeline of human history. Time had begun at some point, had produced Robert E. Lee, had moved on to Garnet Moser Laney, and then it would someday end. Or *not* end—I could extend both ends all around the room until they touched and became a circle, as the arrowheads indicated.

Infinity, the never-ending inside of my room, that white paint that covered all the walls and the doors and made a continuous surface, touched my timeline equally at all points. As far as the interior of my room was concerned, the direction of the line meant nothing. It could be read from right to left as easily as from left to right.

I sat down carefully on the bed, wishing for one of Bill's cigarettes, staring unblinkingly at the pencil diagram until my eyes blurred.

If there is indeed a Consciousness in infinity—God, the Collective Unconscious—then it would make no difference to It that Robert Lee was dead in 1966. Because Infinity touches 1866 and 1807 and 1870 in the same way that It touches me.

They taught us in Sunday School to pray for things to happen; pray for rain so that Daddy's crops won't dry up, pray for Granddaddy to get well. Prayer for future things, that's what they taught us.

But if Infinity has a Consciousness, and if we can indeed influence It sometimes through mental energy or whatever the hell prayer really is, then couldn't I—Couldn't I pray for the *past?*

I sat there looking at Einstein's railroad track, drawn on my bathroom door.

We stood there with him in our seersucker and gingham and madras buttoned-down finery and sneaked little stares at the kids, boys mainly, who ploughed masterfully through the crowd with their short haircuts and dark Republican Brooks Brothers ensembles, gilt monograms on the leather briefcases that they carried like weapons.

"National competitors, young'uns. Git your eyes full," David Dale mumbled deep in his throat. "We look like fleas on a greyhound."

"Yeah," Bubba said.

"Aren't you awful hot in that?" David Dale asked, eying my long granny dress as I pinned my name tag to the gingham. He finished filling out his registration form and handed it to the woman behind the desk.

"Let Garn alone," said Bubba, hands stuck in the pockets of his seersucker suit as he rocked back and forth on his heels and toes in the hubbub around the desk. People filled the place, pouring in the doors of the student center at American University, letting the air conditioning out. "Garnet's a poet. Can't afford to let any of these jerks think she's just another debate queen. Christ, y'all. Would you look at these guys?"

There was both contempt and awe in his voice.

I nodded. "Junior lawyer-land."

"What's your name tag say, Bo?" Bubba leaned over to glance at the name sticker that the woman behind the desk handed to David Dale. "I ain't got one yet."

"Well, git over here and git in line," said David Dale.

"'David D. Baker, Richland Creek High School, South Carolina. Observer,'" read Bubba as David Dale hustled him into a space in the queue ahead of the crowd. "That's right nice. They spelled everything right and everything."

"My buddy here has bad kidneys, y'all let him through," David Dale was telling well-dressed people as he bodily inserted Bubba into their midst. "I won't be responsible if he gives out on us, if y'all know what I mean."

Bubba's face creased up in amused embarrassment.

I laughed. "Where's Damadian?"

David Dale stood on tiptoe and poked his considerable height up above the heads, searching. "Dunno. Little cuss is so goddam *short*. Prob'ly still outside taking one last drag on a cigarette and lockin' up the car."

Bubba pulled closer to me, keeping his place in line with one toe. "You so quiet, Garn. You nervous? We're observers. We don't have to debate anybody unless we want the practice."

I met his friendly eyes. "Ain't got nothin' to be nervous about."

"Think we'll be here next year, graduated, givin' lowlife beginners a thrill before we pack off to Harvard?" David Dale reached for Bubba's tag over several intervening bodies and I watched as Bubba's tawny head bent down. He pinned the tag to his seersucker lapel.

"Maybe." He straightened. "Git me a dark suit and a white shirt and briefcase. Throw out that ol' cardboard envelope I've been using. Git Garn to stop wearin' Beatnik duds. We might make it."

"Don't know where we'll be next year," I countered in a low tone, watching for Bill Damadian. "Don't know. None of us."

David Dale stirred. "Let's move over by the door. I'm gettin' my tie wrinkled."

"Somebody yell 'Fire!'" Bubba laughed as we edged over to the plate glass.

David Dale said, "You wanna see these lawyer suckers move, somebody yell, 'Whiplash!' 'Yell, 'Malpractice!'"

I suddenly glimpsed Damadian. "There he is."

"*Coach!*" David Dale bellowed. Many people looked up startled, irritated.

"He don't look none too happy," Bubba remarked as he saw Bill moving towards us.

"Here we are, Coach," David Dale said as Damadian stepped to the windows with us, "the Cowshit Squad."

"Cool it and cut the clowning." Damadian lit a cigarette. "You yahoos embarrass me and I'll pretend I don't know you."

"*Oooooh,*" said David Dale in a fey voice, "get *him!*"

Bubba fanned Damadian's smoke away from his face. "So what do we do now?"

"All of you get registered okay?"

247

"Yessir."

I saw Bill frown at his watch. "The opening dealies are not until seven. It's only a little after one now. Let me get myself signed in and then maybe we can see about some lunch."

David Dale made a way for the small man to pass. "Can we maybe eat at Sans Souci and gawk at all the big shots?"

Damadian finally grinned. "Not unless you want to pick up the tab. I'm on your basic burger budget."

"Bill?"

We turned, all four of us, to see a smartly dressed young woman with a French-twisted hairdo and understated earrings come glomming onto Damadian's sleeve like a cockleburr, laugh laugh laugh, gush gush gush—

His face creased up and turned pink. "Well, for—Eva Stockfelt!"

They shared a hug, Bill kissing the air beside her cheek to keep from smudging her makeup—a Yankee hug. I had never seen anybody kiss empty air before, why even go to all that trouble if it was bad form to make lip contact?

". . . I wondered if it could possibly be you, William Damadian! I saw this smug face come bopping by—"

"I don't believe it!" He was pinker. "How've you been? Did you marry that sculpture student or what?"

She didn't look at me or the guys. "God no, he turned out to be gay. I'm in Indiana now, teaching speech. Got a *fantastic* team here, but the second affirmative has mono and he might fold on us."

"Betty and I have a little boy. Got married after I got back from Costa Rica with the Peace Corps. We're working down in South Carolina now, went down with the Lyndon Johnson campaign. We're here as observers this year, but next year we might compete, if I can teach my kids to speak English. Catch one of our practice debates while you're here, Eva. I got one girl who can tell you that black is white and make you believe it." He looked away. "Garnet? Garnet?" Bill was pulling me by the arm. I flung my hair out of my eyes. My mascara-clotted lashes felt stuck together. Bill steadied me in front of the woman. "Eva, this is Garnet Laney. My little silver-tongued hellion. Such a mind on this kid! Supernatural."

"'Scarlett', did he say your name was?" Her perfect eyes looked me over.

"*Garnet,*" I muttered, embarrassed. "My grandfather named me. The University of South Carolina's colors are garnet and black."

David Dale stood dead pan. "And he didn't want to call her—"

"Don't say it!" I warned David Dale, turning.

"I shouldn't wonder," mumbled Eva Stockfelt.

"This lovely creature here, Garnet, is Eva Stockfelt," Bill said nervously. "*Was* Eva Stockfelt," he corrected himself, glancing at her married surname on the lapel tag. "My debate partner in college for two blissful years."

"Pleased to meet you," I squirmed, feeling mushmouthed and dowdy in my granny gown.

Bill remembered belatedly the guys who stood behind him. "And, Eva, let me introduce you to—"

"Huey and Dewey." David Dale bowed. Bubba grinned, hands in pockets.

Eva laughed a teacher's laugh. "Bill Damadian, you little do-gooder. How did you ever end up in the sticks?"

"Somebody's got to bring enlightenment to the natives." He grinned pointedly at me. "Guess I'm just a carpetbagger at heart."

I heard Bubba behind me, whispering carefully to David Dale: "I'd give my left nut for a rubber spider."

But somebody was calling Eva's name and she took leave of us with a blithe goodbye. Bill sagged against the plate glass where his cigarette shed ashes all over the plants. "Christ," he said. "Eva Stockfelt. She used to be a lot of fun in the back seat of my Studebaker."

"Gal looks as hot as a Frigidaire," Bubba smirked.

"She didn't look enough like Doris Day," I said. Bill smiled weakly.

"Were you a good debater, Coach?" Bubba pulled chewing gum off the sole of his Weejun.

"Not particularly. Gave it up my sophomore year. I was more interested in Eva Stockfelt than I was in debate. But look where it got me—here with you clowns."

His tone wasn't altogether jocular and I found that my old irritation at him had come back. I was starving. My stomach gurgled.

"Bill?" I tugged at his distracted sleeve. "Is there a place around here where we can eat?"

"I didn't register, did I?" He glanced around. "Let me go sign in and then we'll get out of this zoo for a while."

"I gotta wash up," Bubba said, eyes searching the peopled walls for a men's room sign.

"Ol' son has weak kidneys." David Dale winked. Bubba nudged him.

"Well, I wanna put my hair up." I pulled at the wild strands that draped over my shoulders. My eyelashes still felt stuck together. "Nuts. My purse is in the car."

"Well," said Bill, "you guys meet me back here and I'll—"

I poked him. "My purse is in the car. Hairbrush?"

He rummaged around in his pants pockets and handed me a jangling jumble of warm keys. "It's the round one."

I nodded. "Be right back. Don't go 'way."

I raised my skirts and tripped lightly down the cement steps, thinking of the Victorian appearance I wanted to make at the opening ceremonies. Wondering if I had packed all of my hairpins or had left them in my luggage back at the motel. The day was hot and clear and blooming. I saw the Valiant sitting at the curb a block away and strode down the street to the little car, wrestling at last with the passenger side door that Tommy Damadian had hit with a tire iron back in the spring. My purse lay on the burning vinyl seat cover.

My hairpins were in it, the hairbrush. I sat on the hot seat with my feet dangling sideways out of the open door and hastily twisted my hair up into a chignon at the back of my neck, taking in the clear sharpness of the late summer weather, the knife-edged black shadows under the leafy cherry trees. I checked my hairdo in the rearview mirror and put away my brush, humming and hungry. Then I locked up the car and began to walk briskly back up the sidewalk.

I stopped. Realized suddenly that I was alone and unobserved.

But this was no time to make a break for Arlington, messing up everything for Bubba and David Dale. I jingled Damadian's keys reluctantly, resolving to do my duty, trudging back up the street, feeling a little proud of myself. There would be other opportunities for skulduggery. Was I a trifle relieved?

Damadian, under the influence of La Stockfelt, had signed me and Bubba up for a first-round debate. There went my stress-free lunch.

"It won't *count,*" Damadian kept insisting as I picked at my food in a Greek coffeeshop near campus. Bubba, getting all coffeed up, had his note cards spread all over the tabletop and listened to about half of what everybody else was saying. Only David Dale, safe because he was without a debate partner, chowed down with anything like enthusiasm.

Bubba said nothing. His jaws tightened around a bite of doughnut.

"You might have warned us," I muttered.

"You two have debated this topic at least fifty times this year."

"Not since June, Bill."

"I don't see what the big deal is." He stopped looking at me and tried to make eye contact with Bubba. "It's not like you're in competition or anything. They won't power-match you in Round Two if you win, or anything like that."

That won Bubba's attention. "Round *Two?*"

"I just want everybody to see how good you are." Damadian squirmed a little. "I want you to get a taste of national-level competition. That's all." He made a helpless gesture with his hand.

"Don't sign us up for Round Two," I said, visions of unending debate rising up behind my eyes like nightmares. "We came up here to learn. Not to get massacred."

"I'm the coach," he said, sounding defensive.

"Is Miss Stockfelt gonna look in on us?" asked David Dale.

I didn't like the way Damadian was hunkered down in his chair. Yep, I thought, Miss Stockfelt will be there with bells on. While Bubba and I debate our brains out, maybe win, and then have to do it all over again. And again. And again. When will I find the time to go to Arlington? Will I have this whole tribe with me?

"I ain't doin' no Round Two," I said to the air.

"We'll see." Damadian finished his iced tea.

Bubba scribbled on backs of note cards. He had inkstains on the middle finger of his hand. Three-quarters of a doughnut lay upon his plate, unwanted.

This was not at all how I had envisioned Einsteinian reality.

Round One began in a second floor classroom at two P.M., with a skinny redheaded speech teacher from California serving as judge. Our opponents were two guys from Portland, Oregon—one real tall guy wearing glasses who looked like a tax attorney, one shorter guy with longer hair, who looked more my type. If he had been a girl, I thought, maybe he, too, would have been wearing a granny gown. My blood pressure went down.

Eva Stockfelt had brought several of her non-competitor students to watch us get killed. They sat clumped together in the back rows, paper and pens at hand, intent. Too intent. What in the dickens had Bill Damadian told them?

Old Judas himself sat rattling change in his pants pockets, David Dale right beside him. I absolutely hate this, I realized, fanning my note and quote cards out on the table in front of me. I totally hate debate. I'll be damned if I ever debate anything anywhere ever again. If this is what it takes to go to college, I'd rather dig ditches. I'd rather go to secretarial school.

But I was overstating my case to myself and I knew it. My father had put aside college money for both me and Beth Ann. I did not need to debate, and I did not really hate debate, once it got underway.

This one was underway.

I found myself at the oak podium, soothed by the sound of my own voice, stating the resolution (for the quintillionth time) that nuclear weapons should be banned. It was easy. My reliable, smooth debating voice slid out like syrup, half-an-octave lower than usual. I wondered what it sounded like on a tape recorder, but I couldn't worry about that now. I kept up eye contact with the judge, maintained my posture, and let my prepared opening speech do its thing for both of us.

Not bad at all, Robert, I mentally remarked to my Einsteinian co-spirit as I sat back down, fairly happy. Not bad at all. We're rollin'.

The first negative speaker took the position so many negative teams did, that nuclear disarmament would lead to an imbalance of power which would de-stabilize the world. And the Russians couldn't be trusted in any arms limitation agreements, anyway. Ho-hum. We had heard it all before, lots of times, in southern accents. These Oregonians weren't so tough. I could sense Bubba next to me, cool in his confidence.

He gave his standard second affirmative speech and should have been elected to Congress right there on the spot. I didn't dare turn to see how Miss Stockfelt and company were taking this, but I saw that Damadian had been right in signing us up.

A little tentacle of pride came out of somewhere in me and coiled itself around my heart. Bubba's hands lifted and lowered quote cards without a tremor. His cuffs were immaculate; the elbows of his seersucker jacket bagged not at all. Each controlled movement sent small puffs of air up into his clean blond hair, and the afternoon sunlight coming through the windows gave him an aura of goldenness. He spoke like a media-savvy politician. A star.

You're not thinking about Lee, a detached part of me realized with something like reproach. You're not planning your getaway. I crossed my ankles underneath the table and pressed my lips together.

You're looking at how well Bubba's shoulder seam defines his shoulder. You're noticing how effective he is. How utterly non-nerdlike.

So what? I was irritated at myself. Gimme a break! I'm in the middle of a contest here! Let me have at least a coupla hours in the twentieth century, willya?

Bubba had a tight smile, just for me, when he came back to our table in the sunlight, satisfied, and deposited his notecards and papers onto the tabletop in an unhurried way. Our eye contact was triumphant. I showed no emotion that Oregon could detect, but I heard Bill Damadian clear his throat from his end of the classroom in a very comfortable way.

I was not noticing how Oregon was sneaking up on my blind side. I had not known that I possessed a blind side. And I should have.

Bless their hearts, the Portland guys didn't know they were doing it. What they actually were doing was floundering into the bog of irrelevancy.

The short, Mod one said, "The danger inherent in the Southeast Asian balance of terror is incalculable, if the United States were to unilaterally disarm. The Domino Theory is no theory. In an era of uncertain Sino-Soviet relations, in a decade witnessing the development of a Chinese nuclear arsenal, U.S. foreign policy must be backed up by more than teenaged draftees smoking marijuana in Vietnamese rice paddies. U.S. security must anchor itself upon foundations more tangible than the vague and outdated concepts of duty the . . . uh . . . traditional reliance of gung-ho politicos upon a hidebound military more interested in promotion than national security . . . more interested in . . . uh . . . fighting the campaigns of the past upon the battlefields of the past, rather than positioning themselves upon the high ground of the nuclear future."

I didn't know what he was getting at, and neither did he. It was apparent that he had bypassed nuclear disarmament and was slogging through a quicksand of his own making, contradicting himself at many points to pursue his own agenda. I wondered how his partner was going to effect a rescue.

Bubba scribbled in the margin of our notes: *Do it to him.*

I risked a noncommittal glance at Damadian while the lost Oregonian took his seat. Damadian showed two little hints of dimples at the corners of his mouth. My turn at rebuttal would come before Bubba's, and there sure was a lot I wanted to rebut. But something vague was gnawing at me. I looked over the notes I had taken during the rambling speech, point by point. Was I missing something?

The first negative speaker, tall and lawyerly, began the rebuttal round and tried to make some sense of his partner's arguments. His presentation was quite good. I found it hard to concentrate upon what he was saying.

Here come the dominoes again, Bubba wrote me quietly.

Yep. First negative walked us through the whole scenario, with Vietnam's fall to the Reds followed by India's and Pakistan's and the whole Indian subcontinent going down the toilet. *If* we gave up the Bomb. A big if. But he was terrific, extremely convincing, quoting from his note cards every expert on the subject from General Westmoreland and William F. Buckley, Jr., to Robert MacNamara and Bobby Kennedy and Bob Hope and even the Reverend Billy Graham.

The timekeeper flipped over a time card. This guy had two minutes left to go, and a lot more nails to put into our coffin. I wondered if the judge would remember his partner's foray into no-man's land.

I gathered my notes and walked to the podium, finally, in a swirl of quiet.

"The resolution before us today—" I settled my hands onto the oak beneath my rib cage, settling my eyes upon the judge's own faintly-frowning ones. "—is nuclear disarmament. *Not* the efficacy nor the inefficacy of the American fighting man. *Not* duty. *Not* honor."

Thus, I stepped right into the irrelevancy swamp my own self.

Durn, it was hot up there. The air conditioner was turned down too low or something, the afternoon sun high and blazing and coming through all the windows. The judge shifted in her seat. I saw Eva Stockfelt in my peripheral vision.

Nothing at all psychic happened. I had become so interested in speaking up for myself that I was losing a debate.

"As a student of history," I went on, "I have come to notice, rather, the integrity of the average American fighting man. Even while U.S. foreign policy has more than once become divorced from justice. Vietnam is nothing new. National interests are frequently in collision with ethics, and ethics usually lose out. The American citizen-soldier is called upon to ratify, by his service, his country's claims of moral aims. But he is no puppet, no matter how much marijuana he might have smoked nor how few years of schooling he might've had. He knows what's what. He is quick to see through the bullshit"—(*Oops!* Too late, I've said it.)—"of selfseeking politicians. You don't have to be a nuclear physicist to know when you're being sold a used car, for crying out loud . . ."

I was lost. I had no notes, no quotes to back me up. My brain was saying something about nuclear arms reductions, but my mouth had taken an independent course.

No flop-sweat on me anywhere, though. As a matter of fact, I felt really okay. I felt *good*. Screw debate, screw the rules. I had a chance to make myself perfectly understood to myself, and I had a captive audience.

"It's so easy to take sides," I continued, as rational as a CPA, "*if* you're a moral moron. But if you can *think,* it becomes very difficult. Most of us are not wholeheartedly on one side or the other in any conflict, no matter what it is. When we are forced to side with one view, and to physically champion that view, it doesn't mean that we are blind to the arguments of the other. Many of the duties performed by any citizen—a draftee, nurse, or a teacher to a classful of uninterested clods—are performed with reluctance. Reluctance does not diminish the quality of the performance. In fact, it may be argued that a duty performed in spite of misgivings, performed for what is judged by consensus to be the common good of the community, is all the more honorable.

"I, too," I leaned upon the podium, "am troubled by the I-was-just-following-orders phenomenon, when consensus seems to force the performance of great moral evil upon a dutiful citizen. I cannot, in all honesty, say where honor lies among all the gray areas in between black and white.

"As a Southerner, I come from dishonored citizenry, maneuvered by the antiquated economics of a hundred years ago into fighting a war to defend slavery. *Defend slavery!* Slavery may not be actual genocide, maybe; but it doesn't take a rocket scientist to see that the two are very close relatives.

"So where lay honor for my ancestors who obeyed the call of consensus? What portion of honor is redeemable?" My eyes left those of my judge's. Whatever I was doing, I was no longer debating by the rules. I lifted my head to focus upon Eva Stockfelt, upon David Dale, the timekeeper, Damadian.

The timekeeper, rattled though he might be by my unorthodoxy, nonetheless continued to consult his stop watch and flip over his time cards. I had three minutes left.

"If I worked really hard at assimilating myself into mainstream America," I went on, "I could do it. Alter my *accent*. Become de-regionalized. It wouldn't change my consciousness of original sin, though. It wouldn't take away my guilt, nor the conflicting emotions I have whenever a band strikes up 'Dixie.' Those of us Southerners—and we are many—who understand our evil, are very nervous about getting trapped on the side of the devil again. We spend more time than you can imagine puzzling out things, trying to right wrongs, getting born-again and being preachy. Lyndon Johnson is one of us, remember. And when he makes you all nervous about what he's doing in Vietnam and why, and who he thinks the bad guys are over there—and how hyperactive he is in his pursuit of civil rights for everybody, and how mighty a foe he is of poverty—when he makes y'all nervous and orders draftees out to die for a bunch of capitalist black marketeers in Southeast Asia, and you want to burn him in effigy or burn him for *real,* just remember where he's coming from. That don't mean he's *right,* y'understand. It just means he's explicable, and largely predictable. He's searching for honor."

Somebody in back laughed softly. I smiled to myself. My last time card flipped.

"So what does this have to do with nuclear disarmament?" I said, winding up. "Everything. Honor is everything. Responsible decision-making, upon the part of responsible citizens, is *everything.* Don't let a government maneuver you into a gross violation of ethics. Don't let your pals nor your political party maneuver you into always automatically thinking that the government is wrong, either. When you're old enough to vote, vote. If you're too young, then write letters to the editors of newspapers. But speak up, in some way. Take a stand.

"Slavery is *wrong.* Blowing up the world, chillun, is *wrong.* Get rid of the Bomb. It stinks. It sucks polar bears. Do you really have to be told? We gotta disarm, y'all. My worthy opponents have no case—"

The classroom disintegrated into laughter.

"—and I thank you all very much."

I expected applause; I did not get it. But neither did I get silence. All was subdued hubbub as Mr. Mod, the second negative, got up to take his last swing at bat. From the look on his face, he had been led so far into tangential mine fields that he didn't know, literally, whether he was winning or losing. His coach sat perfectly still, hands in lap, giving nothing away. I saw Bill

Damadian and Eva Stockfelt exchange grinning glances, and I did not give one single rat's ass. I felt light, and giddy, and dancy.

Bubba, the last debater scheduled to speak, would put it all to rights. I stood while Mr. Mod fumbled with his notes, and I squeezed Bubba's nicely-tailored shoulder.

He looked up.

"Gotta go potty," I whispered. "Finish 'em off."

The rules forbade my leaving, but I had already broken most of them anyway. His face was an attractive high-hued pink, his mouth exuberant. He touched my hand with one finger, nodding, watching me dance to the door.

"I don't think Bill is goin' to make us sign up for the second round now," he said, sotto voce.

I laughed. "I'll be right back."

Actually, that was a lie.

The cab let me out upon the lower slopes of the graveyard. I caught a glimpse of the house above me, even larger now and more brooding than it had seemed from the taxi window as we crossed the Potomac into Virginia.

I tried to pay the driver and got the amount wrong—I wasn't accustomed to taxis. Then I undertipped him and he said something evil to me. But I didn't respond. I craned my neck to look up the headstone-studded hill at the American flag flying over Major Custis' empty house.

I patted my silver heart pin to make sure that it was still attached to my dress, and I unpinned my debate name tag and stuffed it into my purse. There might have been signs warning me to stay off the grass but I didn't see them. The shortest way to the summit seemed to lie among the graves, and I hitched up my skirt and jumped off the curb into the short springy grass.

The house receded beyond the curved brow of the hill, beyond slope after slope of small marble markers in neat military rows standing forever at attention, all just alike except for the names.

My quick feet carried me over the dead and I felt nothing for the bodies under my trouncing. Name after name swam into sight and passed on. Name after name, state after state. I spotted South Carolina on tombstones, once or twice, gave an involuntary little nod when I did so, and perspired in my long dress as my hidden legs churned faster.

I was running now, dodging through the graves as I darted uphill, shoulderbag thumping into my hip, my hair blown back in the hot wind. I stopped once, unable to see the house at all now for the curvature of the slope. Washington lay behind me over the river. Far below me were the great gates to the cemetery and beyond them the Memorial Bridge spanned the glinting water to the Lincoln Memorial, a heavy-handed attempt to join the two halves of the country together forever.

I shaded my eyes to stare at the squarish white marble roof, far off, where Abraham Lincoln in statue form sat thinking, eternally austere.

"Fuck you in the heart," I said to Lincoln.

My hair fell and whipped around my face when I spun about on the toe of my good leg; blue gingham ruffles flapped like pennants. The slope ahead held nobody alive. I turned my course uphill and made my feet move faster again. Running.

I burst out of the graves unexpectedly onto pavement: a winding street that joined with others to meander among the tombstones. A small busload of tourists milled about their guide further down. I paused and glanced at some of the street signs as I pattered across the pavement and back onto grass: Sherman Drive, Sheridan Drive, Lincoln Drive.

"Mary would shit," I muttered in disbelief and outrage. "She would just shit."

A stairway of stone steps led off to my right, going definitely uphill. A gaggle of visitors in Bermuda shorts, with cameras slung around their necks, loitered up and down the route. I made for the steps and pulled up my skirts, the only person on the stairs who seemed to know where she was going.

I flung myself off the top step onto a flat plateau, among leisurely tourists who spoke to one another and called their children in strangely reverent voices. The house wasn't on this level after all. I could see the flag above me yet, its red and white stripes flowing in the hot wind. No more steps led upwards from this paved platform, this cul de sac. Damn.

I glanced frantically about myself, every second precious. I pushed a balding man out of my way with a perfunctory, "S'cuse me," and I started back the way I had come. And then I saw it: flat, flagstoned, hidden and revealed and then hidden again by the sweating backs of the people. Saw it, low and even with the ground. It took me a moment to realize what it was and then I flung my wet arms to my sides with an audible slap.

"Oh nuts," I breathed. *Nuts.*

John F. Kennedy lay there at my feet, eternal flame sputtering above him. Cameras clicked constantly all around like the sound of insects.

I thought maybe I should kneel or something, but nobody else was kneeling. I didn't feel like kneeling anyway—the encounter had caught me completely by surprise, and I didn't know how to feel. I saw the pattern in it, saw the synchronized Jungian relevance in the encounter. Knew that maybe I was meant to wind up here. But another part of me treated it as pure coincidence, as pure nuisance, an accidental detour that was even now wasting my irreplaceable time.

I thought about the people back home. Thought about Grandmama. I wanted to feel something now for Jack, wanted to shed a salutatory tear, but I could feel nothing at all.

"You tried," I told Kennedy, unable to put any other value on the meeting. "You tried. Thank you."

I retraced my steps back down the stairs, paused a moment in the sparse shade of a large bush to open my shoulderbag and check my makeup, then I snapped the compact closed and stuffed it back into the purse and started once again willy-nilly up the grass, panting uphill as fast as the heat would let me.

I knew I was getting closer: the gravestones were older up here, larger and more ornate, Victorian cherubs and brave verse carved ostentatiously into their surfaces. Here lay the original Yankees, some of them, buried in Mary Lee's front yard as fast as her husband could kill them off. I was appalled at the inappropriateness of it.

But they wouldn't *want* to be here! I thought. They would have wanted to be buried back in Massachusetts, or Indiana, or New York. Or at least upon the battlefields where they fell. They wouldn't have wanted to be here. Whose warped idea was this? These poor guys deserved better. Somebody used their poor dead bodies to keep Mary Custis Lee from ever coming back.

And of course a few more steps carried me up, and there it was: Custis's Folly. Arlington House. A house so overpowered by its Greek-temple grandeur that it seemed twice as large as it actually was. It seemed in that moment to be the very biggest house in the world, *A house you could see with half an eye,* Robert had once remarked drily.

I stood absolutely still, back straight, and biting my lips. The pillars towered up to hold the roof, brick pillars stuccoed and painted to look like solid columns of marble, and I let my eyes carry me up until I got dizzy and the illusion came, the feeling that the old house was tilting forward and would topple right over me. I leveled my gaze to the cool shade under the portico, the red terra cotta floor and wooden steps.

Arlington! It smelled like evergreen. I breathed it in. Pine. Spruce. Oaks, too. And ivy in the underbrush among the skirts of the trees where the woods crept around the house. Holly. Something that looked like laurel. Cicadas hummed. A daddy-longlegs scrambled over the toe of my sandal.

Constant restoration work had kept the old house in one piece. I wondered how much of what I saw was original and how much was restorative imagination. A crowd of people in polyester swarmed over the portico and through the broad open front doors. I didn't want to go inside just yet.

Children played in the graveled driveway where carriages had once stopped. I tried to hear the crunch of gravel under horseshoes, tried to visualize a dark man in oldfashioned clothes riding up to this very doorway. It was difficult. The children bawling, and the adults calling, "Jeffrey! Kimberley!" in their sharp Northern whines, drowned out the illusion.

I walked backwards two steps and then started around the house's wing. Wasps busily tended their nests under the window arches with no black houseboy now to harry them, no impatient young soldier to stand teetering on a ladder and swat them down with a cane pole, to come crashing down himself in a leap and run laughing down the hill with the children and the dogs until the wasps had calmed down and the nest larvae were available for the very best fish bait. No, I thought, tourists and groundskeepers don't care about the wasps. They don't have to live in the house, they don't have to have the fool things buzzing about the parlor during one of their soirees.

I smiled at the wasps as I went by and saluted them, the only living things I had seen so far that still made the embalmed old dwelling their home. A profusion of roses and day lilies grew in a formal English-style garden some distance from the house. I walked right around the wing until I ended up in back, where the pig pens used to be, wondering if the guides with all of their Old South malarkey ever pointed out the vanished pig pens. Figuring that they didn't. Knowing that tourists would rather fantasize about a plantation redolent of lavender and sachet, instead of a real farm smelling of hogs and humans and diapers, chamber pots and frying meat, somebody's dirty laundry wadded up in a corner of a chifferobe, stables and cows and the turpentine reek of Major Custis's oil paints. A sanitized lemon-wax aroma breathed out of the old place.

There had been cat latrines everywhere at one time; these people had all loved cats. I stood under the shade of an enormous aged spruce tree and wished for a litterbox smell, rubbing my back against the rough bark of the tree and trying to get chiggers. Trying to find something living in the middle of this graveyard.

"How do we get inside?" A sudden voice asked at my elbow. I jumped and looked around into opaque sunglasses.

"Ma'am?"

"Is this the way we go to get inside? We want to take the tour," the woman said in her Midwestern accent. A fat man stood sweating a few paces behind her, his hands full of brochures and leaflets from a dozen historical shrines.

"I don't know, Ma'am." I pointed to the house. "There used to be a back door. I don't know if that's the entrance they want you to use or not."

The woman sighed. "I thought you worked here." She giggled and pointed at my long dress and turned to her husband. "The hostesses wear costumes. I thought she worked here, Hank."

"Go back around to the front," I told them, pointing. "Or to the office entrance through the greenhouse on the side. The front door'll take you into the central hall. The old parlor will be to your right, and the newer one off to your left. The Custis bedroom is on the first floor. The Lee bedrooms are upstairs."

The fat man just stood there. "You *don't* work here?"

"Nossir."

He scratched his nose. "We need tickets or anything?"

"I don't know, sir."

"You ought to be working here, sweetie," the woman said. "You sound more authentic than the other girls. Are you from around here?"

"No ma'am. South Carolina."

"Isn't that sweet."

"I see some people going in the side there, Laura." The fat man tapped her shoulder. His little porcine eyes met mine. "Do we go in that way?"

"She doesn't work here, Hank."

"Too damn hot," he said. "They sell anything to drink around here, any sodas or something?"

I sighed. "I really don't know."

"Didn't they sell Cokes at Mount Vernon, Laura?" The man looked at his wife. "They sold 'em *somewhere*."

"This place bigger than Mount Vernon?" the woman was asking me. She showed no signs of going away.

"I'm not sure. I don't know much about Mount Vernon. But the man who built this house, George Washington Parke Custis, grew up at Mount Vernon. He was Martha Washington's grandson and the Washingtons raised him."

The fat man studied his brochure. "I thought this was Lee's Mansion. They said they were taking us to Lee's Mansion."

I shrugged. "He lived here. When he wasn't on duty. But it belonged to his wife's family. He never owned any part of it."

"He coulda set up a mortar right out here on the front yard and bombed hell out of Washington. That's what I would have done." The fat man wheezed. It must have been a laugh. "You could lob a few shells into a pile of niggers next time Martin Luther Coon gets a mob together over there around the Lincoln thing. You people down South got the right idea."

I got that sick feeling, the same kind of feeling that came over me whenever I saw Civil Rights coverage on national television. Remembered the loaded way accentless reporters pronounced "The South." How much disapproval, how much righteous anger they could put into those two simple sinister words. I nervously pulled some dried pods from the day lilies and rubbed them between my palms.

"Hush, Hank! People might hear you!"

Hank chortled. "Where is Robert E. Lee when we really need him?"

"Buried in exile in the Shenandoah," I answered mildly. "Dying of a genuine broken heart after General Grant intervened to keep you Yankees from hanging him."

The woman's sunglasses gleamed. She tugged at Hank's

yellow nylon shirt sleeve, thrilled. "Listen to that! 'You Yankees!' Do you still call us that?"

I could feel my face getting very red. "Sure."

"Just like *Gone With The Wind!* Isn't that sweet. Did you hear her, Hank?"

"I heard. I heard."

"I was in a race riot back in the spring," I muttered. "You wanna take a picture?"

"I just love the South," Laura of the sunglasses gushed on, the rhinestones in the eyepieces doing a mad dance in the sunlight. "Even if everybody is bigoted and so on. I always stick up for the South at my bridge club. It's hard for you people to change, that's all. If you've never been to school or anything with the negroes—"

"I've been going to school with black kids now for two solid years," I interrupted. "Do *your* children go to school with black kids?"

Eyes behind sunglasses blinked darkly, surprised.

"—Lob some mortar shells right into the communist nigger demonstrations from his own front porch," Hank was wheezing on. "Lee'd get this country into shape in no time—"

I thought I would go starkers. "Do you *know* any black people, lady?" I said. "Do you even know what the heck you're talking about?"

She groped for her husband's hand. "I think we can get into the house now, Hank."

"I don't hate blacks!" I was following them like an avenging angel as they moved off out of the shade. "You don't need to make excuses for us at your bridge club, Madam. Thank you for your kind attention, but we don't require defense. We are not all villains."

We don't even need my own defense, I thought to myself as the couple strode hurriedly around the corner and out of sight. We are not all villains. I've carried this burden of guilt so long that I don't know what it means to put it down. I might not ever be able to put it down.

Listen, Jack Kennedy. I am not a villain and I had absolutely nothing to do with you getting bumped off. And if I live long enough, I swear to God that I'm going to find some way of making myself believe that.

I squared my shoulders, stood up a little straighter, and let the inside of the old house finally call me into its depths. I clutched my lily pods damply in my hand and went off to meet whatever was waiting.

Thirty-Three

*P*ersevere, *and you shall succeed.*

Papa? I cannot persevere anymore, Papa. We are all persevered out, Papa.

None of your sass, damn you, sir. Get up. Fight.

They cannot fight any longer, Papa. I haven't anything to feed them. They are eating the undigested corn from horse droppings, Papa. The living ones. Most of them are dead.

You. Get up. Fight.

Robert awakens. He inventories himself: arthritic shoulders, strong legs, empty belly. He can't remember when he last slept peacefully. His temples burn. The dull pain behind his eyes has no physical cause. Yes, he thinks, I can stand. I can still wield a sword. "Fight."

Right into the enemy lines, Traveller and I and the sword. How badly I want that. With all my heart.

The starving army has been on the move since 1 A.M.: two thousand cavalrymen on skeletal horses, along with General Gordon's two thousand on foot, pushing their way to the front to

268

attempt a breakthrough; sixty-one guns, two thousand artillery-
men, and General Longstreet's six thousand stumbling infantry-
men bringing up the rear. A mere twelve thousand effectives,
perhaps. No one knows for sure. Walter Taylor and the staff can't
keep track of headquarters records, and many are being deliberately destroyed to keep them out of enemy hands.

Robert has no shelter anymore. The wagons containing the
tents are lost. He sits up on his ragged blankets there in the weeds
on this April morning and he empties a canteen over his head. The
cold water prods him back to alertness and he uses a filthy towel to
scrub at his hair and face and body. The water has made mud in the
dust of his clothing. No matter. He will need to change anyway.

Perry the valet has managed to find his good underthings
among the disorder. Robert finishes his cat bath, scrubbing away
the dirt and stink with a ruthlessness that leaves his skin red, and
pulls on a clean shirt over the fresh underwear. He manages to get
collar and cuffs attached but the bow tie defeats him. His fingers
are stiff. They shake.

"Perry?"

The free black man materializes out of the darkness and
attacks the tie without a word. Robert watches the fingers at his
chin, the careful efficiency of the wrists. He looks right into the
man's eyes when the tie is done, eye to eye and no taller after all
than the valet. Only older. And whiter, he thinks now, but no
more a man than Perry is.

He has insisted to President Davis all winter that these people
must be freed so that they can join the army. Davis has demurred;
public opinion is against it. Too bad. Perry would have made a fine
combat soldier. Would've done as much as anyone to keep Grant at
bay. Wouldn't he?

Would he? Lord God, I don't know, Robert thinks now.

Perry brushes at the soft gray wool of the dress uniform tunic
that hangs over his arm, uneasy. Face twitching. Fingers picking
at nonexistent lint in the dim firelight. "You be wantin' your
breakfast now, sir? We got a little cornmeal, sir."

Breakfast. "No. Thank you."

"You ain't eaten anything since yesterday morning, Marse Robert."

But Robert has his back turned now, tucking in his shirttail. "Perry, I shall miss you, son. Thank you for extraordinary service. God go with you."

The valet nods. Licks his lips.

"You must leave me now, please. I can finish dressing by myself." Robert's back is still turned. His voice sounds peculiar.

"Sir?"

He is more explicit. "I've got to be by myself for a while, Perry. Please go. Thank you."

The rustle of weeds and pad of bare feet tells him finally that the valet is gone. He turns after a while, careful, watchful to see if anybody is watching him, because he can't make his face behave. Several deep steadying breaths make him dizzy. A cup of cornmeal mush would probably be a good idea if he could keep it down, but little of the food he has eaten in the past few days will stay put. Too many soldiers eating horse droppings. Too many of them shot to pieces, armless, legless, eyeless, crying, crawling, too spent to fight. Too tough to die easy.

The dry retching comes. Robert has to crouch and crawl into the weeds himself to keep from spitting the bile onto his uniform.

Stand up, damn you! And stop that! You are unworthy, sir.

"Yes, Papa."

You are spoiling the creases in your britches.

Call yourself a commander, do you? You cannot control others until you learn to control yourself, sir!

Where is my towel? he thinks. I cannot allow anyone to see me like this.

His hand finds the saddle in the half-dark, instead, and the left holster and a loaded Navy revolver.

Please, he thinks, fingertips upon the cold metal. Please. Dear God. Sweet Jesus Savior. Only a moment. I know where to put a bullet to insure instant fatality.

Pray God to forgive you, then. Mary will never forgive you. Your children will never forgive you. I will never forgive you.

Robert stands finally, revolver relinquished. He hears far-off gunfire and nearby nightbirds. Papa, he thinks. Papa.

The air is rank with the stench of bloated mule carcasses and burning wagons. He can't see any stars.

His full dress uniform is like some hard shell holding him up, holding him in. Armor. He suspects that if it is once breached this day that he will come flooding out, unmanned. He buttons the tunic all the way up to his tie.

What is to be done, then? What will history say of me if I surrender this army in the field?

We cannot persevere anymore. We reached our breaking point a long time ago, I think. Jackson is dead. Little Jeb is dead. A.P. Hill is dead. Dick Ewell is captured. Richmond has fallen. A few thousand dying boys stand between me and Grant, and every minute that passes brings another death out there among the innocent. Among souls already pushed beyond the limits of human endurance. By me. Even my son Custis is dead, I think.

I have no right to ask this of them any longer. If indeed I ever did. So what then? Shall I go to Grant and let him rape me?

The effort to maintain his composure now is so great that his bad heart batters against his breastbone like a ballpeen hammer. His legs give out and he finds himself on his knees, panting. Yes, comes the answer from within him, better you than they. You are just one stupid old fool. They are many, and they are young, and they are dying for nothing. All of them have died for nothing. Because you asked them to.

"Get up, fool. Stand. Be a man."

It takes him several attempts, but he manages to get to his feet. There is nothing nearby to lean on. No tree, no fence rail. God has turned His back, embarrassed.

It comes down to mortal things like sinew and old bone, and cold adrenaline, and fingers that buckle on a sword while lips repeat, "The Lord is my shepherd. I shall not want."

It was cool in the old house.

My sandaled feet carried me along in the train of tourists, as a hostess led us all from room to room, chatting briskly to us about Robert E. Lee-this and Robert E. Lee-that, the name becoming a label in her mouth—never without the Christian name and the institutional initial, never just "Lee" or the ordinary "Robert Lee" he called himself, but always the full awkward historical label, as if she were referring to that steamboat and not to the man.

I wasn't really listening. I only tuned in when the guide got something wrong. She often got things wrong but nobody but me knew the difference and nobody cared. We wandered into the parlor, gawking, cameras dangling. I studied the rather overly-plush red velvet sofa that Mary had purchased in New York during their West Point days, one of the few pieces of original furniture that had survived the war depredations and time.

I felt strange, numb, as if I wasn't altogether at home in my body, but the déja vu sensations that I might have reasonably expected would not come. I listened to the hostess droning on about the marble mantelpiece, something that Robert had pro-cured himself and insisted upon installing, and I tried to get a feel for my surroundings. I wasn't finding the place unfamiliar, ex-actly; I could fit the things I was seeing into my book-gleaned knowledge. But it wasn't with a sense of anything like unworldli-ness that I viewed the George Washington portraits on the walls.

I scurried over the wooden floors as the herd of visitors clopped around me like so many curious horses. I glanced at the archway under which Mary Custis and Robert Lee had spoken their wedding vows, wondering why the hostess did not point out the place where garlands had once hung and a timid young bride had stood while a thunderstorm raged outside.

There were too many people here, with bratty children who had already been to Mount Vernon and the Lincoln Memorial and the Capitol and the Smithsonian, all hurrying through so they could squeeze in a pilgrimage to the Washington Monument. I listened to them mumble and yawp, heard cooing from the women over some precious piece of bric-a-brac or other that the Lees had probably never owned, and I felt disoriented.

I caught sight of myself in an old mirror, a hungry-looking face and painted eyes and a heart-shaped pin hidden among strangers' big overweight bodies and loud nylon shoulders, alone, seemingly the only person in the group who had come by herself with nobody to make inane remarks to.

The tour ended at the rear of the house. The hostess gave us all brochures with floor plans and told us that we could go upstairs unaccompanied. I pushed through the indecisive herd to the staircase and began to climb, surprised and oddly touched to discover that the walls here were painted a peculiar orange, hearing the guide's voice come thinly floating up, explaining to someone that the walls had been scraped to determine their original colors. I met Laura of the sunglasses and fat Hank on the narrow stairs.

"Don't go up there, honey," he told me in passing. "Nothing up there worth seeing. How do we get to the kitchen?"

And I loved him a little, loved them both for forgetting my earlier rudeness and putting it behind them. I smiled and glanced at the watch dial on the sweaty thick wrist as the man and his wife descended, wondering where Bill was at this second and wondering how long it would take him to figure out where I was.

"The winter kitchen is downstairs, y'all," I called.

Only a few visitors had made the climb and they stood clotted in the wide corridor upstairs where a grandfather clock ticked away the minutes. They were whispering to each other as if they were in a library. I licked my dry lips and consulted the floor plan, noting the playroom off to my left and the boys' quarters ahead on the right.

All of the rooms were barricaded but I stood at the brass-topped fences and peered in, eyes missing nothing, my insides trying to sort out the familiar from the new. The house was less museum-ish up here, more lifelike. I lingered at the doorway of the room that Cousin Markie had shared with Lee's daughter Mary. It was full of big old high canopied featherbeds that left little room to walk, tall armoires that had once held wardrobes of voluminous dresses — almost certainly not the original furniture, but from the right period nonetheless. I felt a hollowness in my gut, nervous twitches like butterflies, as I leaned over the railing and tried to get myself as much into the room as possible. A sudden something like weariness came over me and I yearned to clamber over the unnatural barricade and go in to lie down upon the nearest bed, to snuggle deep into the high softness in the cool, curtain-shrouded light.

I moved down the hallway and marveled at how many people had lived in this house and tried to visualize them coming and going in the mornings from room to room. The girls' bedrooms were crammed full of beds but the knickknacks were missing, the nineteenth century whatnots that had almost certainly once festooned every inch of table and mantelpiece surface all over this dwelling.

The light was failing. Curtains bellied out in a sudden breeze and I heard the low rumble of thunder. I stood by the grandfather clock, brochure in damp hand, feeling the draft clutch at my skirts and blow them against my legs. Woodland smells came inside with the wind, the wet promise of a sudden summer rain.

People began drifting off down the stairs and I was alone now with the ticking of the solitary clock. The shouts of visitor children echoed from below, tinny and removed. I had my eye upon another doorway but I had to check the floor plan once in nervous confirmation. My eyes lifted. Yes.

The master bedroom.

I almost tiptoed across the wide hallway, feeling surreptitious, blood pounding sullenly under my collarbone to the rhythm of the clock ticks. I crept, eyes down, to the open doorway and paused, realizing that the moment was upon me.

Footsteps quick on the floor by your room./ The house is empty . . .

The noises from downstairs receded and I was looking down

at my own bloodless hand that quivered as it touched another brass-topped barricade, my rings making little clinking sounds against the polished metal. I was afraid to look up, afraid and guilty and glad that there was nobody around to see this pathetic display of unwarranted nerves. But I brushed the hair out of my face with a nonchalance I did not feel. And finally, shoulders squared, I glanced levelly up.

It was full of sunlight and it was the emptiest room I had ever seen. At one time there might have been Persian carpets on the drafty wooden floor. Now there was only a small footrug lying before a large rocking chair standing vacant in the sun. An enormous double bed stood against the wall and I wondered if the bed had always stood there, if this was in fact *the* bed.

There was not much else in the room, as if the restorers had not known how to furnish it: how much feminine frippery to mix with how many man-things. I stood there with both my elbows leaning on the railing, feeling the draft from Markie's room, diagonally across the hallway behind me, sweeping into the vacancy, watching the sunlight disappear again suddenly as the thunder outside got closer and clouds blotted up the light.

I speculated endlessly upon this room, where most of the seven Lee children had been sired, wondering about marriages and my own ignorance in such matters, knowing that Mary had moved downstairs after her illness had made it difficult to climb stairs or bear any more children. The breeze behind me stirred my hair, and I wondered if my fellow virgin, Markie, had ever lain awake across the hall and contemplated taking the few steps to this doorway. Silent, guilty steps made without a candle, soft bare feet taking her to the vast expanse of lonely bed where a living man lay huddled and warm.

The rain started up in a loud whoosh and I heard far below me the dismayed shrieks of the tourists who ran for the parking lot.

I've got to get closer, I decided over the roaring. I've got to find whatever it might be that I'm looking for. Sick in the head or not, I've come this far and I've got to see it through.

I lifted one foot and hastily slung the knee over the railing, glancing behind myself, finding no one there, having no plan, no idea of what I would do once I had gained entrance to the forbidden space. Whether I would hide like little Rooney under the bed until the place was locked up for the night, whether I would look for ghosts in the dark or try to reach through time, or whether I would finally stand candleless at the bedside and, in my obsession, see the outline of a sleeping man.

You're like a kid groupie trying to break into Paul Mc-Cartney's hotel room, I tried to tell myself, but the leg over the railing—my good right leg—stayed where it was. Unable to feel ludicrous anymore, unable to feel anything but the honest unstoppable urge to go on. I groped for good handholds and eased my weight up onto the brass rail until I was straddling the barricaded threshold.

Here I come, I thought. Here I come. Do with me what you will.

My weak left leg raised itself from the floor and I balanced, teetering, and then lifted it to swing it over the barrier. The rain splashed against the windows and I lurched suddenly, determined, one quick and desperate motion.

The heel of my sandal fouled in my long skirt hem and I kicked out, hearing the cotton rip, moving one hand down to tug at the ruffles. The other hand slid on the metal and my fingers clutched, too late.

A thousand things went through my mind as I felt my balance going, a thousand things.

I reached wildly for the doorjamb, flailing, hearing somebody calling a name. My name. Somebody's name.

Robert! I thought, a voiceless howl.

Tangled, trapped, I plummeted backwards off the railing and landed upon my hated traitor leg. Something tore.

Thirty-Four

"Mama, we've got to get Pa out of here! Out of Richmond!" Young Rob Lee bends over his mother's rolling chair, face agitated, voice low.

Mary puts her knitting down into her lap and looks up. "And where are we to go? Arlington has been confiscated. Where are we to go? Tell me that."

"It doesn't matter where we go! We've got to go *somewhere*." He brushes the light wavy hair back from his face and beckons to his older brother who stands in the doorway like a sentinel. "Custis. Tell her, man! Talk to her!"

"Ma." Custis crosses the floor and leans over, thinner after his incarceration as a Union prisoner. He puts his hands on the chair arms, pale, bearded face worried and earnest. "Pa's sleeping eighteen hours a day. Eighteen hours a day, Ma. Pretty soon it'll be nineteen."

"He'll die if we don't get him out of here, Mama," Rob hisses. "He'll *die*."

Mary puts a hand over her withered face. The knocker on the front door suddenly clatters a summons.

"Oh Judas H. *Priest!*" Rob smacks a hand against his forehead, frantic. "Another one! Can't they leave us alone?"

"Language, language," Mary clucks disapprovingly.

Custis straightens. "You want this one, Rob?"

"I'll handle it. You talk to Mama."

"Be polite now, if it's one of ours. Just tell him that the general is resting and can't receive anyone. If it's a Yank—"

"If it's a Yank," calls Rob savagely from the hall, "I'll give him three seconds to go back where he came from before I fill his butt full of buckshot! Beg pardon, Mama."

"Be nice anyway! Don't cause any trouble."

Custis and Mary hear him march up the hallway and wrench open the front door. Custis frowns, and then pulls up a chair close beside his mother and sits. "Now, Ma," his voice falls while the sound of Rob trying to be nice to someone comes to them, faint. "What are we going to do here?"

Mary sits very still and toys with the yarn. "I don't know, honey. I just don't know. We're comfortable here, aren't we? Unmolested."

"Ma, Pa won't eat and he won't talk and he can't even go outside in the daylight because people mob him in the streets! And we can't keep everybody away, Rob and I. When Pa's awake, he makes us let them in: Gray ones, blue ones, widows wondering where their men are buried. He makes us let them in here, Ma. That old grizzled Yank sergeant who served with him in Texas and came to bring us food last week. That bunch of Rebs from the mountains who showed up all ragged to offer us their little farm, for God's sake! That one-armed fella from Hood's command who just wanted to shake Pa's hand before he started off walking home to San Antonio. You know what this does to Pa, Mama? Don't you understand what's happening? Mama, it makes him cry. All night long, after he thinks the rest of us are asleep, I can hear him upstairs, walking the floor and—Oh

Dear God Sweet Jesus—the worst sound! He doesn't know I can hear him."

"Well, how do you think *I* feel?" She takes her son's bearded cheeks between the bent fingers of her arthritic hands. "Don't you think I bleed inside, son?"

"Bleeding ain't goin' to help him, Mama." He lights a cigar and sighs.

"He's a wonderfully stubborn man, honey. I've known him a lot longer than you young ones have. You know what he says? He says that they're going to indict him for treason and he'll be damned if he'll run away. Your father is not a profane man, Custis. But that's what he says: 'Damn if I let them see me run!'"

"Well, moving yourselves a few miles out of town somewhere doesn't constitute running! The Yanks'll find him when they want him, sure enough. Every blame soul in the whole world seems to know where he is, looks like."

"Well, where are we to go? Even this house is borrowed!"

Custis socks the palm of his hand with a fist. Teeth clench around his smoke. "Ma! Uncle Carter has *begged* and *begged* youall to go stay with him! And that Mrs. Cocke at Derwent has been having a fit for you to take that little house on her property until you all can find—"

"More charity!" Mary flings down the yarn and turns her wrinkled puffy face to her son's. "Charity! Now, I don't mind, I'm not proud. But your father—"

"Mama," Custis takes her hand in his big one and fondles it. "Rob is right," he says gently. "He's young, and he tends to get hysterical over things sometimes. But he's right. Pa can't live like this. Open your eyes, Ma."

It is with these words still repeating in her mind that Mary wheels herself into the back parlor later that afternoon, squeaky wheels upon polished silent floors. If her husband has heard her approach, he gives no sign. He sits slumped against the wall in a wing chair, looking at nothing, hands folded in his lap.

She glides up to his chair, faces him tentatively. Lays a hand

on the sleeve of his gray suit coat that used to be part of a uniform.
They are still in gray, Mary's menfolk. They own nothing else.
Abraham Lincoln has been shot just weeks ago and feeling runs
high among the Federal occupiers against anything Confederate.
The wearing of Confederate uniforms is now forbidden, and
Mary has had to remove all of the military insignia on the shabby
Lee coats and cover the brass buttons with black cloth. "Even our
buttons are in mourning," Rooney has remarked.

She notices that Robert's cuff is frayed. I'll have to get ahold of
that, she tells herself, once he goes back upstairs to bed . . .

"Robert?"

He doesn't look up. Doesn't move.

"You hungry? Mildred is in the kitchen cooking up a storm.
That batch of nice oysters that little Walter Taylor and his wife sent
from Norfolk . . ."

He turns his head slightly, dark bluish circles under the
bloodshot eyes, face haggard and hollow-cheeked. "No, I don't
believe so. Thank you."

"The Taylors said to give you their best. Walter is such a nice
boy."

He puts a hand to his forehead as if he had a headache. "Yes.
Bless him."

"The garden is lovely, Robert. The flowers are all blooming.
Perhaps you could wheel me out on the porch after supper and we
could get a breath of air." She pats his arm. "Remember when we
used to sneak out into the garden, when Papa wasn't looking,
those times you came courtin'? Remember that little pickaninny
who snitched on us that time? What was her name?—Kitty's sister.
The one who had epilepsy. I recollect you telling her you'd turn her
over your knee and give her a good whuppin' if she ever ran off to
Papa again. Law, how I laughed and blushed and laughed some
more! You could always make me laugh, Robert, you had such a
way about you . . . That was right before you asked me to marry
you. I thought you were never going to ask me to marry you." She
tries to laugh. "You remember?"

He stirs. "That was at Arlington."

She hears the sorrow in his voice, the loss. Tries to think of something else to say, some light subject that she can turn the conversation to, but he has already put both hands over his face now and sits immobile. Her grip on his arm tightens.

"Oh Molly, I am so sorry." She can barely hear his muffled words. "I am so very sorry. Please leave me alone for a few minutes. I am afraid that I am not very good company right now."

"No." Her voice is firm. Her crippled fingers tighten. "No, honey. I'm not going to leave you alone."

He remains motionless, hidden, and she wonders how much more he can possibly grieve, how much more grief can possibly come out of one human being.

"Wheel me out onto the porch." She is scared suddenly. Prods. "Traveller is restless out there in the yard and he'll be glad to see you."

Footsteps sound behind her and she turns. Mildred stands there with an apron tied around her old mended dress, brows lifted and mouth about to open with the question. Mary shakes her head no emphatically, and motions her daughter away with a swift wave of a swollen hand.

"Robert. Please look at me."

He doesn't move.

She reaches up and grasps his wrists and pulls the hiding hands away from his bruised eyes. "Look at me, Robert! Look at my hands. Look at my ankles. I'm becoming worse. I need fresh air."

The eyes turn in their hollow sockets and fall upon Mary's blanketed crippled knees.

She sees that she has his attention now, however briefly, and she plunges on before he can stare at the walls again.

"This city is hard on me, honey. It's too damp here for me. And you know how noisy it is. I couldn't sleep last night, soldiers riding endlessly up and down the streets and folks hallooing at all hours. Now, I hate to complain, and I've tried not to. But my fingers are getting so stiff that I can hardly sew. I was darning something for Agnes today and stuck a needle in my finger." She shows him the small red mark, poking the hand under his face before he can turn away, "and I didn't even feel it. It must be the dampness here. We're too close to the river here."

He takes a shallow breath. "Perhaps Dr. McGuire can give you something if he's still in town."

"No. I need to get away, Robert. We need to talk."

Is he listening? She says a prayer and then summons up her old tone of voice, that whining argumentative timbre that used to drive him up the walls in the past. "It is all very well for you and the children, putting up with this constant hubbub and the strangers that come and go in and out of this house at all hours! You don't have to greet them. *I* do. You can stay upstairs, languishing in bed all day, but I must be forever on duty down here, whether I feel well or not. This place is wearing me out, Robert. I feel like a prisoner in this fishbowl!"

"Perhaps I ought to send you to the Wickhams' for the summer, then. They have asked—"

"There are too many folks there already, Robert! And if any of the chicks came up to see me, Rooney or Agnes or Custis, where would they put us all?"

He turns. Sighs and studies her for a moment. He looks at her hands and she tries to make them appear as contorted as possible. "Well, hasn't Mrs. Cocke issued an invitation to stay in a tenant cottage on her property? Didn't someone mention something about that?"

"Oh, *that*," she sniffs. "It's no palace . . . Guess I could give it a try. The fresh country air might do me good. Agnes and Milly and Mary could do all the cooking."

"Leave me at least one of the girls here to act as hostess in case some tomfool ex-senator or somebody shows up."

"No, you'll have to come along, too."

He shakes his head.

She whines for dear life. "Robert Lee, you know I can't stay out there in that little house in the middle of nowhere in these lawless times with nobody but the girls to act as protection!"

He attempts something that might be a smile. "Molly Lee. Are you frightened of a fate worse than death at your venerable age?"

"Hush up and listen! The boys have their own lives to lead! We can't expect them to go on looking after a helpless old mama."

"*I* looked after *my* helpless old mama."

"Well, you did it because you didn't have a father to do it. These boys have a father."

He rubs at his moustache and looks out of the windows at the night coming down.

"Anyone," she goes on, encouraged, "who needs to find us can find us. We won't be that far away. And Traveller can have some decent stabling; won't have to be cooped up the way he is here."

"Where will I find work out there, Mary? We've got to eat someway."

"What work will you find in Richmond?"

"I don't know." He laughs softly. "I don't know how to do anything. We'll starve."

She pats his hand. "You always used to say that you wanted to resign your commission and farm. I never believed it for a minute. But perhaps this is the time to try it, honey. We'll certainly starve if we stay here. Unless you want to go on living upon the charity of friends."

"No. No."

She wonders if he has planned to go on living at all. She searches her mind for something to clinch her argument. "We can invite people up to see us, after we're settled in. Like the old days. Kinfolks. Your brothers. Cousin Markie."

There. She thinks she sees a flicker of interest in the ravaged eyes. He has always been fond of his brothers. "And if poor Rooney should marry again, and the rest of the chicks find spouses, we'll have ample room for little ones to run and play."

"I wish I could purchase Stratford. My papa's old place."

She sees his lighter mood going with the regret in the name of his lost home and she rushes in to stop the disintegration before he is lost to her again. "That's all in the past," she says firmly. "And the past is gone. Please let it go, Robert. Please. I need you so much."

"Do you?" He takes her hand. His is icy cold. "Do you, Moll?"

"I love you," she says, voice suddenly giving out on her in spite of all she can do to keep it even. "I'm old and I'm helpless and I'm scared to death. I need you. And I do love you so much."

Tears roll down his cheeks into the white beard.

"I don't profess to understand you, Robert. I've never understood you. But we haven't got anything now except each other, and what in the world are we going to do?"

He leans slowly over and lays his head in her lap. She embraces his shoulders with both arms and puts her face down until her hair is mingled with his, white upon white.

"I'll never be with you again, Molly." His lips move against her belly. "I'll always be out upon that battlefield, waking and sleeping. I'll never be free of this."

"I know, love. I don't expect more."

"They will probably hang me. And honest to God, I don't care."

"I know."

"And we have been parted for so long, and are such strangers to each other."

"It doesn't matter, love. I'm no longer a young bride. Romance is forever behind me."

He is very still. "But we had some good times, didn't we?" His arms close around her thick waist. She watches the colorless lashes blink against her ribs.

Some good times? She thinks back. Yes, she can recall a few. Smiles, finally. "Some good times. We surely did."

He is asleep when Rob and Custis tiptoe into the room, Mary

gently smoothing the white hair back from his temple with a soft hand. She looks up at her boys, weary eyes relieved. Her mouth shapes three words: "God be thanked."

"Pack your bags, Rob," whispers Custis, "before he changes his mind."

"You 'way behind, old son," answers Rob. "I got me a spoon and a pair of socks and I'm ready to go."

It isn't long before Robert Lee finds work, taking the presidency of broken-down little Washington College because it needs him, and his experience at running West Point, quite as much as he needs it. The pay will be very low and it will be hard at first there in the ravaged Shenandoah where Stonewall Jackson is buried, but Traveller will have room to run and the family will find a measure of peace. The name and fame of Mary's husband attracts much attention to the college from philanthropists in the North and prospective students in the South. Barefooted boys who served in the Confederate ranks will walk hundreds of miles to get an education from General Lee. To find peace.

Markie writes from the North: *What can I do?*

There is nothing that I want, but to see you, Robert replies. *And there is nothing that you can do for me, but to love me.*

So one day a carriage pulls up at the door and a slender handsome woman of about forty emerges, Pre-Raphaelite hair loosely caught up and exotic handbag stuffed with sketchbooks. Mary intercepts her at the door.

"Yes, I look terrible, Markie," she says without ceremony when she sees the expression on the younger woman's face. "I'm chair-bound now, I'm afraid. But get that horrible look off of your face if you plan to go inside. You must be as bright as ever you can make yourself."

Markie hugs her tightly, nearly upsetting the rolling chair. "Where is he?"

"In the front room with the plans for the new college buildings. He thinks you're arriving tomorrow, that's what I told him. Surprise him."

Markie starts to pull away. Mary holds her back. "Markie. Tell me. Why have you never married?"

The woman blinks. Falters. "I cannot love," she says after a moment.

"Yes, you can. It takes an effort."

She bends, long-lashed eyes earnest. "I love you, Cousin Mary. I love all of you. Isn't that enough? My brother was hanged. It hurts to love."

"Look." Mary's twisted hand grips her cousin's wrist tightly. "Markie. Listen. Robert's changed. You won't recognize him. He's the oldest man in the world. If you cannot cope with that—"

Markie says nothing, just nods. Licks her lips.

Mary lowers her eyes. "Thank you for coming, dear. I know that you have better things to do."

"No." She bends to kiss the cheek that is patterned like a map by its wrinkles. She is trembling visibly and can hardly remove her gloves once she straightens. Mary watches with pity but tactfully stays out on the veranda as the visitor disappears.

They have prepared her well with their letters, Mary and Mildred, but still Markie feels herself unprepared. She pinches at her cheeks to make them red and she steps inside the strange house with its unfamiliar furnishings where the Arlington rugs that she herself saved from confiscation four years ago have been doubled under at the edges to fit these smaller rooms. Her breath comes very short. She is thinking: You spineless fool, what are you frightened of? That he will be terribly changed? Or that he will not be changed at all?

She can tell by his posture that he has heard her approach, but he gives no outward sign. He does not look up as she hesitates in the doorway, just carefully wipes the ink from his drawing pen and lays it down on the table next to the fine straight lines of floor plans and building specifications, and Markie tries not to feel anything about the white hair. She has been well prepared. But they have not prepared her for his pallor, and she realizes now that she has never before seen him when he wasn't burnt a ruddy brown by the sun "like a common labourer," as Mary once complained. Markie is prepared for the masking beard, too; but what of these ugly blue circles under his sunken eyes? She can see his pink scalp through the thin hair on top of his bent head. There is a tiny tremor in the hands reaching up to remove the steel-rimmed spectacles—perhaps not entirely a symptom of age. She understands then that he knows who she is without even looking at her.

She twists her gloves into rags, thinking Dear heavens, he looks so bad.

He folds the spectacles carefully and stows them away in the breast pocket of his black suit coat before he lifts his head. Then he meets her stare and stands slowly, and Markie is face-to-face with the most notorious man in America—not the Byronic cavalier who haunts her sleep, but his shadow-self: the traitor, the stranger, a defanged old lion in a cage. He moves from behind the table in slow motion, hobbled.

Markie has expected to feel some pity, perhaps. She has not expected this awe. But it demands awe, this solemn clear-eyed dignity of his, the lifting of his bearded chin, the stand-tall posture, the shreds of pride he wears wrapped around him like a ragged uniform.

And—Oh God, those heartbroken eyes.

She isn't sure what to do, whether to go to him and hold him, or just to turn on her heel and dash out of the house in her new taffeta to curse him in private for the immolation of himself and her own youth.

He stands mute like a prisoner with his pale hands clasped behind his back.

And then he breaks into a little dance step, a buck-and-wing.

Markie blinks like she's been slapped, startled to the depths of her soul. What on earth—?

But that must not be the reaction he is looking for, because he does it again with a solemn flourish—but cannot maintain the solemnity this time and has to stop in mid-shuffle with a low laugh, hands swinging by his sides, one eyebrow lifted. He shrugs after a moment. "I'm running out of ways to break the ice," he mutters, voice lower and tireder and more hoarse than she remembers. "I could use some help here, Miss M."

But she can't think of anything to say. She looks helplessly into his eyes.

"You look like you've eaten a bad oyster, Miss M., and don't know where to spit it." He holds his arms open, tentative, and then drops them suddenly before she can go into them. It is clear that he expects a rebuff.

She covers her face with one hand to hide the destruction of her composure and gropes for him with the other, gloves flapping in her fist. The gloves fall. He is at her fingertips, his shoulder, and then the warm bushy hair at the back of his neck. She pulls him into her and is enveloped by him, and he is as hard and clean and strong as she remembers.

Mary closes her eyes and dozes in the sun outside. But she awakens to the sound of heartfelt laughter, low and high, coming from the front room.

She smiles, wry. I never knew how to make him laugh, she thinks. But I know how to import someone who can.

The sun shines low at the mountains, making them blue. Mary squints against the brightness, the bright air, the inevitable loss of another day. She rubs at a cheek with her gnarled fingers, sighs, and is glad that no one is around to hear that sigh. Someone might mistake its reason. Might identify jealousy.

I used to think him incapable of love, she muses. Incapable of loving anyone, when it should have been perfectly clear to me that he is capable instead of loving *everyone*. Is that what I really resented? I don't know.

The resentment has gone. When did it go? Life is so brief.

What we need now is time, Heavenly Father. This is what she thinks day after day when Robert saddles Traveller to ride out alone into the mountains. The world presses in on all sides and he flees to find solitude, a paroled prisoner, thinking thoughts that Mary can only guess at. But she thanks God every time he returns, thanking God for the gift of a little more time before the axe falls.

Because the axe is going to fall. She can see it in his face. He will stay with them all as long as he can bear it, but when he can bear it no longer, he will go off to join his dead soldiers.

Two weeks after Markie's visit, Mary wakes in the middle of a rainy night to discover him in her room, sitting slumped and silent on the edge of her bed in his robe and nightshirt. She puts out a hand and he takes it after a while.

"Are you all right?" she asks.

He answers with a question. "Why am I alive?"

"To bind up wounds, love."

"Which I inflicted."

"I swanny, you are the most self-centered man! It took many more people than you to inflict all this misery, Mr. Lee!" She is grateful for the dark. Because her eyes are moist. And because she is terrified.

Thirty-Five

It was immediately apparent that something was very wrong with me.

I had tried to stand at once, my first worry being that the people below had heard my fall and would be soon swarming up the stairs to investigate. I certainly did not want to be found guiltily entangled in the railing.

But my ugly left leg would not bear my weight. A blow torch ran up the nerves to my brain as soon as I tried to put my foot to the floor and I collapsed again, a thudding sound, sure this time that the guides would come. Cussing, I dragged myself over the smooth wood of the floor and leaned back against the wall a safe distance from the barricade. Sticky sweat pouring down the sides of my face, I gave my full attention now to the pain and found it so ominous that I drew inwardly back for a moment, covering the leg with my skirt so that I wouldn't have to look at it, seeking refuge in a kind of giddy laugh and looking out at the dark sky through the windows of Robert's room across the hall.

I think I have broken my shitty leg, I said to myself, repressing the urge to shout it, repressing the urge to laugh wildly. I've broken my rotten ugly shitty leg. And nobody knows I'm up here. It's raining and thundering so hard, nobody has heard me fall. I'll get locked up in here tonight, in the middle of Arlington National Cemetery, with John F. Kennedy and a stupid broken leg.

I did laugh then, aware of the pain-induced hysteria in the sound. I pulled back the blue gingham ruffle to expose an appalling puffy reddened swelling beginning just under my knee. I didn't touch it; touching it was unthinkable. I might feel the jagged ends of bone just under the skin and I wasn't ready to touch anything like that just yet.

Surely You must exist after all, I told God in my mind, leaning back against the orange wall with a dry mouth. And I must say that You have one cosmically warped sense of humor.

I was thinking that I could hear someone calling my name again. I couldn't be sure with the wind-sounds rattling at the windows, but I didn't give in to the notion this time that the calling came from another time and maybe another life. The otherworldly mood in which I had explored the bedrooms was totally gone.

It's amazing how a healthy dose of pain can de-obsess a person, I said to myself, trying to remain perfectly still. It's amazing how a good shot of 100-proof pain can snuff out even the most powerful erotic fantasy. Cold showers definitely have to take a back seat.

Someone yelled my name again. A living voice. The voice of a living breathing person. An impatient angry Yankee voice.

Yanks in this house again, I thought, dizzy. Just won't stay away. Carpetbaggers come to carry me off.

"Up here, Bill!" I shouted at the stairs.

A drumming hollow thudding came from below, feet pounding on the old wooden steps. A dark shaggy head appeared, the shoulders next, and then a small man in a seersucker suit who popped out onto the floor and bounded over to my side.

I looked up at him. Didn't move a muscle. "What took you so long, hotshot? I've broken my dadblame leg."

He stooped down quickly, mad, starting to say something like: For crying out loud, Garnet, you've scared me to death, I thought you'd been kidnaped or—

"I'm not kidding." I twitched back the fabric of my long skirt. "I've broken my leg."

His face went all strange. "Jesus. You've broken your leg!"

"That's what I said. Boom boom. Busted."

His eyes were big and round. "How—?"

"*Don't touch it,* for God's sake. I can't walk. Go downstairs, please, and see if they've got a stretcher or a rolling chair or somethin'."

"How?"

"Fell down the stairs. Up the stairs. It doesn't matter. Should've never worn this idiotic long dress."

He winced audibly. "God! God!"

"Please go get somebody. Tell 'em I won't sue 'em."

He stood jerkily. Licked his lips a time or two. Waved a flapping hand at me. "Stay right here. I'll be right back. Don't move."

"I'm not going anywhere. Depend on it."

He galloped back downstairs, feet shaking life back into the old house. I could hear his urgent voice coming up from below, loud excited shouting mingled with the murmurs of the hostesses. I leaned back against the wall and grinned, eyes closed.

"Bet you haven't witnessed this much excitement," I said to the old house, "since the Yanks threw wild parties here and tossed the furniture out of windows."

Bill's footsteps shook the floors again and he came running back up the stairs, this time with a cup of water in his hand. He crouched and handed me two small white tablets. "They're calling an ambulance. Here. Gotcha some aspirin."

I laughed, disbelieving. *"Aspirin?"*

"You expected morphine? This is the best I could do, lady."

I dutifully swallowed the pitiful offering and gulped at the water. "Oh, oh," I said. "A mistake. Now I'm nauseated."

"Think about something else. They'll be here in a minute. Shouldn't we maybe put ice or something on—?"

"*Don't touch it.* I dunno. I don't know what should be done. I've never broken my leg before." I began to giggle uncontrollably. "Bill!" I shouted between spasms of laughter. "Can you believe it? Can you believe this?"

"Sit still!" he ordered, sitting down on the floor beside me in his rumpled summer suit. "Just don't move."

"My crappy leg. My crappy leg. Can you believe its treachery? I'll have to go to the debate thingies in a goddam *cast!*"

"Have you got any insurance?" He was fumbling at my purse, extracting a wallet. "Have you got an insurance card? Do you want me to call your parents? Where's the number?"

"*Yes,* I've got insurance. *No,* don't call my parents. You worry my parents with this, and I'll tell everybody you pushed me down the stairs." I collapsed against the wall, hands in lap helplessly, and howled with laughter.

"This isn't funny, Garnet."

"I laugh or I puke. Take your pick. Here. Sit still, Bill. I'm not going to sue you either."

An anxious hostess swept up the stairs in a hoop skirt. I was tickled to see that she wore penny loafers. "Oh heavens, oh heavens," she kept moaning, "I've told the park officials that they ought to replace the handrails on these narrow dark old stairs."

"It's all right," I muttered. "It might spoil the look. The barricades at the doorways already spoil the look."

"People would go in and steal the antiques," the girl dithered, looking anxiously at her wristwatch. "What's *keeping* the ambulance?"

"This house is used to folks stealin' from it," I mumbled, looking futilely at the ceiling.

"Can we get you anything, Miss? A pillow?"

I stared at the hostess and she moved off to the head of the stairs, hands twisting at her sides.

The ambulance came and the paramedics hustled up the stairs like the U.S. Cavalry. "I had to pay for the taxi ride out here," I said gaily to Bill while the blue-shirted men carefully lifted me onto a stretcher-like affair. "Insurance didn't cover *that* trip." I craned my neck to look at the route ahead of us and then addressed the paramedics. "You guys really believe you can get this stretcher down that little bitty staircase?"

They said nothing. Just strapped me on and lifted me.

So I was carried down the stairs that Molly Custis had glided over in her wedding dress. Bill Damadian clumped right behind. A small knot of people stood below under the portraits, curious and staring. I waved.

Our entourage stepped out onto the portico and I was loaded hurriedly into the ambulance. Bill moved to my side, the rain plastering his Beatle haircut to the sides of his face. "Hey," said a paramedic, barring his way.

"He's family," I called out, and the ambulance men stepped back to let my teacher inside the vehicle.

I could see the great fake Greek columns recede from where I lay as the ambulance pulled away from the house. Lonely Greek columns in the rain. I haven't found what I came here for, I realized. Turn back. Turn back.

Bill took my hand.

The siren blatted fitfully at pedestrians and then shut off. Tires hummed on the wet pavement of Lincoln Drive or Sherman Drive.

"My great-granddaddy took a shotgun to Sherman's men," I murmured to Bill as the ambulance purred through the graveyard. "He wasn't but nine years old."

Bill pressed close to me. "What did you see back there, lady?"

I was confused. I couldn't get my brain to work right. "What?"

He licked his lips. "Back there at that place. Did you see anything back there at that place?"

I paused. A long thinking pause. "No."

"What happened?"

"Nothing."

"What caused you to fall?"

"Nothing caused me to fall. I'm a klutz."

Neon lights played over his face as we were driven into Washington. Reds and blues.

The hospital was chaos. I was grilled about insurance while a black man bled from a stab wound and a woman in labor went *whuff-whuff-whuff.* Bill waited smoking in the lounge. My dim brain finally understood that they would X-ray me and set my broken bone and certainly keep me overnight. They gave me some kind of shot. My leg was numb now, and I kept looking at it to make sure that it was still there. I was numb all over. Somebody had put me into a dinky little white garment with no back to it . . .

"Bill?" I said suddenly to an unfamiliar ceiling.

A hand took hold of mine. A round worried face materialized over me. "Right here, lady. Right here."

"Bill. Robert's dead, Bill. I don't feel him anymore. I don't feel anything at all."

"What?"

I tried to remember. Groggy. My drugged mind searched itself for the Other. Tried to visualize the young lieutenant at my side. Groggy. There had been nothing at all at Arlington. The face wouldn't come.

"There was nobody at that house. They've given me something, haven't they? Drugs or something. I can't feel him anymore, Bill. He's dead. My mourning fan is back at the motel. Damn."

A nurse's face swam into my unreal vision. "What?" I heard the woman ask my friend. "What's the matter?"

Bill paused. "A death in the family."

"No! Somebody I loved." I heard my own voice trying to tell the motherly face bending over me. "I'm all right. But somebody I loved is dying. Everything is killing him. They've barricaded all the rooms. I can't go inside."

A cold softness wiped at the inside of my elbow. I felt the prick of a needle going in. "Oh, no!" I tried to jerk away. "Oh no, you needn't. I'm all right, really."

"She needs to rest," the nurse said. "I've given her something to make her sleep. You can come back in the morning, Mr. Damadian."

"Oh no, oh no, don't send him off!" I could hear someone pleading. It was probably me. "He's the only one who understands! He's the only one who *knows!* I'm quite all right, I'm so alone . . . I'm so alone."

"Garnet." Bill's strong hand clamped onto my arm. "You sleep now. Understand? I'll be back in the morning. Bubba and David Dale and I'll be back here as soon as this fucking place opens up."

"Bill." I giggled. "Don't say bad words in front of the nurse. Dear Bill. She'll think we're trash." Then: "What about the debate workshop?"

"*Fuck* the debate workshop. I'll be here first thing in the morning, lady. That's a promise."

"Oh Bill." Tears started to run into my ears. I fought sleep, feeling like alien parasites were trying to take over my brain. My head buzzed. "I think he's dead, Bill."

There was breathing in my face. My eyes wouldn't open. The aliens from Jupiter were sitting on them. Finally a quiet voice murmured, "He was always dead, Garnet. He's been dead for a hundred years."

My hands went wildly to my head. I clutched at my disheveled hair. "But not to *me!* Not *up here!*" I pressed at my brain.

"Sleep now, lady."

"I can't concentrate, Bill. It takes an effort to find him. I can't make the effort. He's not with me. He's not up here. And by the time morning comes, I might not be able to ever get him back again."

He squeezed my hand.

"Bill?" I called, eyes shut, to the empty room.

Bill was gone. Everybody was gone. I didn't know how long they had been gone. I couldn't open my eyes. I didn't want to open my eyes.

Am I empathizing? I wondered as I felt myself slipping into dark sleep. Am I living it after all, even now? Am I finally empathizing his death?

Can't a medium choose what she wants to plug into?

Do people really take drugs for *fun?*

I fought it off. Fought off the slip-slide down. Oh God, I prayed to my Einsteinian idea, seeing time lines in my mind all wavering and converging and tangled like spaghetti.

Oh God, I'm so jazzed up with chemicals that I believe in You. I can hear You in the screams of that expectant mother in labor, seven floors away. I can see You in the aliens that are stealing my brain. I can feel Your heart beating in my silver pin.

Oh God of parallel lines. O God of engineers. O God of my grandmother's questions. Do me one favor, God, while I believe: Look around and find the year 1870. There is a man dying in 1870. Look around in that infinite motel room of Yours and find him.

Be good to him, God. Be close to him. Take him gently.

Hold his hand.

The time lines turned neon like the lights of the Washington streets. Parallel lines converged at the horizon like a railroad track. Then the neon went out and I sank, going limply into sleep, repeating Robert Robert Rob—

Thirty-Six

Robert Robert Robert . . .

Someone is calling his name. He opens his eyes.

The October rains rattle against the windowpanes. He tries to speak: Markie? Markie?

Nothing comes out. His lips move.

Mildred drops his hand and scurries from the bedside. Her voice is hushed. "Mama? Mama. He wants you—"

Mary hastily throws down her knitting and grasps the wheels of her chair. Mildred hurries to help maneuver the rolling chair closer to the little bed near the fire where confused dark eyes look out of a gaunt face.

"Robert? Honey?" She takes up his cold hand and lifts it to her wrinkled cheek. "What is it, honey?"

He doesn't speak. His eyes are like black pools of space.

The rain drums at the windows.

"Do you know me, Robert?" She waits. Mildred breathes noisily behind her.

There is a weak pressure of his hand. He nods Yes.

"Were you dreaming?"

He looks into the firelight. His eyes slowly close. Mary caresses his hand. Her fingers close around his wrist. There are runaway horses in his wrist. The weak pulse pounds, screaming.

"Milly." Mary's voice comes out in low even tones. She does not look around. "Summon the doctor. And get Reverend Pendleton in here."

There is a sharp intake of breath behind her and she turns. Mildred has put both hands over her white-lipped mouth.

"Mildred! Go quietly."

The girl flees from the room, soft quick feet first walking. Then running.

Mary sits there holding her husband's hand in a kind of frozen calm. She sits and sits, mind carefully blanked, stroking the wrist as if her touch could soothe the runaway pulse. She is astonished at her calmness, not even trying for it. Not knowing how she could try for it if she had to. It just *is,* this calm.

He was supposed to have been regaining his health, that's why the college had lately sent him south to Florida for a rest in a temperate climate. It had been a stupid idea.

He had traveled by train with only Agnes as companion. The doctors who had imagined that such a journey might be restful were not there to see the mobs of people waiting at every little Southern whistle stop with flowers and bands and babies. Telegraph operators at one town would transmit the news of his advent to the next, and Agnes would look up to see strangers' heads poking through the windows of the railway carriage and hear the everlasting bands striking up "Bonnie Blue Flag", and she and her father would exchange a look. "Well," he would sigh when the mayors came to fetch him, "well . . ."

Raggedy people lined the tracks from Richmond all the way to Florida, standing patiently in the darkness or the daylight with their children sheltered under their greatcoats, the young Woodrow Wilson among them. Elizabeth Ann Cooke stood silent in her shabby widow's black with eight-year-old Liza at the station in

Columbia, South Carolina, where the rains came down and the dripping crowd fell quiet when it saw that figure emerge onto the platform. Hands came up and took away motheaten hats and the water rolled down bare heads and into the beards of the veterans, and some of the water was only water and some of it was tears.

He emerged onto the platform, smaller somehow than the veterans remembered, less erect. Big hands and a plain black civilian suit, face and head all white and bleached: a translucent figure standing hatless in the rain. Transfiguration, bled white of all passion, only the black eyes alive and aware and reflecting love. The band music died to a final tootle. Parents raised their babies in their hands for blessing. The rain came down upon the ravaged streets. "Make your children Americans," he said to the love.

They visited Lighthorse Harry's grave on Cumberland Island in Georgia, and little Annie's grave in North Carolina. Agnes made wreaths of wildflowers. Her father said nothing, just shambled from the tombstones of his daughter and father with one white hand pressed to his waistcoat. Agnes asked him nothing.

It had been a stupid idea, this journey. His heart hurt him and Agnes would watch him press a palm to his breastbone, the luminous eyes seeing something in the burnt and bombed-out landscapes that she never saw.

It was nearly two weeks ago that he was stricken, two weeks since he was laid here in the dining room of the Washington College house with his face to the firelight. He did not smile once in all that time but he dutifully took the medicines that the doctors poured down his throat.

"It is no use," Mary heard him murmur to the doctors. "It is no use."

"*Please,* Pa!" Mildred and Agnes begged. So he swallowed the stuff that they hoped would cure him, while their anxious faces ringed his bed.

Custis mentioned something about Traveller needing exercise and about how Pa must hurry up and get well so that the beautiful horse might be ridden out into the mountains again.

But the man on the bed shook his head. One index finger pointed slowly up to the ceiling. To heaven.

"I don't believe Pa wants to get well," Custis wept into Mary's arms, thirty-eight-year-old strength useless and unavailing. "He's not tryin', Ma. He's not fightin'."

"Law law, son," she muttered, fondling the dark hair. "Don't you think he's fought enough?"

The doctor comes rushing in with his little satchel full of mysterious things. He bends and takes the hand away from Mary, clutches at the wrist with his monitoring pocket watch six inches from his eyes, and then suddenly drops the hand to rip back the bedclothes. He pulls open the fastenings of the nightshirt to expose the chest where the pounding heart lurches visibly under the hairy skin. The patient on the bed has begun to thrash, eyelids fluttering, mouth open in silent torture.

The doctor spins, this man in his undertaker's black frock coat. His hands struggle at his satchel straps. "This is no place for you, Madam," he tells Mary. "Please go elsewhere."

She starts to protest but the Reverend-ex-General Pendleton has come out of nowhere and he wheels her through the curtained double doorway against her will. She is shut out. Mildred and Agnes are pressed against the wall in the rainy daylight, pale faces shining blue.

Mary looks up at the old clergyman, the old ex-soldier, still surprised at her calmness. "I've always left him alone too much, General," she says. "In God's name, let me be with him now."

"The doctor'll call you if he needs assistance," says Pendleton with a professional cheery voice. "You know that doctors prefer to putter around by themselves. Onlookers make them nervous. Let's go in yonder and have a cup of tea and—"

"Milly!" Mary signals her daughter to come push her chair back into the sickroom.

Pendleton blocks Mildred's way, hands on the back of the rolling chair, false cheer gone. "Mrs. Lee. Mary, Mary. We've got to let the doctor do as he sees fit. You must. You *must*."

Agnes leans against the wall. "I thought he was getting better, Mama, I thought he was getting better!"

"And the others can't get here because of the flood! Rob. Mary. Rooney." There is a note of rising hysteria in Mildred's voice. "They can't get here, Mama."

"Make some tea." Mary waves her hands. "Milly, make some tea. Make some tea, one of you. Make some tea."

It is a long time before Doctor Barton emerges from the sickroom to summon his colleague, Doctor Madison. Madison arrives and Mary overhears the two physicians in conference at the front door where the rain splashes in, overhears Doctor Barton saying, "—pulse is very rapid and quite feeble now. Breathing labored. I suggest we apprise the family of the danger."

"I am apprised." Mary rolls herself out of the shadows. Doctor Madison removes his dripping silk hat. "My daughters have brewed some tea, gentlemen. Would you join us in the kitchen? I apologize for its disorder."

She leaves them sitting around the table uneasily with the girls and Reverend Pendleton and she wheels her heavy body back to the parlor where she can still hear their muffled attempts at pleasantries. She has some difficulty with the sickroom curtained doorway but manages to get the chair through without aid. She adjusts her lace cap back upon her white curls and rolls herself quietly back to the fireside where her husband lies.

Young Professor William Preston Johnston, son of late Confederate General Albert Sidney Johnston, blinks at her from the sofa. "I'm relieving you of duty, young man," she tells him. "Go take some tea. I've some shortbread in the kitchen. Help yourself."

"Mrs. Lee—"

"Get out of here, Preston. Don't make me get mean."

He disappears.

She reaches for the graceful hand lying among the linen.

"Robert? Do you know me?"

This time there is no response. Mary leans over and looks closely at the still face on the pillow, remembering all the mornings she would wake up to find that face on the pillow next to hers, the once-black hair streaming over the white cloth.

He does not seem to be in any pain now. That is a mercy. She has come in more than once in the past few days to find him struggling voiceless to turn over, to escape, anguish in the eyes. She bends over now to kiss the cold lips where the breath rushes in and out, fast, panting.

The lips move. He is speaking.

She bends closer. "Yes? Yes? It's Molly, Robert. Molly."

"The guns . . ." His voice is not even a whisper. "Place your guns upon that ridge yonder, Colonel . . ."

He is talking to his soldiers.

In all this time, in all these five years since the surrender, he has rarely spoken of the war. It has been something he will simply not discuss. She has tried to lead him into the subject more than once, she or the children or Cousin Markie during her visits, thinking that if he'll talk about it he might find some measure of peace in the discussion. But he has limited himself to compliance with the new Federal government, has made himself an example to other disfranchised Confederate veterans by burying any subject that might contribute to sectional hatred. The United States has answered his efforts with venom, refusing him citizenship or pardon, denouncing him continually in their newspapers until Mary has had to throw several issues of the New York *Tribune* into the fire in a rage. He has angered her with this seeming ability to forget. Arlington is gone and she will not forgive.

People from all over the world have sent him presents: books dedicated to him by famous English authors; knick-knacks and mementos that he unwraps up in his monastic little narrow-bedded room where his father's sword hangs on the wall.

"Let me see! Let me see!" she begs him when a delivery is made, "I swan, you are the *greediest* man alive—"

"Mama," Rooney has told her once, shoving her rolling chair against the wall, "Some of those packages contain—"

"He takes them immediately upstairs before I even get a chance to—!"

"Mama!" Rooney has hissed, something in his moon face making her blood congeal. "Some of those packages and letters contain *obscene* things, Mama! Things that he doesn't want you to see. Miniature nooses, Mama. Demented things."

Mary has understood, finally. Has allowed Robert to climb the stairs with his packages, with his calm wrinkled smile going back to her from over the banister before he disappears into his room with the brown-papered parcels.

She has wept, understanding. Wishing that she had strength enough to kill. He's been taking more laudanum than is good for him lately.

Now he lies before the fire and talks to his soldiers.

She grips his hand tightly.

"I never went with you to those frightful army camps," she tells him. "I stayed home and sulked like a blame child. But I'm coming with you now."

All that night he murmurs inaudibly. The doctors come and go. Mary sits sleepless in her rolling chair by his side, and the forbidding look upon her long-nosed sharp features discourages anyone who might dare to budge her. The girls bring her periodic cups of tea and Custis comes in to massage her tired sagging shoulders.

Dawn comes rainy and ugly, a smear of clouds crosses the sky.

"They say if a person makes it through the night . . ." Agnes begins hopefully, but does not finish the thought.

And the doctors look at one another, their palms upon the panting chest, and they do not smile.

The war goes on. Sometimes they can understand what he is saying and sometimes they cannot: Grant tries to break through the Bloody Angle lines near Spotsylvania and Lee organizes a countercharge to push him back, placing himself in danger at the head of his men, determined to personally lead them, goading them on until they grab Traveller by the bridle to hustle their protesting commander back from the gunfire, telling him that they'll fix Grant's wagon if he will just *go back* away from the exploding shells. Mary and Custis and Mildred and Agnes hear him arguing with somebody, acquiescing, arguing again. Issuing orders to men long dead.

"He's wearing himself out," Mary hears Doctor Barton tell Reverend Pendleton. "You here to pray? You'd better pray now."

Pendleton opens his prayerbook and begins to read in a voice an octave too high and then they are all on their knees except Mary who can't kneel and won't let go of the cold hand. She hears the whispered orders that issue from the incoherent lips, hears them even over the sad drone of the clergyman's prayers as she sits open-eyed by the bed.

One by one, her children stumble off upstairs to catch a few hours of sleep. The Johnston boy goes home. Mary dozes by the bedside, cramped hand gripping her husband's and soggy with his perspiration.

Someone touches her shoulder. She wakes instantly. The fire is flickering and the windows are very dark with the rainy night.

"Mrs. Lee?"

No one needs to tell her. She can hear Robert's exhausted shallow breath from where she sits, can feel the icy cold of his hand where no heat can warm it.

Doctor Barton stands over her. She blinks up into his bearded face with grave weary eyes.

"Better go wake up your children."

She nods and motions to Pendleton who sits on the sofa with a hand over his face.

He goes out and returns with Mildred and Agnes, wrappers flung hastily over their nightgowns. They clutch each other in a spasm of trembling, long dark plaits of hair intermingled, Custis right behind them carrying a light.

"Tell General Hill he *must* come up," the man on the bed

mutters, oblivious, exhausted, shivering in the grip of the final cold. Struggling for the next breath.

"Goddam," says Custis, and it is more of a prayer than a curse.

The weeping girls gather around the bedside with their brother, and the doctors and Pendleton tactfully leave the room. Mildred tries to fan the fevered face with a flattened newspaper. Agnes moistens a cloth in a basin and holds it to the cracking lips.

He lies on his right side, knees drawn up, hair and linen soaked with sweat. Mary brings the lifeless hand to her lips, studies the blue cast of the nails, looks at the lifeline and knows that there are people who can read the lines in a palm. But she is not one of them. She squeezes the fingers together and kisses the tips.

It is a mystery, she thinks. It is all a mystery. Everything. Come for him, Mystery. He's tired.

Thirty-Seven

🦋

Bubba was the first one to autograph my cast the next morning upon my release from the hospital. He wrote *Charles Hegler Hargett—Future Pres. of the U.S.A.* in large Magic Marker script on my instep and then helped me with my crutches.

"Be healed! Be healed!" David Dale was doing his Oral Roberts routine.

"Cut it out," I muttered, depressed.

Bill had the Valiant at the curb. All the luggage was tied on top, mine included. I regarded my own suitcase under the tarpaulin as Bill sat there with the car doors expectantly open.

"Get in," he said. "We're going home."

Bubba had me by the arm. I turned to him and shook my head. Turned back to Bill, puzzled. "No," I said. "We'll miss the workshop."

David Dale yawned. "Fooey on the workshop."

"No!" I looked from one to another. They looked back at me, zombie-like. "No! Git your butts back there and let's show 'em what we can do! I'll go to the podium in a wheelchair, if necessary.

But don't let anything run us off! Not until we've mixed it up a little with those Harvard-bound preppies and bloodied some noses."

"Ain't you bloodied enough noses, Garn?" Bubba grinned.

"Get in the car, Garnet," Bill said patiently, starting the engine. "We'll come back next year and blow everybody away. I promise. But we're not ready now. We're not up to it."

Bubba maneuvered my heavy cast into the back seat and climbed in beside me. "We'll be back next year, ol' partner," he told me. "Only we'll be comin' as South Carolina State Champs, you and me. Depend on it."

"Bill?" I leaned over the seat as the Valiant pulled away from the curb and nosed out into traffic. "Don't mess this trip up for the guys, just because I broke my stupid leg."

David Dale turned. "We took a vote last night. All of us. If somebody's sick in your family, then we got no business wastin' our money up here."

"Bill!" I banged at his shoulder. "Who's sick?"

"Don't *do* that! You'll make me have a wreck! Look. The guys decided, lady. It was their decision."

Bubba spoke. "We went to the opening shindig last night, Garn. We ain't in those guys' league. Not yet. We'll make fools outta ourselves if we participate, and we're wasting our money if we don't. Let's go home and practice."

"Don't let them intimidate you!"

I saw Bill's face in the rearview mirror. "This isn't war, Garnet."

"We're sorry, Garnet." David Dale turned in his seat once more. "Sorry about your—family thing."

I leaned forward to ask into Bill's ear: "What family thing? Did Grandmama—?"

"Your *cousin*," he said firmly.

I understood, suddenly. "My . . .? Cousin. Yes."

"I think we ought to get you home, lady."

I tentatively felt around in my psyche. Found nothing. Robert was gone. Going. I was not Markie or Mary. I was a silly girl with a broken leg.

Bubba must have seen my face. "It's all right," he patted my hand. "You can cry if you wanna."

"No."

The Valiant sped across the Key Bridge into Virginia.

"Good ol' Dixie!" David Dale rolled down the window all the way and sniffed the air as if it should somehow smell better on this side of the Potomac.

We drove on in silence, the radio humming with static. The guys wanted to stop for lunch in Richmond but Bill met my eyes in the mirror and drove on, finally stopping further on in a little town that meant nothing to me.

I got out of the car and balanced on my crutches, face to the blue wall of the Blue Ridge that barricaded me from the Shenandoah. I was shut out. I was shut out because I no longer had the energy to will myself inside. But the mountains were real. They were real mountains, solid and massive and stone. And I was the victim of the physical world; I was somebody unspecial who could break my leg doing something ludicrous.

Bill helped me into the coffeeshop. "I wouldn't have flipped out just because we stopped in Richmond," I told him while the guys shopped for magazines at the news stand next door.

Bill put down his coffee cup and lit a cigarette. "How do you feel?"

"Perfectly sane, if that's what you mean. Gimme a cigarette."

He lit one for me. I asked the waitress for more coffee.

"Lee still gone?"

"I don't know. The mountains look so solid."

"You sound drugged and spaced-out again."

I took a slug of my coffee. "He's buried on the other side of those mountains yonder. They look so solid. It's a hard impression to overcome, their solidity. I should never have come up here and *seen* and *touched*. There's nothing to see and touch, except mountains and brass barricades at Arlington. I don't know what I'm gonna do with myself now, Bill."

"What did you do with yourself before all this happened?"

"Worried about my crappy leg."

"How many times are you going to need to stop at gas stations, drinking all that coffee?"

I leaned into the cushions in my booth seat and blew smoke into the chilled food–smelling air. "I'm numb. It's like I've had a shock treatment or something. I'll be too numb to pee."

He doodled in the spilled sugar on the formica table top. "You'll have to grieve some, you know, lady. You'll have to get it all out of your system. Before you can put all of this behind you."

There was a void inside me. "Put *WHAT* behind me? What was this thing? What have I been through?"

"You want me to classify it? To label it?"

I stared. "Yes. Call it a neurotic episode. The first of many, perhaps."

He looked troubled. "I can't do that, lady. If this was a movie . . . Oh, they'd give you a label: 'Garnet Laney was a psychic. A medium.' Or maybe, 'Garnet Laney was a reincarnation of somebody else.'"

"Or 'Garnet Laney went a little gaga when she was seventeen years old.'"

"Maybe," he said. "But things don't always have neat little labels. I don't know what this was. We won't ever know for sure. Neither of us. Thank God it's ending, though. You couldn't have lived your life—"

"Yes I could. Yes. Yes."

"Now that's the craziest thing I've ever heard you say," he said severely.

I stubbed out my cigarette in an ashtray. "There is a lot of inspiration in loving from a distance. Look at Dante and Beatrice."

"Bullshit. That's crap. No one can live like that. If Lee were alive, would he want you to live like that? Would he, Garnet?"

I knew the answer immediately. "No."

"You are the damndest woman."

I drained my cup. Put it down. "Maybe this is the last crazy thing you'll every hear me say, Bill. Maybe this is the last crazy thought I'll ever have, but I only wish I could have done something to help him. If part of me once lived in the nineteenth century, I only hope that I helped him."

"This is nuts," he agreed while truck drivers swarmed in around us and put money into the juke box. "This is crazy."

"But he helped me, Bill. He's helped me turn a big corner in my life. And if I ever make something out of myself, it'll be because he lived."

He laughed. Flicked sugar into my hair.

"Stoppit. You're not Southern. You haven't grown up with the inferiority complex that we grow up with. You haven't had the rest of the country always putting you down and telling you how dumb and benighted and stupid and racist you are."

"Okay. Lee wasn't dumb or benighted or racist. Do you know anything about immigrants, Garnet? Do you know what it's like not being a WASP?"

"Well that's not the same thing! It's not cool to make ethnic jokes anymore about Polacks or Jews—"

"—or Armenians," he said.

"I've never heard any Armenian jokes. Hush! I'm trying to make a point! People who tell mean ethnic jokes about immigrants are not cool. But nobody minds if someone wants to poke fun at a redneck. Rednecks aren't supposed to mind. They aren't supposed to have sense enough to mind. They're supposed to just laugh along and say, 'Aw shucks!' Well dammit, I'm not laughing along anymore. I'm sorry if you and Eva What's-her-face find it morally wrong for me to be proud of my traitor slaveholding ancestors, Bill. But they are all the ancestors I've got, and I love them, even if I don't love what they stood for.

"So you can keep Grant and Sherman and all the rest. And put up a statue of Robert E. Lee in the National Capitol Building, if you want. Write about him as the most innovative military mind in American history and speak of his influence upon Doug Mac-Arthur and Dwight Eisenhower all you want to, as if the line was unbroken from American general to American general. Try to co-opt him now, if you want to. You can't. The line has been broken. Y'all did it. You wouldn't claim him after the war. Fine. He's ours, ours alone, forever and ever, by mutual choice. We chose him and he chose us. We were *worth* choosing. So the rest of you will just have to make do with Sherman and Grant and the rest of the second-raters. We haven't had any U.S. Presidents until Johnson. We're used to being a joke. The poorest. The baddest. And we are *bad*. Yes, we're bad. But we've got Robert E. Lee, and you can't have him."

Bill held up his hands at my tirade and smiled. "Lady, my ancestors were in Turkey getting murdered until 1927! Now don't try to accuse *me* of stealing your heritage."

"Well, *somebody* stole it. Or made it ugly. And much of it *is* ugly. And bigoted. And stupid. And backward. But it's all I've got, and I ain't apologizing for it anymore."

"Who do you think separated you from your history, Garnet? What makes you want to go to Greenwich Village and write mediocre poetry for a bunch of unwashed Antioch grads?"

I sat mute.

"Next thing you'll tell me," Bill signaled the waitress for the check, "is that Lee broke your leg."

"He did. Indirectly."

"And that you're glad of it."

"I am. Profoundly."

He looked up into my stare. "Bull," he said. "You've got a cast to hide behind now. But the cast is going to have to come off, lady."

I waited until the waitress left the table but then I reached over and grabbed Bill's hand, fierce. "I've got a *reason* for it now. The hardest thing to bear about this stupid leg has always been the fact that I never knew why it was made this way. My grandmother used to drive me starkers, asking 'What's the matter with your leg?' all the time. Do you know what that's like? To be afflicted with something, and not even have a clinical diagnosis for it? It's been like having leprosy. Stupid. Nebulous."

Bill had his chin in his hands, face solemn, watching me. The waitress came back to get the money for the meal and he didn't move.

I paid her. "This time next year, when I'm packing up to go off to college," my voice was getting a little treble, "I won't have to be so scared of meeting new people. I won't have to avoid their questions. I can tell them that I once broke my leg. And we can let it go at that. Everybody understands a broken leg."

He took my hand. Squeezed it.

"I have a reason for it now, Bill. And who cares if the results happened before the reason? I don't think I'll ever pay any more attention to time as long as I live."

I could see the guys coming back with their *Playboy* magazines and lumpy paper-sacked bundles under their arms. I pulled my hand away from Bill's and took several deep breaths. "Y'all ready to roll?" asked Bubba.

Damadian nodded.

"I just wish I could have helped him in some way," I muttered again to him as he helped me to the car. "I loved him. I just wish I could have helped him a little." I stopped. Listened to myself. "That sounds insane, doesn't it?"

"Who knows? Maybe it works both ways," Bill answered in a low voice as he pulled back the seat for me and guided my cast inside with the new crutches. "There's a strong streak of the Romantic in me. I like to believe that ordinary human love can transcend anything. Even time. Maybe he's felt you close, just once, the way you've felt him. Maybe you were alive then, and did your duty by him. Who is to say?"

"Not if I was Markie. He wrote her one last letter and told her to hurry. She didn't make it. She didn't come. I don't know why she didn't come."

"Garnet," Bill muttered, real low, "it's the wife who has the rightful place at a deathbed. That poor woman Markie did the only right thing there was to do, even if it meant that she would never get to say goodbye. Maybe that's what all this has been about. Saying goodbye."

"Through me?"

"I don't know." He sighed. "Now I sound kin to looney myself . . ."

Bubba ran over and scrambled in beside me, gently trying not to bump my cast. It didn't really hurt, it was too rigid to hurt. But something itched inside.

David Dale climbed into the front seat with Damadian and we were off.

"You got fleas in this car, Bill," I said after a moment. "You and that doggone Irish setter."

"Time to go home, then," he called back to me. "Time to see Betty."

I wondered what it was time for me to do. Time to do what? I hated time.

The sun was getting low. Bill adjusted his auto visor and I slumped in the thinning rays, feeling empty and sad as we neared the North Carolina state line. Reality was beginning to close in upon me. Every mile brought Grandmama closer, brought boredom and my worried parents closer. Every mile left more and more of Virginia behind.

David Dale squirmed and bent down until I could see only the top of his head. He was stirring around under his seat. A paper bag crackled and he sat up with his earlier purchase in his hands. He smirked over the back seat at Bubba, stuck his hand into his parcel, and drew out a still-cool can of Miller High Life beer with dew on its sides.

"Got a church key on ya, son?" he asked.

Bubba sat up a little to fish around in his pockets. I saw Damadian look back at us. "Hey! Hey! Hey!" he hollered.

"Want a brew, Coach?"

"Put that stuff away. Your parents'd have my ass."

David Dale took the can opener from Bubba and punched two little triangular holes in the top of the Miller. Foam bubbled out all over his hand. "My parents aren't here. My ol' man don't care, anyway."

"Where'd you get it?" Damadian sounded very weary.

"Man back there at the news stand. Didn't even ask to see my driver's license. I'm so big, I can pass for forty-two or however old you have to be here in ol' Virginny . . ."

"Put it away, David Dale."

The big boy took a slug. "Coach, I'm eighteen years old. Old enough to do anything I want to in Carolina, swear on a stack of Bibles. Want one?"

I saw Damadian's lips form a silent cussword. He shook his head no.

"Want a brew, ol' Bubba?"

"Don't mind if I do, ol' David Dale."

"You clowns are going to catch it," said Damadian as David Dale handed Bubba a beer over the seat back.

"Whatcha gon do, Coach?" David Dale guffawed. "Th'ow me outta the car? All two hundred pounds of me?"

"Jeez." Damadian whistled low and passed a truck. "I could have gone full time to graduate school. But NO, Betty wanted to link up with the Johnson people and go South to make sure everybody got his civil rights. JEEZ."

I had to laugh. He could be so stagy.

"Want one, Coach?" David Dale waved a beer under Bill's nose. "I got three six packs. I'm gonna put 'em in your Coke cooler, if you don't mind . . ."

"Maybe I'll have one later. Once we stop for the night. I'm driving now. I don't want to meet my Maker just yet."

"Garnet?" David Dale was looking at me.

I hesitated. I had never tasted anything alcoholic.

"Give Garnet a beer," Damadian said suddenly. "She needs one."

I met his eyes in the mirror.

"You're the most wound-up and nervous person I've ever met," he told me. "Take a few sips. Without aspirin. Maybe it'll help."

I took the can from David Dale and took a swallow. It tasted dreadful. But I kept my distaste to myself and dutifully began to drain the smelly bitter contents, trying to figure out why anybody in his right mind would voluntarily drink this stuff.

David Dale belched. Lifted his second can in salute. "Here's to Debate."

"Debate!" chorused Bubba. "Th'ow me another un, Bo. I'm dry."

"Debate" I muttered, nauseated. Lifted my can.

"And here's to good ol' Bill Damadian, even if he is a Damn Yankee smart-ass!" David Dale hollered.

Bubba hooted. "To good ol' Bill Damadian!"

"And here's to the future!" David Dale raised his can yet again.

"Screw the future," Bubba said. "You an me are gonna be vacationin' in beautiful Vietnam in the future, Bo."

He casually put his arm around me and I leaned back against it, feeling the hardness of his biceps and shoulder.

I've never gotten to know you, Charles Hegler Hargett, I thought at him, throwing my empty beer can over the seat divider and beckoning to David Dale for another. Here comes the future: Vietnam and what? I'm allergic to the future. Gimme another beer.

"And here's to ol' Virginny!" David Dale waved his third can and pointed to a highway sign, reading: "'You are now leaving the Old Dominion—'"

"North Carolina!" crowed Bubba. "Smell them tar heels?"

But I was sitting up and then trying to turn around and crawl into the back window, slamming Bubba with my cast, pressing my face and arms and shoulders into the glass and watching everything recede, recede, recede . . .

"Garnet, sit down!" Bill ordered.

I let the beer spill down the seat back and I began to dissolve with dignity, wondering how drunk a person needed to get before forgetfulness set in. A few final memories flitted past, fleeting, memories of those strange familiar black eyes shut forever and broad shoulders that tried to carry more for us than they could bear.

"Goodbye," I told him as the memories faded with the Virginia state line. "Goodbye."

Bubba did not have any idea what was wrong with me but he pulled my head over against his chin and stroked my cheek the way all the cool guys did in the movies.

"For cryin' out loud!" I muttered, ambivalent. "Can't a person have a little nervous breakdown without everybody getting all self-conscious?"

We drove on in a silence broken only by my sniffles.

I finally sat up, slipping out from under Bubba's arm. Punched David Dale on the shoulder. "Gimme one more. Just one more. I'm tired of crying."

"What's the matter, hon?" he asked.

"I saw John F. Kennedy's grave," I told him.

Bill Damadian said nothing when David Dale handed me the beer.

The radio was all staticky. It was dark outside now and the radio buzzed like a hive of bees.

"Durn," said Bubba. "Can't ya'll find any music on that thing?"

Bill reached over and spun the dial. A flurry of bluegrass music flew past and was gone. Something Rolling-Stones-ish came out now.

I sat up immediately and leaned over the seat back. "No no. Go back. Turn it back."

Bill's fingers touched the knob and banjo music flooded the car. Flatt and Scruggs. The "Foggy Mountain Breakdown."

"Whatcha wanna listen to that ol' shit-kickin' music for?" Bubba asked me, grinning.

"Gentlemen," I addressed both of my colleagues in turn, "we are shit-kickers. Get that through your heads. And we're gonna come back up here next year and kick the shit out of those li'l Harvard-bound preppies."

David Dale screeched, a wild hallooing that made Damadian nearly swerve right off the road.

Bubba took it up, self-consciously at first, but the beer unloosed both his voice and his restraint. He stuck his head out of the window, wind whipping at his light hair, and screamed out into the night where his voice wavered over old graves and echoes came back.

"Don't tell me!" Bill was shouting over the hullabaloo, eyes meeting mine in the mirror. "That must be the Rebel Yell."

I leaned vindictively over the seat, heavy cast unwieldy, and turned up the radio to ear-splitting volume. The music rocked the car: "Pike County Breakdown," "Miller's Reel," and after them "The Southern Rose Waltz."

David Dale was tossing beer cans out of the window, making hog-calling noises at anybody he saw and waving at the ones who shouted and waved back.

Our Valiant raced down the Dixie highway, its Lyndon Johnson and Ban The Bomb bumper stickers flashing under passing headlights, an absolute bedlam of noise and music and flailing. I was satisfied. This was the way Lee's wake should be conducted.

I lay down in the back seat and put my head in Bubba's lap. Stuck my broken leg out of the window. And listened to the wild drunken hooting and that jangling music with its minor chords that spoke of love and lonely places and hardscrabble farming and defeat, but with a heady driving even-so rhythm that was capable of putting laughter back into the laughless, of putting heart back into a whipped chicken, of healing burned babies and putting

318

strength back into a crippled ego. Of even putting arms around black brothers someday, maybe, and finding a way to share the burdens of sharecropping and mosquitoes and loud-mouthed politicians. Groping. Groping towards each other.

I raised my beer can to the sky. Here's to you, Robert, I said to him with tears of drunken glee running into my ears and down Bubba's fly. Here's to you, love, wherever you are. I ain't forgettin'.

I prayed for him then. Really prayed for him. And if God could not hear that astounding Valiant, if it was not verily shaking the foundations of heaven, then there is no God at all and we might as well give up and bomb ourselves to smithereens.

A strange yodeling sound swept back to me.

Bill Damadian had poked his mouth out of the car and was yelling out into the hot country air, getting his mouth full of bugs, yelling for all he was worth, for Chrissake.

For everybody's sake.

Thirty-Eight

It is very strange.

He is at Petersburg again. Petersburg, where his few hungry ragged men hold their desperate lines against Grant's many thousands. It is the winter of 1864 again, December, and very very cold. He can see his breath, can feel the cold biting through the thin worn fabric of his coat. His soldiers haven't enough to wear and several of them freeze to death on the picket lines each night, just freeze to death with their rifles still in their hands. They lie there dead in the trenches in stiff attitudes of watchfulness while their living comrades lift weak voices to greet their commander as he inspects the ravaged lines.

But today, it is very strange. The usual sniping from the Union lines is not forthcoming. The morning is very still and there is no sound of musketry. New-fallen snow muffles the blasted landscape.

Am I dreaming? he wonders. Nothing looks quite real.

He sees a girl standing on a parapet. He cannot imagine what she might be doing there, what a civilian would be risking such an exposed position for. Her skirts blow about her legs and he spurs Traveller.

Nobody is shooting. Nobody goes up to take her down. He dismounts and makes for her at a run, leaps upon the parapet, grasps her arm and pulls her down into the trench in one fluid motion.

"Miss, I don't know how you got here in one piece, but this is no place for you." He is careful to be polite but he won't keep the firmness out of his voice.

"Pa?" she says, gaily pulling back the blowing dark hair out of her face and uncovering a scarred eyelid.

"Annie?" He grasps her shoulders, unbelieving. *"Annie?"*

"I've been looking for you," she says. Shiny red cheeks. Happy white teeth.

His voice quavers. "But they told me you were dead, Annie! They sent me a letter—!"

"I've come to find you, Pa."

He hugs her. She is real. He can feel her little heart beating in her breast. He starts to weep but Annie is laughing, holding him, laughing and laughing.

"It's Christmas, Pa," she says. "You never spend Christmas with us. Come home with me for Christmas."

He cannot believe what he is hearing. He pulls away from her a little. Her face is like a light. "Annie, Annie—I can't go any-where now, Grant is somewhere out there planning his next move. My men don't even have shoes—!"

She looks at him quizzically. Says finally, slowly, "No no. It's all over. Don't you know?"

He blinks rapidly. Searches her face. "All over? What's all over?"

"Everything."

He tries to shake the fog out of his brain. "The campaign?"

She nods.

"The war? The war is over . . . ?"

She nods. Smiles.

He grabs Traveller's bridle and walks hand in hand with his daughter in the stillness. Nothing disturbs the silence except a few birds rummaging for seeds in the snow. The trenches are empty, the dead bodies and the starving soldiers miraculously gone. He blinks and blinks, confused.

She pulls him on, young feet wanting to hurry. He leads Traveller, walks along in a daze with her to the rear. She is leading him back to headquarters.

"All right, Miss Annie. All right. I'm coming with you. But you've got to cue me. Tell me what to say and what to do, now. I don't want to make a fool out of myself."

She laughs, a tinkling sound.

"I am wretchedly confused, you know. The war. The war. When did it stop?"

"It's ending right now," she says.

A woman stands with her back to them and Lee is just beginning to notice something familiar about the set of the shoulders when—

When she turns, and presents her loving radiant face. The small dark-eyed face, with features much like his own, go instantly to his heart and stab him there with such a thrust of unbearable poignance that he is sure he will faint.

He is totally undone, no longer careful about making an appearance, incapable of anything but the one small questioning word: "Mama?"

"Oh Robert." She is in his arms and she is real, standing unaided on her small feet, kissing him over and over as he sobs into her dark hair. Time loses all meaning for him. He could be holding her like this for a second or for an hour or for years. Don't cry, she is telling him. It's all right, darling! It's all right. We've been waiting for you and we are so proud of you, Robert. So very proud.

Annie tugs at his sleeve. "We've got to push on, Pa. We've got to get home. Give somebody some orders. They won't listen to me. Grandmother'll come with us. Don't worry."

He looks up out of his mother's hair and controls his voice sufficiently to summon a faceless orderly. "Strike the tent," he tells the young man in a tone made strong through a concentrated effort.

And Mary and the children who wait at his bedside will hear the words clearly. Not mumbled in the dying voice of a prematurely old man, but words enunciated decisively in the resonant deep voice of General Robert E. Lee. They will sit up straight, marveling at the sound, sensing the passing of an era.

I went home to South Carolina, back to the farm where my grandmother languished confused in a sickbed. For a time, my injury kept me indoors as the rest of the 1966 summer played itself out. Indoors where Bubba Hargett stopped by quite frequently to bring me candy bars and issues of *U.S. News and World Report*. I put away my mourning fan.

My parents had myriad problems, with two invalids on their hands. Beth Ann was kept hopping. Grandmama Moser sat in front of the television set and whined about nobody needing her, until one day I could stand it no longer.

"Grandmama?" I spoke, hobbling back from my bedroom with my shoulderbag dangling against my crutches. "I've got something to show you."

The old lady wasn't interested. But I sat next to her with my heavy cast propped up on a footstool, I forced her to watch me as I reached into my roomy purse to take out a crumpled handful of something that had lain forgotten for weeks in the bottom.

"You know what these are?" I asked my grandmother then, spilling the dried shriveled husks into her sunken lap.

Grandmama only looked at me, eyes like a bird's.

"These are lily heads that I pulled off of the flowers in Robert E. Lee's garden. At Arlington. Isn't that something?"

"There's something the matter with your leg," the old woman croaked by rote. "Azalee!" she called to my mother in the kitchen. "There's something the matter with this child's leg!"

"I broke it," I answered. I took a withered old claw hand and stirred it among the lilies.

"I want to plant these out in the garden out yonder, Grandmama. Show me how."

Bewildered old eyes met mine.

"I don't know nothin' about flowers, Grandmama. I don't know if I should plant anything this late in the year or not. You're good with flowers. Tell me what to do."

"What are they?" the wispy voice finally asked, rheumy blue eyes questioning.

"Day lilies. From Robert E. Lee's house."

The name sank in at last and caused ripples in the depths of a deep place. "My grandmother met Lee once," the old lady offered. "He was good to her."

"Yes'm."

Trembling blue-veined hands went down to brush against the sleeping husks.

"I want to plant them," I explained. "I need you to help me, Grandmama. No one but you can help me."

Fingers rustled among the waiting blossoms.

"What month is it?" Grandmama asked me finally.

"August. The end of August. Is that too late?"

"No, no. No, no. They've dried out already. They were ready to fall off of the stalk themselves. Put 'em in the ground and let the heat take care of them. The rain. And next spring you'll have yourself a heap of blooms."

I pointed down at my leg. "I can't walk so good, Grandmama. Can't bend. Will you come with me out into the garden and help me?"

The old lady sat still for a moment. I found myself holding my breath. Then she handed the lilies back to me, slowly drew down the counterpane, and swung her feet over the side of the bed.

"Fetch me my sweater," she said.

And then we tottered out into the sunny garden together, old woman and young girl, to scratch at the ground with a spoon.

Let there be a seed.